BLUE
BLOOD

ALSO BY DAMIEN BOYD

DI NICK DIXON

DI BOB WILLIS

A DI Nick Dixon Novel

BLUE BLOOD

DAMIEN BOYD

THOMAS & MERCER

Published by Thomas & Mercer, Seattle

www.apub.com

Amazon, the Amazon logo, and Thomas & Mercer are trademarks of Amazon.com, Inc., or its affiliates.

EU Product Safety contact:
Amazon Publishing, Amazon Media EU S.à r.l.
38, avenue John F. Kennedy, L-1855 Luxembourg
amazonpublishing-gpsr@amazon.com

ISBN-13: 9781662524660
eISBN: 9781662524653

Cover design by @blacksheep-uk.com
Cover image: © Robert Harding Video © Kevin Cass / Shutterstock;
© Mark Owen / Arcangel Images

Printed in the United States of America

For Nats and Jonny

Prologue

The instructions were complicated, not that he was in any real hurry. One step at a time, attention to detail; just like building an Airfix model, really.

Finding the right nails had been a bit of a struggle. Twelve-gauge, according to the instructions, but that was an American measurement. It turned out to be one inch, with a 0.281 inch head and a 2.680 millimetre diameter. Nice that they mixed imperial and metric – made it bloody difficult in B&Q.

The tools had been expensive – capital outlay, they call it – but he'd make it all back with his first sale anyway. Drill bits, two, three and eight millimetre to go with his old man's Black and Decker; a grinder, a file, sandpaper. Epoxy glue and acetone too. After that it had just been a packet of elastic bands – different colours to match. They had to match, otherwise the gun would look like a water pistol.

Not forgetting the 3D printer, of course. That had been nine hundred and ninety quid.

Five spools of e Tech PLA Plus to be on the safe side. Printing on the maximum density setting and he didn't want to run out halfway through.

Dark grey for the first one, although he might try something a bit more exotic after that.

Taulman Bridge nylon filament for the barrel. The instructions said either that or insert a two and a half inch piece of copper pipe, glue it in place with the epoxy cement. He'd try the Taulman Bridge first – less hassle. Only bother with the copper pipe if the barrel ruptured when it was fired. After all, he was increasing the calibre from .22 to 9mm, and nobody wanted the bloody thing blowing up in their hand.

The bloke in the YouTube videos had been wearing a chain mail glove, and it seemed a good idea. He'd got a pair of cut resistant gloves on order, due tomorrow by 1 p.m.

Test firing the gun would have to wait until then – that's if it had finished printing by lunchtime. Eleven different parts, and then he'd have to assemble it.

A thousand pounds for the gun and five rounds of ammunition. Seemed like a nice round figure and the bloke hadn't even flinched at the price, even wanted two of them. Perhaps he'd throw in a pair of gloves as a goodwill gesture?

A profitable little business. Five spools of polymer at ten quid each, a single spool of Taulman Bridge for the barrel at thirty quid. The cartridge cases had been thirty quid for two hundred and fifty; after that it was just smokeless powder, primers and lead – cheap as chips on that dark web forum.

A healthy profit margin, they call that.

And it kept him busy.

Asking the bloke what he wanted the guns for had been a mistake, though. Wouldn't do that again.

Somewhere remote on the Levels for the drop off.

Oh, and the burner phone. He really ought to have included that in his costs; another thirty quid.

A message telling the bloke where to leave the money, then another telling him where to find the guns, chuck the phone straight in the river.

Nice and easy.

Yes, bright pink for the next one.

Keep it for her.

Bitch.

Chapter One

'Have you done any rowing before?'

'I had a go on the machine at the gym,' he said, with an apologetic shrug. 'Does that count?'

'Not really. This is a fixed seat and you've only got one oar to worry about, but I'm sure you'll get the hang of it.'

It had seemed like a good idea at the time – late on a Friday night after a Chinese and a few beers.

'Yeah, gig rowing. Fancy having a go?'

'I'd love to.'

'We'll be going out in the morning then, about ten.'

Bravado, topped up with Dutch courage, and here he was, standing on the jetty at Burnham Yacht Club, looking down at the pilot gigs bobbing about on the small waves rolling up the River Brue. A freezing cold February morning, the wooden seats in the gigs soaking wet.

She tried a reassuring arm around his shoulders. 'You won't notice the rain when we get going, and it'll be lovely out there this morning.'

'I'll take your word for it.' He swallowed hard, trying to keep his breakfast down more than anything; two Solpadeine Max and a bowl of muesli. It was going to be touch and go whether he'd hang on to it as it was, and that was before he'd even set foot in the gig.

Being out in Bridgwater Bay in an open boat was one thing; doing it in the pissing rain with a steaming hangover was another altogether. The things lads do to impress a girl. He zipped his coat up to the collar; waterproof, it said on the label, but it was showerproof at best. He'd be soaked to the skin before they got out to Stert Island.

It might not be a date, but it was the next best thing. And it was Valentine's Day after all, so maybe he'd try his luck when they got back in? A nice meal somewhere, although he hadn't booked a table; didn't want to presume.

'Here,' she said, handing him a large rectangular cushion. 'It fits on the seat with these Velcro straps. Just try to keep it dry.'

'Thanks.'

'Haven't you got any waterproof trousers?'

'No.'

'Did you bring a change of clothes?'

'You didn't say . . .'

'No, I didn't, did I,' she said, with a mischievous grin. 'You can always come back to mine to dry out afterwards.' She hesitated. 'If you'd like.'

'That would be great, thanks,' he replied, a sudden spring in his step, not that he'd been walking anywhere, just shifting uneasily from one foot to the other.

'You never know,' she said, 'you might actually enjoy the rowing.'

A little suffering is good for the soul, he thought, deciding it was best left unsaid.

'Who's this, Erica?' The woman was small and wearing a wetsuit, even a surfing hood underneath a bobble hat. Not a good sign.

'Penny, meet Steven,' replied Erica.

'A new member?'

'Just here to try it out, see if he likes it.'

'We'll stick him in the bow in that case. Come on, let's get going.' She was clearly used to giving instructions. 'Tide's perfect.'

'Penny is the cox.' Erica checked Penny was still within earshot, raised her voice a little. 'She sits at the stern shouting at us all the time.'

'Whatever.'

'Do we need wetsuits?' Steven asked, nervously.

'She gets splashed by the oars, isn't rowing either, so she gets cold. Don't panic.'

'She's wearing a life jacket . . .'

'That's just in case we throw her in,' replied Erica. 'Rowers don't wear them, they restrict the stroke. And if you're going to puke, make sure you do it over the side.'

'I'll try to remember.'

'You'd better. I'll be sitting in front of you.'

The other gig had already left the jetty, turning out across the current. 'Hurry up!' shouted the cox. He'd already forgotten her name, not that he'd made much of an effort to remember it in the first place. He had far more important things to be worrying about.

'Where are the oars?' he asked, trying to ignore the sighs from the four rowers waiting not-so-patiently to get going.

'In the bottom of the gig.'

'He's a new bloke,' said the cox. 'Here for a taster session.'

There really is no going back now, he thought, stepping across into the boat.

Seat cushion secured in place, he sat down.

'You brace your feet on the stretcher,' Erica said, pointing to a wooden bar in the bottom of the boat.

'Locate oars!'

'Yours is number one.' She was helping him slide the oar out from under the seats. 'Hold it vertically, and when Penny gives the signal, lower it on to the gunwale between those pins. After that, just follow number three. Do what he does when he does it and you won't go far wrong. All right?'

Number three was looking over his shoulder. 'It's easy, mate, don't worry.'

Steven stretched his shoulders, tried to look confident.

'Right hand under the handle, palm facing up. Left hand, palm down,' said Erica. 'The opposite of me, because I'm on the other side of the boat.'

'Right,' he said, pretending to know what she was talking about.

He watched someone on the jetty untie the mooring line and drop it into the bow. Then the man shoved the gig out across the current with his foot.

Everyone else was lowering their oars into position, so he did the same; ignoring the shouts from the cox, not that he understood them anyway, instead copying number three in front of him. Erica was sitting to his right and in front of him. Occasionally he'd catch her glancing over her shoulder, smiling, not that he could read much into that; she'd just be checking he hadn't fallen overboard or something daft.

His hangover was soon forgotten, and he was even starting to enjoy the rowing. He'd missed a couple of strokes and nearly gone over backwards a few times, the blade not in the water when he pulled on it, but he was getting the hang of it now. Keeping time with number three, despite his arms and stomach muscles screaming at him.

'You'll feel it tomorrow,' said Erica, grinning at him over her shoulder. 'You won't be able to move.'

He finally felt able to take in the view when they were passing Stert Island, Hinkley Point nuclear power station behind it; on the port or starboard side – he didn't know which was which. The flashing lights on the pavilion at Burnham penetrating the gloom to his left.

Then he heard the thud.

The gig had hit something, the bow lifting slightly underneath him.

The cox heard it too. 'Ship oars!'

The rowers in front of him raised their oars into the air, but he had already dropped his, the cox lurching over the side of the gig to grab hold of it. He had turned on his seat and was leaning forward, kneeling on the pilot seat in the bow, peering over the gunwale into the murky water.

The mooring line was lying next to him; instinctively he reached over, threading it through the thick nylon belt.

'What is it?' shouted the cox.

'A body,' he replied, oddly matter of fact, but then he'd seen a few in his time.

'Get a rope on it.'

'I have.'

'Male or female?' asked Erica.

'Male, I think. It's face down.'

'Roll him over and have a look.'

Steven took hold of the belt, heaving the body on to its back. 'Oh God.' He turned away, vomited – still leaning over the side of the boat, as luck would have it.

'It's not too late to change your mind.'

'Thanks, Roger.' Detective Chief Inspector Nick Dixon decided not to take the bait. Not today.

He was standing in the porch at Berrow Church, staring out into the drizzle, trying to keep the rain off his morning suit – it had to go back to the shop on Monday, after all – hoping for a glimpse of a white Rolls-Royce sweeping into the car park. Jane's father had insisted.

'My daughter is getting a proper send off,' Rod had said. 'And that's all there is to it.'

A small crowd had gathered in the car park, standing under umbrellas, listening to the bells. A Valentine's Day wedding always attracted a crowd of well-wishers, according to the churchwarden.

Dixon's best man, Home Office pathologist Dr Roger Poland, was standing under a golf umbrella, waiting for a signal from one of the ushers sheltering in the lychgate.

'It was raining cats and dogs on my wedding day,' said Poland.

'And look how that ended up.' Dixon let out a long slow sigh. 'You've used that line before.'

'Have I?'

'Please tell me it's not in your speech.'

Poland smiled. 'You'll have to wait and see.'

Dixon looked at his watch. 'She's late.'

'Fashionably so,' replied Poland. 'Now, stop fidgeting.'

He checked his pockets: empty. 'Let me have my phone, will you, Roger.'

'Jane said no phone, on pain of death.'

'I need to check my blood sugar.' It was a lie, but the best Dixon could come up with.

Poland wasn't having any of it. 'We had a full English. There's no way your blood is going low.'

'My hands are trembling.'

'That'll be nerves, old chap. Nothing to do with diabetes. Trust me, I'm a doctor.'

'All your patients are dead.'

'Just keep your hands in your pockets until we go in, and don't forget to breathe.'

Dixon was watching the ushers for any sign of movement. Detective Constable Mark Pearce, a longstanding member of his team, and Police Constable Nigel Cole, one hand still bandaged after his brush with the cider bottles. Both good lads.

Cole had cut himself to ribbons on broken glass to save the life of a colleague – and there she was, PC Sarah Loveday, sitting at the back of the church in a wheelchair, an order of service in one hand, a dog's lead in the other, Dixon's large white Staffordshire terrier stretched out on the stone floor next to her. She'd managed to cover her bandages with a hat.

'There's a phone buzzing in your pocket,' Dixon said. 'Mine's on airplane mode, so it must be you.'

Poland slid his phone out of his inside jacket pocket, careful not to dislodge the white rose in his buttonhole.

Dixon had felt this nervous only once before, standing in the dock at Taunton Magistrates' Court charged with murder, listening to his solicitor making a bail application. Best not dwell on that, perhaps.

'Yes, Lucy,' said Poland. He'd turned away deliberately so Dixon couldn't hear what was being said.

Lucy was Jane's half-sister and her bridesmaid. They'd met at their mother's funeral less than a year ago, Jane having been adopted at birth, with Lucy in and out of foster care all her short life. They'd become the best of sisters in the months since, although it felt more like mother and daughter sometimes.

Poland turned to Dixon and feigned a look of concern; eyes wide. Dixon hoped he was joking, anyway.

'Five minutes,' said Poland, ringing off. 'They had a bit of trouble with the dress.' He shrugged. 'She's nearly seven months pregnant, so that's to be expected, I suppose.'

'Yeah.'

'We'd best get in there.' Poland was signalling to the ushers, who came trotting along the path. 'She's coming along the Berrow Road now.'

'Good luck, Sir,' said Cole, extending a bandaged hand.

'I don't need luck, Nige,' replied Dixon, patting him on the back.

Heads turned as they walked down the aisle, Dixon passing his parents, their smiles forced, unable to hide their disapproval even now. He wasn't sure whether it was Jane or the pregnancy they disapproved of, or both, but then they tended to disapprove of everything, so he'd given up wondering.

His promotion to acting detective superintendent had been disapproved of because it was only temporary, the fact that he was the Avon and Somerset force's youngest ever detective chief inspector overlooked for some reason. Still, they seemed to approve of everything his younger brother did, so that would have to do.

Assistant Chief Constable David Charlesworth was there in full dress uniform, sitting with his wife – on the groom's side of the church, at Jane's insistence.

'You invited him.'

Actually, Dixon hadn't. He'd just sort of invited himself, although Poland had invited him to the stag do, so perhaps that was it.

The stag do. Dixon had lost count of the times he'd put his hand over his beer glass and said 'I'd better not, I'm diabetic.' They'd even had a whip round to get him a T-shirt with it printed on, but then put the money in the drinks kitty instead. Dixon had been the only one still upright at the end of the evening.

'She's on the way, I gather,' said the vicar, appearing at the top of the steps. 'I had a text from Lucy.' Reverend Jonathan Philpott was godfather to Lucy's boyfriend and practically part of the family.

'A couple of minutes,' replied Poland. He leaned over and whispered in Dixon's ear. 'It's surprising how close the "Funeral March" is to "Here Comes the Bride". You listen. Just speed it up a bit and Bob's your . . .' He grimaced. 'Sorry, my phone's buzzing again.'

'What is it?' asked Dixon.

'A text from work.'

'I thought you weren't on call this weekend?'

'I'm not supposed to be, but Davidson is off sick.'

'Marvellous.'

'It'll have to wait,' said Poland, sliding his phone back into his pocket.

'What will?'

'The gig rowers have fished a body out of the sea. The RNLI are on their way out to bring it in now.'

Chapter Two

Detective Chief Inspector Janice Courtenay stared at the smartphone buzzing on her desk at Express Park.

Managing DCI suited her, and she liked it. Performance reviews, training schedules, webinars, the work no one else wanted to do. It was a different sort of stress, seeing to it that CID ran like a well-oiled machine. The ACC had been kind enough to say so on several occasions. 'In spite of the challenging situation' was the phrase he had used; not enough people, far too much work.

Allocating resources hadn't been easy recently either, with several high profile major investigation teams and then that regional task force taking officers she couldn't spare. Glamorous maybe – *sexy* even – but the routine work still needed to be covered: the shoplifting, pub fights, thefts. Dull as ditch water, perhaps, but it was her job to see it was done.

Today she was standing in as duty SIO, everybody else at that bloody wedding.

It had been a quiet morning and she was praying it would stay that way, at least until four o'clock when her shift ended. She'd always hated being the senior investigating officer; everybody looking to her for direction. It was a confidence thing, according to her husband anyway. It didn't help that she hadn't done it for the best part of a year.

The phone stopped buzzing and then started again.

Sod it.

'Janice Courtenay.'

'We've got a body, ma'am,' said the voice.

Hopefully it would be an unexplained death, something routine she could send someone else to sort out. 'Where?' she asked.

'Bridgwater Bay, floating face down. The RNLI are on their way out now.'

'Any evidence of foul play?'

'He was found by some rowers. They rolled him over and there's a hole in the middle of his forehead, apparently. Looks like a bullet hole, but there's no exit wound. One of them's a paramedic and that's what it looked like to him, anyway.'

Marvellous.

She managed to stifle a sigh. 'I'm on my way.'

'They're bringing him into the yacht club, they said. Away from prying eyes at the town jetty.'

Pretty much everyone else had beaten her to it by the time Janice arrived at Burnham Yacht Club half an hour later. An HM Coastguard Land Rover was parked across the entrance, two ambulances on standby as well. Three police patrol cars had blocked the road, uniformed officers turning dog walkers away from the footpath that led past the pontoon.

A CID officer she recognised from his performance review was walking towards her as she parked her car on the grass verge. Janice knew his name and remembered the review; she must've done over seventy in the last couple of months and it stood out for all the wrong reasons. Twerp.

'They've got him on the lifeboat, ma'am,' he said. 'They'll be here in about ten minutes.'

'Thank you.'

'You need to have a word with Steve Yelland. He's the bloke from the Coastguard, wanted to know who was in charge. I told him I was, but now you're here . . .'

'Where is he?'

'He went along the path to the pontoon with a couple of paramedics.'

The pontoon extended about thirty yards into the river, then turned parallel to the bank, yachts moored either side, a few gaps where some had been craned out for the winter. Janice recognised the familiar sound of yachts moored in the wind: the clink of ropes rattling against the masts. It didn't drown out the seagulls, but near as damn it.

Yelland was talking into his radio, but saw her on the pontoon and walked up to meet her.

'Who are you?' he asked.

'Detective Chief Inspect—'

'That's better,' interrupted Yelland. 'I was beginning to think your lot hadn't realised what's going on. That young bloke said he was in charge.'

'He isn't,' replied Janice. 'And what is going on?'

'You'll be able to see for yourself in a minute. The body's been in the water for a couple of days maybe, dead for about the same time, I'm told. It is a bullet hole, though. Plain as day. The paramedics will confirm life extinct, then it's over to you.'

Janice was on the phone to Scientific Services when the large 'D' class lifeboat roared into view at the entrance to the River Brue. She walked down the pontoon, glancing across to the line of spectators along the sea wall. Blue lights always attracted the nosy parkers.

'Forensics are on their way,' she said, appearing next to Yelland, who was waiting adjacent to a gap in the line of moored yachts, waving to the lifeboat helmsman. 'Can we keep the body in the lifeboat until they get here?' she asked. 'At least he'll be down in the boat and out of view.'

'An hour max,' replied Yelland. 'We can't risk the "D" getting stuck here when the tide goes out.'

'Forensics will be here before that.'

The lifeboat pulled into the gap between the yachts, the mooring rope thrown across to Yelland.

'Do you want to see him?' he asked.

'Let the paramedics do their bit first,' replied Janice. She stood back, allowing them to step into the boat.

She looked away, up to the sea wall, the line of ghouls gawping, their view blocked by the large yacht in front of the lifeboat.

It didn't take long to confirm life extinct.

'About three days, I reckon,' said the helmsman, turning in his seat. 'Takes that long for a body to float.'

'About that,' replied one of the paramedics, handing his case up to his colleague who was already back on the pontoon.

Yelland waited until Janice was in the lifeboat before he pulled back the foil blanket. 'See? It must be a bullet hole. Can't be anything else.'

Bloated, the skin grey, wrinkled; his eyes wide open, the man still managed to look surprised in spite of two or three days in the water. A clean hole in the middle of his forehead that could only be a bullet hole, surely?

'Take the blanket back a bit further,' she said.

Yelland pulled it back, revealing the man's torso.

'Oh, for fuck's sake,' hissed Janice. 'You never said he was one of ours.'

15

'They call it "punching above your weight".' There was a glint in Poland's eyes, watching for a reaction. 'When you marry someone far more attractive than you are.'

'I get it, Roger.'

The first sign Jane had arrived was Monty almost pulling Sarah out of her wheelchair. Then Dixon's future mother-in-law, Sue, crept into the church, the music starting when she sat down in the front row.

'It doesn't sound anything like the "Funeral March",' said Dixon, louder now no one could hear him, but there was an unfamiliar tremble in his voice all the same. He held his hand out in front of him.

'You're not still shaking, are you?' asked Poland.

'Have you got the rings?'

'That's the fourth time you've asked me.'

Lucy had to step in to stop Monty jumping up at Jane, but then he hadn't seen her for all of twenty-four hours, so it was to be expected, perhaps. Separation anxiety. There was a lot of it about.

'You haven't brought your dog, surely?' his mother had said when she'd seen Monty stretched out on the stone floor, the remark ignored.

Jane's father, Rod, looked well, considering he'd had a heart attack a couple of weeks earlier. A bit red in the face, perhaps, but that might be the occasion.

The aisle seemed oddly long for such a small church, nestled in the dunes behind the golf course.

It was a favourite spot for dog walking, following the path across the fairways to the beach. Sheltering in the porch when it rained. Not even the severed head in the green side bunker behind the church had ruined his enjoyment of that.

He blinked away the memory, instead watching Jane walking slowly towards him.

That had been their first night together, oddly enough; still in bed when he got the call that Sunday morning.

They'd found the rest of the body in a burnt out car on the beach.

'You all right?' asked Poland. He spoke quietly, lips fixed in a smile.

'Yes, fine.'

'What are you thinking about?'

'Don't ask.'

'You might want to consider smiling back at her, she's starting to look worried.'

A deep breath. Big smile. Rod shook Dixon's hand and then sat down next to his wife.

'You look—'

'I know.' Jane gave a lopsided grin. 'Don't look too closely at the dress. Mum had to stitch a strip of pillowcase into the back. You'll need a pair of scissors to get me out of it.'

'I'm sure you'll manage,' said Poland, mischievously.

'Dearly beloved,' said Jonathan, loudly. 'We have come together to witness the marriage of Nicholas and Jane . . .'

The odd word or phrase got through after that – love and trust, joyful commitment to the end of their lives, children are nurtured – but Dixon had heard Jonathan's introduction at the rehearsal. He was miles away, remembering a man who had murdered those he held responsible for the deaths of his wife and child.

Somehow it had become Jane in the vision that was repeating on a loop, like one of those Instagram reels, slipping a rope around her neck and jumping from a hotel balcony.

At the time it had seemed simple enough. Black and white. The man had committed murder and it was Dixon's job to bring him before the courts.

'Bring him to justice' was the old cliché, but what was justice?

He was watching Jane, wondering how he'd feel in the same situation. How he'd feel in the same situation *now*.

'Marriage and fatherhood change a man,' Roger had said. Dixon was about to do both at once. Almost. Not that he had the slightest hesitation, mind you, but he wondered whether anything would ever seem quite so *black and white* again.

Funny, the things you think of at a time like this.

'First, I am required to ask anyone present who knows a reason why these persons may not lawfully marry, to declare it now.' Jonathan was looking around the congregation expectantly.

Someone hadn't switched their phone to silent mode. Charlesworth, as it turned out. Dixon spun round to watch him sheepishly fumbling in his inside jacket pocket. Several other phones had buzzed at the same time, all of them in the pockets or handbags of police colleagues.

There was a buzzing coming from Poland's jacket pocket too.

'That's not yours, is it?' whispered Jane, glaring at Dixon.

'Mine's on airplane mode,' he replied.

'It's mine. Just another text. Whatever it is, it can wait,' said Poland.

'The vows you are about to take are to be made in the presence of God.' Jonathan was raising his voice over the sound of footsteps in the congregation, someone making a hasty exit down the aisle.

Jane was the first to look over her shoulder. 'Charlesworth,' she said, her voice barely audible. 'Something's going on.'

'Nicholas, will you take Jane to be your wife?'

The question 'will you?' didn't seem right somehow, but Dixon had been overruled at the rehearsal. 'Will you . . . ?' implied at some point in the future, surely? 'Do you' was much better, immediate, and then the answer would be 'I do', which was what he had always thought he'd be saying when the time came. Still, it made no real difference. He did, and that's all there was to it.

'I will.'

Their vows were punctuated by footsteps and murmured apologies behind them. Charlesworth returning to his seat, probably.

Poland had remembered the rings, which was a relief.

Church services had always dragged for Dixon. Time seemed to pass much more slowly than usual; everything seemed to take longer. Not today though, and he was wondering what might be important enough to have interrupted Charlesworth's afternoon off. He must've told his office only to ring in an emergency.

Then he heard the magic words. 'I therefore proclaim that they are husband and wife. Those whom God has joined together let no one put asunder. You may kiss the bride.'

The congregation were singing 'All Things Bright and Beautiful' while they signed the register.

'I thought you were going to burst into tears at one point,' said Jane. 'I was watching you. Miles away, you were.'

'Trying to keep my composure,' mumbled Dixon.

Poland was taking the opportunity to check his phone. 'Bloody hell.'

'What is it, Roger?' asked Jane.

'That body the gig rowers fished out of the sea,' he said, curling his lip. 'It's a police officer.'

Chapter Three

'Sorry to drag you away,' said Charlesworth. 'I thought your speech went well.'

'Thank you,' replied Poland.

They were sitting in the back of Charlesworth's chauffeur driven car, not that either of them had drunk too much to drive. Poland had known what was coming as soon as he'd seen the text message in the vestry and had limited himself to the obligatory glass of champagne for the wedding toasts. The fact that he still hadn't properly recovered from the stag night was neither here nor there.

Forensics had done their bit at the yacht club and the body was now waiting for him in the pathology lab at Musgrove Park Hospital.

'Did you meet his mother?' asked Charlesworth. 'Bit of a tartar, isn't she?'

'You could say that.'

'Jane looked—'

'Yes, she did.'

'Look, I'm sorry about this, Roger. I'm not going to tell you what's going on. Suffice to say it can't wait until the morning.'

'I quite understand, David.' Poland shrugged. 'Besides, it's got me out of having to dance with Jane's bridesmaid.'

'We've got an ID. He's a uniformed constable out of Bristol, but I don't want to tell you any more than that at this stage. I don't want to risk influencing your findings.'

'You won't do that.'

'I thought not.'

Janice Courtenay was waiting for them when they pulled into the car park at the pathology lab just after six, standing under the canopy at the front entrance, sheltering from the rain.

'D'you know DCI Courtenay?' asked Charlesworth.

'We've met.'

'She's the office manager at Express Park. Just holding the fort for today.' The car pulled up across the entrance, allowing them to slide out under cover of the canopy. 'Best wait for me, Stephens,' said Charlesworth to his driver.

'Yes, Sir.'

'I'll go and get myself sorted out,' said Poland. 'You're welcome to come in or watch from the anteroom. I'll leave it to you.' He glanced at the reflection in the small pane of glass in the lab door, watching Charlesworth and DCI Courtenay behind him. The conversation was animated to say the least, although Janice Courtenay looked more like a rabbit caught in headlights.

Something was going on, Charlesworth had said as much, but Poland hadn't heard anything on the grapevine. Dixon hadn't mentioned anything either. No doubt he'd find out soon enough.

The body had been laid out on a slab, two lab technicians buzzing around like flies. Poland was tying an apron behind his back when he barged through the swing doors a few minutes later, but he noticed the hole in the middle of the man's forehead straightaway, lit up by the flash of a camera.

He slid his mask into position and leaned over the body, examining the neat hole. Definitely a bullet, judging by the brain injury visible despite the shadow he was casting over the forehead.

Still traces of powder burns around the wound too, even after a couple of days in the sea, so the gun had been fired at point blank range; pressed to the forehead, probably.

A gloved hand either side of the head; he tipped it forward and looked at the back of the skull.

'No exit wound,' he said, lowering it back down gently. 'Bullet must still be in there.' He turned to the lab technician standing next to him with a clipboard. 'Do we know when he was last seen alive?'

'His shift ended at eight on Wednesday evening. That's the last sighting of him, leaving Bridewell police station.'

'That's about right. Anything from his wife or partner?'

'Divorced.'

Something was wrong about the legs, both broken by the looks of things, but with no corresponding bruising; after he died, then.

'We'll start with the head,' Poland said, turning at the sound of tapping on the window of the anteroom. 'I'm guessing that's the bit they're interested in.' He opened the door.

'Well?' demanded Charlesworth.

'It's definitely a bullet and there's no exit wound so it'll still be in there. Looks like gunshot residue on the forehead; fired at close range, which means low velocity, otherwise it would have blown straight out the back of the skull, taking most of it with it.'

'We need the bullet for ballistics.'

'Of course you do,' replied Poland. 'Would you like to watch?'

Charlesworth glanced at Janice Courtenay, who looked white as a sheet. 'We'll wait here,' he said.

'There's tea and coffee in the machine out there. Fresh air outside.' Poland let the door slam behind him.

Procedure, every step documented for the record, photographs, dictated notes; it took him forty minutes to remove the top of the skull even with an electric saw, the brain intact, cleaned of blood by seawater that had washed in through the bullet hole.

The lab technician swabbed away the last of the murky water, grey tinged with pink running into the drains either side of the slab to reveal the bullet, buckled, the tip flattened where it had struck the inside of the parietal bone at the back of the head. Definitely low velocity.

Poland held it up in a pair of forceps for Charlesworth and Janice to see, then placed it gently in a stainless steel bowl. 'Let's have a look at it under the microscope,' he said.

Charlesworth could contain himself no longer, appearing at Poland's elbow. He'd remembered to put on a mask and clearly knew where the jar of Vicks VapoRub was.

'It ricocheted around inside the skull making a right mess of the brain,' said Poland, squinting into the eyepiece. 'I'm no ballistics expert, but there are no striations on this bullet, no rifling marks at all.'

'Fired from a smooth-barrelled weapon.'

'Looks like that to me.'

'Any other injuries?'

'Both legs are broken, but that happened after death. I'll know more when I've had a closer look, obviously, but it could've been done to get the body in the boot of a car, perhaps, or when he was disposed of.' Poland looked up. 'A low velocity, smooth barrelled weapon, David. Looks like you've got someone 3D printing guns on your patch.'

'And using them to kill police officers.'

REFRAIN

Dixon wondered whether he could do it to his new wife on her wedding night; whether he *should* do it.

23

A seven letter word on a triple word square; eight if he used the 's' Jane had just put on the end of 'panic'. He'd tried adding up the points in his head, but lost count before he'd got to the fifty point bonus for using all his tiles.

'Are you going, or what?' she demanded, taking a sip from her orange juice.

He took a few minutes shuffling the letters on the stand in front of him, well hidden, despite Jane craning her neck when she thought he wasn't looking.

The first four out of the bag had spelled out 'FRAN', which was the first time he had thought about her all week, in the excitement of the big day.

That was the way it should be, of course.

They'd been engaged to be married, even though they were only seventeen at the time. Told no one, either. Then Fran had been taken. Finding her body and her killer had helped him move on. Guilty pleas and a whole life tariff had saved him the trauma of reliving it all in the witness box. And another serial killer would die in prison.

The chapter was closing – closed even – and he might not have thought about her at all, had it not been for those letters appearing at random. Odd sometimes, how things worked out.

She'd have liked Jane; would have approved. Dixon knew that much. And that was enough.

It was gone midnight, the dull thump of music still coming from the function room at the Red Cow, opposite the cottage. They'd made their grand exit a couple of hours earlier. No need for a car with 'Just Married' sprayed all over it, no trailing tin cans; they'd just walked across the road.

A quick change into jeans and a T-shirt, his tails safely in the bag ready to go back to the hire shop. A pair of scissors to get Jane out of her wedding dress and now here they were, listening to the party gradually winding down. They'd got a late licence until twelve-thirty, so it wouldn't be long until it all went quiet. Taxis had been coming and going with greater frequency, as best of three had become best of five.

'We need to get one of those timer things they use at chess matches.' Jane was drumming her fingers on the table.

Another car outside, this time close enough to the cottage for Monty to start barking. Footsteps on the pavement outside, then a knock at the front door.

'Who the bloody hell is that?'

'Don't look at my tiles,' said Dixon, standing up.

'Sorry to call so late,' said Charlesworth, when Dixon opened the door. 'I'm not interrupting anything, am I?'

'We were playing Scrabble, Sir.'

'On your wedding night?'

'My wife is seven months pregnant.' It sounded good, *my wife*.

'Yes, but you could still . . .' Charlesworth thought better of it.

'Come in, Sir.'

'You sod!' Jane had leaned across the table and picked up Dixon's tiles. 'You've got a seven letter word.' Then she clapped the board shut, scattering tiles across the table. 'That's it, two all it is,' she grumbled, packing the game away.

'A good place to leave it, I'd have thought,' said Charlesworth.

Actually it was three-one, but Dixon would let it go. He stepped out into the darkness, looking for Monty, who'd taken his chance and was sniffing around the neighbour's backyard.

He'd been expecting a visit from Charlesworth, albeit in the morning, but he wasn't surprised to find him standing on his doorstep in the early hours. A police officer with a bullet hole in his forehead. If ever there was anything that was going to interrupt his wedding night, it would be that.

The ACC was still in his full dress uniform. He looked embarrassed, shifting awkwardly from one foot to the other, his face flushed. 'Roger said you weren't going away.'

'We had a honeymoon booked last time,' replied Dixon. He had hold of Monty by the collar and was leading the dog back into the cottage. 'Went anyway, even though the wedding got cancelled.'

'We'll go somewhere when I've had the baby.' Jane raised her voice over the soft click of the Scrabble tiles she was dropping into a cloth bag. 'When the weather's a bit better.'

'Look, I'm sorry to do this to you, Nick—'

'Drink, Sir?' asked Jane, her voice flat. She was struggling to hide her disappointment. Dixon had booked a couple of days off, and both of them knew what was coming.

'No, thank you.'

'Who is he, the dead constable?' asked Dixon, breaking the silence that followed.

Charlesworth appeared grateful for the opportunity to keep the conversation moving. 'Russell Lock. He worked out of Bridewell, Bristol city centre. Last seen leaving after his shift finished on Wednesday evening. Roger recovered the bullet from his skull and it's on the way to Ballistics now. Fired at point blank range; there are powder burns and traces of residue on Lock's forehead.'

'And the bullet was still in his skull?'

'Largely intact,' said Charlesworth. 'Low velocity, fired from a smooth-barrelled weapon. Roger looked at it under the microscope and there's no rifling on the bullet at all. Ballistics will confirm but it's looking like a—'

'3D printed gun,' interrupted Dixon.

'Precisely.' Charlesworth shook his head. 'We can't have those on our patch, Nick.'

'No, Sir.'

'Two drug dealers were murdered using one a couple of weeks ago and there's an investigation ongoing out of Bridewell. DCI Keith Hunt is the SIO, but he's getting nowhere with it. Do you know him?'

'I do,' said Jane. 'He's a tosser.'

'You wouldn't expect me to comment on that.'

'No, Sir,' said Dixon.

'That said, I'm not going to argue with it either. Just between you and me.' Charlesworth cleared his throat. 'Anyway, I need you to take over both investigations, Nick. Drug dealers killing each other was bad enough. We've even had some bloody idiot telling everyone there's a vigilante on the loose; cleaning up the streets of Bristol because we're incapable of it, apparently.' He raised his hand, silencing Dixon before he had drawn breath. 'You'll find out. But we can't have 3D printed weapons being used to kill police officers. You're still acting detective superintendent, so you have the authority and I'll speak to DCI Hunt in the morning. You've run two teams before?'

'No, Sir.'

'You'll manage. I want those guns off the streets.'

'You said *officers*, plural.'

'Lock's regular partner, Darren Canter, hasn't been seen since Wednesday evening. You'll need to liaise with Professional Standards about the pair of them – might give you a head start. In the meantime, the usual missing person enquiries are in hand, and I've lined up the Coastguard and the RNLI. They'll be starting a full search at first light.'

Charlesworth had made his way back to the front door, closely followed by Monty, hoping to nip out again when he got the chance. 'I'll arrange for Deborah Potter to meet you at Bridewell in the morning to sort out staffing. You can take personnel from the Bristol teams. As many people as you need, we'll find them. Anything else?'

'No, Sir.'

'Good. I'll leave you to it. A lovely day, by the way. I hope you'll both be very happy.'

Chapter Four

Breakfast in bed was a nice touch, even if he said so himself. Not that Jane had taken much notice. Rolled over and gone back to sleep, probably, leaving Monty to eat it. Bacon and egg. Toast. Hopefully, he hadn't eaten the roses.

Greedy little bugger.

It had still been dark when Dixon crept out of the cottage, the rain replaced by clear skies. A few squirts of de-icer on the windscreen of his Land Rover and he was soon on his way, parking on the pavement outside a small block of flats on the edge of Nailsea half an hour later.

A new development, cars left on street corners and pavements; even double parked in places. He'd only just managed to squeeze through, and how they'd got the Scientific Services van through was beyond him.

It was as good a place to start as any. PC Russell Lock's rented flat, the added advantage being that the senior Scientific Services officer, Donald Watson, was there.

Prams tucked under the stairs in the entrance lobby; bicycles chained to the railings. A folded free newspaper had been wedged under the front door, light streaming out into the front garden, gravel covered in wheelie bins.

Dixon's footsteps echoed on the hard lino floor, despite his best efforts, although lights were on in both ground floor flats.

'Up here.'

He pulled on a pair of latex gloves as he climbed the stairs, Watson waiting for him on the landing.

'Happy honeymoon,' Watson said.

'Thanks.'

'It's not the murder scene, before you ask. And there's nothing of interest. Not that I can find, anyway.'

'Do I need overalls?'

'No. We've nearly finished, so make yourself at home.' Watson followed Dixon into the flat. 'Bedroom on the right, sitting room on the left. He rents it from a housing association. There's a garage; nothing in there either, except a set of golf clubs gathering dust.'

'Talk to me about 3D printed guns.'

'You need Ballistics for that.'

'They're in Birmingham.'

Watson stifled a sigh. 'What d'you want to know?'

Dixon was opening the bedside table drawers one by one. 'Everything,' he said.

'I'm guessing he's a bit of an optimist, is our PC Lock,' said Watson, when Dixon opened the top drawer, revealing a packet of condoms.

Bedsheets that hadn't been washed in weeks, piles of dirty washing on the floor. And the smell: socks and trainers. An optimist maybe, but dead all the same. 'Is there a girlfriend?' asked Dixon.

'Not as far as I can see. We haven't got his phone either, which doesn't help, but we'll get his call records from his mobile provider.'

'You were going to tell me about 3D printed guns.'

'Well, where to begin?' Watson took a deep breath as he followed Dixon into the living room. 'An ordinary printer prints in two dimensions. You ask it to print a picture of a rabbit and you get a picture of a rabbit on a piece of paper. If you ask a 3D printer to print a rabbit, you get a plastic rabbit, sitting there looking at you. That's about it, really.'

A television on a stand, games console sitting on the carpet in front of it, a tired leather sofa, a small table against the far wall. Dixon was looking at the birthday cards on the windowsill. There were only three. Mum, dad, and someone called Sam.

'That one's from his sister,' offered Watson.

The family had been spoken to, Dixon knew that much. While he'd been enjoying his wedding reception, they were being told their son had been murdered; the father doing the formal identification while Dixon had been playing Scrabble.

'It uses melted plastic, or polymer, to print objects,' continued Watson. 'Three dimensional things, building them layer by layer. There are all sorts of applications, joints for orthopaedic surgery is just one, but it was never going to be long before some scrotum started printing things he shouldn't.'

Dixon had moved on to the kitchen, not that he was going to venture in without a hazmat suit; standing in the doorway was close enough. 'How much is a 3D printer?'

'About a grand will get you a decent one, capable of printing gun parts.'

'And the polymer?'

'Freely available online,' replied Watson. 'Cheap too. It comes on spools like fishing line, all sorts of different colours, thicker though. PLA, or polylactic acid, is the best stuff and most commonly used. There are various brands: a Tech PLA Plus, Diamond PLA. A single spool is about a tenner.'

A plastic crate full of evidence bags was sitting on a dining chair. Dixon lifted the bags up one by one and held them up to the light bulb hanging from the ceiling. 'What's this lot?'

'Credit card bills. All of them up to the limit. About forty grand in total. There's a bank loan in there too.'

'So, how would I go about printing a gun?'

'Download the files from the internet, one file for each of the parts, and away you go, really. The Liberator was the first one doing the rounds in the early days. It was a pistol, just a rudimentary handle and then a rectangular box. Blew up when it was fired, more often than not, but using a metal barrel and reducing the velocity of the cartridge got around that.'

'Some parts are metal then?' asked Dixon.

'The firing pin needs to be, but an ordinary nail would do it. A bit of nine-millimetre copper pipe for the barrel – five quid online – and hey presto. Everything else can be plastic. The technology's moved on now though.'

'Which means the guns have got better, I suppose.'

'Much better,' replied Watson. 'The polymers are stronger, and if you print in high definition you don't even need a metal barrel any more. And you can print assault rifles now. They even look like proper guns too. The Liberator was a funny looking thing, more like a water pistol.'

'How long does it take to print one of these guns?'

'The Liberator took about twenty hours, but some printers are quicker than others. Some guns have more parts than others too. The Songbird takes about twenty-four hours.'

The look on Dixon's face was enough.

'It's a handgun, looks just like a nine-millimetre Browning, only there's no magazine in the handle. The barrel pushes out of the side, you load the cartridge into the end of it and then push it back in. An ordinary woodworking nail and an elastic band does the business when you pull the trigger.'

'Does the cartridge eject?'

'No. I know where you're going with that, but if it was a Songbird, you won't find a cartridge at the scene. You have to take it out by hand when you reload, sometimes even push it out from the other end of the barrel with a screwdriver. It can get stuck. Remember, when you pull the trigger, there's a mini explosion going off inside these things.'

'And what does one of these printers look like?'

'They're pretty big: a base – or build plate, they call it – steel rods, a sort of frame for the nozzle to move up and down and from side to side; some of them are enclosed in glass like a large square fish tank.'

'What's that door?' asked Dixon.

'The bathroom,' replied Watson. 'You really don't want to go in there.'

'The ACC said two drug dealers had been killed in Bristol using a 3D printed gun.'

'Didn't go to that one, myself. Let's just say two drug dealers were put out of their misery by a 3D printed gun. Right here.' Watson pointed to the middle of his forehead with his index finger. 'Hands cable-tied behind their backs, badly beaten. The colleagues who went are still off sick; both of them are having counselling. And, as you know, we see some sights.'

'Have you come across 3D printed guns on our patch before?'

'No. They're either buying them in, or someone's decided to set themselves up in business as a gunsmith. No serial numbers, they're effectively untraceable.'

'What about the bullets?' asked Dixon. He was making his way towards the front door; places to go, people to see. 'Can Ballistics do anything with them?'

'There's no rifling, of course, but there'll be microscopic traces of the polymer melted on to them, so they can tell it's been fired by a 3D printed gun. They should also be able to identify the polymer used to print the gun, even the specific batch, so you might be able to find out where and when it was bought if they can find a match.'

'But we could have a different gun printed from the same batch of polymer?'

'Exactly. Then there's the firing pin; depending on how the nail is mounted, it might leave a distinguishing mark on the base of the cartridge, but you'd need the cartridge for that and they're not ejected.'

'That batch of polymer it is then.'

'Good luck,' said Watson, when Dixon was at the top of the stairs. 'You'll need it,' he muttered under his breath. Too loud, as it happened.

A cul-de-sac of two smart houses on the edge of Banwell. They'd been built in the back garden of a bungalow, by the looks of things, or a small paddock behind it, perhaps. There was still a timber stable block rotting away in an area the size of a tennis court, last year's ragwort in amongst the long grass; hardly enough room to keep a horse now anyway.

The one on the right, the message had said. A white Jaguar and a grey Audi two-seater on the drive, blocked in by the family liaison officer's car. Dixon had been told to look out for a black Ford Focus, standard pool car issue.

He hated these meetings; parents trying to stay optimistic, him trying not to burst their bubble, but how do you sugar-coat it?

'We'll find him, don't worry.'

'Dead or alive?'

'Er . . .'

The FLO answered the door. 'Superintendent Dixon?' he asked, his voice hushed.

He nodded his reply.

'They're both retired doctors, although she still does a bit of locum work,' said the FLO, stepping out and pulling the door to behind him. 'Trying to stay positive, but they're not daft, Sir. They know about Russell Lock, so they're starting to fear the worst.'

'Do they have any other children?'

'There's a daughter at uni.'

Might be some consolation, thought Dixon.

'They haven't told her anything yet,' continued the FLO.

'Let's go in.'

Crumpled figures, sitting either side of the kitchen table, hunched over mugs of coffee.

'Have you got any news?' asked the man, more in hope than expectation.

'Not yet, Sir,' replied Dixon.

The FLO made the introductions, explained that Dixon was taking over the investigation. Julian and Diane Canter seemed young to be retirees, although they'd have aged ten years at least in the last twenty-four hours.

'Do you know Darren?' asked Diane.

'I don't, I'm afraid. I'm based at Bridgwater usually, so don't know many Bristol officers.' It was an ordinary family kitchen; try as he might, Dixon couldn't see anything out of place. 'That might be why I've been assigned the case, of course.'

'What's that supposed to mean?' Julian this time, the hostility born out of fear. The fear of losing his son.

'Just that it gives me objectivity, if I don't know anyone involved.'

Julian mumbled something that sounded like, 'Yeah, I suppose.'

'Can I see his room?'

'I'll show you,' said Diane, standing up. 'This way.'

Not up the stairs, surprisingly, Dixon following Diane along a corridor to an en suite bedroom that he thought was probably behind the double garage, the window overlooking the back garden.

'We bought a house with a granny annexe for when Julian's mother can't cope on her own,' said Diane. 'Until then, Darren's got it.'

Room for an armchair and a television, a games console on the floor; a double bed, wardrobe, desk with a computer.

'Does he have a girlfriend?'

'Spends all his time on that thing,' Diane said, gesturing to the computer.

'Doing what?'

'Side hustles, he calls it. He's always trying to make a bit of extra money online, although it's more of a hobby than anything else, I think. Trying to pay for his bloody car.'

'Can we take the computer?'

Diane frowned. 'Is that really necessary?'

'It is.'

'Do what you have to do, in that case.'

Dixon sat down at the desk and began opening the drawers one by one. 'Have you met Russell Lock?'

'No. Darren's never really spoken about him, either. Never says much about his work, to be honest.'

'I'm told they're under investigation by our Professional Standards department.'

'News to me,' replied Diane, a defensive edge to her voice. Not surprisingly. Dixon had been expecting it. 'What for?'

'I don't know yet, I'm afraid.'

'What the bloody hell have you been doing, then?' demanded Diane. 'I thought you were in charge of the search for our son.'

'I was assigned the case at one o'clock this morning,' said Dixon, calmly.

'Oh, right.'

Several photographs of the same car had been stuck to the wall above the computer. A souped-up BMW of some sort, metallic green.

'That's the car,' said Diane. 'His pride and joy. It's an M3 Competition. The all-wheel drive version. Nought to sixty in two-point-eight seconds, as he never tires of telling us.'

'Expensive to insure for someone twenty-four years of age.'

'It's a bit cheaper for a police officer, but still crippling. He doesn't pay rent or anything like that, though.'

'Is it fitted with a black box?'

'No. No GPS tracker either. We've thought of that. Tried Find My iPhone too, but it's switched off. Nothing.'

Dixon stood up. 'What about friends?'

'There's a lad he was at college with, but we've spoken to him. He's not seen Darren since last weekend.'

'And when did you last see him?'

'Tuesday night. He'd gone to work before we got up on Wednesday morning.'

Dixon took two steps towards the door, but Diane stepped in front of him, blocking his path. 'Look, don't say anything in front of my husband, but nobody's told us how Russell Lock was . . . was killed. All we know is he's been found dead and foul play is suspected, which means he was murdered, right, but *how* was he murdered?'

'There's no reason to believe your son —'

'I'm not an idiot, Superintendent.'

Wanted to know what probably happened to her son. Fair enough. Dixon would want to know too.

'He was shot in the head.' No need to explain further, not to a doctor.

Diane closed her eyes, nodded, apparently comforted by the knowledge her son would have been killed instantly, assuming he'd suffered the same fate as Russell Lock.

'D'you think my son's out there too?' she asked. 'In the sea.'

'We'll find him, don't worry.'

'Dead or alive?'

Chapter Five

'Use the multistorey car park behind the station. Rupert Street,' Charlesworth had said. 'Claim it back on expenses.'

Nice, but it meant Monty couldn't come.

Another brand new, purpose built police station, the old one still sitting empty. Steel cladding and glass, this one, with red window frames, it looked more like an office block, shutters and roller doors on the ground floor.

It must be like working in a goldfish bowl, thought Dixon, standing on the pavement outside, trying to count the floors; five landings visible in the vast atrium, but there might be more. There'd be an underground too, the custody suite, probably.

'Detective Chief Superintendent Potter is expecting you, Sir,' said the receptionist, when Dixon emerged from the revolving doors into the brightly coloured reception area. Lilac and lime green armchairs; a student union, possibly, but definitely not a police station.

'What d'you think?' asked Potter, leaning over the balustrade above him. There was mischief in her voice, mercifully. 'I know. It's supposed to be a warm open space where people feel welcome and relaxed. A new concept, apparently.'

'Whose?' asked Dixon.

'The Police and Crime Commissioner's.' Potter opened the glazed security door from the inside. 'Soft furnishings, a vibrant colour palette, corporate graphics. You couldn't make it up.'

'Someone has, Ma'am.'

'It's Deborah. I've told you about that before. Congratulations, by the way. For yesterday. Not this. You're not going to thank me for this. Word's got round Lock's colleagues, and you can cut the atmosphere with a knife. I've seen it before; a toxic mix of fear and anger.'

Dixon was following her across the waiting area, weaving between coffee tables covered in glossy magazines.

'Lift's this way. CID are on the fourth and fifth floors,' she said, jabbing the button. 'We've given over the whole of the fifth floor to your incident room. DCI Hunt was up there already with his team, so it made sense.' Potter waited until the lift doors closed behind them. 'You should know he's left already, so DS Redgrave will deal with the handover; Hunt didn't fancy being moved aside for a superintendent younger than his children, he said. That's a rough translation, anyway.'

I bet it is, thought Dixon, not that he had anything useful to add anyway.

'See how you get on with DS Redgrave to begin with,' continued Potter. 'He can be a pain in the arse, but he does know what he's doing.'

Dixon was old enough to remember proper offices, with doors on them. He still hadn't got used to open plan working at Express Park, and the lift doors opened to reveal much the same layout here. An area the size of a tennis court, perhaps, green and grey striped carpet to match the lime green pillars; long lines of desks facing each other, the tops of heads visible over the low partitioning between them. He understood the rationale behind it, of course he did. You were less likely to put your feet up if everyone could see you. It was cheaper too. But, he hated it all the same.

'Let me introduce you to Glen Redgrave first,' said Potter. 'His team are down the far end. Glen, come and meet Superintendent Dixon.'

The 'acting' had gone; red rag to a bull, probably. A visible sigh, but then Redgrave had exaggerated it, if anything. Fiercely loyal to his DCI, probably. There was certainly no attempt to hide it.

A team of twelve, the five officers at their workstations looking him up and down as Dixon shook Redgrave's hand.

'I've heard a lot about you,' said Dixon, lying. Actually he hadn't; just that Redgrave was a pain in the arse. He'd give him the benefit of the doubt, all the same.

'Don't believe a word of it. We've got a team meeting at two. Everybody will be back for that, Sir.' Redgrave's *Sir* was a bit laboured perhaps. 'Everything's on the system, and if there's anything you need to know, just ask.'

'Thank you.'

'We'll be in the Montpelier Room.' Redgrave gestured to rooms with glazed partitioning along the back wall, most small with round tables and four chairs, but one had a long table and more than enough chairs.

'Good idea, Glen,' said Potter. 'Saves you going through everything twice. And in the meantime, you can get up to speed with the other part of the operation, Nick.'

Dixon had already walked past the other part of the operation, all but three of the workstations empty at that end of the room. That was as it should be, of course.

'I asked DCI Kendall to make herself available,' said Potter. 'We took her entire team from downstairs and reassigned them. That's her at the photocopier. She's got everything up and running overnight and is off to Portishead tomorrow. I'll introduce you and leave you to sort out the handover. You don't want me hovering around like a mother hen all day.'

'Thank you.'

'One last thing, Nick,' said Potter. 'You've got Redgrave and his team on the drug dealer murders, Liz Kendall's team on Lock and Canter, but you'll need to give some thought to possible connections between the two investigations and who's going to focus on that.'

Dixon had sent the text messages from a lay-by on the A38; hadn't had time to check for replies, but then Mark Pearce and Louise Willmott were in the lift. Glass everywhere had its advantages.

'We are, Deborah,' he said.

'We're doing everything you'd expect, Sir,' said Kendall, a little defensively perhaps. A two piece grey trouser suit, just like Potter's; dyed hair in a bob, just like Potter's. No wedding ring.

Dixon wasn't entirely sure why he'd noticed that. He didn't usually look. Maybe it was his own? He was still getting used to it, twiddling it around his ring finger. After all, he'd only had it on since yesterday.

'Mobile phone traces on both of them,' continued Kendall. 'We've got people tracking them on CCTV, but there are hundreds of cameras to check. Number plate recognition cameras too. House to house in the area of Lock's flat. We're speaking to their colleagues, neighbours, friends; going back through their recent arrests.'

'What about proof of life for Canter?' asked Dixon. They were sitting in one of the smaller meeting rooms, on chrome chairs with lime green upholstery, a band of frosted glass in the glazed partitioning giving them some measure of privacy from the open plan office, although people would be able to see their feet. Yet another design gimmick.

'Nothing,' replied Kendall. 'He hasn't touched his bank account. We've checked his email too. We're just waiting to hear from his phone company.'

'That car of his is going to stick out like a sore thumb, isn't it?'

'We've got pictures of it everywhere, asking people to keep an eye out for it. It's going on the evening news too.'

'Any connection with . . . ?' It suddenly occurred to Dixon that he didn't know their names, the two drug dealers who'd been murdered.

'Justin Hampton and Andrew Paul. Not as far as we can see,' replied Kendall. 'They've got form, obviously, and Keith checked their arrest records. No mention of Lock or Canter being the arresting or interviewing officers.'

'They were being investigated by Professional Standards?'

'It's a death in custody. I've arranged a meeting at five. A Superintendent Carlisle and a DI Larkin are coming over from Portishead to brief us on it. You'll take that meeting, of course, Sir.'

He smiled to himself. Carlisle and Larkin. Again. Small world, and all that. 'I will, thank you,' he said. It was Carlisle and Larkin who had arrested him for murder only three and a half short months ago. A night in the cells, a Magistrates' Court appearance, bail application; Dixon could still taste the vomit, grateful to that prison officer for the Extra Strong Mint.

No, he bore Carlisle and Larkin no ill will. There was no grudge. *Gits.*

'Russell Lock was up to his armpits in debt,' said Dixon. 'Credit cards and loans; about forty-five grand all told.'

'Was he?' Kendall looked surprised.

'There was a pile of statements at his flat. Scientific were bagging them and sending them over. We'll need to find out what he was spending his money on.'

'Yes, Sir.'

'The card statements were mainly cash advances.'

'Drugs, you think?'

'I'll check with the pathologist,' replied Dixon. 'He was the best man at my wedding. Still got a hangover, probably.'

'Congratulations, Sir.' Kendall looked surprised. 'When was it?'

'Yesterday.'

Dixon had remained in the meeting room, tapping out a message to Roger Poland:

Any sign of drug usage on Russell Lock?

He was watching the speech bubble, Poland typing a reply, when Mark and Louise walked in and sat down. They'd made themselves a coffee and had spent the last half an hour standing in front of the whiteboards, one at each end of the open plan office, trying to make sense of the jumble of photographs and arrows.

Louise leaned across and placed a mug in front of Dixon.

'Thanks, Lou,' he said, his phone buzzing.

No. Tox screen all clear. David C asked if you were going on honeymoon . . . put me on the spot. Sorry!

Dixon would reply later, something about ruining their wedding night and owing them a curry.

'Thanks for coming,' he said, turning to Mark and Louise.

'How was last night?' asked Mark, with a lopsided grin.

'Fine, until David Charlesworth turned up,' replied Dixon. 'We were playing Scrabble.'

'Yeah, right.'

He thought it best not to argue the point. 'We've got two drug dealers murdered with a 3D printed gun, a police officer also murdered with a printed gun, and another police officer – his partner – is missing. There are teams already working on both investigations, with us sitting in the middle. It'll be our job to find the connection between the two. They've checked the drug dealers' arrest records and, on the face of it, their paths hadn't crossed.'

'The gun's the obvious connection,' said Louise. 'If it was the same one.'

'A big *if*, and we may not be able to tell, anyway. Forensics can identify the batch of polymer, but it may have been used to print more than one gun.'

'Yeah, I suppose it could.'

'Mark, I need you to review the CCTV images from both investigations.'

'They're going to love that.'

'You're going to need to be careful, Sir,' said Louise, tentatively, not that she was usually reticent when she thought Dixon had got it wrong. 'Last time out you were in charge of a regional task force, which was fine. This time you're running two teams. You're going to need to delegate and let them get on with their j—'

'She's right, Sir,' interrupted Mark.

Louise was talking, but it was Jane's voice Dixon could hear.

'Have you spoken to my wife?' he asked.

'She rang me to see what was going on.' Louise's face reddened. 'She asked me to remind you . . .'

'Jane's right, of course,' said Dixon, trying not to sound impatient. 'We'll act as liaison between the two teams, focusing our efforts on any connection between the two investigations.'

'That sounds much better.'

'There's another thing. I want the gunsmith. Someone is printing these bloody weapons and I'd like to welcome him to this warm and open space, see how he likes its soft furnishings and vibrant colours.'

Chapter Six

'There's someone on the phone from the ballistics lab in Birmingham, Sir,' said Louise, her hand over the mouthpiece. 'Said she's been asked to give you a call by Donald Watson.'

'Put her on.'

'You'll have to take it here. I haven't got a clue how to use this phone system.'

'Nick Dixon,' he said, standing by her workstation.

'Susan Reynolds,' said the voice on the end of the line. 'Donald said you'd got someone printing guns on your patch. Bit of a specialist subject of mine.'

'Looks that way. We've had three murders, so far. Nine-millimetre bullets, point blank range, no exit wounds.'

'Certainly sounds like it in that case. Rather you than me, Gunga Din.'

'Thank you.'

'Nine-millimetre, you say? Could be a Songbird in that case. They've been test-fired up to three-fifty-seven magnum without shattering.'

'Where will they be getting the ammunition from?' he asked.

'It's probably homemade. You can buy empty cartridge cases online; twenty quid for a hundred used ones that can be repurposed. Either that or new ones at thirty quid or so for two hundred and fifty, depending on the calibre. Then you need some smokeless powder, primers and the projectile itself, which is just a lump of lead and a mould. There are plenty of videos on YouTube that'll show you how to do it. After that it's a matter of getting the amount of powder right, so the gun doesn't blow up in your hand. We always fire them from clamps and stand well back. In the field, I'd suggest using a chain mail glove or something like that. Wear glasses too, goggles preferably.'

'Tell me about the Songbird then. Who gives these bloody things their names, for a start?'

'The designer. Has a nice ring to it, don't you think?'

Dixon waited.

'The files are all online so you download them. The Songbird comes in eleven parts, each one with a separate file. It prints on its side, which means there are internal supports that need to be cut out, filed down. Ordinary PLA will do for everything except the barrel. That can be metal held in place with epoxy, or Taulman Bridge nylon filament printed on the highest setting will do it. I heard of one lasting sixty-two shots when they used that. The latest set of downloadable files say to use Taulman Bridge. The firing pin is a standard twelve-gauge roofing nail. That's a diameter of two-point-six-eight-zero millimetres, with a nought-point-two-eight-one head. Then you've got to grind the tip down for zero-point-zero-four-zero profusion.'

Dixon had leaned over, slid the pen out of Louise's hand, and was scribbling on her notepad.

'What else d'you need to know?' Susan didn't give him time to answer. 'Takes about twenty hours to print, then another couple of hours to put together. I guess where I'm going with this is you need to know what you're doing.'

'Will any printer do it?'

'Pretty much. It needs an eleven-inch diameter build plate, that's the base, so that's not that big to be honest.'

'How much do they change hands for?'

'A bloke in London was selling them for a thousand pounds each, with five rounds. He's doing twelve years now.'

'Thank you.'

'There's a video on YouTube of someone in America firing one in his garage. I suggest you look at that. In the meantime, let me know if there's anything else you need.'

'You'll have all heard the news by now, I'm sure,' said Dixon, looking around the conference table in the Montpelier Room. 'Does anyone know Russell Lock or Darren Canter?'

'Only socially' seemed to be the gist of the murmuring.

'Well, if you know anything you think might be remotely useful, speak to DC Willmott. PC Canter is missing, not seen since his shift ended on Wednesday evening. PC Lock's body was pulled from the sea off Burnham yesterday morning. A single gunshot wound to the head, from what looks like a 3D printed gun, so the same as Hampton and Paul. We're still waiting for Ballistics to confirm that though.'

Dixon had spent a couple of hours reading up on the murders of Justin Hampton and Andrew Paul, their bodies found in a flat in Crofts End. The post mortem reports confirmed what Charlesworth had said – the gunshot wounds being the fatal injuries that 'put them out of their misery'. They'd taken a beating first, confirmed by the forensic analysis of the murder scene, blood spatter in particular.

And the photographs.

The witness statements hadn't taken long. Neighbours had complained the victims were known drug dealers, with people coming and going from the flat at all hours. Regular reports of antisocial behaviour had resulted in several police visits to the property in the past but nothing had been done.

No one had seen or heard anything the night of the murders apart from a commotion an hour or so earlier described as 'just the usual', before the anonymous tip-off came in at 11.37.

Conveniently.

Hunt's Policy Log hadn't been terribly enlightening either. It was supposed to be a daily record of the SIO's decision-making process as the investigation progressed. Instead, there was a single entry: 'Proceeding on the assumption it is a gangland killing, turf war'. A man of few words, clearly.

'We did check, but haven't found a connection, have we?' asked Redgrave, looking around the table.

'No, Sarge,' said the detective constable sitting to Redgrave's left. Redgrave hadn't bothered with introductions, not that Dixon would have remembered the names anyway. The niceties could wait. 'I checked Hampton and Paul's previous and there's nothing to connect them with Lock or Canter. Phone, email, WhatsApp. Nothing.'

'Where have we got to with the CCTV image of the car?'

'High Tech weren't able to enhance it any better than it is now,' said the constable.

Dixon had seen the image, pinned to the whiteboard. Grainy, a car illuminated in street lighting leaving the general area – that was the best that could be said about it; three frames before, it went behind a tree, the camera mounted on the corner of an office building covering the car park, the road visible in the background. There had been other cars, of course there had, but they'd been picked up on ANPR cameras at traffic lights, the drivers spoken to and eliminated from enquiries. This one had turned off somewhere, avoiding the number plate recognition cameras.

A dark SUV of some sort. Not a BMW, no matter how hard Dixon squinted at the photo.

'What about informants?' he asked.

'Adamant there's no turf war, Guv,' replied the officer sitting to Dixon's left. 'It's all quiet at the moment, everybody's minding their own business.'

'That would be a first,' said Redgrave. 'What about that lot trying to muscle in when the Albanians moved out of Whiteladies Road?'

'Mancs. They were seen off by the Clifton crew.'

It reminded Dixon why he preferred rural areas. Policing cities was a thankless task. Gangs fighting over turf, witnesses frightened to say anything. Then you had the general public apparently happy with drug dealers killing each other. *'Why don't you just let them get on with it?'*

It was clear Hunt's investigation had been getting nowhere. A conclusion jumped to far too early, evidence sought to confirm it, nothing found. All too common, sadly. Dixon would have to tread carefully.

'Anything else?' he asked.

He listened attentively to three keen young detectives listing everything they'd done in the last twenty-four hours, everyone they'd spoken to; trying not to wince every time he was called 'Guv'.

Redgrave's frustration was starting to show. Arms folded, the sighs getting louder.

'I think we need to consider the possibility it's not gang-related, Guv.' The officer sitting on Dixon's right looked up from her notepad. She had been doodling throughout the meeting, a horse's head gradually appearing on the corner of the page. 'Maybe there really is a vigilante on the loose; someone whose son or daughter has died—'

'That's bollocks, Anna, and well you know it,' snapped Redgrave. 'It's just that prick York using it to further his bloody election campaign.'

That explained the photograph in the top right corner of the whiteboard. Sohail York, the annotation scribbled underneath reading, simply, 'TWAT'.

'A gangland killing was a reasonable assumption, but we've looked at that and I think we can rule it out.' Dixon was treading carefully; trying to, anyway. 'I looked at the ballistics report and it confirms the bullets were fired from a gun or guns the barrels of which were printed from the same batch of Taulman Bridge nylon filament. We need to track down everyone who has bought that in the force area in the last two years.'

'There could be hundreds,' protested Redgrave. 'A lot of effort for a couple of bloody drug dealers. The DCI said—'

'It's not just drug dealers now, is it, Glen?' said Anna.

'Start with the suppliers, get their customer lists, and work through them one by one.'

'Who do you want to put on that?' asked Redgrave.

'All of you,' replied Dixon. 'Find the gunsmith, find the killer.'

He was standing in front of the whiteboard, staring at the photograph of Sohail York, when Anna appeared at his elbow. 'He's an independent candidate, standing to be the PCC at the election in May, Sir. Seems to think there's a vigilante out there, doing our job for us.' She was looking over her shoulder, nervously. 'It's a line of enquiry we haven't even looked at and I keep saying we should at least be speaking to anyone who's lost a loved one to a drugs overdose, surely? Especially if the drugs had been supplied by Hampton or Paul.'

'We checked that,' said Redgrave, arriving to shut the conversation down. 'There's no evidence Hampton or Paul supplied the drugs to a deceased addict anywhere in the force area in the last twenty-four months. If there was, we'd have looked at it, of course we would.'

'I'd like to visit the crime scene,' said Dixon, affording Anna the opportunity to slip away to her workstation.

'Yes, of course, Sir,' replied Redgrave. 'You don't need me for that, do you?'

'No.'

'Forensics have finished and it's all locked up. Anna will get you the keys.'

◆ ◆ ◆

'How were they?'

'Defensive.'

'Hardly surprising,' replied Louise. 'Their DCI has been shunted off to God knows where and some young superintendent they don't know is parachuted in. We'd have been the same if they'd done that to you.'

'Thank you,' replied Dixon, sure there was a compliment in there somewhere.

'It's not exactly a big team, either.'

'We can rule out a gangland killing. They've pretty much exhausted that line of enquiry and got nowhere.'

'Which leaves what?'

A good question. 'Anything else,' was the best he could come up with. 'Forensics have identified the polymer the gun barrel was printed from, so Redgrave and his team are going to be tracking down and speaking to everyone who bought some in the last two years. DCI Hunt thought it was too much effort for a couple of drug dealers, from what I can gather.'

'How many people is that?'

'No idea.' Dixon pulled into the nearside and looked across to an office block: cars in the car park, a camera mounted on the corner of the building. 'That's the camera that got the dark SUV, going that way,' he said, looking over his shoulder.

'How far are we from Hampton's flat?'

'It's just around the corner.'

'Could be the killers then, making their getaway.' Louise had turned in her seat. 'Maybe the polymer will turn up something?'

Dixon turned into Plummers Hill and parked in the bus stop opposite a terrace of small houses, a block of four flats at either end, the porches larger with doors at the side and front.

'It's number forty-one,' said Dixon, 'so that block there.'

'Nineteen eighties, maybe.' Louise was scrolling on her phone. Rightmove, probably. 'Barrett, I reckon. The houses have two bedrooms, the flats only one.'

Dixon was about to ask how much they changed hands for, when . . .

'The houses are about two-forty these days,' continued Louise. 'The flats maybe one-seventy.'

Most of the front gardens had been gravelled; wheelie bins and rotary washing lines, rubbish strewn among the dead weeds. An old barbecue, four tyres, a motorcycle engine, a laundry basket full of empty bottles. Two of the houses in the terrace had neatly manicured lawns, pruned roses; the neighbours who'd complained, probably, although that was a lazy assumption.

The door at the side of the porch, a flight of stairs behind it, grubby carpet, the handrail loose. Dixon had brushed the pile of junk mail and freebie newspapers aside with his foot; a letter from Bristol City Council, another from Bristol Water.

'Council tax and a water bill,' said Louise. She'd put on a pair of latex gloves and picked up the pile, shuffling it into some sort of order. 'That's it. Rest is crap.'

'Leave it for the landlord.'

'This place is rented?' Louise dropped the post on the bottom step, followed Dixon up the stairs. 'Bloody landlord should be ashamed of themselves.'

'You're assuming it was in this state when they let it out.'

'Yeah.'

'Remind me about the downstairs flat.'

'There's someone in there now, but it was empty at the time of the murders.'

A student let, originally, but Hampton had dropped out of university. Four rooms: a living room, kitchen, bathroom and a bedroom. 'Paul dossed on the sofa,' said Dixon.

'Nice.'

The sleeping bag was still there, unzipped and lying open on the floor, heavily bloodstained. Dixon looked around the room. Television – flat screen – games console, beer cans. He could have been standing in PC Russell Lock's living room. 'What is a drug dealer's living room supposed to look like?' he asked.

'Is that a trick question?'

'Let's assume the killers took the drugs and whatever money there was.' Something wasn't right about it. Dixon knew that much. 'And ignore the blood.'

A large pool of dried blood had congealed on the carpet in front of the sofa, more spattered up the wall behind it. Even on the ceiling, from a weapon wielded during the lengthy beating that must have preceded the execution.

Dixon tipped his head. An odd choice of word that, *execution*.

'No weapons were found,' said Louise. 'The killers must have taken them.'

Everybody had assumed there were two, or more than one certainly. Hunt, for a start, although there were two figures visible in the unidentified SUV, so again a reasonable assumption, perhaps. And how would one person be able to overpower two drug dealers? They'd be expecting trouble every time someone came into the flat, wouldn't they?

A gun pointed at them changed things, though. Yes, one person could've done it.

Dixon blinked away the image of Paul's body lying on the floor, his legs still in his sleeping bag, hands behind his back. The killers – or killer – had used cable ties, thick white ones, pulled tight. Hampton in the bedroom first, then Paul, perhaps. And once restrained it would have been easy.

A knife of some sort and a piece of wood – baseball bat, possibly. There were burns too.

Odd that not one of the neighbours had heard anything out of the ordinary. Although that begged the question: what was *ordinary*?

The bedroom painted a similar picture. The blood-soaked sheets were still there, the mangled corner of the duvet encrusted with Hampton's saliva, stuffed in his mouth at some point, presumably to stop him screaming.

'Did you see the photos?' asked Dixon.

'Yeah.'

'Strange that there was no meaningful DNA found; plenty from the victims, some from their customers who've been traced, but nothing that looks like it should have come from the killers.'

'They were careful.'

'Very.'

The contents of the bedside table had been emptied on to the floor next to the bed, the drawers then thrown in the corner. Both wardrobe doors were standing open, the top shelf emptied on to the floor too. After death, given the bloodstains on the carpet underneath.

'Had a good rummage, by the looks of things,' said Louise. 'Looking for the drugs and the money, I suppose.'

'Did you have a look at their previous convictions?' asked Dixon.

'Hampton's got two for possession of class B, and one intent to supply class B.'

'How much on the intent to supply?'

'A hundred grams,' replied Louise. 'Paul was clean.'

'Clean?'

'He'd been cautioned for drunk and disorderly, but there's nothing else.'

Dixon took a long, slow breath. 'We've got two lads who look like they've been turned over by a cartel, and one's clean and the other's dealing a bit of cannabis to his friends, probably. A hundred grams is hardly big league, is it?'

'He didn't even get a custodial sentence, Sir,' said Louise. 'They may have branched out though. You never know.'

'Have you seen their photographs?'

'Yes, Sir.'

'Not exactly the Kray twins.'

Louise picked up the end of a cable plugged into a socket on the wall, the cable draped across the chest of drawers. 'Looks like he had a laptop. This is for a MacBook, my husband's got one,' she said. 'The killers probably took that as well.'

'Hello?'

The call came from the bottom of the stairs.

'I'll go and see what she wants,' said Louise.

'Are you estate agents?'

'Police, Madam.'

Dixon was listening from the bedroom, trying to work out the number of blows from the blood spatter on the ceiling; seventeen, the report had said.

'Only, I live next door and we were wondering what's going to happen to the flat.'

'Mrs Kimber, isn't it?' asked Dixon, appearing at the top of the stairs with his best disarming smile painted on.

'Yes, dear.'

'Lock up, Lou,' he said, dropping a set of keys into her hand. 'I'll be next door.'

◆ ◆ ◆

'Nice garden.'

'I sometimes wonder why I bother.' The old lady shook her head. 'Look at this place.'

'When was it you complained to us about drug dealing in the flat, Mrs Kimber?' asked Dixon, taking a bit of a flier perhaps, but it seemed a safe enough bet.

'Look, I don't want you to think I'm some sort of nosy parker.'

'Far from it.'

'They were fine when they first moved in. There was a bit of student high jinks, the odd party, but then Justin dropped out last summer and that's when it all got a bit much.' Mrs Kimber was standing on her doorstep, her arms folded, craning her neck to look along the terrace.

'What did?' asked Dixon.

'The thieving, to begin with.' Her eyes narrowed. Dixon could understand the anger, although it might have been pity. He couldn't tell. 'Had to keep our doors locked after that, we did. I'm sure I had cash taken from my purse. I used to leave it on the hall table and he must've opened my front door, the little sod.'

'And the drug dealing?'

'That started about six months ago. You've got people turning up at all times of the day and night, some in a right old state, shouting and lurching about all over the place, using our gardens like a public toilet. You wouldn't believe what I've had to clean up of a morning.'

Maybe Hampton and Paul had 'branched out', to use Louise's phrase.

'Twice I rang your lot. And Doris, two doors up. Never heard a thing back, although there was a visit, for all the good it did.'

'What about the night of the murders?' asked Dixon. 'Did you hear anything?'

'No, dear. I take my hearing aids out at night. Sleep like a baby.'

Chapter Seven

An empty shop. It still had the stencilling on the window, 'CLOSING DOWN SALE', although someone had tried to cover it with banners stuck to the inside.

Sohail 4 PCC

People in there. It seemed too good an opportunity to miss. There was even a loading bay to park in.

'Who's this?' asked Louise.

'He's standing as an independent in the PCC election,' replied Dixon, pulling on the handbrake. 'Been telling everyone there's a vigilante killing drug dealers and we've lost control of the streets.'

'Elected Police and Crime Commissioners.' Louise sneered. 'Which bright spark thought that was a good idea?'

'We've got time for a quick chat.'

'Before what?'

'A meeting at five with Carlisle and Larkin from the PSD. I'll need you to sit in on that.'

Louise stifled a chuckle. 'Referee it, you mean?'

'Something like that.' Dixon glanced in the shop window. A couple of desks, filing cabinets, boxes of leaflets, posters on the wall; sharp suit, beaming at the camera – a professional photo shoot, obviously. 'He's getting funding from somewhere,' Dixon said. 'Let's see if he knows something we don't.'

'Welcome to my campaign headquarters.' York's arms were outstretched, quickly sagging at the sight of warrant cards. His smile wasn't far behind them either.

The face said 'what now?' but he was clearly anxious not to appear hostile. 'How can I help you?' York asked, loud enough to drown out the sigh from his assistant.

'I'm investigating the murders of Justin Hampton and Andrew Paul, Sir,' replied Dixon. 'And you appear to have information that might assist the enquiry. I've seen various newspaper articles, interviews you've given to the local press in the last few days.'

'I don't know anything in particular,' said York, nervously.

Dixon waited, allowing the awkward silence to hang until York felt the need to fill it.

'I thought it was a reasonable assumption based on what I do know.'

'And what is that?'

'Look, I'm not sure I should be seen speaking to you.'

Dixon allowed himself a laugh of disbelief. 'You're standing for election to the office of Police and Crime Commissioner, but don't think you should be seen speaking to the police?' He let that hang for a while too. 'How's that going to work then?'

'It's not a good *look* for me, is it?' said York. 'I'm happy to talk to you about policing generally, just not an individual case. I'll look like a grass.'

'I'm trying to find the killer or killers of Justin Hampton and Andrew Paul, Sir. I'm not interested in politics.' Dixon was trying to stay patient; failing. 'The other alternative is I arrest you and we continue this down at the station.'

'You wouldn't dare.'

Probably wouldn't, no. Wouldn't want to give him the free publicity, but he wasn't telling York that. 'Try me.'

'Go ahead. You'd have a riot on your hands.' York sat down behind the vacant desk. 'All right, all right. This is getting us nowhere. The word on the street is it wasn't gang related, there's no trouble at the moment, everyone just doing their own thing.'

'And you know these people, I suppose.'

'I live in the community, Superintendent. Of course I know them. Most of them came to the youth club I ran when they were kids.'

'Were Hampton and Paul drug dealers?'

'Small time.'

'So, who killed them?'

'I don't know. I'd say if I did.' York was shuffling the pens on the desk, lining them up, avoiding eye contact. 'I just thought a vigilante was a possible explanation.'

'And it got you some column inches in the local paper.'

'Are you telling me there definitely isn't a vigilante?'

'It's a line of enquiry we haven't ruled out, Sir,' replied Dixon. 'Equally, I would have to describe it as highly unlikely.'

'Then we'll have to agree to disagree, won't we?' A defiance had crept into York's voice. 'I suppose you're going to lecture me about claiming you've lost control of the streets next?'

'Not at all, Sir. You're perfectly entitled to your opinion, and if it's a line that appeals to your voters, then so be it.'

'What's that supposed to mean?'

'It's not *supposed* to mean anything, Sir. If you're elected, you'll quickly find things aren't nearly so simple, but then, what are the chances of that?'

'I'm trying to start a conversation.'

'Who with?' Dixon couldn't help himself; probably should have, mind you.

Dixon allowed the door of York's campaign office to slam behind him.

'Do you want me to check him out?' asked Louise.

'Don't bother,' he replied, unlocking the Land Rover. 'He won't have any previous – any convictions and he'd be barred from standing.'

'He's on the phone already.' Louise opened the passenger door casually, spoke without looking up. 'Complaining about you, probably.'

'There were no traces of cocaine found anywhere in Hampton's flat.' Dixon was sitting in the driver's seat of the Land Rover, waiting for Louise to put on her seatbelt. 'If you were going to rob a drug dealer, pinch his drugs and money, you wouldn't pick a small time weed dealer, would you? You'd go for someone higher up the food chain, where the reward was worth the risk.'

'Low reward, but low risk, I suppose. You wouldn't kill them like that, either, if it was just a robbery.'

'Let's see if Lock and Canter attended any drug deaths, any overdoses, in the last two years.'

'Almost bound to, I'd have thought.'

'We know they didn't arrest Hampton or Paul, but their paths might've crossed some other way.' Dixon turned the key, the diesel engine rumbling into life.

'You're thinking the two cases really are connected, then?'

'Hoping they are, Lou,' replied Dixon, allowing his voice to be drowned out by the engine. Almost. 'Hoping they are.'

'Superintendent Carlisle and DI Larkin are here, Sir,' said Kendall, when Dixon and Louise stepped out of the lift. 'I've put them in the Montpelier Room.'

'Thank you.'

'They've been waiting about fifteen minutes.'

'Any news of Darren Canter?'

'Nothing yet.'

Deep breath, count to ten. Nice and professional at all times.

Carlisle and Larkin stood up when Dixon opened the door of the conference room. 'Good afternoon,' they said in unison, Larkin tagging a 'Sir' on the end.

He'd almost forgotten he held the same rank as Carlisle now. 'Sit, please,' he said.

Carlisle remained standing, his hand outstretched. 'I feel we ought to clear the air.'

'Not at all. No need. We're all just doing our jobs as best we can. No one can ask for more than that.' He wasn't sure who looked more surprised, Carlisle or Louise. A firm handshake, all the same. 'Now, what have you got for us on Lock and Canter?'

Carlisle sat down and opened a file on the table in front of him. 'They're both the subject of a conduct investigation arising out of an arrest made near the Clifton Suspension Bridge on New Year's Eve. The individual they arrested later died in custody, and there's a separate investigation ongoing in relation to that. The custody officer concerned has been suspended and the matter referred to the Independent Office for Police Conduct.'

Dixon had sat down on the same side of the conference table as Carlisle and Larkin, turning his seat to face them. Somehow the other side felt confrontational. He'd avoided sitting at the head of the table too. It was a little like those new interview rooms at Express Park, where the interviewing officer and suspect sat side by side to help build a rapport. Bollocks, of course, but perhaps it was time to build a rapport with Carlisle and Larkin?

'Is there bodycam footage?' he asked.

'Yes, Sir,' replied Larkin, opening a laptop and turning it to face Dixon and Louise. 'The two individuals you see in the background called emergency services. An ambulance was despatched at the same time, but Lock and Canter got there first. The report was of a person in a wheelchair brandishing a knife.'

Dixon clicked Play. 'Who's wearing the camera?'

'This is Russell Lock's,' replied Carlisle. 'Canter's isn't any better, I'm afraid.'

The bodycam footage had been filmed by a camera mounted on the left side of PC Lock's stab vest, right about the height Dixon had worn his buttonhole only the day before.

Time flies, and all that.

The footage bounced around as Lock walked towards the small group on the pavement, his arms visible from time to time in the frame.

'What's her name, the person in the wheelchair?'

'Bryony Beech. She was well known to police and had a long history of mental health problems. It's all in the file.'

Dixon turned back to the screen.

'What've you been up to then, Bryony?' asked Lock, both officers standing back from her wheelchair, out of arm's reach.

'Leave me alone.'

'We've had reports you've been waving a knife about, Bryony. What's that all about?'

'Nothing.'

'Where is it?'

'She's still got it,' said a voice from across the narrow road.

'We're going to need to search you, Bryony, if you don't hand it over.' Canter that time, out of shot to Lock's right.

'Just fuck off and leave me alone.'

'I've seen enough,' said Dixon, clicking Pause. 'Just tell me how it ends.'

'Basically, with Bryony face down on the pavement, Canter kneeling on her. There's a lot of spitting and she's trying to bite them at one point too.'

'Did they find a knife?'

'A small kitchen knife,' replied Larkin.

'It escalated pretty quickly and there's a complaint from the family,' said Carlisle. He was watching Louise making notes, trying to read them upside down. 'They're also alleging that the restraint played a part in her later death in custody.'

'What do the witnesses say?' asked Dixon.

'They're largely supportive of Lock and Canter, to be fair. Bryony was uncooperative, aggressive, but that's still no excuse for Lock and Canter's conduct in my view. They lacked empathy, they were impatient, and allowed the situation to get out of hand when it needn't have done. It doesn't amount to gross misconduct, but my recommendation to the panel will be a written warning and further training. I'll also be recommending that they're separated, we'll get one of them transferred to another station. Or at least we would've done if . . .' Carlisle's voice tailed off.

'What happened later?'

'Bryony was taken down to the custody suite at Express Park. It was the only space available at that time on New Year's Eve.' Larkin closed the laptop. 'Further restraint was necessary when she was checked in and it seems to have got a bit out of hand at one point. She had complex needs, medical issues that weren't addressed, and was found unresponsive in her cell in the early hours. An ambulance was called but she was pronounced dead on arrival at Musgrove Park.'

'No one was monitoring the video feeds and she wasn't checked as she should have been, seems to have been the failure,' said Carlisle. 'The restraint is all on film. It looks justified and proportionate to me.'

'What can you tell me about the family?'

'Both parents are alive and there's a sister. They live in St Paul's. I know what you're thinking and it's possible. Certainly the sister. She's Sohail York's assistant. Militant, argumentative, and very angry about her sister's death.'

'The custody officer has been suspended?'

'Paid leave while the IOPC investigation takes place. His name's Edward Grady and he lives at Burtle out on the Levels.'

'We need to do a welfare check, Lou,' said Dixon.

'Now?'

'Now.' He turned back to Carlisle. 'Have you got Lock and Canter's personnel files?' he asked.

'These are the originals, we've kept copies.' Sliding two folders along the table. 'This is a complete copy of our file, as well.' A lever arch file this time. 'I can email you a secure link to view the footage of both incidents.'

'Have Bryony's family seen the videos?'

'They have.'

'That went well,' said Louise, when the lift doors closed behind Carlisle and Larkin. 'You'll be putting them on your Christmas card list next.'

'What about that welfare check?' asked Dixon.

'Express Park are sending someone over there now.'

'How are you getting on, Mark?' he asked, stopping behind Pearce, who was sitting hunched at a workstation, staring at a screen.

'Nothing yet. They've isolated quite a lot of images, but I haven't seen anything so far. This is interesting, though.' Pearce leaned back, gesturing at the screen. 'We've had the stuff through from Canter's phone. Nothing in the calls, but there are some odd messages. The last one was timed Wednesday at five-twenty-one. It reads: *overpaid disgraced detect 11.30.*'

'It sounds like a cryptic crossword clue.' Louise raised her voice over the kettle. 'My grandad used to drive us round the bend with them.'

Dixon had downloaded the app to his iPhone months ago. One of those ones that looked useful, and you might need one day if you ever got lost or had an accident in the middle of nowhere. Or you were luring your victim somewhere remote to commit a murder, perhaps.

He opened the What3Words app on his phone, clicked on the microphone in the search bar and said, 'Overpaid, disgraced, detect.' Loud and clear.

Three options to choose from, one in Canada, another in Spain. No, far more likely was the exact match: Newport, South Wales. And there it was. A little square on the map just east of the city, right on a bend in the River Severn coast path.

'What time was high tide at Newport on Wednesday evening?'

'Give me a sec,' replied Mark. 'Eleven-twenty. High too, by the looks of things. That's assuming the measurement is the same that side of the estuary. Nearly twelve metres.'

Chapter Eight

'Darren Canter's BMW is there,' said Louise, her phone lighting up the passenger compartment of the Land Rover as Dixon sped over the Prince of Wales Bridge. 'In a lay-by opposite the Seawall Tearooms. The local lot have spoken to the owner, who said it's been there a couple of days. She was going to ring us if it was still there in the morning, apparently.'

'Is there any CCTV on the tearooms?' asked Dixon.

'No idea, but satnav says we'll be there in twenty-two minutes.'

'Has someone been out to the What3Words square?'

'A uniformed constable with a torch,' replied Louise. 'Couldn't see anything, but they've got forensics on the way with arc lamps.'

'Let's see if the Coastguard have any experience of where bodies going into the water on this side of the estuary usually wash up, will you?'

'I'll ring them when we get there, if that's all right. Off here.' Louise was following the satnav on her phone, the roads gradually getting narrower as Dixon drove down towards the coast, the Newport Retail Park behind them.

He was making an assumption, of course he was, albeit the obvious one, and it wouldn't do any harm to check. After all, Russell Lock had been found in the water.

A narrow lane, open countryside on both sides, lights in the distance across the water.

'Odd, seeing it from this side,' said Louise. 'Where's Hinkley Point?'

'Can't see it from here,' replied Dixon. 'It's out of view, round the corner. That's Clevedon, and that's Minehead you're looking at over there.'

Blue lights up ahead, a patrol car blocking the lane, the uniformed officer waving them through. 'Plenty of room to park down there, Sir.'

'We'll need a flatbed lorry to pick up Canter's car,' said Dixon, sliding his warrant card back into his pocket.

'Already on the way,' replied Louise. 'Give me a minute and I'll ring the Coastguard now.'

'There's his car.' Dixon drove past it and parked at the end of the lane, leaving Louise sitting in the Land Rover. He walked up the steps to the top of the sea wall, a vast expanse of wet mud glistening in the moonlight in front of him.

The grass was wet, slippery, the bank much like the one on the River Parrett; tons of rubble on the seaward side, coated in slime, the high tide line clearly visible and alarmingly close to the top of the wall.

'That's him up there.' Louise's voice, so someone was looking for him.

'Superintendent Dixon?'

'Yes.'

'Sergeant Williams, Sir. I've got Mrs Jenkins from the tearooms, if you'd like to have a word with her now. She seems rather keen to go to bed.'

'Have you been out to the meeting spot?'

'Not personally, Sir, no. I've got a PC Jones out there keeping an eye on it.'

'The car's locked, I take it?'

'Yes, Sir.'

Metallic green, with custom wheel arches and tyres to match.

'Nice car, it is,' said Williams. 'Must've cost him a pretty packet. Those tyres must be two-seventy each on their own. And the road tax, insurance.' He puffed out his cheeks. 'I'd like to know where he's getting his money from.'

Side hustles, Canter's mother had said. No doubt High Tech's report on his computer would shed more light.

'Mrs Jenkins is through here, Sir,' continued Williams, pushing open the front door of the house adjacent to the tearooms. 'Nice spot, it is, down here. I quite often bring the dog for a walk.'

Dixon hadn't thought it was that late, but Mrs Jenkins was already in her dressing gown. She was sitting at her kitchen table, puffing on a cigarette.

'Tell me about the car,' he said, when Williams had finished making the introductions.

'It was there when I got up on Thursday morning and it's been there ever since. Hasn't moved and I haven't seen anyone going to it, either.' She leaned over and flicked her ash into the grate behind her. 'It does happen though. Some people leaves their cars here and walks the estuary path. Not often though, and not this time of year, really, thinking about it.'

'Did you hear anything on Wednesday night, say between eleven and midnight?'

'Fast asleep, I'd have been, at that time of night.'

'Is there much shooting around here?'

'A bit, on the fields. Pigeons and rabbits, I think.'

'And is it busy in February?'

'Not really. We only open if the weather's nice, and at half-term like. We gets plenty of dog walkers, bird watchers at the low tides and fishermen on the high tides. It's a good spot for winter cod, so they tells me. Not sure I'd want to eat it, mind. Not out of that water. Sometimes you gets three or four of them lined up along the top of the wall there.'

'I asked her about CCTV, Sir,' offered Williams. 'And there isn't any.'

'I've got a camera covering the outside seating, but it's only switched on when we're open. It's so I can see if any of the tables need clearing, really.'

'Were there any cars here on Wednesday night?'

'A couple maybe. There was one with the windows steamed up. I think that was a courting couple, if you know what I mean?' Mrs Jenkins dropped her cigarette into the grate, a wisp of smoke rising. 'We gets a few of them down here.'

'Did you recognise any of the cars?'

'There was a van I've seen a few times. I think he's an angler.'

'Scientific are here, Sarge.'

The shout came from the outside, so Dixon made his excuses and left Mrs Jenkins to go to bed.

'You can hitch a ride, Sir,' said Williams. 'The gate's open. I'll hang on here, keep an eye out for your lorry.'

'Thank you.'

'What did the Coastguard say, Lou?' asked Dixon, when they'd climbed into the passenger seat of the van, the driver creeping along the rough track behind the sea wall, equipment rattling in the back.

'They sometimes get them at Newport Wetlands and the mouth of the River Usk. Sudbrook is another possibility, but that's above the bridge we came over. They'll start a search in the morning. They get quite a few, he said. Jumpers mainly.'

There was a light up ahead, on the top of the sea wall.

'That's PC Jones,' said the driver. 'So, that's your spot up there. I'll get the lamps set up first, then have a look with luminol. I'm guessing it's blood you'll be looking for.'

A bend in the sea wall, lights from the flat above the tearooms just visible through the trees. No anglers yet, but then the tide was too far out.

'It's a three-metre square, Sir,' said Jones, when Dixon had scrambled to the top of the bank. 'I've marked what I think is just about the middle of it with that cone.'

Plenty of footprints in the wet grass. Jones's probably.

'There won't be any blood,' said Dixon. 'Not here.'

'Why not?'

'You might meet someone up here, but you wouldn't shoot them here. You'd have to carry the body across those boulders down to the water's edge. If there was going to be blood, it'd be down there, but the tide's been in and out three times since Wednesday night.'

'Where d'you want them?' asked the Scientific Services officer, appearing at the top of the bank, struggling under the weight of an arc lamp.

'Light up the whole area and we'll have a look anyway,' said Louise.

'What about cartridge cases, Sir, if he was shot?' asked Jones.

'They don't eject from a 3D printed gun. And if I'm right, it'd be down amongst those rocks.'

'I've got a metal detector in the van.'

An arc lamp at either end of the general area lit up nothing except wet grass. Same for the luminol. Nothing on the concrete plinth at the top of the boulders.

'Do you want me to go down there?' asked the Scientific Services officer. 'If so, it's probably best done in daylight.'

'Thank you,' replied Dixon. 'We'll need a couple of officers at the gate down there, speaking to dog walkers and anyone else passing by, seeing if they saw anything suspicious on Wednesday evening.'

'I can organise that, Sir,' said Jones.

'House to house, such as it is, and a look at the nearest ANPR cameras. We could try a post on local shore fishing Facebook pages too, see if any anglers were out that night.'

'There's a Newport Sea Anglers group. A fishing tackle shop too. Leave it with me, Sir.' Jones again.

Dixon trudged back towards the tearooms along the top of the sea wall. He wasn't entirely sure what he had expected to find, apart from Canter's car. It was that assumption again – that Canter's body was in the water, and he wouldn't know one way or the other unless and until it washed up somewhere.

'What d'you think, Lou?' he asked, idly.

'I reckon he's in the water,' she replied. 'Shot down at the edge, like you say, and straight in. You don't seem convinced.'

'I'm not.' Dixon had stopped and was staring out to sea, his hands thrust deep into his pockets. 'There are too many assumptions. Ask yourself, what do we actually know?'

'His car's here.'

'But we don't know who drove it here.'

'He got that message with the What3Words geocode in it.'

'We don't know he got it because we don't have his phone. All we know is it was sent. He might've been dead already.'

'Yeah, he might.'

'The whole thing might be an elaborate set-up to send us in the wrong direction, away from the murder scene.' Dixon picked up a stick and sent it spinning out across the mud, listening for it landing with a splat. 'And that's assuming he's dead.'

It was just after midnight when Dixon finally got away from Bridewell police station; just before one when he got home. Lights were on inside, so Jane had waited up for him; asleep on the sofa, probably, but it still counted as waiting up.

The microwave door slammed just as he opened the back door of the cottage.

'How was your day, dear?' she asked, with a cheesy grin.

'I'd rather hear about your day.'

'I've bunged a curry in for you. I bet you haven't eaten.'

'Where's Monty?' he asked, deflecting. Always best not to start off married life on a lie.

'Asleep on the end of Lucy's bed. I'm dropping her at the railway station in the morning. Usual drill.'

The smell of the curry sauce would get his dog up sooner rather than later. Then a turn around the field behind the cottage.

'Mum and Dad bought us that,' said Jane, gesturing to a large rectangular box leaning up against the back of the sofa. 'You've just got to put it together.'

Dixon tipped his head, the word 'cot' telling him all he needed to know. 'Please tell me you didn't lift it in from your car.'

'Dad dropped it off this evening. There's a pile of clothes on the dining table too.'

Life is a game of contrasts, thought Dixon. Happy families, building a cot, sorting out baby clothes. There were two piles on the dining table as it happened, one pink, one blue. Jane's mum hedging her bets, probably. Then there was his day; four murders – and it was four, even if Canter's body still hadn't been found – grieving families, post mortem reports, crime scenes, blood.

'Is there a beer in the fridge?'

'I'll bring it over,' replied Jane. 'You sit down.'

The television on pause. Whatever it was, it was in colour, so it was unlikely to be one of his films. 'What's this?' he asked.

'Some true crime thing on Netflix.' She handed him a can of beer. 'I'm going to be home a lot so I thought I'd give it a go.'

'Yes, but true crime?'

Jane's turn to deflect. 'There's no mango chutney,' she said, placing a tray in Dixon's lap. 'So I've sliced you a banana.'

Footsteps on the stairs before he had taken the first mouthful, and Monty hopped up next to him.

'Has he been out?' Dixon asked.

'Dad took him out earlier, just round the field.' Jane was lowering herself on to the sofa, one hand on the arm, the other in the small of her back. 'So, what's the story?'

'I thought you rang Lou?'

'I just wanted to know if she was . . . she was in the car with Mark on their way up, so that answered that.' Jane coughed, to hide her embarrassment more than anything. 'Did you meet Keith Hunt?'

'Gone before I got there. Didn't want to hand over to a superintendent younger than his children, apparently.'

'Sounds like him. And how's your blood sugar been?'

'Fine. The alarm hasn't gone off.' Dixon thought it best not to tell her he'd switched it off. Lies about his diabetes he could live with; they were almost expected anyway.

If he hadn't known better, he'd have thought she was putting her arm around him, but actually, she was just checking the sensor was still there, stuck to the back of his left arm.

'Any sign of a motive?'

'A death in custody that might explain the two police officers, but there's no connection with the drug dealers that I can see.'

'Maybe they're not connected at all; just by the use of a 3D printed gun?'

The thought had crossed his mind.

Among others.

Chapter Nine

Timelines. CCTV tracking. ANPR images of Canter's BMW on the Second Severn Crossing. Social media profiles. Mobile phone triangulation. Bank statements. The first statements from buyers of Taulman Bridge nylon filament; four down, thirty-seven to go. That was just those identified in the last twenty-four hours, in the immediate force area.

It had been a double briefing. Both teams, starting at eight, which had meant leaving home at six-thirty.

He'd managed to get out of the cottage without waking Jane. First sign of movement, though, and Monty had been scrabbling at the back door.

Commuting. It had never been part of Dixon's plan.

He'd been relieved to see Charlesworth sitting in. If nothing else, it would save him the bother of having to go through it all again.

'I gather you've been out and about quite a bit,' said Charlesworth, sidling up to Dixon once the briefing had broken up. 'That's not really the role of a superintendent. It's more of a deskbound job, Nick, supervising your teams from the central hub of the station, marshalling your forces, providing guidance to the investigating officers on the ground.'

'That's not really the way I work, Sir.' It'd been 'David and Sue' at Dixon's wedding reception less than forty-eight hours earlier, but this was the middle of an open plan incident room, after all.

'It was different last time. You were running one team.'

Something was going on, Dixon knew that. Charlesworth was building up to it, whatever it was. He knew the way Dixon worked well enough, and if he'd wanted a desk jockey to run the investigation he would've appointed someone else. Time for a little mischief, perhaps. 'I've got a mobile phone, Sir,' he said.

'Well, it's not really about that, is it?'

'What is it about?'

'I had a call from the PCC last night. Apparently, you've been harassing one of his opponents, and Hugo's worried how it might look if it got out before the election. Mr York is a well-respected member of the Bristol community, a high profile activist and campaigner. We can't be seen to be harassing him as it is, leaving aside that he's a candidate to be the Police and Crime Commissioner.'

Dixon had expected it; was ready for it. 'As you know, Sir, he's made public statements to the effect that there's a vigilante on the streets of Bristol killing drug dealers, and I thought it only right and proper to see if he actually knew anything substantive. It was hardly harassment.'

'And did he, know anything substantive?'

'No. He was more worried about being seen talking to the police. My view is it was just a cynical ploy to gain electoral advantage from the murders of two young men.'

'Hopefully you were able to reassure him there isn't a vigilante on the loose?'

'No, Sir. For the simple reason there could be. We don't know yet one way or the other.'

'Be that as it may, I can tell the PCC you'll be able to leave Mr York alone from now on?'

Louise appeared at Dixon's elbow, handing him a mug of coffee, her eyebrows raised just about as high as they would go. Enjoying the show, it seemed.

'Sadly not, Sir. I had a meeting with Professional Standards yesterday and Police Constables Lock and Canter are, or were, under investigation for misconduct arising from an arrest and subsequent death in custody over New Year. The deceased was the older sister of Mr York's assistant, so I will be going back to his office today to speak to her.' Dixon took a sip of coffee. 'I think you'll agree, she has motive, and it would be remiss of me not to interview her.'

Charlesworth lifted his horn-rimmed glasses off his nose, examined the lenses and replaced them; buying time more than anything else. 'Can't you send someone else?'

'Given Mr York's high profile in the Bristol community, and his status as a candidate in the PCC election, I think it's only right that his office is afforded the courtesy of being dealt with by a senior officer.'

'I heard about your meeting with Professional Standards,' said Charlesworth, changing the subject. 'Superintendent Carlisle was most impressed with your professionalism.'

Actually, Dixon would've cheerfully throttled him, but thought it best to keep that to himself. 'We all have a job to do, Sir,' he said.

'What about Darren Canter? I said I'd go and see his parents today. Is he in the water?'

'The Coastguard and RNLI are out looking, just in case, but I suspect not. I think the car was left there and the What3Words message sent to point us in the wrong direction. He was probably dead before the message was sent.'

'What makes you say that?' Charlesworth kept glancing at the kettle, Louise resolutely refusing to take the hint.

'Nothing specific, Sir,' replied Dixon.

'One of your hunches, I suppose?'

'We'll soon find out, one way or the other.'

'Let's hope so.' Giving up on a coffee, Charlesworth was edging towards the door. 'And you've still not found a connection?'

'No, Sir.'

'Let's hope there isn't one. Police officers getting mixed up with drug dealers isn't exactly a good look for us, is it?'

Then he was gone.

'Where to first?' asked Louise, as Dixon drove down the ramp of the multistorey car park behind Bridewell police station.

'Bryony Beech's parents. They live in a high rise in Bedminster.'

'Still no obvious connection between the two sets of murders,' said Louise.

'There's the 3D printing if nothing else.'

'Yeah.'

'Was there anything in Lock and Canter's personnel files?'

'Not really.' Louise was plugging her phone into the cable dangling from the dashboard of the Land Rover. 'They knew each other before they joined the police, both played for the same football team, local stuff, nothing exciting. Organised shouting, my husband calls it. There's a football field about half a mile from us and you can hear them on a Saturday afternoon, yelling and screaming at each other. I've learned new words.'

The Beeches' flat turned out to be on the seventh floor. The lift was working, but they opted to take the stairs when the lift doors opened. Someone needed to get in there with a mop and bucket.

A loud shout of 'Hang on' greeted Dixon's knock on the front door of flat 28. Two locks, a bolt top and bottom, then a chain. 'Push it open, will you?'

Dixon did as he was told, slowly, as a wheelchair was inched back.

'Frederick Beech?' he asked.

'Yes.' The man was looking over his shoulder as he reversed his wheelchair through an open door at the far end of the corridor, no room to turn. Brown corduroys, a check shirt with food down the front – tomato soup, possibly – hand-knitted cardigan.

'We're—'

'I know who you are. Come in and shut the door behind you.'

The living room was dark, the curtains closed, not even the lights on. 'It's my wife's eyes,' said Mr Beech.

'I've got glaucoma,' said the woman sitting in the armchair on the far side of the room. Freda Beech, in the shadows.

Fred and Freda. Easy to remember.

'Our solicitor said we weren't to talk to you without him being here. There's a civil case pending.'

Dixon tried a conciliatory smile. 'Look, I'm not here to talk to you about what happened to your daughter. I've seen the footage and I'm not going to try to justify it, or excuse it either. All I can say is it wouldn't have happened if I'd been there.'

The old man softened. 'Shame you weren't.'

Dixon nodded.

'What d'you want then?' asked Mrs Beech.

'One of the officers who arrested Bryony that night is dead, the other is missing.'

'Dead how?'

'Shot, with what we believe to have been a 3D printed gun.'

'And you think we did it?' Mr Beech was starting to bristle now, sitting up in his wheelchair, puffing his chest out. 'You're all the same, you see black skin and suddenly we're guilty until proven innocent.'

'Not at all, but I have to ask all the same. I have boxes to tick; anyone connected to the victim, however remotely or unlikely. You know how it is.'

'We were here,' said Mrs Beech, patiently. 'Whenever it was, we were here. We never go out, unless it's to the hospital for something or other.'

'Wednesday night, between eight and midnight,' said Dixon.

'Didn't you hear what she said?' snapped Mr Beech, an impatient edge to his voice now.

Dixon had sat down on the sofa, conscious that he hadn't been invited to do so, but better that than tower over Mr Beech in his wheelchair. 'And what about your other daughter, Faith? She lives with you?'

'She does.'

'She'd have been out with Sohail,' said Mrs Beech. 'Some meeting or other. There's a calendar on the wall in the kitchen. One of those tall thin ones.'

Dixon glanced at Louise, who made for the door.

'Are they in a relationship?' he asked.

'I think that's their business, don't you?' Mr Beech again.

Dixon could understand the hostility, sympathise with it even.

Mr Beech took the opportunity of the pause in the conversation while Louise fetched the calendar. 'They knew her history and yet they got our disabled, mentally ill daughter out of her wheelchair, face down on the ground. They hit her with a Taser and then put a spit and bite guard on her when they knew she was asthmatic. It's unforgivable. And as for that bloody custody officer who left her to die. I'm sorry, but if they're dead, that's the best news I've had all week. Hopefully it was painful and slow, like Bryony's.'

'Fred!' Mrs Beech looked apologetic. 'He doesn't mean that.'

82

'Yes, I do, Freda. I bloody well do.'

Dixon had watched the bodycam footage in its entirety; distressing enough for someone unconnected, but for a parent to have to watch their daughter being treated in that way was unimaginable. Motive enough for murder, he was in no doubt about that.

Mercifully, Louise appeared holding the calendar. She passed it to Mr Beech, who snatched it from her.

'Faith was at a St Paul's Community Forum meeting with Sohail,' he said, holding it up to the dull light from the lamp on the table next to him. 'Eight till ten.'

'What time did she get home?'

'She came in when we were having breakfast in the morning, so she probably stayed with Sohail,' said Mrs Beech. 'Which answers your other question, doesn't it?'

'It does.'

'We do intend to pursue this through the courts,' said Mr Beech. 'We want justice for Bryony.'

'I wish you luck with that,' said Dixon, standing up.

'We'll need it, you mean?'

'I suspect not, but don't quote me on that. We'll show ourselves out.'

'Slam the door behind you,' Mr Beech said. An odd choice of word, but then no doubt he would have liked to slam it behind them himself.

Louise waited until Dixon had shut the door, firmly. It did stick, as it happened. 'You can understand the bitterness,' she said.

'Plenty of motive, but not the opportunity.'

'Some bugger did that to Katie and I'd . . .' Louise let her voice tail off.

Dixon was starting to understand the feeling. Perhaps it was the sight of the cot and baby clothes on the dining table the night before? And 'the bump' seemed a bit bigger every time he saw Jane. He'd always been able to identify a motive before and could still. What was new was that he was starting to sympathise with it.

Understand it.

Nothing seemed clear cut any more.

Fatherhood would change him, was changing him already. It was just a question of how much.

'Sohail's not here.'

Dixon allowed the front door of the shop to slam behind him, the bell jangling noisily. 'We're looking for you, actually, Faith.'

'Me? What have I done?'

She was folding leaflets, several piles on the desk in front of her, each neatly wrapped in an elastic band; the printer behind her churning out still more. There was a pile of maps too; delivery routes, probably.

'Nothing, I hope,' replied Dixon.

Mid-thirties, possibly. A black fleece with 'Sohail 4 PCC' embroidered on it, unzipped and revealing a T-shirt with his picture front and centre. Dixon had spotted the box on top of the filing cabinet.

'We've spoken to your parents,' continued Dixon. 'About Bryony.'

Faith looked up sharply, suddenly curious. 'What about Bryony?' she demanded.

'One of the officers who arrested her on New Year's Eve is dead, the other is missing.'

'What's that got to do with me?'

'We're just eliminating people from our enquiries, Faith. You'll appreciate I have to ask, where were you on Wednesday evening between eight and midnight?'

'Our solicitor said—'

'I know what your solicitor said, and he's quite right, but I'm not here to discuss what happened on New Year's Eve. Nor am I going to try to justify it.'

'Because you can't.'

'No, I can't.'

'Have you seen that bloody tape?' asked Faith. 'Hang on a minute, if they're dead, does that mean our complaint won't be pursued?'

'You're going to need to speak to your solicitor about that,' Dixon replied. 'I'm just interested in where you were on Wednesday evening.'

She looked away, her hostility turned to embarrassment. 'I was at a St Paul's Community Forum meeting with Sohail. That went on until about ten, then we went back to his place. You can ask him if you don't believe me.' Defensive too, but then that was to be expected.

'How long have you been working for him?'

'I came to see him after Bryony died. He was very helpful and I ended up volunteering to help his campaign.'

'Volunteering?'

'There isn't any money. Not a lot anyway, just what the local community donate, and times are hard. The shop was empty and the landlord has given it us for free until after the election in May. The shirts and fleeces were free.' She frowned. 'Which one is dead?' she asked.

'Russell Lock.'

'Murdered, otherwise you wouldn't be asking where I was, would you?' A smirk crept across her face. 'Can't say I'm surprised. Or sorry.'

Dixon turned at the sound of the bell behind him.

'You again.' York let the door close behind him, raising his voice over the jangling. 'I spoke to Hugo Napier last night about your harassment. I was told you'd be spoken to.'

'I was spoken to, Sir,' replied Dixon. 'But you wouldn't expect that to get in the way of a legitimate investigation, would you? And we're here to talk to Faith, not you.'

'About what?'

'A private matter, although you can help us with one thing. Faith's whereabouts on Wednesday evening.'

York looked at Faith and raised his eyebrows, her nod almost imperceptible.

'She was with me,' he said. 'All night. First at a meeting, then at my home.'

'Thank you, Sir.'

'Now, is somebody going to tell me what this is about?'

Faith beat Dixon to it. 'The officers who arrested Bryony. One's dead, the other is missing.'

York took his time, composing his reply. 'You'll appreciate I've been helping Faith and the family with this matter, Superintendent. Obviously, the civil case against the force will proceed, as will the IOPC investigation, even if disciplinary proceedings against the deceased officers do not.'

'Only one of them is deceased, Sir, as far as we are aware.'

'Of course. My mistake. Faith did say "missing". But their treatment of Bryony was appalling, all the same. I've seen the footage.'

Dixon was edging towards the door, hoping for a suitable gap in the conversation, although York didn't draw breath.

'They inflamed the situation, raised their voices, they showed no patience at all.'

'Well, in fairness, Sir, they had been alerted by the 999 call to the fact that Bryony had been seen brandishing a knife, so you would expect a search in that situation. And one thing that is apparent from the tape is Bryony resisted that search.'

'She had ADHD, anxiety, depression,' said Faith. 'They knew that. They knew she had asthma and they put a spit hood over her head.'

Louise opened the door, the bell jangling again.

'I think you know my view, Faith,' said Dixon. 'And if you'll forgive me, I'll take my leave before we stray into areas we really shouldn't be discussing.'

Chapter Ten

'We know all we need to know about Hampton and Paul, surely?'

'Apart from who killed them,' replied Dixon. He had parked across the drive of the large house on the edge of Bradley Stoke; two cars on the gravel drive, both SUVs, both new. 'Well?' he asked.

'I'm not really familiar with the market north of Bristol,' replied Louise. 'Maybe seven-fifty? New windows, looks like a new roof. Double garage, good-sized plot. Yeah, seven-fifty. Maybe a bit more. The cars are five-nine-nine a month each if they've leased them. Seventy grand to buy new.'

A mine of information.

The Pauls weren't the first family whose son had gone off the rails, and they wouldn't be the last. What interested Dixon was just how far off the rails.

'Are they expecting us?' asked Louise, over the noise of the gravel beneath their feet.

Her question was answered from the open front door. 'Police?'

'Yes, Sir,' replied Dixon.

'We were expecting you,' said the man, presumably Andrew Paul's father. He'd put a tie on too; rare anyone bothers these days, thought Dixon, adjusting his own. The inner door was shut, but Paul's father still spoke quietly. 'My wife's in the kitchen. Go easy on her, will you? She's finding this all rather hard. The doctor's put her on antidepressants.'

'Of course, Sir.'

His name was Philip, but then Dixon knew that from their witness statements. A firm handshake too, one of those Masonic ones.

Stained glass panels in the inner door; a central staircase like something out of *Gone with the Wind*.

'Maybe nine hundred,' whispered Louise.

'We paid one-point-one two years ago,' said Philip. 'There's a timber stable block out the back and a small paddock. About five acres in all.'

Louise's face reddened.

'Very nice,' said Dixon. 'What is it you do for a living?' he asked.

'I'm retired now, but I was in merchant banking. The City. Back in the days when we got juicy bonuses. I saved mine and here we are.'

Late forties, early fifties at most. Yet another reminder Dixon was in the wrong business.

'Sophie's in here.'

They followed Philip through the hall and into the large kitchen. One of those ones with the black marble worktops and a large island in the middle.

'Sophie, the police are here.'

She looked up from a mug of coffee, her eyes a touch glazed over if anything, but then Philip had warned them. Antidepressants. Hardly surprising.

Dixon made a beeline for the mantelpiece over the wood-burning stove, looking along the line of framed photographs. Happier times; three children, mercifully.

Mounted on the wall above the fireplace was a large framed picture, a photograph with a filter applied to it so it looked like a painting: three children giggling.

'We had a devil of a job getting them to sit still for that,' said Philip, working hard to keep his composure. 'That's Andrew in the middle. Zoe and Daniel are boarding this term. We thought it best.'

'Where are they?'

'Clifton College.' Philip was filling the kettle. 'Would you like a coffee? There's a fancy machine that I'm not very good at, or out of a jar.'

'Jar's fine, thank you,' replied Dixon. He'd moved on to the French window and was admiring the large garden, paddock at the far end, open fields beyond.

'We have someone in to do the garden, and there's a girl from the village who keeps her horses here, so she's looking after Reuben. That's Zoe's horse. There are a couple of rescue donkeys as well.'

Some of Dixon's questions had already been answered; Andrew Paul had clearly gone a long way off the rails.

'So, you've taken over the case?'

'Yes, Sir,' replied Dixon.

'I saw on the news that a police officer was found in the sea at Burnham and a murder investigation has been launched.'

'He was killed with a 3D printed gun.'

'Like my son.'

'Yes, Sir.'

Louise had sat down at the kitchen table, opposite Sophie Paul. Her mouthed 'D'you mind if I . . . ?' answered with a dismissive wave.

'That explains the detective superintendent. Have you spoken to that shit telling everyone my son was a drug dealer killed by a vigilante?' Philip turned round and leaned back against the worktop, his arms folded tightly across his chest. 'There's no evidence of that whatsoever. He's just exploiting my son's death for a bit of publicity.'

'I have spoken to Mr York and, you're right, there's no evidence of a vigilante at large.'

'I thought not.'

'Justin Hampton did have a conviction for possession with intent to supply.'

'It was a small amount of weed he was selling to friends. He wasn't even making a bloody profit. That's all it was.' Philip ignored the kettle boiling behind him. 'We pushed Andrew too hard. I pushed him too hard. And he railed against it. We only found out he'd dropped out of university when he was dead. Kept that from us.'

'I knew,' said Sophie. 'He was too frightened to tell you.'

'You knew?' asked Philip. 'What does that say about me, I wonder?'

'He'd been thrown out of his halls of residence, and that's how he ended up falling in with that Hampton creature. I begged him to come home.'

'Why did he drop out?' asked Dixon.

'He couldn't get on with the course, so I said to him, just change, take a year out even, go travelling, start again on a new course. Sport and Recreational Studies he was doing, and he hated it.'

'He wasn't the brightest of students,' said Philip. 'Lazy with it. We sent him to what we thought was one of the best schools, Sherborne, but he spent his time mucking about, drinking in the local pubs. I'm sure he was using cannabis too, then he flunked all his A levels. Had to resit them, one of them twice.'

There was a lot of it about. Dixon stifled his grimace; best keep it to himself. Resits. It conjured up a world of nightmares and bereavement long past, but not forgotten. He could so easily have gone the way of Andrew Paul. So very easily.

'After that, the best he could do,' continued Philip, with a sneer, 'was *Sport and Recreational Studies*. "Fruit and veg" we used to call it when I was at uni.'

'And what did you study, Sir?' asked Dixon.

'Law.'

And there it was, in a flash. The reason Andrew Paul hadn't been able to tell his father he'd dropped out of university. Sneering snobbery and ridicule. From father to son. Nice.

'Can I see his room?' asked Dixon.

'What about your coffee?'

There was a nasty taste in Dixon's mouth as it was, bitter, and coffee would only add to it. 'We'll leave the coffee if that's all right, Sir, thank you.'

Sophie stood up. 'I'll show you his room,' she said.

The landing at the top of the stairs was bigger than the living room at his cottage in Brent Knoll, not that he felt envy. It wasn't that. *Money can't buy you* . . . whatever it was. Dixon blinked away the hideous old cliché.

Just don't make the same mistake with your own children when the time comes.

'We've left it as . . .' Sophie's voice wobbled, her breathing suddenly louder. 'As he left it, really.'

There were posters on the wall, much the same as any child's bedroom, only these ones had been mounted in frames and hung, rather than stuck on with Blu Tack. A double bed, but then the room was large. A desk, but no computer. Dixon remembered the statements; Andrew had had a laptop, and there'd been no sign of it at the murder scene. Stolen or sold to buy drugs had been the assumption.

'D'you have children?' asked Sophie.

'My first is due in about eight weeks,' replied Dixon.

'Don't make the same mistakes we made.' She was lighting a cigarette. 'I gave up twenty years ago,' she said. 'Started again when Andrew was murdered.'

There'd been a search of the room in the immediate aftermath of his death, but Dixon wasn't looking for anything specific. Just an impression of the boy.

'How long have you been married?' asked Sophie, glancing at the ring on Dixon's finger.

'Two days.'

'Some honeymoon. You must have an understanding wife.'

'She's a police officer as well, so she knows the job,' replied Dixon. 'I'm guessing you met Andrew without your husband present, if he told you he'd dropped out of university?'

'We met for a coffee a couple of times in the city centre. There's a Costa.'

'When was the last time you saw him?'

'The Saturday before. He seemed fine, his usual self.'

'Was he dealing drugs?'

'No. Your predecessor seemed to think Hampton had got himself mixed up with those county lines gangs, but Andrew wasn't dealing, and he wasn't using either.'

'What did he do for money?'

'I gave him quite a bit, thought it might keep him out of trouble, and he still had some left of his student loan. I think he was stealing things as well, but he never admitted it, not in so many words, anyway.' She shrugged. 'Snatching phones and bikes. Nothing more than that. I got the impression he thought it was all a big game.'

'And what about Hampton?' asked Dixon. 'Did you ever meet him?'

'No.' Sophie opened the bedroom window and flicked her ash outside. 'Didn't want to, either. We didn't like the sound of him, to be honest, even though he'd given Andrew somewhere to live. We rather wish he hadn't, actually. Andrew might have come home. Seen enough?' she asked, locking the window.

'Thank you.'

'So, are you trying to find our son's killers or are you just interested in who killed your colleague?'

It was a blunt question, but Dixon could understand it, sympathise with it even.

'I'm trying to find both,' he replied. 'And the person who printed the gun.'

'I didn't go to see him in the mortuary. Philip wouldn't let me. Haven't seen the post mortem report, either. Would we usually get to see that?'

It was the one meaningful entry in the Policy Log that Hunt had made: 'The victim's father has made the decision to withhold details of injuries from the mother. We have agreed to respect that.'

Dixon took a deep breath, silently through his nose.

'Not usually,' he said. Lying.

'What did you make of that?' asked Dixon, making the turn at the end of the road, a safe distance from the house.

'The husband seemed like a nice bloke when we got there, but fancy treating your child like that?'

'Paid the price for it. So did the mother. Let's see if we can speak to someone on the drug squad.'

'Wasn't their intelligence on the file?'

'There was enough for Hunt to jump to his conclusions, but I'm not sure it's telling us the whole story. Sophie was adamant her son wasn't a drug dealer and I'm inclined to believe her.'

'I'll see if someone can meet us later on today.'

'What did the husband say to you when I was upstairs?'

'Excuses, mainly. That he was trying to do the best for his son, that he needed driving on, kicking up the backside; a bit of ambition instilling in him. Computer games and Netflix wasn't going to set him up with a decent career, that sort of stuff.'

'See if you can find out where we've got to with Darren Canter as well.'

Louise was fumbling in her coat pocket for her phone. 'Where are we going now?'

'Clevedon,' replied Dixon. 'I want to speak to Hampton's mother. If they weren't dealing drugs, then it wasn't gang related and they're unlikely to have been targeted by a vigilante, unless it was mistaken identity.'

'What does that leave?'

'Robbery, but if there were no drugs and no money, then what was there to steal?'

'I'll ring Mark, see what's going on at Bridewell.'

'After Hampton, we'll go and see Russell Lock's ex-wife. I ought to go and see her, as the SIO.'

'Feels a bit close to home, doesn't it?' Louise was dialling a number on her phone, talking idly. 'A young mother with a newborn.'

'Taking it seriously now one of your own's been killed?'

Sophie Paul had said much the same thing, although she had been slightly more polite about it, perhaps. It was a fair point all the same, and Dixon had expected it from Justin Hampton's mother. It was how it looked. Charlesworth must have been aware of that when he interrupted Dixon's honeymoon. No doubt it would come up at the press conference too, although Charlesworth hadn't mentioned holding one yet. It had a certain inevitability about it, though. That, and another run-in with the head of corporate communications, Vicky Thomas.

Something to look forward to.

They were standing in the small staffroom of a bakery in Clevedon High Street, watching Justin Hampton's mother dabbing her eyes with a piece of kitchen roll she'd torn from the holder on the wall above the microwave.

'My Justin was a good boy,' she said. 'The first in the family to go to university. And your Mr Hunt said he was a drug dealer.'

'Had he ever—?' Dixon felt he had to ask, not surprised to be cut off mid-sentence.

'No.' Mrs Hampton slammed the microwave door so hard it bounced back open. 'He'd had the odd joint, of course he had. All students do, don't they? He wasn't dealing, though.'

'What was he studying?'

'Design.'

'And you knew he'd dropped out?'

'Yes. I wasn't surprised, to be honest. He was a misfit. Always has been.' She caught herself. 'Always *was*, I should say. I think he had ADHD, but I was never able to get a doctor to take him seriously; never had a formal diagnosis or anything like that. He just never fitted in. Ever. Anywhere. It would never have occurred to him to deal drugs. He just wasn't wired that way.'

'He has a conviction . . .'

'Possession with intent to supply, they said, but it was just a tiny amount of cannabis. Hardly *Breaking Bad*, is it?'

'And what about Andrew Paul. Did you meet him?'

'Once or twice. Justin came home for a bit of supper sometimes and Andrew tagged along. Nice lad. Well spoken, from a posh family, Justin said.'

Louise had sat down at the small table against the wall, under the noticeboard.

'What can you tell me about their relationship?'

'It's all in my statement.'

'I've read it, don't worry.'

'There was nothing sexual, before you go getting any ideas. They were just friends. Andrew was sleeping on Justin's sofa.' Mrs Hampton glanced at the clock on the wall. 'It's nearly lunchtime. You don't mind if I . . . ?'

'Not at all.'

Something from the fridge, bunged in the microwave. 'They met through the online gaming. There was some club at the uni. *Call of Duty*, or something like that. Andrew wasn't getting on well, either, some sport course or other, and they were just sort of thrown together, really. Became quite good friends, I thought. And it was nice for Justin. He'd never really had many, or any, friends, come to think of it.'

'Were they involved in any side hustles or money-making schemes on the internet, that sort of thing?'

Louise looked up sharply, surprised at the question, that the connection was being made.

'Not that I know of.' Mrs Hampton looked puzzled. 'He never said anything, if he was. His phone was stolen. He had a reconditioned laptop I got him for his studies, but that was taken as well.'

'What was he doing for money, in that case?'

She took the pot from the microwave, stirred the contents and then put it back in. Chicken soup, judging by the smell. 'Look, let's just say he'd always been a bit light-fingered. It was part of his condition. He got in trouble at school and stuff like that. I know he was pinching stuff and selling it online. He did a fair bit of shoplifting, but had never been caught. Actually, that's not true. He got nabbed by a security guard at a store on Cribbs Causeway once but got away somehow.'

'Was he able to pay his rent just from that?'

'No. He still had his student loan, and when that ran out he said he was coming home. Sadly, it was not to be. Someone killed him, and now I've got to listen to that tosser telling everyone he was a druggie killed by some vigilante cleaning up the streets of Bristol.'

'There is no vigilante, Mrs Hampton,' replied Dixon. 'And I've spoken to Sohail York about that.'

'Good.' Mrs Hampton crumpled. 'I blame myself, really. I never should have let him go off to university on his own. He was never going to survive. He should have stayed at home and even gone over by bus every day, but he was determined to lead a normal student life, he said, whatever the hell that is. I tried to convince myself he'd be fine, that it'd be fine, and look where that's ended up.'

'Is there any possibility he was getting himself in deeper with the county lines gangs? In too deep?'

'That's what DCI Hunt said and I never believed it. There's just no way. And I know you'll find this hard to believe, but Justin would have told me. He used to tell me everything.' Stirring her soup now. 'How d'you think I knew about the shoplifting?'

'Making money online?'

'Lock and Canter were at it.' Dixon was sitting in the driver's seat of his Land Rover, eating a sausage roll he'd bought at the bakery on their way out. 'Trying it, anyway.'

'It could be the connection we're looking for, I suppose.' Louise was brushing crumbs from her pasty into the passenger footwell.

'They must be connected. We haven't had a 3D printed firearm in the force area before and suddenly we've got three people killed by a gun or guns made from the same batch of polymer.'

'Sounds like the "c" word to me.'

'Coincidence?'

'Why not? The last case was riddled with them.'

'Although none of them turned out to be coincidences in the end.'

'Yeah.'

'And if this isn't a coincidence, then they're connected. Somehow.'

Chapter Eleven

'Sounds lovely, doesn't it? Sleep Lane.'

'What number?' asked Dixon, slowing as he made the turn.

'Thirty-seven.' Louise was looking out of the passenger window. 'Odds this side. It'll be a bit further up.'

Dixon glanced at her phone. Rightmove again. All it had taken was the sight of a 'For Sale' board cable-tied to a fence post.

'Three-twenty, that one,' she said. 'Eight years old. Taylor Wimpey.'

'How did Charlesworth get on when he came to see them?'

'Fine, I think.' Now she was pointing. 'It's that one there.'

Two cars on the drive, another parked across it. Dixon opted for the pavement opposite.

'There's a family liaison officer,' continued Louise. 'Tessa somebody.'

The front door opened, a young woman in jeans and a pullover stepping out into the drizzle. 'DS Beatty, Sir,' she said. 'I was told to keep an eye out for a Land Rover, so . . .'

'How are they?' he asked.

'Bearing up, I think. They've got Russell's ex-wife here, seeing as you were coming. They split up a while ago, but there's a baby; eighteen months old, he is. Nice little lad. Sits on the floor playing with his zoo animals, seems to cheer them up.'

A figure appeared in the window.

'We've been spotted,' said Louise.

'The only thing to know is that the father is ex-job, Sir. Retired about eight years ago. A drug squad DS out of the old Bridewell station. Before my time, I'm afraid.'

'And mine,' said Dixon. 'Let's go in.'

'The family are through here, Sir,' said Tessa. She'd closed the front door behind them and pushed open the living room door.

Dixon noticed the look of surprise on the face of Russell Lock's father. A big man, tinges of grey in his moustache and hair. He stood up, careful not to tread on the plastic animals littering the rug in front of his chair. 'Young for a superintendent,' he said, his hand outstretched. 'Means you must be good.'

Dixon shook his hand while Tessa made the introductions. Then she offered to make tea and disappeared.

'Are you? Good, I mean,' asked Russell Lock's father. Michael, as it turned out. Definitely not Mike. 'I've heard of you, so I suppose you must be. And the ACC assured us you're the best.'

'I shall certainly do my best,' said Dixon. 'We all will.'

The living room was small, or it felt small with six people crammed into it, including the baby asleep in his carrier. Two armchairs, a sofa, all positioned around an electric fire in a fake fireplace. Dixon had spotted the framed photograph of Michael in full dress uniform, a photograph of Russell on the other end of the mantelpiece. A police family, and proud of it.

'Please, sit down,' said Linda, gesturing to the vacant armchair.

Louise had sat down on the window seat, her notebook already on her knee.

Russell's mother, Linda, was mid-fifties. Dyed hair, a large bunch of sodden tissues in her hand. She was sitting on the sofa next to a younger woman: Tracey, Russell's ex and the mother of Luke.

'I always thought it would be Michael,' said Linda. 'I spent our entire married life waiting for the knock on the door and it never came. Thought I'd got away with it, until Russell went into the police. Then it all started again, the waiting.'

'I noticed lots of horses on the way in,' said Louise. 'Fields full of them.'

'That's Horseworld,' replied Michael. 'It's a rescue centre, just over the back there. We walk Luke round in his pushchair to see them sometimes.' He leaned forward and picked up a plastic horse from among the giraffes and elephants on the rug. 'If he goes in the force, he'll be on horseback.'

'He won't go in the force.' Linda's voice was suddenly abrasive. 'I've had enough of the bloody police to last a lifetime.'

Russell had been an only child. Dixon knew that. And now Luke was their only grandson. He could understand the sentiment.

'Do you have children, Superintendent?' asked Michael.

'Due in about eight weeks. And DS Willmott here has a four-year-old girl.'

'It changes things.'

'So I'm told.'

'It did for me anyway.' Michael's eyes glazed over. 'There's nothing you won't do for them. Nothing. You'll find out.'

'And he's left us this little lad.' Linda was sobbing quietly, so as not to wake the baby.

'I do need to ask you about Russell,' said Dixon, with an apologetic smile. 'Did he ever mention the incident on New Year's Eve?'

'He spoke to me about it,' replied Michael. 'I don't think he was particularly worried. I told him complaints are an occupational hazard. If a police officer goes a year without a complaint being made against him then he's not doing his job properly, is my view.'

He was fiddling with the television gizmos; lining them up along the sideboard next to his chair. 'How many have you had?' he asked.

'One only, yesterday, as it happens,' replied Dixon. 'I've been harassing Sohail York apparently.'

Michael clearly recognised the name. 'That little shit. Standing to be the PCC, and God help us if he gets elected. God help *you*, I should say. At least I'm out of it now.'

'He seems to think there's a vigilante on the loose in Bristol. Two boys with a history of low-level drug dealing were killed with a 3D printed gun.'

'Like Russell?' asked Linda.

'Yes.'

'I don't get this 3D printing,' said Michael. 'I've googled it and there are loads of videos on YouTube, but I still don't get it.'

It was the weapon that killed their son so they were bound to have questions. '"Printing" is the wrong word, really,' replied Dixon. 'It's a machine that builds things in three dimensions by laying down layers of molten plastic. I'm not sure why they called it a *printer*.'

'What else would you call it?' asked Linda.

'No idea, I'm afraid.'

'There you are then. A printer it is.'

'It doesn't bear thinking about if these weapons become widespread.' Michael was looking up at the photograph of himself on the mantelpiece. 'It'll be carnage out there. We'll have to arm the police. I'm glad to be out of it.'

Time to get the conversation back to Russell. 'So, Russell never mentioned anyone he thought might—'

'Police officers make enemies all the time. You know that. Every time you make an arrest, but no, he never mentioned anyone specific.'

'What about to you, Tracey?'

'No.'

That was the first word she'd uttered since Dixon and Louise had arrived. Time to keep her talking. 'And how long were you with Russell?'

'Two years.'

'When did you split up?'

'Just after Luke was born.'

'And why did you split up?'

Sharp intakes of breath from Michael and Linda. 'Not our son's finest hour,' she hissed.

'I found out he'd been . . . how can I put it . . . visiting sex workers. There were messages on his phone and he didn't deny it. Couldn't.'

Dixon glanced at Louise, furiously scribbling in her notebook. 'Were you living at his flat?'

'He moved there when we split up. We've got a little place on the other side of Whitchurch. He was still paying the mortgage on it. I don't know what I'm going to do now.'

'We'll sort something out.' Linda held Tracey's hand. 'We can't have you out on the streets, can we?'

'Did you ever meet Darren Canter?'

'Quite a few times,' replied Tracey. 'They were friends as well as work colleagues. Known each other for years. They used to play football together as lads.'

'There was a boy called Darren, I remember,' said Michael. 'But I never put two and two together, I'm afraid.'

'Which football team was this?' asked Dixon.

'Clevedon United,' replied Tracey.

'We were living over there then,' said Linda. 'We moved here when Michael retired.'

'Russell played for the under-eighteens to begin with. Then the first team.' Michael smiled at the memory. 'He was pretty good too, even had a trial for Bristol City, but it was all forgotten when he went in the police.'

'What about Darren?'

'Darren was crap,' replied Tracey. 'Or so Russ used to say. Ended up in goal and was useless at that. That was their little joke anyway.'

'Did they join the police at the same time?' Dixon knew the answer – he'd seen their personnel files – but asked it anyway.

'About a year apart, I think. Darren was already in when Russ joined.'

'And what sort of police officer was he?' Dixon knew the answer to that one as well – he'd seen Russell's performance reviews.

'What sort of question is that?' demanded Michael, loud enough to wake the baby.

Linda leaned forward and lifted Luke out of his carrier, cradling him in her arms. 'It wasn't as if he'd been convicted of rape or anything,' she said.

'He was a good officer,' said Michael, diving in. 'Conscientious, hard working, and loyal.'

Dixon nodded. 'He must've had money worries, I should imagine. He was paying rent on his flat and the mortgage on the house.'

'Things were tight,' replied Tracey. 'Him and Darren had some schemes on the go, to try and make a few extra quid. They'd tried all sorts. Drop shipping was one; you name it. They were members of some forum, the Ninja Forum or something like that, and there was always some money-making scheme they were trying. The latest was importing cheap dashcams from China and flogging them on eBay.'

'Dashcams?'

'Six quid each to bring them in and they'd sell for sixty. That was their plan.'

'How far had they got?' Dixon was watching Michael and Linda; it seemed to be news to them as well.

'Last I heard there was a container due in at Portbury Docks, maybe six weeks ago. That was what he told me when he missed the last mortgage payment, anyway.'

'I warned him that unmanageable debt was a disciplinary matter,' said Michael. 'And that he had a duty to report it. He didn't though, I'm guessing.'

'Unmanageable debt can place police personnel in a vulnerable position and more likely to become engaged in corrupt activities.'

Louise was sitting in the passenger seat of Dixon's Land Rover, reading from the force's Debt Policy.

'A recognised tactic employed by criminal groups to coerce . . .'

'What's the definition of "unmanageable debt"?'

'When the level of required repayments cannot be met through normal income streams.' She frowned. 'Are side hustles normal income streams? I suppose so, if they're legal.'

She'd already made the telephone call about the container at Portbury Docks. 'Tell Mark to drop everything,' Dixon had said.

'Hard working and conscientious, his father said,' he muttered.

'He would, wouldn't he, but it doesn't accord with what's in Russell's personnel file, does it?' said Louise. 'Poor attitude, it said at the last review, although the financial stress he was under might explain it, what with rent and the mortgage to pay.'

'Let's have the father's personnel record out as well.'

'Really?'

'See if "like father, like son" has any truth to it.'

'That was an odd remark the mother made,' said Louise. 'Came out of nowhere.'

'*It wasn't as if he'd been convicted of rape or anything.*'

'I wonder what that was all about.'

'Michael was quick to leap to his son's defence too, although you'd expect that, perhaps.'

'There was certainly nothing in his record. And he'd never have got past the database checks to become a police officer in the first place.'

'Your phone's buzzing.'

'Yes, Mark,' said Louise, answering the call. 'He's driving. We're on the way back to Bridewell. Yeah, I'll tell him.' She rang off. 'Mark says Charlesworth's at Bridewell with the PCC, looking for you, and there's a container over at Portbury. He's sending a team over there now. The bloke was locking up the yard, but he's going to wait.'

'Put the docks into your satnav, will you?' asked Dixon.

'What about Charlesworth and the PCC?'

'They can whistle.'

Chapter Twelve

Everyone's seen Portbury Docks from the M5 northbound, the cranes and hoists visible from miles away, vast container ships moored at the dockside. Then, looking down from the bridge at the huge areas, sometimes empty car parks, sometimes full of new cars and vans.

'I thought this was all Avonmouth,' said Louise.

'They're north of the river. South is Portbury.'

'Where do we go now, I wonder?' she asked, as Dixon sped around the roundabout under the motorway.

'I'm following that blue light,' he said. 'They seem to know where they're going.'

Dixon had flicked his headlights on as they passed under the Clifton Suspension Bridge, racing out along the dual carriageway, glancing up at the cliffs of the Avon Gorge, shrouded in darkness now, memories of days spent rock climbing there overshadowed by death and pain. Five months had passed and so had the pain, although he felt a dull ache in the middle of his chest at the mention of crossbows. Some bright spark had even asked him whether he wanted to keep the bolt as a souvenir.

Twat.

The car parks were empty as they raced along the access road towards the bright lights in the distance. Cranes climbing into the night sky, a container on a hoist.

'Look at the size of that thing.' Louise was marvelling at the stern of a ship. 'I saw a programme on the telly about these ships once, with that bloke off *Top Gear*. That's a small one compared to some. Massive, they are.'

'That must be the office block over there,' said Dixon.

The patrol car had stopped in front of the single-storey building, the blue light switched off, two uniformed officers climbing out and speaking to someone who looked as if he'd been waiting for them. Must be it.

The security guard raised the barrier at the sight of a warrant card and, seconds later, Dixon parked outside the office block.

Portbury Docks Limited – the right place then.

'The super's here,' said one uniformed officer to the other, when Dixon climbed out of the Land Rover.

'Yes, Sir,' said the other, spinning round. 'This is Mr Marler. He was just about to show us where it is.'

'The container's registered to a haulage company in Stroud, although no one's been to collect it, so we dumped it in our graveyard. We tried ringing, but got nowhere. They gave us the name of their client, a Mr Canter, but we got nowhere with him either.'

'What d'you do if no one collects it?'

'Keep it for a while, then auction off the contents to cover our costs. It doesn't happen often because most people pay up front.'

'We'll need details of the hauliers,' said Dixon.

'I copied the paperwork for you just in case,' Marler said, holding a bundle in his outstretched hand.

Louise stepped forward and took it from him.

'Is it locked?' asked Dixon.

'There was a padlock on it, but we cut it off, so we could check the contents for perishables.'

'When was that?'

'A month ago, maybe.'

'Where is this container then?'

'It'll be easier if we drive round.'

'You can go,' Dixon said to the uniformed officers, before climbing back into his Land Rover, Louise on the bench seat in the back, Marler in the passenger seat.

'Has anyone been to the container since it arrived?'

'You'd need to ask the security guard at the gate,' replied Marler. 'Left here. Now, we're dockside, so you need to be careful, hoists moving and all sorts.'

Containers piled six high, lines of them. Lorries with empty trailers queuing to be loaded up.

'This one's come from Shanghai,' said Marler. 'Be gone by morning.' Then he was pointing. 'We're aiming for that far corner of the yard. That's where we dump the strays.'

There were six containers in a dark corner, lined up along the chicken wire fence topped with coiled razor wire.

'It's that end one,' said Marler, Dixon driving slowly along the line.

He turned and parked, headlights illuminating the large steel doors at the front.

Tarmac, so there wouldn't be any footprints to worry about. Dixon pulled on a pair of latex gloves.

'What are you expecting to find?' asked Marler, nervously.

'Dashcams,' replied Dixon.

'You need rubber gloves for that?'

'How do I open it?'

'There's a sliding bolt, then the two handles together. Both doors open.'

Dixon was standing in front of the container now, his own body casting a shadow from the light behind him, but there had been something trickling under the door at some point, a small dark stain visible on the tarmac when he stepped to the side, allowing the light to fall on it. Not a good sign.

He slid the bolt across, then released both latches, turning the handles and allowing one of the doors to swing open with a metallic screech from the hinges.

He saw the feet first, the rest of the body hidden in the shadows behind the still-closed door on the left of the container. Dark trousers and standard issue boots.

Pallets wrapped in clear plastic all but filled the container, the two nearest the door cut open and boxes removed, the pallet on the right completely empty, only the plastic left, the body slumped across the last few remaining boxes on the other side.

Dixon leaned in and shone the light on his phone at the body.

Police Constable Darren Canter.

A bullet hole in his forehead.

Louise had climbed out of the Land Rover and was leaning around the steel door, peering over Dixon's shoulder.

'Is it him?' she asked.

'Looks like it,' replied Dixon. 'Call it in, Lou. We'll need Scientific, the pathologist and Hari Patel – what would we do without our crime scene manager.'

'A 3D printed gun, you think?'

'Must be.' Dixon sighed. 'Otherwise his brains would be all over that pallet of dashcams.'

'You were right about his car then,' said Hari, one hand on the open boot of his own car as he wriggled into a hazmat suit.

'Something just didn't feel right,' replied Dixon. 'It felt contrived, and the location unlikely.'

'We only wasted a day on it.' Then came the hairnet. 'Have you been in the container?'

'I opened it with gloves, poked my head around the door. That's all.'

'Good.' Hari was scribbling notes on his clipboard. 'The pathologist will be here in twenty minutes. Is there anything in particular you need to know?'

'Just if there's an exit wound.'

'Thought you might say that.'

Louise was standing by Dixon's Land Rover, her notebook open on the bonnet, taking a statement from Marler. 'He wants to know how long we're going to be,' she said.

'About two days, tell him,' replied Dixon. 'And while you've got him, ask him where the nearest water is, will you?'

He could see the hand gestures, then Louise turned back to him. 'That way is the dock; open water is about a hundred yards that way.' Pointing into the darkness beyond the containers. 'He says there's a hole in the fence.'

'Is there any CCTV?'

'Only dockside.'

The hole in the fence was easy to find, and he ducked through it into the undergrowth on the far side, a path of sorts winding through the long grass and brambles. He was holding his phone in front of him, using the light as a torch, then it buzzed, a text flashing up from Jane:

How are you getting on? Jx

The path opened out on to rough ground; large stones and rubble beneath his feet. A torch in one hand, gun in the other. Perfectly possible to lead a man out here to his death. One bullet and into the water. Dixon was standing on the edge of an old timber wharf, the water hidden in the darkness maybe fifteen feet below, the beam of light from his torch too feeble to reach it. The familiar stench of estuary mud stinging his nostrils, he picked up a stone and lobbed it into the gloom, a count of three before it hit water with a splash.

Open water, Marler had said. An outgoing tide, and who knew where a body might end up? The Severn Estuary certainly, then into the Parrett Estuary on an incoming tide.

Footsteps behind him.

'What've you got?' asked Hari.

'I reckon this is where Russell Lock was killed,' replied Dixon. 'We'll need a search of the area. Fingertip.'

'Leave it with me.'

'And be careful. That's the Avon down there.'

'Your DC was looking for you. Said she'd got the ACC on the phone.'

The containers were a hive of activity when Dixon ducked back through the gap in the fence. Two Scientific Services officers were unloading arc lamps, the Bristol pathologist was suiting up by the back of his car, the mortuary van parked a discreet distance away. Several members of Dixon's new team had arrived too, not that he could remember their names.

'We'll need someone to take a statement from the security guard at the gate,' he said. 'We'll soften him up on the way out, give me ten minutes.'

'Yes, Sir.'

'*Soften him up?*' asked Louise, as they drove out past the dock.

'He's been letting Lock and Canter come and go as they please, fetching their dash cameras. It's free storage, isn't it?'

Dixon pulled up by the barrier and slid out of the Land Rover, leaving the engine running. 'Busy tonight,' he said, tapping on the glass.

The security guard had been watching something on his phone, oblivious to his approach. 'Sorry, mate.' The phone slammed face down on to the desk in the kiosk. 'Always busy when we've got a boat in. Then there's your lot, of course. Still, passes the time. D'you want me to let you out?'

'Thank you.'

Dixon waited until the security guard was lifting the barrier. 'Someone will be along in a minute to take a statement from you.'

'Of course. Happy to help.'

'How many times did you let Darren in to fetch some of his dashcams from the container?'

'Most nights.' The blood drained from the man's face. 'I shouldn't have said that, should I? He was a police officer. What was I supposed to do?'

'Did you know him?'

'We played football together, back in the day. I hadn't seen him for years, mind, then he just popped up here, asking if I'd turn a blind eye while he fetched some stuff from a container.' Now he was out in the open he took the opportunity for a puff on an e-cigarette. 'I wasn't going to say no, was I? Not to an old mate, and a copper.'

'Were you here on Wednesday night?'

'Yes. Busy night it was. We had a car transporter out and this one in,' he replied, gesturing to the ship at the dockside.

'Did you see anything unusual that night?' asked Dixon.

'Nope.' The security guard turned his face away and exhaled, a thick cloud of sickly smelling vapour carried away on the breeze.

'Hear anything?'

'Over that racket? You must be joking.'

It was a fair point. The noise of the cranes, containers clanking, lorry engines revving. A 3D printed gun wasn't exactly a loud bang.

'Do you go out, on patrol?'

'On my own? No way. There's a van that does the rounds and they've got a dog, but they only come once in a blue moon.'

Chapter Thirteen

A new police station, a new receptionist, and Dixon still hadn't found the back door.

'Ring me as soon as he arrives,' Charlesworth would've said, and the bloke had only been following orders.

Sod it.

The back stairs were no use; glass everywhere.

Louise was jabbing the button, summoning the lift. 'Might as well,' she said. 'It's the fifth floor.'

Dixon saw the movement as they passed the third floor. A small meeting room, the table littered with coffee cups; Charlesworth and, presumably, the PCC standing up when they saw him in the lift.

An ambush, then.

Dixon had thought he might abstain in the election for the Police and Crime Commissioner. Deliberate abstention, rather than *can't be bothered*. That could change, though. He might even spoil his ballot paper. A few well-chosen obscenities, possibly.

'Let's see what this fellow's got to say for himself, shall we?' he muttered, when the lift doors opened, Charlesworth pushing open the double doors to the incident room.

'The Montpelier Room,' said Charlesworth, stalking past him, the PCC hot on his heels and avoiding eye contact.

'Give me a minute, Sir,' said Dixon.

'Now, please.' The 'please' was new, but then staff were watching and he had been a guest at Dixon's wedding only forty-eight hours earlier.

Dixon stopped at Mark Pearce's workstation. 'Anything on the CCTV?'

'Nothing to write home about,' replied Mark.

'What about the intelligence on Sohail York?'

'There isn't any. I checked with the intel team downstairs, and there's none on the system. Nothing at all.'

'Is there really nothing at all, or has it been deleted?'

'Does it matter?'

'It matters a great deal.'

'Leave it with me,' said Mark, but Dixon already had, and was opening the door of the Montpelier Room.

Charlesworth was sitting at the head of the conference table at the far end, the PCC his right hand man. Tempting, but Dixon thought it best not to sit at the opposite end.

Both of them stood up, Charlesworth making the introductions. Dixon knew the name, of course, every police officer did, even if they had nothing but contempt for the office. Actually, *contempt* might have been a bit harsh, perhaps. More like *indifference*.

It seemed that Hugo Napier knew his name too. 'I've heard a lot about you,' he said. 'You have your own way of doing things, I'm told.'

Actually, Dixon had never really thought of it like that. He followed procedure, always completed the Policy Log, although operational matters were hardly the PCC's remit anyway. Hopefully, he wouldn't have to remind him of that.

'I'll need to go and see PC Canter's family,' said Charlesworth. 'It was a 3D printed gun?'

'I'm waiting for a call from Hari Patel, Sir,' replied Dixon. 'The pathologist was going in as I left. Looks like it, though. There

116

didn't seem to be an exit wound, which means it was low velocity, much the same as Russell Lock. My feeling is they were both killed at the same time and that's where Lock went into the water. The Coastguard will be advising on the tides, and I've asked for a search of the water's edge. It looked like an old wharf to me in the dark, but we'll get a better look at first light.'

'And what's the story behind the dashcams?'

'Unmanageable debt. Lock, in particular, was up to his armpits in it, paying rent on a flat and the mortgage on a house where his ex-wife and young son live. My impression is that Darren Canter liked to live beyond his means, but the end result was the same. They needed the money.'

'At least they didn't turn to corruption.' There was just enough sarcasm in Napier's voice to be noticeable. 'I suppose we should be grateful for that.'

Charlesworth had spotted the sarcasm too, frowned.

'A decent pay settlement might have helped,' said Dixon.

Pick the bones out of that, you tosser.

Dixon made his mind up about people quickly and was rarely wrong; *never* wrong, actually.

Napier was bristling now. 'You went to see Sohail York again when you were told not to.'

'I wasn't *told* anything of the sort. And I didn't go to see Mr York, I went to see his assistant. She's the sister of Bryony Beech, who is at the centre of an IOPC investigation into Lock and Canter following her arrest and subsequent death in custody. It's called *motive*, and in operational policing we take it seriously. Anyone with a motive is spoken to and eliminated from our enquiries – or not, as the case may be.'

'Sohail York is one of my opponents in the election, for heaven's sake. I specifically asked that he be left alone.'

'I'm sure you did, but I'm also sure you wouldn't wish to interfere with a murder investigation.'

'How d'you think it looks?' Napier was sitting up, his chest puffed out. 'He'll scream blue murder; tell everyone who'll listen that I'm arranging for the police to harass him, trying to get his name off the ballot paper. That I'm running scared.'

'I don't care how it looks,' replied Dixon. 'Ask yourself how it would look getting arrested for obstruction.'

'If York gets elected it'll set policing in this city back years. It'll be them and us all over again, with that idiot on *their* side.'

'I think we can all agree on that.' Charlesworth cleared his throat loudly. 'Gentlemen, this is getting us nowhere. I'm sure, Nick, you didn't mean to suggest that Hugo is attempting to interfere—'

'That's exactly what he suggested, David,' interrupted Napier.

'That is exactly what I meant, Sir, yes,' replied Dixon. 'That's how it'll look when the story is leaked to the press, and you know what police stations are like. They leak like sieves.'

'I know you better than that, Nick.'

'I wouldn't do it, Sir. Never have, never will. But there are plenty of people around here who feel they were shafted in the recent pay negotiations.'

'So, let's be clear,' said Napier. 'Sohail York is not mixed up in this?'

'As far as I'm aware at this stage . . .' It was his solicitor's training, loading everything with caveats – old habits, and all that. 'His involvement is limited to telling anyone who'll listen that there's a vigilante out there, killing drug dealers. I have spoken to him about that and I'm hoping the issue won't come up again.'

'And what about his assistant?'

'She has an alibi for the murders of Russell Lock and Darren Canter.'

'You'll be able to leave them alone from now on then, in that case?' Napier's eyes were pleading almost.

'Vicky Thomas is organising a press conference for the morning and the issue might come up at that, Hugo,' said Charlesworth. 'I was going to mention the press conference in a minute, Nick.'

'Superintendent?'

'I have no reason to believe that I will need to speak to either Sohail York or his assistant again.'

'Let's keep it that way.'

'I'll drop you home when we've finished here,' said Dixon.

'You'll have to pick me up in the morning in that case,' replied Louise. 'I've left my car in Bristol.'

'What number is it?'

'Five.'

They were driving along a terrace in Burtle. Old railway workers' cottages, from the days of the old Edington Burtle station.

'That's it, there.'

'Two hundred and twenty thousand,' said Dixon.

'About that.'

They'd passed a patrol car at the end of the lane – local officers out of Express Park. They'd recognised the Land Rover, given a flash of their headlights before moving on. Dixon had asked for a visible presence, just in case.

'His name's Edward Grady.' Louise looked blank. 'Can't say I know him. Probably seen him around, but I can't put a face to the name.'

'Me neither.' Although Dixon knew the custody officers better than most. Some of them, anyway.

Union Jack pyjama bottoms and a red T-shirt, a can of Stella in one hand, a gaming controller in the other.

Yes, Dixon knew him. That night in custody; it had been Grady on duty the following morning. Grady who Dixon had had to ask for his insulin injection.

Grady who had handcuffed him in the afternoon for his transfer to the Magistrates' Court; Grady who had clearly found it amusing to be handcuffing a DCI.

He was just doing his job.

'A patrol car's been past about five times tonight,' said Grady, waving his can of beer towards the end of the lane.

'I've asked for an increased presence in the area,' replied Dixon.

'Why?'

'Can we come in?'

'Yeah, I suppose.'

If Grady didn't mention it, then neither would he.

The television was on; Dixon had seen the flickering light through a gap in the curtains. The hall light had come on when he'd knocked on the door. Otherwise the cottage was shrouded in darkness.

'Let me switch the living room light on,' said Grady, the shaft of light illuminating the hall.

A two-seater sofa, bean bag on the floor in front of the giant screen. It looked like he'd just shot a zombie with a crossbow, the image freeze-framed.

Nice.

'D'you mind switching that off?' Dixon's tone left Grady in no doubt that it wasn't optional.

'My federation rep said I shouldn't be speaking to anyone without him present.' Grady dropped the television gizmo back on to the coffee table, the screen now dark.

'We're not here to talk about what happened on New Year's Eve. We know what happened on New Year's Eve.' A little brutal, perhaps, but Dixon would forgive himself. 'What concerns me is that both of the officers who arrested Bryony Beech are now dead.'

'You've found Darren's body?'

'In a container at Portbury Docks, killed with a 3D printed gun, just like Russell Lock.'

'Fuck.' Under his breath.

'How well did you know them, Mr Grady?'

'Call me Ed.'

'I'll stick to Mr Grady, if it's all the same to you.' After all, the tosser had insisted on calling him 'Mr Dixon'.

'Not that well. They'd been down from Bristol a couple of times when the cells were full up there. We've got the largest custody suite in the force area, so it was fairly common. Express Park takes people from all over the place.'

'You didn't know them socially?'

'No.'

'Have you met Bryony's family, spoken to them?'

'No.'

'Have they tried to contact you?'

'No.'

'So, what are you doing with yourself?'

'Not a lot. I'm suspended on full pay, the weather's shit, so I spend most of my time playing on this thing.' Grady leaned over and switched off the games console. 'And drinking, I suppose. My rep reckons it's going to be at least a year too, and there's no guarantee I'll still have a job at the end of it.'

The street had been lined with cars. Dixon had looked for Grady's Vauxhall Vectra but hadn't seen it. 'Where's your car?' he asked.

'In the car park at The Duck.' Grady slumped down on to the sofa. 'I'd had a few, thought I'd better leave it there. Don't want bloody drink driving on top of everything else, and there are police everywhere in the village.'

'And where were you on Wednesday night between eight and midnight?'

'Is that when they were killed? You don't seriously think I . . . ?'

Dixon didn't, as it happened. It was about the fear factor, and watching Grady squirm.

'I was here, all night.'

'On your own?'

'Yes.'

'D'you have a partner?'

'Not any more.' Grady took a swig of beer. 'She left. Went home to her parents. She worked from home, and with me here all day, every day, it just wasn't working out, was it?'

'Has anyone threatened you?'

'No.'

'Is there anyone you can think of who might wish to do you harm?'

Apart from me.

'Nope.'

'Right, well, we'll be keeping the patrols going just in case, but I'd suggest not going out until you hear from us further. Do your shopping online and have it delivered. All right?'

'If you say so.'

Dixon glanced around the hall while Grady fumbled in the darkness for the lock on the front door. A pile of junk mail on the floor, shoes, a coat thrown over the banister, post on the bottom step for his ex-girlfriend, probably.

'Be on the alert,' said Dixon, stepping out into the lane. 'Ring us if you see anything unusual.'

'I will, thank you.'

'Tosser,' he muttered through gritted teeth, when Grady slammed the front door.

'I'm guessing it was him looking after you when you were in custody?' asked Louise.

'He didn't let on he remembered.'

'Too embarrassed, I expect.'

'Enjoys his job a little too much, if you ask me.'

'He had one of those smart meters on the mantelpiece, did you see it? They keep pestering us to have one put in, but you read such horror stories. Have you got one?'

'No fear.'

Louise climbed in the passenger seat of the Land Rover and was putting on her seatbelt. 'Where to now?' she asked.

'The Duck first, then I'll drop you home.'

'It's a bit late for the pub, surely?'

'I just want to see if his car's got a cheap dash camera in it.'

'Had a good day, dear?' Jane was standing in the open back door of the cottage, watching Monty sniffing around the backyard in the light from the window.

She was sideways on, the light behind her, the bump bigger, if anything.

'I managed to rub the PCC up the wrong way, which was fun,' replied Dixon.

'You've found the missing officer. I saw it online. It's the lead story on the *Bristol Post* website. There was even a photo; I saw the Land Rover in the background, but I couldn't see you.'

'There's a press conference tomorrow at eleven.'

123

'I'll record the lunchtime news in that case. I thought I might go and see Sarah. See how she's getting on.'

'Has Monty been out?'

'He's been out and about all day,' replied Jane. 'Came with me to my parents'. I'm guessing you haven't eaten?'

'No.'

'I'll bung you a cottage pie in the microwave.'

Dixon put his arms around Jane's waist, pulled her as close to him as the bump would allow. 'Hardly the start to married life we'd hoped for, is it?'

'Doesn't matter to me.' She kissed him on the lips. 'We both know the score, and besides, we've got plenty of time.'

'Yeah.'

'So, what's the story?'

'Two double murders now. Apparently unconnected by anything other than the weapon used. That's about it, really.'

'You've got no idea what's going on?'

'Nope.' Dixon sat down on the sofa, picked up the gizmo and clicked Play. 'He'd have more of an idea than I've got,' he said, watching Peter Sellers fall over backwards into a swimming pool.

'I always thought you modelled yourself on Clouseau,' said Jane, from the kitchen.

'I'll have some ketchup with my cottage pie, please, unless you've bought that sugar-free crap again.'

'Sorry.'

'I had a brilliant idea earlier. What d'you think about you going back to work after the baby's born, and I stay at home. I could be one of those house husbands.'

'There's a slight difference in salary to take into account.'

'We'd manage.'

'That's a worse idea than you becoming a corporate finance lawyer,' Jane said, placing a can of beer in Dixon's hand.

'Why would all police intelligence about a PCC election candidate have disappeared from the system?'

'No idea.'

'I've been warned off by the PCC himself, told to leave the bloke alone. Napier doesn't want it looking like he's getting the police to harass one of his electoral opponents.'

'What's the PCC like?'

'A bit of a pillock. So's the candidate, come to think of it, so we're buggered whoever wins.'

'Anything I can do?'

'Find out everything you can about Sohail York. I'd better not do it on a police computer.'

'I'll get Sarah to help me,' said Jane. She was carrying a tray with a steaming cottage pie on it and a dog following underneath it. 'It'll give her something to do, keep her busy.'

Chapter Fourteen

'The pathologist has confirmed it's a printed gun,' said Mark when Dixon walked through the double doors of the incident room the following morning. 'No rifling on the bullet and there's polymer residue, so he's sent it off to the lab.'

'What about Russell Lock's car?'

'Still no sign.' Mark ducked behind his computer. 'And Vicky Thomas was looking for you. Wants to prep you for the press conference this morning.'

'Lucky you,' said Louise, her laugh almost drowned out by the kettle.

'You ought to see this as well, Sir,' said Mark, gesturing to his screen. 'I found it last night in amongst a wagonload of stills from the CCTV footage we've got. It's not been catalogued or followed up at all, as far as I can see.'

It was not like any CCTV image Dixon had seen before. A large photograph of Justin Hampton running along the pavement towards the camera, something tucked under his arm. Then, above that, two smaller images: his police mugshot, presumably taken at the time of his arrest for possession with intent to supply, and next to that an enlarged image of his face from the photo below it. 'Captured Face'. Match Details, Score 64%.

'Looks like facial recognition to me.' Mark was pointing at the screen. 'AFR Reason is left blank, but AFR is Automatic Facial Recognition. I googled it.'

'Warrant Info', 'Occurrence/Ref' and 'Police National Computer ID' had all been left blank.

'Are there any other images?' asked Dixon.

'I haven't found any yet, but I'm still looking.'

Louise had given up on the coffee and was standing behind Mark. 'One-fifty-two on the seventh of January,' she said, 'so that's three weeks before he was killed.'

Mark leaned back in his chair, his hands behind his head. 'I didn't think we were using facial recognition technology on the streets yet.'

'We're not.' Dixon straightened, taking a moment to let the implications sink in. 'Officially.'

'The ACC's in the lift.' Louise turned away, trying to look casual. 'With Vicky Thomas.'

'Print that off for me, will you, Mark,' said Dixon. 'Then make several colour copies and hide them about your person.'

Mark grinned. 'Think it might disappear now we've stumbled on it?'

'Something like that.'

'We'll be in the Montpelier Room, Nick,' said Charlesworth, on the way past Mark's workstation, although Dixon had leaned over and minimised the window on the computer screen, leaving Charlesworth to glance at the Avon and Somerset Police logo on the intranet home page.

'It's that printer over there,' said Mark.

'See if you can find out where it was taken, the location.'

'Yes, Sir.'

'D'you want to take a coffee in with you?' asked Louise.

A mug in one hand, a colour copy of Justin Hampton's AFR image in the other. Dixon knew it was going to be an uncomfortable meeting for someone. Charlesworth, hopefully. Probably.

'Sit down, Nick. Vicky's going to take us through the arrangements for the press conference, but before she does that, I was just wondering what progress you've been able to make?'

'Well, Sir,' replied Dixon. 'We've managed to find an image of one of the victims taken three weeks before he was killed. I was hoping to use it in the press conference this morning, coupled with an appeal to members of the public who may have been there on the day and might remember what happened, and in particular what Justin Hampton might have been running from.' He slid the photograph across the table.

Charlesworth studied the image, then slid it across to Vicky Thomas, giving her a concerned look.

'I thought we weren't using facial recognition,' said Dixon, matter of fact.

'We're evaluating it.'

'And I thought the images were deleted when there was no match with someone on the watchlist.'

'They are.'

'Well, they're clearly not being deleted, are they, Sir? Justin Hampton had no outstanding warrants, wasn't a suspect in any ongoing investigation, nor was he a missing person, so he wouldn't have been on a watchlist and this image should have been deleted.'

'Yes, it should.'

'Not that I'm complaining,' said Dixon. 'It might hold the key to this whole thing.'

'You can't use it.' Charlesworth's face had reddened. 'Not in the press conference. Not only do the public not know about the AFR, but if it comes out we're not deleting images when we should, that puts the force in breach of the Data Protection Act. We could be prosecuted by the Information Commissioner, and how would that make us look?'

'It would be a PR disaster. And if it comes out that we've got a facial recognition van on the streets of Bristol, there could be riots.' Vicky Thomas was the head of corporate communications, not that the police force was a corporation. No doubt the new job title had come with a hefty pay rise too. Dixon wasn't sure where there was more starch, either. On her hair, or her pinstriped suit.

'Its use is strictly controlled, Nick,' said Charlesworth. 'There's guidance on where it can be used, who can go on the watchlist, and then there are the data protection implications to consider. It's a bloody minefield, and as I said, we're just evaluating it at this stage, no decision has been taken yet about whether it's rolled out more widely in the force area.'

'Whose decision will that be?'

'The Chief Constable and the PCC, so nothing's going to happen before the election, you can be sure of that. Now, what progress have you been able to make with the investigation?'

'Very little, Sir.'

'And we're supposed to tell the press that, are we?'

'I was hoping you would, Sir. I've got places to go, people to see. You know how it is.'

'It's a side turning off Whiteladies Road,' said Louise. 'On the right. Lower Redland, then it's on the left. Mark said the camera was facing west. Are you sure about this?'

'He's come out of one of the shops and he's running towards the camera.'

'Looks like a laptop to me,' said Louise. She was holding a copy of the AFR image of Justin Hampton running. 'You could be right. He's nicked it and is making a run for it.'

'Let's see if anyone remembers anything.'

Dixon had slowed and was making the turn on to Lower Redland Road, cars parked on both sides.

'Is it on the list of places the AFR van is allowed to go?'

'The list that officially doesn't exist for the camera van that's not being used, you mean?'

'Yeah.' Louise turned in her seat, looking over her shoulder. 'The van must've been parked about here, looking back that way,' she said. 'He's going, there's a space over there.'

A minute or so later and they were standing on the pavement, the image in Dixon's outstretched hands. 'He came out of that coffee shop.'

'Burra,' replied Louise. 'I could murder a latte.'

A white painted shopfront, two tables on the pavement outside, a handful inside, the familiar smell of roasted coffee. Pastries, cake stands. It seemed to be doing more trade in takeaway coffee, those in the queue in front of them wrestling with the lids on their cups and making for the door.

'Can I help?' asked the barista. Dixon knew that's what they called themselves from the job advert Sellotaped to the inside of the front window. He usually avoided these places like the plague, opting for tea on the rare occasions when Jane managed to drag him into one. Posh coffee was a mystery to him, unless it came out of a jar. That was bearable.

'Skinny latte, please,' replied Louise.

Whatever the hell that was, thought Dixon.

'How about you?'

'Some information, please,' he said, flashing his warrant card.

'Oh, right.'

130

It had taken a few seconds with a pair of scissors to cut out the image of Justin Hampton running, removing any reference to the facial recognition. Louise had even laminated it.

'Have you seen this person before?' asked Dixon, handing the picture to the barista.

'No,' he replied, shaking his head.

'Were you here on the seventh of January?'

'I'm here every day. It's my place.'

'We think the person photographed had just stolen a laptop and was making a run for it.'

'I do remember it, in that case.' He was holding his card machine out to Louise, who was paying for her coffee with a wave of her phone. 'We had a bloke sitting in the window seat there, on one of the stools. He'd gone to the loo out the back and left his laptop on the table.' He tore off the receipt and handed it to Louise. 'The shop was crowded, a bit of a queue, you know, and the next thing I know he's running out shouting, "The little shit's stolen my laptop," or words to that effect.'

'Had you seen this man before?'

'Once or twice maybe. He's not a regular.'

'Did you ring the police?'

'No, I'm afraid not. I assumed he would. Actually, I was expecting him to come back into the shop to ask if anyone saw anything, could recognise the bloke, but he never did. He just picked up his empty laptop case and walked off.'

'Do you have CCTV?'

'No. Nothing worth nicking, except the takings I suppose. Are you sure I can't interest you in a coffee of some sort?'

'No, thank you.'

'How about a hot chocolate?'

'Diabetic, sadly. And I've got one of these bloody sensors in my arm now, so my wife will know.'

◆ ◆ ◆

'You haven't forgotten you've got a team on this?' said Louise.

'I want to see for myself,' replied Dixon. 'And besides, if I go back to Bridewell now, I'll get dragged into that bloody press conference.'

They were sitting in a meeting room in the High Tech Unit, looking through the glass partition at an open plan office space, all of the workstations occupied. A desk job, was High Tech; hours and hours staring at a screen, examining God knows what. In this case it was side hustles, money making schemes – nothing too disturbing.

'You know there are more officers from High Tech receiving counselling than any other unit?'

'I'm not surprised.'

'I think I'd rather stick pins in my eyes than look at some of the stuff this lot have to look at,' said Louise.

It was a fair point, although specially trained officers catalogued the worst of it, and certainly not in an open plan office.

'You have to wonder about human beings sometimes,' she mumbled, her voice softening as the door opened.

A relaxed dress code too.

'DS Barrett, Sir.' Jeans and a T-shirt, not that it mattered. Bleary eyes, worn out.

'What have you got for me?' asked Dixon.

'Darren Canter was industrious, to say the least. A twenty-first-century snake oil salesman. You name it, he's tried it.'

'Made any money?'

'Not that I can see.' Barrett opened her notebook. 'He started off with drop shipping. That was about four years ago; just about broke even. They've sent over his bank statements so I can match payments in and out to his internet activity.'

'What's drop shipping?' asked Louise.

'Specialist wholesalers hold stock and send out individual items direct to the consumer. So, I set up a website, or a listing on an online auction site, then when I make a sale I send the details to them and they send the item direct to the buyer. Say I sell it for thirty quid and the wholesaler charges me twenty, then I've made ten quid less the auction fees.'

'It sounds too good to be true,' said Dixon.

'It is. A few people make some money at it, but you've got to find the right items and advertise heavily on social media. It's about volume. Most of the time you're making pennies on the deal. And some of the wholesalers charge membership fees on top. Canter was paying twenty-five quid a month just to be a member of one platform.'

'What was he selling?'

'Nothing illegal, in fairness to him. Household items on eBay, irons, ironing boards, kettles, stuff like that. I've got all the records off his hard drive and it'll be in my report, which you should have by the end of tomorrow. One of the kettles sold quite well, but after auction fees, he was only making one pound ten for each one he sold.'

'Was he paying his tax?'

'He didn't make a profit from what I can see, so there wasn't any to pay.' Barrett was flicking through her notebook. 'He stuck at it for about six months, trying different products, but moved on in the end. Most people do. The margins are just too tight, and if you do happen to stumble on a hit product, everyone else piles in and the market's saturated within days, everybody undercutting everyone else.'

'What did he try next?'

'Forex trading. The internet's plastered with ads from people promising you instant risk-free profits, pictures of their flashy cars

– hire cars mostly. It's basically just trading on the foreign currency exchanges, and that's hardly risk-free in any conventional sense. You're betting on movements in the market. It's a full time job for traders in the City of London, but for someone like Darren Canter it's a nightmare. You set up your day trade, start your shift, and what happens if the market moves against you while you're at work? You're buggered, that's what.'

'How much did he lose?' asked Dixon.

'Just over two grand. He'd bought some system called Forex Trader Elite, paid two hundred and ninety seven quid for it, believe it or not. Soon made his money back though.'

'Really?'

'The system paid fifty per cent for new sign-ups so he moved on to selling it and raking in the affiliate commission. Still not doing anything illegal. Trouble is, Russell Lock bought it and lost about five grand. Quite a few people lost money; I've sent over the emails.'

'A motive to kill him, perhaps,' offered Louise.

'I wouldn't kill someone over five grand.'

'Were there any bigger losses?' asked Dixon.

'No. From what I can see, most people buying these systems are desperate and haven't got the money to lose. They're betting small, so the losses are generally small. Important to them, but enough to kill for?'

'We'll speak to them anyway.'

'Of course you will.'

'I'm just amazed he was able to do all this in his spare time,' said Louise. 'He'd have been better off doing overtime if he needed the money.'

'That's the lure of get-rich-quick schemes. Some of them claim to be passive income, so you set it up and just sit back. Easy money, or so they claim.'

'Anything else?' asked Dixon.

'Oh, yes. A pyramid scheme, and this is illegal. Probably. He came up with a tool kit for driving traffic to websites that displayed adverts, called it Traffic Generator Gold, priced it at four hundred quid and offered a two hundred quid affiliate commission. Then he just sat back and raked in the cash while everybody sold it to everybody else. There's no evidence I can see that anyone made any money actually *using* the system, just selling it, and that's classic multi-level marketing.'

'What happened to that?'

'It lasted a few months until the reviews got too bad and sales dwindled. It even popped up on the Scam Watch website. Paid for his BMW though; the deposit anyway. After that he had some stake money set aside and so moved on to the dashcams, which you know about. He was in partnership with Russell Lock this time, trying to get him his money back, probably. And no, he didn't pay his tax.' Barrett turned several pages in her notebook. 'Russell Lock was a very different animal. He had a mortgage to pay, and rent. Plus he seems to have had a habit of visiting sex workers; pages and pages of messages which you needn't trouble yourself with. I've read them; it's just setting up meetings, stuff like that.'

'Anything on their phones?'

'I sent what I've got over to Mark Pearce. We haven't got the phones themselves, so there will be gaps in the information, but they both went offline on Wednesday evening at Portbury Docks at ten-fifty-seven. Both at the same time exactly, so my guess is the phones went into the water together.'

'Any connection with Hampton and Paul?'

'Canter and Hampton were both members of the Ninja Forum, an internet marketing thing, but there are thousands of members and there's no evidence they ever communicated with each other.'

'Mobile phone triangulation?'

'At the time Hampton and Paul were murdered, both Canter and Lock were in Bristol city centre.'

Dixon had noticed the woman walking towards the meeting room. It was her hair that caught his eye; either bleached or pure white naturally. Shoulder length and straight. Must be dyed or bleached, surely? Louise would know.

The woman stopped in front of the door. Knocked.

Barrett leaned over and opened it.

'You've got Detective Superintendent Dixon in here, I gather,' she said. Tall, although that was the heels. A two-piece trouser suit.

'Yes,' replied Barrett. 'We've nearly finished, I think.'

The woman turned to Dixon. 'The PCC is asking for you, Sir,' she said. 'We heard you were at HQ. I'm his personal assistant, Julia. I'll walk you over to his office when you're ready.'

'I'll wait in the car, if it's all the same to you, Sir,' said Louise, her hand outstretched.

Dixon stood up, dropping his car keys into the palm of Louise's hand. 'You can finish up here, Lou. Get the team to focus on anyone who lost money in the Forex trading thing.'

'It's all in the emails,' said Barrett. 'There are about six or seven who felt strongly enough to rant and rave at him.'

'Making progress?' asked Julia, idly.

'What's it like working for Mr Napier?' asked Dixon, ignoring the question. He was following her across the grass to the main entrance.

'Knowing that everyone here hates him, you mean?'

'Not everyone, surely? The grounds staff must like him.'

'He takes the credit when things go well, passes the buck when things don't. That's what people say, isn't it?'

'All Police and Crime Commissioners do that.'

'Yes, they do, but don't quote me on that.'

'I won't.' Early fifties, possibly, but she didn't look it. Contact lenses; dental implants, must be. Nobody's teeth could be that straight. Funny, the things you notice, thought Dixon. 'How long have you worked for him?'

'A year. I was at a law firm in Bristol before that.' She turned around, pushed open the swing door with her backside. 'You've made quite a name for yourself,' she said, with a flirtatious smile.

Yes, flirting with him. Definitely.

'Thank you,' he said.

'We keep a league table of sorts. Unofficially. Senior officers and their arrest records. Since you joined ASP you're on a hundred per cent. Never failed yet.'

'Give me time.'

Up the stairs, across the landing, 'Office of the Police and Crime Commissioner' etched into the glass doors.

'You got married recently?'

'On Saturday, as it happens.'

Knew that and still flirted with me.

'Congratulations.' She leaned over the desk and pressed a button on her phone. 'He's here, Hugo,' she said, when Napier answered the intercom.

'Send him in.'

'He's in a foul mood.' Julia shrugged. 'Sorry.'

Napier sat bolt upright, watching Julia, waiting for her to leave his office. 'You can't use the facial recognition image, Dixon,' he said, as soon as the door had closed behind her 'It's not in use operationally and we don't want it coming out that we're even considering it at this stage. Is that clear?'

'No, it's not.' Dixon was fucked if he was calling Napier 'Sir'. That was reserved for officers more senior than him, not elected bureaucrats. 'It's evidence in a murder enquiry, whether you like it or not.'

'Look.' Napier was clenching his fists. 'We've not undertaken the required risk assessments, we're just evaluating the effectiveness. No arrests have been made, even where there's been a match with someone on the watchlist.'

'So, there is a watchlist?'

'Unofficially, yes. It's just a random sample from the police national computer of people living in the force area, the aim being to see how many matches we get. If it's considered to be value for money, based on the number of positive matches, then it'll be my job to find the funds for it.'

'Assuming you get re-elected.'

'That's right,' replied Napier, his voice taut. 'And I won't get re-elected if it comes out we've been trialling facial recognition technology covertly on the streets of Bristol.'

'How did the image of Hampton come to be submitted to the enquiry?'

'I don't know. It must've been done in error by someone working on the AFR project. Either way, none of the guidance is in place yet and we simply cannot use it. I'm not sure it would be admitted in evidence anyway, given that it was obtained illegally.'

'It's not illegal to use AFR,' said Dixon. 'Provided the proper safeguards are in place. The Court of Appeal ruled it was proportionate interference with human rights.'

'I forget you're a solicitor, aren't you. Anyway, the reality is those safeguards are not in place at the moment, because we're not using it. We're evaluating it. If we do decide to adopt it, then there will be an announcement, the public will be made aware, and all of the guidance will be in place before the vans go out for their first operational deployment.'

'After the election.'

'Yes, after the election.' Napier stood up, facing the window, his back to Dixon. 'There'll even need to be signs on lamp posts telling the public that AFR is being used in this location. It will be strictly controlled, but in the meantime, you cannot use that image of Hampton.'

'It should have been deleted.'

'It should.'

'A bit of a coincidence that Hampton was murdered three weeks after the image was captured, isn't it?'

Napier turned, looked puzzled. 'Are you saying his death might be connected to the AFR?'

'Not that no, but he stole a laptop. We've got a statement from the coffee shop owner.'

'But you can't use that without revealing the existence of the AFR trial. That's how you found out about it, isn't it?'

'Bit of a conundrum that.'

'It's an illegal search, and everything that flows from it would be ruled illegal as well.' Napier's voice was gathering momentum, his face turning a shade of crimson. 'The whole episode will be inadmissible in court.'

'You've been watching too much American telly.'

Chapter Fifteen

'How did you find it?'

'Don't ask.' Mark was sitting on a stool in the window of Burra, watching the steam rising from a mug of coffee; watching a van parked further along the road too. 'I used to work in Bristol back in the day,' he said. 'Know a few of the lads.'

'That's the van, is it?' asked Dixon. He was doing his best to act casual, not to look too obviously.

A white Transit van with tinted windows at the back.

'That's it, Sir,' replied Pearce. 'There are cameras front and back, so it's looking in both directions. Nice work if you can get it. Sitting there all day drinking tea and watching porn on their phones, probably.'

'What if you need a widdle?' asked Louise. 'Have we got time for a coffee?'

'No,' replied Dixon. No taste for it either, but that was a different matter.

'They'll know you're coming, if you're on the watchlist,' said Mark.

'We're on the watchlist?'

'We all are, for testing and evaluation purposes.'

'Then they'll know it's me when I bang on the door, won't they.'

Seconds later Dixon was doing just that, his warrant card pressed to the tinted rear window of the van. 'Open up.'

Silence.

Louise had walked to the front of the van and was looking in the driver's side window, her hand shielding the reflection. 'There's a screen, so I can't see into the back. You can see the camera, though, if you look closely. They'll have to do better than that. People will spot it a mile off if they're looking for it.' Shouting now. 'You'll have to do better than that.' Her sentence was punctuated by a bang on the driver's door. 'People will spot you a mile off.'

A small crowd was gathering on the pavement, watching the commotion, a few with smartphones in their outstretched hands.

Dixon tried the sliding door at the side.

'Shall I move them on?' asked Pearce, gesturing to the handful of spectators further along the pavement.

'Don't bother, Mark.'

Then they heard movement inside the van, the door sliding open a few inches.

'This is a covert operation, Sir,' said a voice, nervously, the face hidden.

'It *was* a covert operation. Now open the bloody door and let me in.'

It was one of those tall vans that you could stand up in. Swivel chairs fixed to the floor in front of a bank of computer screens along the offside panel, cameras mounted on tripods in the rear windows, another fixed to the inside of the screen behind the cabin. It was much like a mobile speed camera van, although unmarked, and with three people crammed into the back rather than just the one.

Mark was looking in the side door. 'Crikey,' he said. 'The three of you in here all day. I hope nobody had a vindaloo last night.'

'Shut up, Mark.'

'Yes, Sir.'

'Do you mind if we shut the door, Sir?' said a man wearing a fleece with the Avon and Somerset Police logo on it. 'We don't really want everybody and their dog knowing what's going on, do we?'

'They'll find out soon enough.'

The man was shutting the door anyway, pausing to allow Mark and Louise to step back.

'We'll be in the coffee shop, Sir,' said Louise, just as the door was closing.

'Who are we all then?' asked Dixon, once the door was shut.

'I'm DS Finn from High Tech, Sir,' replied the man in the fleece. 'And this DS Hancock from the camera unit and Alan Platt from Facetech Solutions. It's their set-up. We're here to see whether it works or not.'

'And does it?'

Hancock reached forward and tapped the mousepad on a laptop, the screen coming to life showing a photograph of Dixon walking along the pavement taken moments earlier, above it two thumbnail images: one his police identity card photograph, the other of his face from the image of him on the pavement.

'Why only an eighty-one per cent match?' he asked.

'Maybe you've put on a bit of weight, Sir,' replied Hancock.

'It's purely for testing purposes,' said Platt. 'All the images are deleted at the end of each day. At this stage, it's just about the number of matches to the watchlist and the accuracy achieved.'

Dixon reached inside his jacket pocket and took out the screenshot of Hampton running towards the camera, the laptop tucked under his arm. 'If that's the case, why was this one kept?' he asked, handing the piece of paper to Platt.

'I don't know.' He glanced at it before passing it on to Hancock.

'The young lad in the photograph was found murdered a few weeks later, so you'll understand my interest. I'd also like to know

142

how this image came to be among hundreds of CCTV images submitted to the enquiry.'

'That was me, Sir,' replied Finn. 'This particular image was retained by me because I thought the subject was acting suspiciously and a crime may have been committed. I couldn't reveal myself at the time, for obvious reasons, but I did retain the images when the rest were deleted at the end of the day. Just in case.'

'We have a statement from the coffee shop owner confirming that a laptop had been stolen,' said Dixon.

'I thought as much.'

'And how did this image find its way to the enquiry?'

'I was collating other CCTV images and thought this one might be relevant, so I sent it over on the QT. After all, it's not supposed to exist, is it? If the ACC finds out I kept it, I'll be in deep shit.'

'Explain to me how this works.'

'The cameras are recording video footage,' replied Platt. 'Then there's an algorithm that isolates the facial features of each individual and compares it to the watchlist. If there's a match it flashes up. The Met are using the technology in London and they have uniformed patrols on standby to make an arrest.'

'What about data protection?'

'We had to jump through a few hoops, but provided all images where there's no match are deleted, we're fine. The Met have their got risk assessments in place, all the necessary guidelines. It's working really well.'

'What about false matches?'

'It has happened.' Platt licked his lips. 'They say we've all got a doppelganger, don't they?'

'So, this image came from video footage?' Dixon reached over and retrieved the picture of Hampton running that Finn was still staring at.

'Yes, Sir.'

'And you deleted that, I suppose?'

'I'm afraid so, Sir,' replied Finn, with just enough hesitation to be noticeable.

'What about the stills isolated immediately before and after this one?'

'They'd have been deleted as well.'

'Can't the images be retrieved from the hard drive?' Dixon frowned. 'I thought it was all but impossible to delete everything from a computer.'

'We use special software that deletes the images and wipes . . .' Hancock's voice was lost in an exaggerated shrug.

'So, this is all I've got?'

'Yes, Sir.'

'What about you?' asked Dixon. 'You were here, you saw what happened.'

'Well, I did and I didn't. After all, we're not supposed to be here at all, are we? And if I gave a statement I'd have to say what we were doing here, then I'd run into all sorts of trouble with the ACC. It's bad enough that I kept that image.' Finn swallowed hard. 'Does the ACC know?'

'He does.'

'Shit.'

'So, what happened?'

'Not a lot. The lad snatched the laptop and ran, then someone came out of the coffee shop in pursuit, quickly gave up and walked off in the opposite direction. That's all I remember to be honest.'

. . . to be honest.

Dixon was sitting in the corner of the Red Cow, waiting for his fish and chips. And for Jane to go to the loo. Again. Something about a baby pressing on her bladder.

144

Nice.

Monty was stretched out on the rug in front of the fire that was burning out. Dixon checked that no one was watching, reached over and dropped a couple of logs into the flames.

'There you go, matey,' he said, rubbing the dog's ears. If it hadn't been pouring with rain, they'd have been out on the beach.

He'd spent several hours reading the latest statements that had been taken and uploaded on to the system, none of them terribly enlightening in either case. The briefings had been disappointing too, neither team making much progress.

The enquiry into the Hampton and Paul murders was still identifying more people who'd bought 3D printing polymer in the force area – Dixon couldn't bring himself to call it 'ink'. It was up to ninety-three now; seemed it was far more widespread than Dixon had thought. Not all of them would be printing guns, mind you.

Some progress was being made speaking to those who'd lost money in Darren Canter's Forex trading scheme – or was it 'scam'? – alibis being checked and double-checked. Wasn't going to be that, though. If it was, why murder Russell Lock as well, unless he'd just been in the wrong place at the wrong time?

'How are you getting on, running two teams?' asked Jane, squeezing on to the seat opposite him.

Dixon dragged the heavy table towards him a bit to let her in. 'A lead in one of them would be nice.'

'Still not found a connection?'

'Nope.' A swig of beer

'God, it's hot in here,' grumbled Jane. 'Have you put more logs on the fire?'

'Someone came and did it,' he replied, marvelling at how easily the lie trotted off the tip of his tongue. It was only a small one and hardly consequential, but it was a timely reminder: most people lied, most of the time. 'Like a cheap watch' was the old saying.

He was being lied to. He knew that; knew who was doing it, and why. The time-honoured reason: covering his own arse.

'I'm making more enemies than usual this time,' he said.

'Who?'

'The PCC. Charlesworth too.'

'Oh God, what now?'

'One of the murder victims was caught on a facial recognition camera stealing a laptop a few weeks before he was murdered.'

'Are we using facial recognition?'

'Apparently not. It's just a trial.'

Jane was sniffing her tonic water without much enthusiasm.

'Just pretend there's gin in it.'

'Yeah, right,' she grumbled. 'I haven't seen any publicity about facial recognition.'

'There hasn't been any. It's hush-hush. The PCC doesn't want it affecting his re-election chances, which leaves me with an image I'm not supposed to have and can't use.'

'You really don't want to find yourself on the end of a disciplinary. Not now,' said Jane, rubbing her bump.

Actually, there was a conversation to be had about that, but now was not the time.

'She kicked!'

'It was *he* last time.'

'How the hell am I supposed to know?'

'Can't you tell?'

'No, I bloody well can't.'

Fatherhood changes a man, Poland had said. Marriage too. Lines become blurred; good and evil, right and wrong. What can be justified and what can't.

That severed head in the golf course bunker again . . .

'So, are the cases connected, or what?' asked Jane. 'That's the first thing you need to sort out, whether it's one investigation or two.'

A swig of beer.

'What does your gut tell you? Because that's never wrong.'

'It's one,' said Dixon. 'They're connected. I just don't know how yet.'

'Not just the 3D printed gun?'

'No.'

It made a pleasant change, Dixon's phone buzzing just as they finished their food. Usually it would happen before it arrived, sometimes when he took the first mouthful.

A text from Louise, as it happened:

We've got a body. Two shots to the head. No exit wounds.
BA6 8DY. On way now.

Dixon recognised the postcode.

'Fancy a trip to Glastonbury?' he asked.

'What for?' replied Jane.

'Another body.'

Chapter Sixteen

Jane hadn't needed much persuading. She'd only been on maternity leave a couple of weeks but boredom had been mentioned more than once. Most people reminded her to make the most of the peace and quiet, of course, but that didn't seem to stop the complaining.

Once a police officer, always a police officer. That was another cliché that had been trotted out with monotonous regularity; one that Dixon was beginning to hope wasn't true.

Road signs and knowing the way got them to the edge of Glastonbury; following the blue lights took them to Meadow View. No need for satnav.

The rain had stopped, Glastonbury Tor silhouetted against the night sky, the dark expanse of the Levels stretching away to the south.

An ambulance, three patrol cars, Hari Patel's van, Roger Poland's Volvo. A Scientific Services van had been following his Land Rover, but the road was well and truly blocked. A cul-de-sac of bungalows with a grandstand view, if only Dixon could see it.

Lights were on in the surrounding houses, curtains drawn, figures standing in windows watching the drama unfold. Not that there was much to see now. Hari had set up a cordon, a large tent in the middle of the road, arc lamps inside and out.

Dixon parked outside the roadblock and they walked the rest of the way, Louise striding towards them along the pavement.

'We've got several witnesses, Sir,' she said. 'It was just gone six, so there were lots of people about. Roger Poland's in the tent over there, but you'll never get past Hari.'

'Who's the victim?'

'Liam Smith. Lives in number four with his mother. She's being looked after by the neighbour at number six.'

The front door of number 4 was standing open, Scientific Services officers filing in with equipment.

'We've got the mother's permission,' said Louise. 'Sounds like it could be a professional hit, if you ask me. He came out of the house, was hit by a car, then the driver got out, stood over him and shot him twice while he was lying in the road.'

'Let's go and see what Roger's got say to about it, shall we?'

They were intercepted by Hari before they reached the tent. 'You're on maternity leave,' he said to Jane. 'What are you doing here?'

'We were out for a bite to eat,' she replied. 'Came straight here.'

Hari clearly didn't need to know the pub was just across the road from their cottage.

'Can't let you in, I'm afraid.' Hari turned to Dixon. 'You can go in. Three max, and there's the pathologist and a photographer in there at the moment. Overalls are in the crate. Stick to the stepping plates, there are shards of polymer everywhere. Looks like the 3D printed gun disintegrated when it was discharged. You may find the shooter has a hand injury.'

Overalls, latex gloves and overshoes; there were even some hairnets in the crate, but Dixon pretended he hadn't seen them.

'What've we got, Roger?' he asked, pushing open the tent flap with his elbow.

'Twenty-eight-year-old male. Hit by a car first, then shot twice at point blank range. He was facing the car when it hit, both legs are broken from a frontal impact, then he pitched forward, his head hitting the windscreen. That shattered and there are bits of glass embedded in his scalp.'

'Then shot?'

'Twice. Low velocity. I had a look under his head and there are no exit wounds, so the bullets will still be inside. Fits with the 3D printed weapons we've encountered already.' Poland stood up. 'Having a nice honeymoon, I trust?'

'Lovely,' replied Dixon.

Poland had been kneeling on a sheet of plastic beside the body, the photographer standing behind him, both of them obscuring Dixon's view. Now he could see the entry wounds, one right in the middle of the forehead, the other off to the left. If Dixon had to guess, the one on the left had been fired first, the victim turning his head to the right at the last second, hence the need for a follow-up shot.

It would be interesting to see if any of the witnesses saw the shooter reload. Most 3D printed guns were single-shot. Maybe firing twice in quick succession was too much for the polymer, which might explain the disintegration, as Hari had called it.

Worse than that, though, was the angle of the legs. Stomach-churning. Best to focus on something else.

'Where are these shards of polymer Hari was talking about?'

'We picked them up and they're in an evidence bag, but they were on or around the victim's head,' replied Poland. 'So, the shooter was about here.' Poland was standing on a stepping plate adjacent to the victim's shoulder, his fingers making an imaginary gun barrel in his outstretched right hand. 'Splinters of grey plastic. Ballistics will have a better idea, but my guess is the gun blew up in his hand.'

'Probably just the barrel,' said the photographer. 'There weren't that many of them. No blood on them, either. Not that I could see, anyway.'

'Sounds about right,' Poland said.

'Post mortem?'

'In the morning. Unless you're in any particular rush?'

'The morning's fine.'

'I'll ring you when I've got the bullets under a microscope.'

'Thanks,' replied Dixon, backing out of the tent.

'Where's Jane?' asked Dixon. He was rolling his overalls into a ball before stuffing them into a bin liner.

'In number six with the neighbour and the victim's mother,' replied Louise. 'They were worried about a woman in her condition standing out in the cold, they said.'

'Nice of them.'

'You need to speak to Mrs Warren first. She lives at number one, on the corner there. She was out in the garden, putting some food out for the birds, got the best view.'

Her front door was unlocked, Louise pushing it open with a shout of 'Hello?'

'In here, dear.'

A television fell silent in the room on the left.

Louise led the way, made the introductions. 'Just tell him what you told me,' she said.

'It was the weirdest thing,' said Mrs Warren. 'It was like fireworks going off, not a real gun at all.'

'Where were you?' asked Dixon.

'Standing by the bird feeders,' she replied. 'I'd been out all day with my daughter and hadn't filled them. They come to rely on it, you know, so I filled a jug with sunflower hearts and was filling up one of the feeders when I heard Madge's door go and Liam came out. He's a nice lad.'

'How well did you know him?'

'I've known him since he was a boy.' She shuddered. 'They moved here when he was about four or five, I suppose. Just neighbours, though, to say hello to, that sort of thing.'

'What did he do when he came out of the house?'

'He was crossing the road towards his car. That's when I heard the car coming.'

'What sort of car was it?'

'One of those . . . what d'you call it . . . big things.'

'An SUV?' asked Louise.

'That's right. A dark SUV. They all look the same though, don't they, so I couldn't tell you what sort it was. Anyway, he just stood there and it hit him.'

'Did he have time to move out of the way?'

'Yes, I think so, but he seemed to freeze, like the proverbial rabbit in the headlights.'

'Then what happened?'

'He was thrown on to the bonnet, the windscreen shattered – I remember that – then he was thrown forward, like a rag doll, landed in the road in front of the car. That's when the driver got out, walked over to him, and I heard the popping sound. There were two, I'm quite clear about that.' A cat had hopped up on to the old woman's lap and she was stroking its head. 'He's a house cat, in case you were wondering,' she said. 'If I let him out, he eats my birds.'

'Was the driver a man or a woman?'

'Oh, I couldn't tell, dear. My eyesight's not great without my glasses, and it was dark, just the streetlights. I couldn't see any facial features so I did wonder if they had their face covered. They were wearing a hooded jacket too.'

'What colour was the jacket?'

'No idea, I'm afraid. It was a dark top and dark trousers, come to think of it, but as for what colour.' She shrugged. 'Who knows?'

'And have you seen the dark SUV before?'

'I don't usually notice cars, I'm afraid.' She shook her head. 'I don't think so, but then they're pretty common, aren't they?'

'Was anything said?'

'Not that I remember.'

'When was the last time you saw Liam?'

'I'd not seen him for weeks, three or four, possibly. I thought he may have gone away, but his car was there, so . . .'

'Last question,' said Dixon. 'Then we'll leave you in peace for now. You said there were two pops. Did you see the driver reload the gun before they fired the second shot?'

'No, dear. They had two guns, definitely, one in each hand. The first shot made a slightly different sound, muffled almost. Then they fired again with the other gun.'

Another house, another set of latex gloves, another dead child's bedroom. Not that Liam Smith was really a child at twenty-eight, but he was still his mother's son. And Dixon would have to face her sooner rather than later. Rescue Jane too.

A Scientific Services officer was photographing Liam's desk against the far wall, opposite the single bed.

A built-in office space. Perhaps he worked from home?

'What did he do for a living?'

'A techie of some sort. Programming,' came the reply. 'Freelance, from what I can see; there's some correspondence from an agency, so that might be a good place to start.'

Louise was making notes.

153

'The computer's on,' said the officer. 'Password protected though. I'll get it off to High Tech as soon as I can.'

'Is that his phone?' Dixon was gesturing to a smartphone lying face down next to the keyboard.

'His mother said so. It'll be going off with his computer.'

'What's his date of birth?'

'Third of December 1996.'

Dixon picked up the phone and tried his luck with the passcode. Straight in.

A deleter of emails, which was a shame. Nothing in Messages or WhatsApp either. He'd know how to delete stuff properly, as well, so High Tech would have their work cut out. Sensible enough to use a burner phone if he was up to no good, probably.

Everyone was a bloody expert these days. God bless Netflix and all their true crime stuff.

'The passcode's his birth date,' said Dixon, dropping the phone into an evidence bag being held out in front of him.

'Thanks.'

It was a sparse room, but then the younger generation didn't tend to frame photographs and hang them on the wall. They were all on smartphones, these days. Not that Dixon would exactly describe himself as old, at thirty-five. Jane would tell him he was old-fashioned, but that was a different thing altogether.

A turn around the living room, which seemed to be where his mother spent her time. An old TV, DVD player, landline. A few photographs on the mantelpiece; one of a football team, not that Dixon could tell which one was her son. He'd looked different lying in the road. Dead.

Loughborough University First XI.

Liam had a degree then; Computer Sciences, if Dixon had to guess.

There were other pictures too. A young girl, so hopefully he wasn't an only child.

Funny, the things that go through your mind when your life revolves around death, thought Dixon. It was something that hit home in the darkest moments that seemed to be engulfing him more and more often. Most fathers would be looking forward to the birth of their first child, but he found himself thinking it might be better to have another one, just in case.

Chapter Seventeen

Time to face the grieving mother.

The bungalow next door was a mirror image, even the same shade of pink, as far as Dixon could tell in the streetlights. He knocked on the front door, waited, Jane answering it. On maternity leave, maybe, but acting family liaison officer.

Once a police officer, always a police officer, etc, etc.

'The mother's in here,' she said. 'In bits, as you can imagine. One thing strikes me as odd—'

'Just one?'

'You know what I mean.' She was speaking softly, closing the front door loudly. 'She said he hadn't been out of the house for three weeks. Couldn't get him to either, for love nor money.'

'Tallies with when Hampton and Paul were killed, our so-called drug dealers.'

'Still looking for a connection?'

'I'm always looking for a connection.'

Two older ladies, sitting side by side on the sofa. A tray of tea on the table in front of them: bone china cups, doilies, Rich Tea biscuits.

'There's more in the pot, if you'd like a cup,' said the one who wasn't crying.

'This is Mrs Lavender,' said Jane.

'I saw a picture of a young girl on the mantelpiece next door . . .' Dixon said hesitantly, dreading the follow-up.

'That's the daughter, Emily. I spoke to her on the phone and she's flying down from Edinburgh in the morning.'

'She's Liam's half-sister.' Mrs Smith was speaking through a crumpled tissue she was holding to her nose. 'My daughter by my first husband.'

'Both husbands are dead,' mouthed Mrs Lavender.

Two husbands and a son. Dixon glanced at Jane, leaning over Mrs Smith with the box of tissues in her outstretched hand. Perhaps it was because life was so good that moments like this were suddenly so difficult?

'You mentioned to Sergeant Winter—'

'We thought Jane was your wife?' asked Mrs Lavender.

'She is. Sorry, I was being formal.'

Actually, it's a defence mechanism. Formality. A bit like a uniform; something to be hidden behind.

'Mentioned what?' Mrs Smith was looking up at him now.

Not much more than sixty years old. What was that statistic again? Fifty per cent of women who reached sixty reached ninety-five. Something like that. Decades in front of her, with one daughter left and she lived hundreds of miles away.

'You mentioned that Liam hadn't been out of the house for several weeks.'

'Wouldn't go.' Mrs Smith blew her nose softly. 'He works from home and doesn't go out much these days anyway. People grow up and move on, don't they? And the lads he used to knock about with have all gone; here, there and everywhere. He was the last one still living at home with his mum.'

'Did he say why he wouldn't go out?'

'Never said a thing. It only really dawned on me after a couple of weeks. I asked him about it and he just fobbed me off, said nothing was wrong and I was imagining it.'

'And were you?'

'No.' She pulled another tissue from the box, dabbed her eyes. 'He only went out this evening to see if his car started. I told him the battery was probably dead.' The word pulled her up short, the tears flowing again.

'Did he keep a diary, or a journal, anything like that?'

'No.'

'We're going to be sending his computer and phone to our High Tech Unit, if that's all right?' Dixon asked, but it wasn't really a question, a fact not lost on Mrs Smith, mercifully.

'You won't get anything off them. I used to call him "secret squirrel". He had programs to delete things and all his messaging was encrypted. He even used a thing to redirect all his internet traffic.'

'A VPN,' offered Jane. 'A virtual private network.'

'That's it. He said it made it secure.'

'High Tech are going to love that.' Jane raised her eyebrows at Dixon.

'And what work did he do?' he asked.

'He was a programmer of some sort. Freelance through an agency. Did very well at it. He worked on games mostly.'

The curtains were open and Dixon was looking across the road, trying to see the car parked on the other side. He hadn't noticed it on the way in.

'It's an old BMW,' said Mrs Smith. 'He was into motorbikes. There's a carbon fibre Honda Fireblade in the garage. His ambition was to compete in the Isle of Man TT, but he never did; said he didn't want to put me through that.'

'Did he have many friends?'

'Not really. They'd all moved away and then the friendships just drift, don't they?' A sad shrug. 'He used to be thick as thieves with a couple of lads he played football with.'

'Names?'

'Darren and Russell. They're police officers now, I think. Up Bristol way.'

◆ ◆ ◆

The living room door opened slowly. 'The ACC's here, Sir,' said Louise. 'Wants a word.'

'You will find whoever did this,' said Mrs Smith, when Dixon was making his way to the door.

'He will,' replied Jane. 'He always does.'

'Thank you.'

There hadn't been many occasions in the past when Dixon was relieved to have been summoned by David Charlesworth, but this was one of them. The joy of starting his own family made a harsh contrast with the grief of someone whose family had just been torn apart.

Perhaps the time had come to act like a proper detective superintendent, and sit behind a desk; spare himself the emotional rollercoaster? Or maybe being a corporate finance solicitor wasn't that bad after all?

There'd be time enough for that conversation when this was over.

'Roger tells me it looks like a 3D printed gun again,' said Charlesworth, turning when Dixon was still crossing the road towards him.

'Yes, Sir.'

'Any connection with Hampton and Paul?'

'No, Sir. But he was friends with Darren Canter and Russell Lock. Thick as thieves they were, when they were younger, according to his mother.'

'Really?' Charlesworth was watching two mortuary technicians carrying a stretcher into the tent, an empty body bag ready and waiting on it. 'Soon be moving him,' he said. 'A professional killing, possibly, I'm told?'

'That's just a neighbour speculating,' replied Dixon.

Charlesworth hadn't come all this way for small talk. Important it might have sounded to anyone listening in, but something else was coming, and Dixon knew exactly what it was.

'What are you doing about it?'

'We've got house to house going already, houses with lights on, which is most of them as you can see. Doorbell camera footage, dashcams. We're checking traffic cameras in the area for a dark SUV, but the end of the lane there, turn left and you're out on to the Levels. Forensics are doing their stuff and the post mortem's fixed for the morning.'

'Good. You seem to have it covered.' Charlesworth's eyes were darting from side to side. Checking whether anyone was within earshot, probably. 'There are too many people here,' he said. 'Walk with me.'

A dressing down about the facial recognition van, as if I give a bloody shit about that, thought Dixon.

Charlesworth stopped out on the main road, beyond the police roadblock, in the darkness of a blind spot in the streetlighting. 'What the bloody hell are you playing at?'

'I don't know what you mean, Sir,' replied Dixon, feigning innocence.

You're going to have to spell it out, you twat.

'You know very well what I mean. Banging on the side of the AFR van like that. What the hell were you thinking? There's

160

footage all over social media, the *Bristol Post* has picked up the story and we've had a complaint from Facetech Solutions. They've even referred it to the Home Office, which is funding the trial.'

'Five people are dead.'

'Are you telling me it started with that stolen laptop?'

'It's a line of enquiry I have to pursue. I'd be negligent if I didn't.' Time to let him have it. 'Not only that, but there's a strong chance anyone trying to suppress the image will find themselves on the wrong end of a conspiracy to pervert the course of justice charge.'

'Are you threatening me?'

'Stating a fact.'

'We know who leaked the image to the enquiry.'

'He did the right thing, and if he finds himself on a disciplinary charge I will personally appear—'

Charlesworth raised his hands in surrender. 'He won't. I'll see to it.'

Time to press home his advantage, if he had one. 'The image was a still from video footage,' Dixon said. 'It's my belief that the footage has not been deleted as it should have been. And I want it.'

'Am I allowed to ask why?'

'What would you do if you were sitting in a coffee shop and someone snatched your laptop?'

'I'd run after them.' The penny had dropped, mercifully.

'I want the footage.'

'If it exists.'

Dixon waited. Charlesworth needed time to mull it over. 'The PCC will block its release. If it exists, and at the moment I don't know the answer to that one way or the other.'

'Fuck the PCC. It's an operational matter, none of his business.'

'If it comes out we haven't been deleting the footage when we should have been, the bloody human rights lobby are going to have a field day.'

'Your answer to that is it's just a trial and all the necessary safeguards will be in place – as specified by the Court of Appeal – before it's introduced operationally within the force area. Anyway, that's not my problem,' said Dixon. 'Five murder victims are my problem.'

Charlesworth grimaced, a long sigh close behind it. 'Put a request in tomorrow morning and I'll see it's not blocked. But if you pull a stunt like that again . . .'

'Thank you, Sir.'

Although Dixon had a better idea.

'Where are we going now?' Jane had asked, sitting in the passenger seat of Dixon's Land Rover.

'I'm dropping you home, then I've got to nip over to Weston.'

'At this time of night?'

Now he was parked on the pavement outside a bay-fronted terraced house; half an hour later and gone midnight. The lights inside were still on, downstairs at least.

Louise had done the necessary. Detective Sergeant Sean Finn's home address. One phone call was all it had taken.

Dixon turned the key, switching off the diesel engine, the curtain twitching in the bay window. Then the front door opened.

'I know why you're here,' said Finn. Tracksuit bottoms and a hoodie. Snappy.

'There's been another murder,' said Dixon, squeezing down the side of a car parked on the drive.

'I heard.'

'Which makes five, and it all starts with that laptop.'

Finn was looking up and down the street.

'Expecting someone?' asked Dixon.

'My wife. She's a nurse and her shift finishes at midnight. I always wait up for her when she's on lates.'

'I need the footage.'

'I told you I deleted it.'

'And I didn't believe you.' Dixon tried a reassuring smile. 'Live footage of a crime being committed? No police officer I know is going to delete that.'

Finn took a deep breath. 'If they find out I sent that image to the enquiry team, let alone the video footage.'

'The ACC knows who sent the image.'

'Did you—?'

'No, I didn't tell him, so I don't know how he knows, but he knows. My guess is the bloke from Facetech told him, but be that as it may, he's assured me you will not face disciplinary proceedings either for failing to delete the image or for releasing it. And the same applies to the video footage.'

'What about the PCC?'

'It's an operational matter and none of his business.'

'Actually, it is.'

'How?'

A car had pulled in behind Dixon's Land Rover.

'Look, my wife's here,' said Finn. 'I really don't want her worrying about this. I'm on duty at six and I'll send over the clip then.'

Chapter Eighteen

Dixon sat down at a workstation at Bridewell police station just before six the following morning, switched on the computer and logged into his email. He looked over his shoulder to find Louise standing on one side, Charlesworth on the other.

Funny that.

Mark Pearce was there too, and several of the officers working on the Hampton and Paul investigation. Or was it the Hampton and Paul *part* of the investigation? Dixon still wasn't sure whether it was one or two separate cases – leaving the guns aside, of course.

That familiar ping.

Finn was as good as his word.

Dixon opened the email and clicked on the attachment. Then pressed Play.

A twenty-four-second clip, the AFR van no more than twenty yards from the coffee shop, the footage clear as day; none of that grainy CCTV crap to contend with here.

People were walking towards the camera. They had no idea they were being filmed, no idea the footage had been retained. Most wouldn't care, probably.

Why should I mind? I've got nothing to hide.

It was a common enough reaction, but that didn't make it right. The solicitor in Dixon knew enough to mind, that the safeguards existed for a reason. After all, it wasn't a police state.

Yet.

Hampton appeared, walking past the van, his back to the camera as he headed towards the coffee shop. The forward-facing camera would have got him, possibly, but then that footage probably had been deleted.

He stopped in the window of Burra, noticed the laptop on the table, realised he had an opportunity. Then he darted through the open front door, emerging seconds later with something tucked under his arm, turning back towards the camera. Sprinting.

Then a figure emerged from the coffee shop, shouting, but there was no sound. He stopped on the pavement, looking left and right; ducked back inside to retrieve his empty laptop case, before walking slowly away.

'The Montpelier Room,' said Charlesworth. 'Now.'

Charlesworth slammed the door behind them, the glass partition rattling in protest.

'We've got no evidence of any wrongdoing on his part,' he said. 'He's a private citizen, and if he chooses not to report a crime then that is entirely a matter for him.'

'And what example does that set?' replied Dixon. 'The Police and Crime Commissioner has his laptop stolen and doesn't report the theft. How's that going to look?'

'Like he doesn't have confidence in his own force to investigate the theft,' mumbled Charlesworth.

Neither of them sat down for what would no doubt be a short meeting, all eyes in the incident room watching them through the glass partition.

'It's worse than that, though,' said Dixon. 'Think about it. The PCC has his laptop stolen and three weeks later the boy who stole it is murdered.'

Dixon let that one hang in the air for a moment.

'I'm going to need to speak to him,' he continued. 'From where I'm sitting, he's a suspect in the murders of Hampton and Paul.'

'You must let me speak to him first,' said Charlesworth.

'That'll just tip him off I'm coming for him, Sir.'

'I suppose it would.'

'It might also explain why he was so keen the AFR trial shouldn't come out, that the image of Hampton stealing the laptop shouldn't be used. It wasn't about the election at all. And that's bordering on perverting the course of justice, that is.'

'Just go carefully. I don't want you steaming in there, both feet first.'

'He was probably keeping an eye on the bloody camera van. I'll bet that's why he was in the coffee shop.'

'I'd give my back teeth to know what was on that laptop,' muttered Charlesworth.

'Whoever killed them probably stole it, assuming they hadn't sold it on already. I'll get High Tech to check for auction accounts, see if they've got any completed auctions. We've had some success with that before, on a different case.'

'Just go carefully, for God's sake.'

Chapter Nineteen

'Who are you visiting, Sir?'

'The High Tech Unit.'

A little white lie, perhaps, but it got them past the security gate at Avon and Somerset Police headquarters without a phone call being made to the PCC's office.

'You'll go to hell, you will,' said Louise.

'It'll be very crowded.'

'Yeah, it will.'

They were walking across the grass in front of the main building before Dixon spoke again. 'Remember, we treat him just like any other suspect in a murder investigation. All right?'

'Yes, Sir.'

'And if anybody ends up on a disciplinary, it'll be me, not you.'

'I'm not worried about that.'

Dixon left his reply – *Well, you should be* – unsaid. Always best.

The first test would be getting past the PCC's personal assistant, Julia. There she was, sitting at her desk outside Hugo Napier's office.

'Is her hair bleached or naturally that colour?' whispered Dixon as they walked across the landing.

'I'll let you know,' replied Louise, without moving her lips, now that Julia was watching them.

One half of the double doors was standing open, Dixon nudging it with his elbow so it closed behind them.

'Is Mr Napier available, please?' he asked, formally.

'He's got the Assistant PCC with him at the moment,' replied Julia. 'Can it wait?'

'No.'

She appeared taken aback by Dixon's curt reply. 'Oh, right,' she said, standing up. 'Give me a minute.'

A soft knock on the door, closing it behind her, so Dixon couldn't hear what was being said.

'I don't want you steaming in there, both feet first,' Charlesworth had said. Dixon would try to remember.

'You can go in now,' said Julia, leaving the office door standing open.

Napier's Assistant PCC was standing with his back to the filing cabinets. White shirt, black tie, red braces framing a beer belly. He wouldn't have looked out of place in the organised crime squad.

'What is it, Dixon?' demanded Napier, when Louise had closed the door.

'The image from the AFR camera—'

Napier stood up sharply, sending his swivel chair into the window frame behind him. 'Not that again. I thought I'd made myself abundantly clear on that. You cannot use it.'

Dixon unfolded yet another copy of the image, dropped it on Napier's desk. 'You can see in the picture that Justin Hampton has a laptop under his arm.'

'So what?'

'A laptop that we know from the owner of the coffee shop he'd just stolen.'

'I say again, so what?'

'Your laptop.'

Napier looked at the Assistant PCC, then back to Dixon. Lost for words, apparently, so Dixon thought it best to keep the conversation moving.

'We've got the video footage from which that still is taken. A twenty-four-second clip, which shows Hampton going into the coffee shop, running out with your laptop and you in pursuit. Needless to say, it hadn't been deleted.'

'You need to leave my office.' Napier's voice was getting louder as he spoke. 'Now!'

'There are two ways we can do this, Mr Napier,' said Dixon, impassively. 'Either you can talk to me now, or we can do it at Bridewell police station under caution.'

'You're bluffing.'

Both feet first.

'Three weeks after your laptop is stolen, Hampton is murdered, which makes you a suspect. *Prime* suspect, actually.'

'You'd better cooperate, Hugo, otherwise you can kiss any chance of re-election goodbye.' Wise words from the Assistant PCC, still leaning against the filing cabinets, his hands thrust deep into his trouser pockets. Hardly surprising. If the PCC lost the election, then his Assistant PCC would be out on his ear too.

Napier slumped back down into his leather chair, folded his arms. 'Fire away,' he said, with a heavy sigh.

'Let's start with the incident itself, shall we? Did you recognise Hampton?'

'No.'

'You've seen the AFR image since, got a better look at him from that. Have you ever seen him before?'

'No.'

'Why didn't you give chase?'

'He was too far away by then and I'd never have caught him. I'm not exactly light on my feet these days.'

'What sort of laptop was it?'

'It was an old Acer I kept for personal stuff. My work one is here,' he said, gesturing to a laptop open on the desk in front of him. 'This one never leaves this office unless I'm doing a presentation somewhere.'

'And what was on the stolen laptop?'

'Personal stuff. I was writing a book, if you must know, but the manuscript was backed up to the cloud anyway, so I haven't even lost that. Apart from that, there was nothing of consequence. I didn't use it for internet banking or anything; that's all on my phone. Look, it was hardly worth worrying about.' Napier frowned, glared at the Assistant PCC. 'Hang on a minute, are you seriously suggesting I murdered Hampton or whatever his name is because he stole my laptop? Me, the duly elected Police and Crime Commissioner for Avon and Somerset?'

'It's a line of enquiry, and not an unreasonable one from where I'm sitting.'

'D'you know how utterly ridiculous that sounds?'

'Why were you in that particular coffee shop? Burra, it's called.'

'I was interested in the AFR trial, if you must know. I was watching the van, seeing if anyone spotted it.'

'Hardly likely; an unmarked van, hidden cameras.'

'That's right. If and when we use it for real, the van will be marked and the cameras visible on the roof, but you never know, sometimes the Big Brother Watch lot are out and looking to stir up trouble.'

'*Trouble* is an inflammatory word,' said the Assistant PCC. 'There's a balance between intrusive surveillance and the reasonable use of new technology to improve public safety. It's about finding that balance, with all the appropriate safeguards in place to make sure we bring the public with us. We police by consent in this country, after all.'

'I've seen his election leaflet, thanks,' said Dixon. He turned back to Napier. 'So, you're keeping an eye on the AFR trial and someone you don't recognise steals your laptop. Why didn't you report the theft?'

'It was an old laptop, of no value, and I thought it would be wasting police time and resources.'

'Even though you knew the AFR camera was there and we'd be able to identify the thief in an instant?'

'I didn't want a fuss made. The PCC having his laptop stolen is news, isn't it?'

'In an election year,' offered the Assistant PCC.

'It might also have come out that we're trialling live facial recognition, although that's well and truly out there now, thanks to you banging on the bloody van.'

'What's your book about?'

'My memoirs.'

Either Louise coughed, or she stifled a chuckle, Dixon couldn't tell which.

'Here, you can have this,' said Napier. He leaned forward, slid a piece of paper across the desk to Dixon. 'It's a Facebook post calling for a demonstration tonight outside Bridewell police station to protest against the fascist state and its use of surveillance cameras. All thanks to you. Well done.' His voice was loaded with sarcasm.

'The responsibility rests with the idiot who authorised a covert AFR trial,' replied Dixon. 'And then tried to hush it up when it produced evidence in a murder investigation. If I was them, I'd be worried I might find myself on a charge of conspiracy to pervert—'

'Are you threatening me?' snarled Napier.

'Steady on, Hugo,' said the Assistant PCC. 'We're all on the same side here.'

'Are we?'

'I'm on the side of the lad who was murdered three weeks after stealing your laptop,' said Dixon. 'He was beaten up, then shot in the head at point blank range.'

'I'll have you drummed out of this police force.' Napier had stepped out from behind his desk, squaring up to Dixon. Almost. Another step forward and then, maybe.

'If I find Hampton and Paul are dead because of what was on that laptop, then you and I will speak again, Mr Napier. Under caution, at a police station. Is that clear?'

◆　◆　◆

'Bleached,' said Louise, once they were sitting in Dixon's Land Rover. 'Did you believe what he said about what was on the laptop?'

'I don't know,' replied Dixon, turning the key, the diesel engine rumbling into life. 'My starting point is the bloke's a git and I don't believe a word he says.'

'Mine too.'

'If he's telling the truth, then it's pure coincidence that Hampton and Paul were murdered three weeks later. And we've got no evidence to suggest they were murdered for the laptop.'

'A laptop was stolen from the flat though,' said Louise. 'There was that power cable, wasn't there?'

'Yes, but his parents said he had his own for his university course.'

'Bet he'd already sold that.'

'You may be right.'

'Where to now?'

Chapter Twenty

'I need time to think.'

Louise knew what it meant, offered to keep him company, but Monty would do that. Being alone was the whole point.

It had been a soul-destroying couple of hours back at Bridewell police station. Roger Poland had confirmed low velocity gunshots had killed Liam Smith, and there were signs of polymer on the bullets themselves. They were already on the way to the lab, with the shards of plastic found next to the body.

And, yes, Canter, Lock, Hampton and Paul had all been killed by a gun or guns made from the same batch of polymer, but confirmation of that was the only step forward. All of the other steps had been backwards. *One step forward, two steps back.* Bollocks. It felt more like one forward and eight back.

It wasn't as if the batch of polymer had come as much of a surprise. He'd have bet his house on it, and he'd only bought it off his landlord last Friday, completion taking place the day before his wedding. No, more than one gunsmith would have been too much of a coincidence.

A couple of grainy CCTV images of a dark SUV, the only eyewitness a woman in her late eighties with dodgy eyesight. You couldn't make it up, you really couldn't.

Interesting that whoever killed Smith had had two guns, didn't need to reload. Only one left now, though, assuming one had disintegrated when it was fired. At least that was one gun off the streets.

Somewhere different for a change. Dixon didn't want to go back to Berrow Church for a while anyway, in case the churchwarden was there. No confetti was the rule, set in stone, but one well and truly ignored by their guests. It had been biodegradable, not that that had calmed him down much. Best to wait until it had disappeared.

Dixon parked at the end of Trinity Rise and took the steep path up and over the dunes, coming out on to the beach opposite the low lighthouse. A series of high tides had washed away the base of the dunes, leaving a steep drop on to the beach below. Only a few feet, and someone had slid down it before him, so he followed their footsteps. Monty had jumped it and buggered off, already sniffing around the base of the lighthouse.

Wednesday lunchtime, during the school term time, everybody at work. Lovely.

There were a couple of other dog walkers in the distance, so Dixon walked straight out to sea, not that he'd reach the waterline, the tide was miles out; wading across the channels in the sandbanks, then turned north for Brean Down, not that he'd get that far either. There really wasn't time for that.

Jane had been at the cottage when Dixon called in to pick up his dog, handed him a few pages of stuff that Sarah Loveday had found on the internet about Sohail York. There hadn't been a lot to find that wasn't about the PCC election; York was of that generation that didn't post every detail of their lives on social media.

Some people would upload stool samples if they could. They really would. That was another of Mark Pearce's jokes – with a shred of truth in it, possibly.

A clear blue sky; one of those cold and crisp February days with not a breath of wind, following his dog along the flats, twirling a tennis ball launcher like a baton. These were the moments that made it all bearable.

It all.

All the death. And a life spent up to his neck in other people's misery.

Jane had been sorting out babygrows. His mother-in-law, Sue – *mother-in-law*, that would take some getting used to – couldn't help herself and kept buying them. Pink and blue, just in case. But it had been the look on Jane's face, the joy of it all. Thank God she knew the job, knew what he was going through. Knew enough not to expect a smiling face.

The two sets of murders must be connected, surely? Two major investigation teams, God knows how many hours, and all they'd come up with so far was Canter and Hampton being members of the same online marketing forum. Along with 1.6 million other people, as it turned out.

Connected, but how?

If they weren't, then Dixon really was running two separate major investigation teams.

Not forgetting the gunsmith, of course. Although even then it was possible two people with 3D printers had bought polymer from the same batch and printed guns with it.

He threw the tennis ball along the beach, watching Monty kicking up the sand as he set off after it.

Clarity of thought was needed. Two gunsmiths was unlikely. Actually, it was the 'realms of fantasy', as Captain Mainwaring would've called it.

So, two cases connected by the one person providing the weapons.

Or one case?

Start with what you know. Jumbled thoughts, Dixon strolling along the sand. There was a warmth to the sunshine; early spring or late winter. Who knew?

A person or persons unknown walked into Hampton's flat, tortured Hampton and Paul, killed them with a single shot to the head from a 3D printed gun, stole this and that, and then left.

Two weeks later, Canter and Lock were killed at their container at Portbury Docks by a gun printed from the same batch of polymer. Canter's body left in the container, Lock thrown into the sea.

Dixon knew what had happened. *Exactly* what happened.

He also knew what didn't happen.

'Have you been running?' Jane had asked when Dixon dropped Monty back at the cottage. Clearly the few minutes in the car hadn't been enough to settle his breathing. Still red in the face too, and wearing his muddy wellies.

'Do me a favour, will you? Text Lou and Mark and get them to meet me at Severn Beach, under the bridge.'

Jane knew the look, knew better than to ask.

'When?'

'I'm on my way there now.'

The stench was the same; tide out, exposed mud, further up the estuary so that was to be expected perhaps. Dixon was sitting on the riverbank in the sun, looking across to Wales, where Darren Canter's BMW had been found only a couple of days earlier. He'd spotted the CCTV cameras on the works compound under the bridge and had kept out of view.

It was a place he knew well, but that was another story. Another tale of death and misery; of sadness, and a family destroyed.

The tops of high-sided lorries were visible from time to time on the bridge above, crossing into Wales.

What didn't happen?

It felt like an odd question to be asking. What did happen was the one they concentrated on more often than not, but this time it was what *didn't* happen that had unlocked it.

Possibly.

At the moment it was just a theory. Not one that he'd want to share with the wider teams either. Not yet.

'There he is.' Mark's voice.

Dixon turned to see Mark and Louise picking their way along the path, stepping over driftwood and Christmas trees left by the high tides.

'What's going on, Sir?' asked Louise.

Dixon stood up, brushing the grass off his backside with both hands. There was a metaphor if ever there was one.

'Why are we meeting here?' asked Mark.

'Away from prying eyes and walls with ears. It's just a theory at this stage, a line of enquiry, and we need to keep it to ourselves for the time being.'

Mark and Louise waited.

'Someone went into Hampton's flat, tortured and killed Hampton and Paul. Forensics haven't been able to confirm it either way yet, but it's reasonable to assume it was more than one person.'

'It could've been one,' said Mark. 'They had a gun.'

'Yes, it could.' Dixon nodded. 'But I'm working on the assumption that it was two. There was a commotion. We know that from the neighbour. Then an anonymous tip-off was received at eleven-thirty-seven and police attended twelve minutes later, finding the bodies.'

'Yeah, we know what happened,' said Louise.

'Ask yourself what didn't happen,' replied Dixon.

Silence.

'One of the neighbours heard a commotion an hour or so before the call came in, but no one dialled 999 and reported it. Why not?'

Louise shook her head. 'I don't know.'

Dixon took a deep breath. 'Because the police were already there.'

Chapter Twenty-One

'Hang on a minute. Are you saying that Police Constables Darren Canter and Russell Lock murdered Justin Hampton and Andrew Paul?'

'That's exactly what I'm saying, Mark.'

'Fucking hell.'

'Yeah, but . . .' Louise glanced at Mark, her mouth open, eyes doubtful.

'Don't look at me,' he said, thrusting his hands into his jacket pockets.

'We need to speak to the neighbours again,' said Dixon. 'But what I don't want is word going around Bridewell until we're sure. I'm not going to be updating the Policy Log either. We're outsiders and they had friends and colleagues in that station; lots of them. It's just a line of enquiry at the moment and I might be wrong.'

'That's never happened before.' Louise was still letting it sink in.

'Well, it's going to happen one day. That I can guarantee.'

'Why though?' asked Mark.

'That's stage two. Let's find out if they did it first. I want you to check their phone signals for the time of Hampton and Paul's murders, Mark. You'll need to be discreet. I'll sign off on it, but don't tell anyone what you're doing.'

'Yes, Sir.'

'Check CCTV and ANPR cameras looking for their cars in and around the murder scene at the time as well. If I'm right, they'll have been off duty and in their own cars, otherwise the GPS tracker on their patrol car would've picked it up. We'll speak to the neighbours, Lou, but I need to have a chat with Roger first.'

'Can't you just ring him?'

Dixon ignored the question. Truth was it had only occurred to him while he was sitting on the grass at Severn Beach. And, no. No phones. It was best dealt with in person.

The receptionist had tried her best, in fairness. 'He's in the middle of a post . . .'

Dixon had hoped Poland would've come out of the lab when he banged on the window of the anteroom. Instead he got a waved invitation to go in. Poland had looked up, his apron and arms smeared with blood, and beckoned him with a scalpel. Nice.

'You can wait here, if you'd like, Lou.'

'Thanks.'

Dixon pushed open the door. 'Do I need the VapoRub?' he asked, nervously.

'No. Nice and fresh, this one,' replied Poland. He may have been grinning behind his mask, but Dixon couldn't tell.

A man; early thirties, possibly.

'Motorbike accident,' said Poland. 'They reckon he was doing over a hundred. Went under a lorry.'

Dixon was standing a safe distance from the slab; the smell of fresh blood wasn't as bad as decomposition, but bad enough. 'I wanted a word in private,' he said.

'Laura is the soul of discretion,' replied Poland, stepping back to allow her to take a close-up photograph of God knows what.

'Have you got Russell Lock's body here?'

'Yes, he's in the fridge.'

'I want his hands tested for GSR.'

'Gunshot residue?' Poland's frown was visible below his fetching hairnet. 'Er, yes, we can do that.'

'I'm not holding out much hope,' continued Dixon. 'We found no fingerprints, so he was probably wearing gloves, and he'd been in the water.'

'Might still show up. You never know, he may have test-fired the guns somewhere, but they wear chain mail gloves when they fire these things, don't they?'

'Where are the clothes he was wearing?'

'They went off to Scientific.'

That was another conversation then, with Donald Watson, although whether Dixon could rely on his discretion was another matter.

'We need to get Darren Canter tested as well, but he's at Bristol. Can you speak to Leo Peterson and organise that?'

'Can't you do it?'

'It needs to be discreet.'

Poland straightened up slowly. 'You suspect Lock and Canter murdered the other two, those drug dealers, don't you?'

'It's a line of enquiry.'

'Don't give me that flannel.' Pointing the scalpel at Dixon now. 'You be very careful making allegations like that. David Charlesworth will go ballistic.'

An interesting choice of word, *ballistic*.

'Only if I'm wrong. That's why it needs to be done quietly first, why I'm asking you to have a discreet word with your colleague, have the test done without any fanfare.'

'All right. Leave it with me.' Poland turned back to the body on the slab in front of him. 'It might not be such an easy conversation with Donald Watson.'

Dixon knew that. If he was right, there would come a point when it became general knowledge, when he might find he'd overstayed his welcome at Bridewell police station.

'You need to be sure before you go public with this,' said Poland. His parting shot as Dixon made for the door.

'We asked Mrs Kimber, in that one,' said Louise, pointing at a small terraced house next door to Hampton's flat. 'We spoke to her, remember?'

The flat was still locked up, police tape zig-zagging across the front door, new wood where the frame had been repaired, a large notice stuck to the glass.

'Said she didn't hear a thing. Took her hearing aids out and went to bed.'

'That's right. There's a statement from her in the file, and one from a Doris Capel in that house there. She heard a commotion just after ten-thirty, but thought nothing of it and went to bed.'

'She's the one we need to see then.'

It was a simple enough question, but no one had asked it, or so it seemed.

'Did you phone the police?'

'No.'

'Why not?'

Dixon had read her statement. Whoever had taken it needed further training, and a kick up the backside. Lazy at best. If the question had been asked, as it should have been, the statement would have said something along the lines of 'I didn't phone the police because . . .'

Every question had an answer, and every answer was converted into a sentence in the witness statement.

'What did you see then?'

'Then I saw . . .'

Take the person through it line by line, step by step. Simple enough, surely?

Louise was knocking on the old lady's door, waiting patiently as the figure inside loomed slowly in the frosted glass, a distinct limp. At least she was in.

'Who is it?' Nervous, a hand resting on the door handle.

'Police, Mrs Capel,' replied Louise, pushing her warrant card through the letterbox.

Net curtains in the window, to the left of the front door, just enough of a gap in the middle to look through. No twitching needed here.

'You do the talking, Lou,' said Dixon, while Mrs Capel was unlocking the door, bolts top and bottom. It was taking a while.

'Is it about the murders?' asked the old woman, handing Louise back her warrant card.

'Yes, it is. Can we come in?'

'Of course.'

Dixon followed. Yes, a pronounced limp. A stairlift too, although the sofa was gone in the living room, replaced by a bed at some point. There was an electric armchair too, the old woman taking hold of a switch on the end of a cable and pressing the button, the chair returning to the customary upright position. Then she sat down.

'You'll need to sit on the edge of the bed, I'm afraid,' she said, with an apologetic shrug. 'I don't get many visitors.'

'We wanted to ask you about the night of the murders, Mrs Capel.'

'I gave a witness statement.'

'You did, but we have a couple more questions, specifically about the commotion you said you heard at about ten-thirty. You described it as "just the usual" in your witness statement.'

'There was always something going on in there,' she said, with a shake of the head. 'Noisy buggers, they were. Shouting, breaking glass, people coming and going at all times of the day and night, banging on the door. Music, if you can call it that.'

'What about that night?'

'It started with a banging sound. I thought it was someone trying to get in, then it went quiet. Shouting started a few minutes later. I think I heard someone screaming at one point, then it went quiet again.'

'What about gunfire?'

'No. There were two popping sounds at about twenty to eleven, maybe twenty-five to. Sounded more like fireworks to me, so I didn't really think anything of it. They were always letting off fireworks.'

Dixon nudged Louise's arm, gestured to the gap in the net curtains.

'Did you look out of your window at any point?'

The old lady's face reddened. 'Yes. Several times.'

'And what did you see?'

'People on the path. Two of them, walking away they were.'

'And did you phone the police?'

'No. There was always something going on in there. Besides, there was no need. When I looked out, they were there.'

'What time was that?'

'Like I said, just after twenty-five to.'

Louise was making notes, her notebook resting on her knee. 'We received an anonymous tip-off at eleven-thirty-seven, Mrs Capel. Officers responded to that call and arrived on the scene at eleven-forty-nine. That's over an hour later, isn't it?'

'So, who were those officers I saw on the garden path?'

'What were they doing when you saw them?' asked Dixon.

'Walking away from the flat.'

'Quickly?'

'No, walking normally.'

'Were they carrying anything?'

'One of them had a bag in his hand, a holdall. I thought it was just stuff they'd confiscated or something.'

'They were in uniform, I take it?'

'It was definitely police uniform – dark trousers, white shirts, and those stab vest things you all wear,' she said.

'Could you see any blood on them?'

'No, dear. It was dark and they were walking away from me, remember.'

'And where did they go?'

'They walked out on to the main road and got in an unmarked car. I couldn't tell you what sort, couldn't really see it from here. All I can say for sure is there were no blue lights on top.'

'I'm confused, Mrs Capel,' said Louise. 'Why didn't you mention this before?'

'Nobody asked me. I answered the questions I was asked. And besides, I assumed you'd know about the officers being here. Everything's supposed to be logged these days, isn't it?'

Chapter Twenty-Two

'Are you sure about this, Sir?'

'Far from it.'

'Then should we really be wading in there, accusing their son of murder?'

It was a fair point, although Dixon had intended to be a little more subtle about it, perhaps.

'The FLO isn't even there,' continued Louise.

'We don't need a referee, Lou. And nobody's wading anywhere.'

There were sitting outside Darren Canter's parents' house on the edge of Banwell, only the Audi two-seater in the drive this time.

Julian Canter answered the door, which was a surprise, perhaps; lazy assumptions about who drove which car.

'There's only me. My wife's gone to work.' Mid-afternoon, bleary eyed, a strong smell of alcohol. 'She does a bit of locum work at local surgeries, covering for holidays, stuff like that, and it's more important to her than her family apparently,' he said, over a sigh.

'Can we . . . ?'

'Yes, of course.' Julian took a step back, almost lost his balance. 'Go through. There's a bottle of Pinot Grigio open if you fancy joining me?'

'We're on duty, Sir,' replied Dixon, trotting out the standard response.

'Coffee then.' Julian was filling the kettle, most of the water missing the spout.

'We were very sorry about your son,' said Dixon.

'Thank you. At least you found his body. We're grateful for that. They said it's going to be a while before we can bury him.'

'I'm afraid so, Sir.'

A slurp of wine, two mugs banged down on to the worktop, the kettle gathering steam in the background. 'I know how these things work. I was a GP for thirty years, certified many a death. Never got used to it. Not really.'

Funny that. Me neither.

'When was the last time you saw Darren?' asked Dixon.

'I'm guessing you mean before I identified his body in the mortuary?' Julian raised his hand, silencing Dixon before he could reply. 'Sorry. I was being stupid. It was that morning. I was in here. He came in, grabbed a banana for breakfast and went off to work, his usual monosyllabic self.'

'And how had he been in the weeks leading up to his death?' asked Dixon.

'Sugar?'

'No, thank you.'

'He'd been stressed. We knew that, and we'd had words. It occurred to us later it must have been down to the Professional Standards investigation you told us about. We hadn't known about that and he never mentioned it, but it explains a lot to be honest. He was short-tempered and downright bloody rude to his mother, on several occasions.' Milk, spilled all over the counter. 'We had a blazing row one night when he came in late, stinking of booze. Driven home too. I was bloody livid, I can tell you.' Another slurp of wine.

Louise noticed the irony too, shaking her head almost imperceptibly.

'I know he never said anything about the misconduct investigation, but did he say anything else that might be relevant, about what was going on at work, perhaps?'

'No. We had to find out from you about the misconduct thing,' replied Julian. 'I keep thinking about that poor woman dragged out of her wheelchair. What was he playing at?' He shook his head. 'We certainly never brought him up to behave like that. We taught him compassion and empathy. That was soon knocked out of him by you lot, wasn't it?' He was filling the mugs with boiling water, concentrating. 'Not you personally, obviously. I meant the police generally.'

'It's fine, Sir.'

'I guess it's the job. Probably got to him.'

It gets to us all. Some quicker than others.

'Mine got to me. It's like working in a call centre now, getting rid of patients on the phone, playing Russian roulette with your professional indemnity insurance. I couldn't wait to get out.' Julian placed two mugs on the kitchen table in front of Dixon and Louise, spilling both. 'They're the same, white, no sugar,' he said. 'I'll get some kitchen roll for that.'

'Tell me about the blazing row. When was it?'

'Three weeks ago, maybe. His shift was supposed to end at eight and we were expecting him about eight-thirty. Diane had done a stew and his was in the oven, keeping warm. No phone call, nothing, and he comes in roaring drunk at nearly one o'clock in the morning. Wakes us up, demands that Diane put his uniform in the wash.'

'Did he say what had happened?'

'There'd been a fight, he said. I can't remember the name of the pub, but him and Russell had gone in to try to calm things down when everyone turned on them. They were lucky to get out alive, he said, wouldn't have done if reinforcements hadn't turned up.'

Dixon was looking at the calendar on the wall, one of those large ones with a wire spine and a hook, a picture of what looked like the Highlands. Glencoe, possibly. Most of the entries were Diane here, there and everywhere. Banwell, Nailsea, Weston-super-Mare; locum engagements, probably.

'Diane was starting at Nailsea that morning, I seem to remember. A week, filling in for someone going skiing. So, it might have been the night before that.' He lifted the calendar off the hook, flipped it back a month. 'Yeah, twenty-seventh of January. It was that night, I'm sure of it. She started at Nailsea on the twenty-eighth.'

'And he wanted his clothes put in the wash?'

'Straight away, he said. They were covered in blood; none of it his, I might add. Someone got glassed in the . . . brawl, I suppose you'd call it. Quite a few arrests were made. He said the bloke with the glass would go down for GBH, the rest of them for affray, is it?' Julian rolled his eyes. 'He made it sound like something out of an old John Wayne film.'

Too much coffee, not enough milk. Even Louise had turned her nose up at it.

'What was he like as a child, growing up?'

'Quiet. Worked hard at school. Didn't want to go to university and I can't say I blame him for that, being saddled with all that debt for the rest of your life.'

'Did he ever get into any trouble?'

'Not really.' Julian had drifted off, just for a second. 'He couldn't have done, could he? Otherwise he'd never have got in the police. He did get in with the wrong crowd for a time when he started playing football, drinking. But he soon snapped out of it.'

'What did he do before he joined the police?'

'Not a lot really. He did a stint as a delivery driver. Then he started an engineering apprenticeship, but didn't stick at that. Loafed about at home for a while.'

A key was being inserted in the front door.

'God, is that the time?' said Julian. 'That'll be Diane.' Lid on the bottle of wine, in the fridge just as his wife appeared in the doorway.

'What's going on?' she asked.

'They just wanted to ask some questions about Darren,' replied Julian.

'You didn't tell them about—?' She glared at her husband.

'Yes, I did. I told them about the blazing row.'

'It was nothing,' she said, looking relieved, albeit fleetingly. 'And now we know what stress he must've been under, it all makes sense. Gross misconduct proceedings.' She dropped her bag on the table, slung her coat over the back of an empty chair. 'If only he'd told us about it, we could have helped him; paid for a solicitor or something.'

'Julian said it was the night before you started at Nailsea on the twenty-eighth of January.'

'That sounds about right. I did a week's holiday cover for someone. It's my old surgery, so I know them over there anyway.'

'Was he injured in the pub fight?'

'Didn't seem to be. I checked him over.' She shrugged. 'It wasn't the first time it'd happened. He said it went with the job.'

'That was the night Hampton and Paul were murdered,' said Louise. 'He gets home late, covered in blood, and gets his mother to stick his clothes in the washing machine.'

'Not a mark on him either,' replied Dixon. 'Which means he used a weapon to inflict the beating. I wonder what he did with that?'

'Could've disposed of it anywhere.'

'Had a few beers somewhere to calm his nerves too. We'll need to check there wasn't a shout at a pub in Bristol that night.'

'I'm not holding my breath. Are you?'

'No.'

There was more to it than that though. Dixon knew what had happened that night, was more interested in what didn't happen. Now he was more interested in what Darren Canter's parents *didn't* say; that was even more interesting than what they did say.

He was drumming his fingers on the steering wheel, waiting for the traffic lights in front of him to change, pretending not to notice his phone buzzing. He'd plugged it into the charger, left it in the cup holder.

'It's David Charlesworth,' said Louise, tipping her head to see the screen. 'He's left a message. D'you want me to—?'

'Don't bother. He'll just be passing on another earwigging from the PCC. Either that or he wants to know why I haven't updated the Policy Log today.'

'And we know why that is.'

They were on their way to Whitchurch, to see Russell Lock's parents. Clutching at straws, probably. Dixon had much the same questions to ask them, but he wanted to see if what they didn't say matched what Darren Canter's parents didn't say.

Or maybe they would say it, if they thought the Canters had done. A sly trick, perhaps, but it might work.

'Russell Lock's parents won't have seen him that night, though, will they?' said Louise. 'He'd have gone home to his flat.'

'What did Diane Canter say when she walked in?'

191

Louise was flicking through the pages of her notebook. '"You didn't tell them about . . ." but she didn't finish the question. Then he said he'd told us about the blazing row.'

'He did,' replied Dixon. 'That wasn't what she was asking about, though, was it?'

'Wasn't it?'

'There's something else. *You didn't tell them about* . . . She didn't say it, and neither did he.'

Chapter Twenty-Three

No Tracey this time. And no baby Luke.

Luke Lock.

Nice.

It was a conversation he'd had with Jane: baby names. His suggestion of Richard for a boy had been greeted with amusement, mercifully, Jane getting better at spotting his jokes. Dick Dixon was not to be inflicted on anybody.

No, a boy, and he'd be called Peter, they'd agreed on that, after . . . another life shattered.

He checked the cars in the drive. No family liaison officer either, it seemed. Just Russell Lock's parents.

'I was about to ring,' said Michael, standing in the open front door. 'See what's going on, now you've found Darren as well.'

'How the hell do we explain that?' whispered Louise, hiding behind Dixon. Almost.

'We don't.'

The photograph of their dead son Russell in uniform had been moved and was now taking pride of place in the middle of the mantelpiece in the living room. Someone had cut a piece of black ribbon, draped it across the corner of the frame.

The fire was on in the fake hearth, just the lightbulbs, red, illuminating the glass coals.

Michael was ex-police and would spot the 'various lines of enquiry' line a mile off, but Dixon thought he'd try it anyway.

'Don't try and fob me off with that,' said Michael, dismissively. 'That's what you say when you don't want to tell someone what's going on. You found Darren in the container at Portbury Docks, didn't you?'

Dixon was softening him up, getting him to the point where he'd be eager to talk . . . about anything. Shameless, really.

'Well, what else did you find?'

'Nothing of note. Forensics was clear, but we think it was where Russell went into the water, off the old wharf.'

'What about the family of that girl who died in custody? New Year's Eve.'

'Both parents are housebound and the daughter has an alibi.'

'What about the bugger printing these damn guns?'

'We're working through anyone who has purchased that particular batch of polymer, but there are a lot of them and it's taking time. Plus we're finding new ones each day. I don't hold out much hope of that to be honest. If I was going to be printing weapons with the stuff, I'd get it on the black market, the dark web probably.'

'Somewhere it's untraceable.' Michael curled his lip in disgust.

'Exactly.' Dixon turned to face the picture of Russell. 'The Canters mentioned an incident that took place some time ago, wondered if that might have any relevance,' he said, casually.

'It was something and nothing.' Linda had been sitting in the armchair, leaving the talking to her husband, but listening intently, barely hiding her frustration at the apparent lack of progress. 'He—'

'It was nothing,' interrupted Michael.

It reminded Dixon of the last time Linda had volunteered something, only to be shut down by her husband.

It wasn't as if he'd been convicted of rape or anything.

It had seemed an odd thing to say at the time, leapt out at Dixon and Louise. He was close now. Time to stick his neck out.

'Tell me about the allegation of rape,' he said, matter of fact.

'There was no allegation of rape.' Michael, indignant.

A loud sigh came from Linda. 'Yes, there was, Michael. What use is denying it? What harm can it do Russell now? And besides, it might be relevant.'

Her husband was pacing up and down on the rug in front of the fire. He paused next to Dixon, who had turned around from the mantelpiece, fixed him with a steely glare.

'They know anyway,' continued Linda. 'The Canters have told them.'

Actually they hadn't, but the Locks didn't need to know that.

What Dixon knew now was that there had been an allegation of rape involving both Russell Lock and Darren Canter.

Getting somewhere at last.

He waited. Push them now and they might clam up. Michael had a decision to make and needed time to make it.

'I need a drink,' he said, pouring himself a tumbler of whisky. He took a swig. 'It was a long time ago and they were just kids, really. It took us all a long time to get over it, put it behind us, and I'd really rather it wasn't all raked up again now.'

'And what if it's relevant to his murder?'

'It can't be.'

There was a reason for that. All he had to do was wait.

'Both the girl and her mother are dead now.'

'What about the father?'

'There never was one, not in any conventional sense. The bloke was never part of their lives is what we say these days, isn't it?'

Dixon ignored the sarcasm. 'It's a line of enquiry,' he said.

'I know, I know.' Another swig of whisky. 'Russ was eighteen. The football team went on a group trip to the Glastonbury Festival.

It was *alleged* they raped a girl in their tent. Drugged her first and then raped her. They were just kids, for fuck's sake.'

'Were the police involved?'

'They made a report but decided not to pursue it, withdrew the complaint a few days later. I was involved, wasn't I?' He sat down on the arm of his wife's chair. 'Russell and Darren said it was consensual, so I persuaded the girl's mother it would be her daughter's word against theirs; two against one. Actually, it was three against one, there was another lad there. There was evidence of sexual activity, of course there was, but Russell and Darren were adamant it was by consent.'

'Were there drugs in her system?'

'Yes, there were, but they were all experimenting with them. It was Glastonbury!'

'And you were a drug squad officer at the time?'

'Yes, I used my position. I know that, but all I really did was save us all two years of agony before it went to court, saved her the stress of having to give evidence and they'd both have been found not guilty anyway.'

'That's what you've told yourself, is it?'

'Look, you do what you have to do for your children. All right? I'm not proud of what I did, but I'd do it again. You'll find out when you have your own children. It changes things.' Refilling his glass.

'Russell was adamant it was consensual,' said Linda, her voice weak. 'He wouldn't have lied to us. Not about something like that.'

A cheap watch . . .

'What was the girl's name?'

'I don't remember.' Michael getting in first before Linda drew breath.

'And you expect me to believe that?'

'Her name was Jess,' said Linda, her eyes fixed firmly on the rug in front of her. 'Jessica Burroughs. Her father was Jamaican and the mother hadn't seen him since she told him she was pregnant. Buggered off back to Jamaica, she thought.'

'Name?'

'Carl.'

'The mother's name was Flora,' said Michael. 'Came from Wiltshire way, I think, but was living in St Paul's at the time. It was all very upsetting, very stressful, and we dealt with it the best way we could. You know what it's like once these allegations are made. A young lad's life is destroyed, whether it's true or not.'

'A young woman's too,' said Dixon.

'I know that.'

'You said Jess and her mother were dead.'

'You really want your pound of flesh, don't you?'

Another comment to ignore.

'Jess developed anorexia,' said Linda. 'Took her own life a couple of years later. Flora died in a fire in Jamaica about a year after that. On a boat, I think it was. She must've gone looking for Carl.'

Michael fixed Dixon with cold eyes, gave a colder smile. 'I looked them up on the police national computer before I retired.'

And breathed a sigh of relief, no doubt.

A curt 'We'll be in touch' and Dixon had walked out of the house into the rain, closely followed by Louise.

'He wouldn't have lied to us. Not about something like that,' hissed Louise, when the front door closed behind them. 'Are they for real?'

'No one thinks their son is capable of something like that.' Dixon stopped in his tracks. 'Actually, that's bollocks, isn't it? Plenty of people think their children are capable of anything.'

'Plenty of people's children *are* capable of anything.'

'Quite.'

Louise was standing by the passenger door of the Land Rover, waiting for the central locking. 'Are we going back to the Canters'?'

'We'll do some digging first.'

Sitting in the seat now. 'I've got a list,' she said. 'The initial police report, assuming the records have been kept. Medical records for mother and daughter. Glastonbury Festival organisers, for any reports of an assault. It would've been St John's Ambulance at the event I expect, so check with them. Police in Jamaica, obviously. Relatives. Anything else?'

'The football coach for a team list.'

'Yeah.'

Dixon turned the key. 'It only explains so much, doesn't it?'

'What d'you mean?'

'It gives us a possible motive for the murders of Russell Lock and Darren Canter, but what it doesn't tell us is why they killed Justin Hampton and Andrew Paul.'

'And you're sure they did?'

'Yes.'

'Couldn't the same person have killed all four?'

'Why?'

'I don't know.'

'Hampton and Paul would've been ten years old ten years ago, and hardly likely to have been at Glastonbury. And that's before you add Liam Smith into the mix.'

'Where are we going now?'

'Rattle the PCC's cage again. We've got time before the briefing at eight.'

◆ ◆ ◆

'It could be a coincidence,' said Louise, tentatively. 'Hampton was stealing stuff all the time.'

Dixon was on hold, waiting for his call to be transferred to Donald Watson. They were parked in the visitors' car park at Portishead, only a short drive around the campus to the Scientific Services lab, but he wanted to keep it low key; attract as little attention as possible. A superintendent turning up at the lab and everybody would want to know what that was about.

'Watson.'

'You've got their uniforms, Donald – Darren Canter and Russell Lock?' asked Dixon.

'They've been tested for DNA but there's nothing of interest.'

'What about gunshot residue?'

'It wasn't requested.'

'Well, it's being requested now.'

'Er, yes, we can do that.' Watson hesitated. 'You think they fired a gun.' Dixon could almost hear the frown. 'Think they killed the other two?'

'This needs to be done on the quiet, Donald,' he said.

'Leave it with me.'

Dixon rang off, slid his phone into his inside jacket pocket.

'Are you sure about this?' Louise was trying again as they walked across the grass to the main entrance of the police headquarters, and the PCC's office. 'He'll be complaining we're harassing him at this rate.'

'Anybody else, and we'd be interviewing him down at the station, under caution,' replied Dixon. 'We're sparing him that. The least he can do is answer our questions.'

The receptionist reached for the phone as Dixon and Louise walked straight past the desk, heading for the stairs.

His personal assistant, Julia, was there, standing by her desk, coat and gloves on, rummaging in her handbag. 'He's not expecting you,' she said, leaning over and picking up a desk diary, flicking the page. 'Is he?'

'No, he isn't,' replied Dixon.

'Give me a minute.'

The soundproofing needs work, thought Dixon, although the voices were muffled, only the expletives unmistakable. Then the office door was wrenched open from the inside, the PCC marching out into the lobby.

'Here to arrest me?'

It was a rhetorical question.

'You've got a bloody cheek coming here. Again.'

'We need to speak to you about the murders of Justin Hampton and Andrew Paul.'

'Have you any idea of the trouble you've caused?'

Julia was waiting in the sanctuary of the PCC's office.

'We've got Big Brother Watch crawling all over the city, looking for AFR vans, and we're monitoring several social media groups calling for a demonstration outside Bridewell police station tonight.' Napier was working up a head of steam. 'Not only are we going to have to police that demonstration, but how the hell d'you think it makes us look? You've set policing in this city back years.'

'We can do this out here, if you'd like,' said Dixon, impassively. 'Or we can do it in your office, although the soundproofing's not great.'

'Do what?'

'The other alternative is that we do it down at the station. Under caution.'

'I've cooperated with your investigation, answered your questions.'

'I have more,' replied Dixon. 'The investigation moves on, more things become relevant.'

'Like what?'

Dixon gestured to Julia, now standing in the open doorway of Napier's office. 'Were you going home, Julia?' he asked.

'I'd just been to the canteen,' she replied. 'I can stay if you need me.'

'You go home.'

Dixon waited until Julia had left, Louise closing the door of the PCC's office behind them.

'So, your laptop was stolen and you decided not to report the theft.'

'Like I said, it was an old laptop, probably worth no more than fifty quid, if that, and it just had personal stuff on it, so I thought it would be a waste of police time.'

'It had nothing to do with the facial recognition trial that was going on?'

'Yes, of course it did. There was no way I wanted that coming out. I'd have to explain what I was doing there, for a start.'

'Then, three weeks later, the person who stole the laptop, Justin Hampton, and his friend Andrew Paul are both murdered.'

'I've told you before, that's got nothing to do with me.' Napier had sat back down behind his desk, his arms folded tightly across his chest.

'How well did you know Darren Canter and Russell Lock?'

Napier frowned. 'I didn't know them at all. I know *of* them, obviously, but I'd never met either of them.'

'What do you know about them?'

'Well, leaving aside their recent murders, they were involved in the arrest of that poor woman on New Year's Eve and are, or were, facing disciplinary proceedings.'

'Have you been following the case?'

'Of course I've been following the case. I'm the Police and Crime Commissioner and there was a death in custody. It's the highest-profile thing we've got going on at the moment, or it was until you outed the AFR van. There have been several press conferences. I've even had a meeting at the Home Office about it.'

'Were you involved in the disciplinary proceedings?'

'No. And I haven't interfered with them, either, if that's your next question.' Napier shook his head. 'I have had several conversations with the IOPC about it. They wanted to know if it was indicative of wider problems in ASP, things like that; whether a full inspection was warranted. I assured them it wasn't.'

'And you didn't attend the misconduct hearing?'

'We don't, as a matter of routine, attend disciplinary proceedings; only where there's a public interest. I know people like to think I stick my oar in, but they are considered operational police matters. And the hearing hasn't taken place yet anyway. It won't until the IOPC investigation is complete. There was a preliminary hearing and I sent Julia to take notes for me, but I didn't go.'

'Are the IOPC aware of the facial recognition trial?'

'They are now. In view of the public response, I've asked David Charlesworth to make a referral. We put a press release out this morning to that effect, hoping it might head off this demo tonight, but it hasn't.'

'Have you ever been to the Glastonbury Festival?'

'What sort of bloody stupid question is that?'

'It's a question I want the answer to, please.'

'No, I haven't.'

Mid-fifties, so there was no way he'd have been there with Canter and Lock anyway.

'Do you play football?'

'Golf, if you must know. David Charlesworth is my regular golf partner. We play at Burnham and Berrow.' Napier stood up, slid his office chair under his desk. 'Now, I've answered your questions. Is there anything else, before I get over to Bridewell? Sohail York is going be there and there's a chance I might be able to defuse the situation before it gets out of hand.'

Chapter Twenty-Four

Not even a hundred people; it was more of a peaceful protest than a demonstration, and certainly not a riot. Not yet, anyway. Somebody with a loudhailer, a few placards, although Dixon couldn't see what they said from where he was. It was hardly the civil disturbance the PCC had feared.

No, far more irritating was that the road was closed, and he didn't know Bristol well enough to find the back way round to the car park behind the police station.

Then the chanting started, the person with the loudhailer leading the crowd:

'What do we want?'
'No intrusive surveillance.'
'When do we want it?'
'Never.'

Dixon could sympathise. Those with nothing to hide had nothing to fear from cameras, was the old cliché, but it was never that simple, the lawyer in him knew that. It was about checks and balances; it was a free country, after all. And those with nothing to hide had nothing to fear from microchips under their skin. Where did it all end?

That said, it made his life a bit easier, perhaps. CCTV everywhere, doorbell cameras and dashcams. Mobile phone signals.

They'd never have known Hampton had stolen the PCC's laptop without the AFR van.

People were becoming more tech savvy though, mainly thanks to the explosion of true crime stuff on Netflix.

'Everyone's a bloody expert these days,' Donald Watson had said.

Hide your face from the cameras, wear gloves, leave your mobile phone at home; hardly rocket science. Even DNA wasn't the silver bullet everybody seemed to think it was. Dixon had lost count of the times he'd had the same conversation:

'It's proof of—'

'It's not proof of anything. It's evidence, that's all.'

Scientific had come up with a DNA trace at Hampton's flat, Donald Watson suitably pleased with himself. Police Constable Darren Canter's DNA; it was a match, but then the logs showed he had visited the premises twice in the six months leading up to his suspension, once responding to reports of a disturbance, the second time assisting the drug squad with a search.

So, what did his DNA at the scene prove then?

Nothing.

It was evidence that he'd known *of* Hampton, perhaps. That when the PCC had given him a description of the person who had stolen his laptop, Canter knew where to look.

That was Dixon's working hypothesis, and why he kept 'harassing' the PCC.

'Harassing' had been Louise's choice of word, and she must have used it five times on the drive over from Portishead. Not that he'd shared his theory with her. Not in full, not yet.

It all started with that laptop.

Whoever had killed Hampton and Paul had cleared the flat of electronic devices; not a single phone, iPad or computer of any sort had been left behind. Not even the bloody games console.

No, it was about that laptop – or, to be more precise, what was on that laptop.

He'd never find it now. It would have gone in an incinerator, or water possibly. If the information on it was such that someone was prepared to kill to get it back, they were hardly going to be stupid enough to have kept it, were they?

Thoughts, jumbled.

Blackmail was the obvious motive. If that was the case, then Hampton and Paul might have been tech savvy enough to have backed up the information. But where?

The PCC had got Canter and Lock to kill Hampton and Paul, recover the laptop, then he'd killed Canter and Lock to cover it up, tie up loose ends, etc, etc.

Dixon knew better than that, though. Life – and death for that matter – was never that simple. And there was still the thorny question of proving it.

Finding the gunsmith, too.

'I can see Charlesworth in the upstairs window,' said Louise, looking up at the front of Bridewell police station. 'Are you sure you want to go in?'

'We've got the briefing at eight.'

'Yeah.'

Dixon wound down the window of the Land Rover, waved his warrant card at the constable walking towards him.

'That way, Sir,' she said. 'Keep turning left and you'll come out the other side of the demo, then it's straight across.'

'Thank you.'

Napier had come out of a side door and was in an animated conversation with Sohail York on the pavement outside the police station. Arms waving, fingers jabbing and pointing. A good-tempered election then.

'Are there any other candidates in the election?' Dixon asked.

'A couple,' replied Louise.

'Thank God for that.'

The demonstration had grown in size and volume by the time he parked in the Rudolph Street car park and crept in the back door of the police station. Maybe one hundred and fifty people now. A second loudhailer. Someone must have had some fireworks left over from New Year, letting them off at the back of the crowd. Dixon watched from the window as uniformed officers closed in, made the arrest.

If it was going to turn into a riot, it would start now, but then they didn't really look like the crowd for that. There were a few agitators around the fringes, the ones who would start the trouble then run for it, but the crowd remained largely peaceful.

'You'd better hope it doesn't kick off,' said Charlesworth, appearing at his elbow.

'Why me?'

'It's thanks to you we've got this bloody demo to contend with, getting yourself filmed banging on the side of the AFR van.'

Dixon had known that one was coming. The PCC had said as much earlier. 'I think you'll find it's thanks to the idiot who authorised the covert AFR trial in the first place. It was always just a matter of time before it became public knowledge, Sir.'

'Be that as it may—'

'And I wasn't the one attempting to suppress evidence in a murder investigation.'

'It was never about that.'

'Wasn't it?'

'What time is the briefing?' asked Charlesworth, clearly deciding a change of subject was called for.

'Now.'

'I'll sit in at the back, if that's all right. Hugo wants to sit in as well.'

'No.'

'I beg your pardon.'

'From where I'm sitting, he's a suspect in all five murders. And you'd be well advised to distance yourself from him, Sir.'

'Distance myself?'

'It all starts with his laptop, his failure to report the theft, and then his attempt to pervert the course of justice by suppressing—'

'I get it. Thank you.'

Darren Canter and Russell Lock had made quite a few friends at Bridewell, judging by the reception Dixon received at the briefing when he announced they were suspects in the murders of Justin Hampton and Andrew Paul. It was a briefing he would remember for all the wrong reasons, not least the chants from the crowd outside that continued for the whole hour and ten minutes.

Still no news on Russell Lock's car. Or their phones, but their call records had arrived from the mobile phone companies. Not terribly enlightening, as it turned out. Nothing to place them at Hampton's flat, apart from the neighbours saying that the police had already been there.

Dixon was taking a flier, he knew that, and didn't need sarcasm from Redgrave or Redpath, or whatever the hell his name was.

'You didn't know them, Guv.'

He hated being called 'Guv' too.

'They were good lads, highly regarded around here.'

Objectivity. Easier for him, perhaps, because he didn't know them from Adam. Had never met them, never known them. Never made judgements about them; about what they were or weren't capable of.

Dixon thought it best not to mention what had happened at Glastonbury. He didn't really know himself yet, although Mark and Louise were already working on it. Discreetly.

The gunshot residue tests might come to his rescue. Evidence that one or other or both of them had fired a gun recently would silence the doubters, but those tests were going to take time. Until then he was sticking his neck out, making enemies, but that was what senior investigating officers did.

Make decisions. Record them in the Policy Log, so there'd be evidence against you when it all went wrong, when it turned out you'd made the wrong decision, sent the team in the wrong direction. Arrested the wrong person, let the killers get away.

It would be a while before he came to Bridewell after this. Accusing two of their own of murder was one thing, but now the station was being pelted with eggs. No doubt the pictures would be all over the news.

The PCC a murder suspect too. Dixon hadn't mentioned that at the briefing, but it didn't take much to work it out. The bloke's laptop had been pinched and three weeks later the lads who stole it were found dead.

'Sort it out, and sort it out quickly,' Charlesworth had said. 'I don't care which way it goes, but we can't have this hanging over us for too much longer. If it gets out, we'll have the Home Office sending in another force to sort it out and the PR damage will be even worse.'

An hour spent reading new witness statements that had been uploaded on to the system, updating the Policy Log; no mention of the PCC. Dixon was sensible enough to know things got printed off, leaked to the press.

The demo had broken up by the time he left the station just after ten. Someone was out with a pressure washer, removing the spray paint from the front windows; an obscenity or two on the pavement as well. A couple of cars had had their windows smashed, a high price to pay for parking on double yellow lines. At least the protestors had left the parking tickets.

It had never been much of a commute, Brent Knoll to Bridgwater. One junction on the motorway, fifteen minutes at most, even in an old Land Rover. At least the roads were quiet at this time of night. Time to unwind. He'd heard people say their commute was the best part of their day, thought it sad, but now he understood; couldn't even answer the phone. Not that it rang.

He'd sent a text:

On way Nx

Jane sensible enough to know he'd be driving, so she hadn't replied. Dixon had often wondered how many people had been killed in road traffic accidents trying to read a text message that said *drive carefully.*

Death again. He'd got this far without worrying about it too much; couldn't work out why it seemed different now. Being a husband and father might explain it.

One step at a time.

He pulled into the yard behind his cottage, the barking starting before he switched off the engine. Then Jane was standing in the open back door, her fingers hooked in Monty's collar, the dog pulling like a train.

'Let him go,' said Dixon.

'I made a fish pie,' said Jane. 'I'm guessing you haven't eaten.'

Don't make a fuss, it reinforces the excitable behaviour. Bollocks to that, bloody dog trainers. Dixon squatted down, his arms around Monty, the dog greeting him as if he'd been away for months.

'How is it?' asked Jane. 'The case.'

'Different,' replied Dixon, straightening up, wiping his face on the sleeve of his coat. 'Has he been out?'

'I took him to the beach for a while this afternoon.'

'Lucky you.'

There were rules; what you could and couldn't discuss with people not involved in an investigation, not serving officers. Bollocks to that too. Jane was his wife. She'd understand.

'The fucking PCC?' Jane thrust a can of lager into Dixon's hand. 'You'd better be right, because if you're not, your career's over.'

Dixon was beginning to wonder if that would be such a bad thing; that conversation for another day rearing its head again.

'It all starts with his laptop.'

'What was on it, I wonder?'

'He said he was writing a book.'

'You don't have people killed because you're writing a bloody book. But, if you're right, it certainly gives him a motive.'

'And the opportunity. He knew who Canter and Lock were, knew they were facing a gross misconduct hearing, probably told them he'd help them out, see to it they got off, if they got his laptop back.'

'I bet he says he never knew they were going to kill Hampton and Paul.'

'Now who's jumping the gun?'

Chapter Twenty-Five

It was a short text from Louise that arrived the following morning, while Dixon was out in the field behind the cottage with Monty. Just a number and a postcode.

He knew what to do with it, though. His reluctance to embrace satnav had been gradually beaten out of him over the last year or so, and he'd downloaded some free thing to his phone. Live traffic reporting too, and it was someone to talk to in the mornings on the way to work, now Jane was on maternity leave.

He was sitting outside a large Victorian house that had been converted to flats, a couple of streets back from the seafront at Clevedon, parked in a 'residents only' area, the blue light on top of the Land Rover to deter any officious traffic wardens. He'd resisted the temptation to ask Louise why Clevedon. There'd be a good reason.

A tap on the driver's window.

'Douglas Sanders,' said Louise, when Dixon opened the door. 'Coach of the under-eighteens football team ten years ago. Retired now, lives in number four B, which looks like it's round the side.'

An old man, white hair, a pair of grey pinstriped trousers from a suit, vest underneath a check shirt with stains down the front; cardigan, the pockets stuffed full of God knows what. Teeth missing. Bobble hat.

'Mr Sanders?' asked Louise. 'My colleague spoke to you last night.'

'Yes, come in.'

Dixon would have preferred to stay outside. In the fresh air. He paused in the doorway, slid his warrant card back inside his jacket pocket – the old boy hadn't bothered to look at it – took a deep breath, held it.

Cats, must be.

The flat was cold, too cold for a man of this age. An electric radiator was mounted on the wall in the hall, switched off at the socket. Even the electric fire in the living room was off, a smart meter on the hall table registering marginal usage – twelve pence for today – from the fridge probably, although the old boy could have kept his chilled stuff on the table and saved himself even that electricity.

A freezing morning in February.

'I'm sorry it's so cold,' he said. 'They took my winter fuel payment and I've only got my state pension.'

'Savings?' asked Louise.

'A couple of thousand, but I've got to keep that for my funeral.'

'You'll be eligible for Pension Credit in that case.' Louise was scribbling in her notebook. 'I'll get someone from Age UK to call you, help you with a claim.'

'Thank you.' The old man sat down in his armchair, gestured to the sofa. Then pulled a rug over his legs.

'I'll make you a hot drink while I'm here, as well. Is it all right to put the kettle on?'

'I'll be fine, don't worry.'

'We wanted to ask you about the football team ten years ago,' said Dixon. 'There was a trip to the Glastonbury Festival and an incident took place in a tent.'

'It was a good team that year. They'd done well in the league the previous season and we had high hopes. Some of them were due to go up to the first team. Liam and Russell. Darren was hopeless, to be honest, but he was a good team lad and we needed a goalkeeper.'

Dixon hadn't mentioned the names. Deliberately. 'You remember the incident at the festival?' he asked.

'I do,' replied Sanders, through a heavy sigh.

'Were you there?'

'God, no. Glastonbury is hardly my scene.'

'Nor mine.'

'We'd had the club's annual dinner the night before, awards ceremony, that sort of thing, the Thursday I think it was, then they went off to Glastonbury the following day. Someone had hired a minibus. I can't remember who drove it. There was a mix of first team players and some from the under-eighteens.'

'How did you hear about what happened?'

'The following week, I got a call from the parents of one of them. They'd instructed a solicitor and could I give a statement; a character reference, really, I suppose it would've been.'

'Who was that?'

'That was Liam Smith's father who asked me. It never came to anything though, because the girl dropped the allegation. I think Russell Lock's father was involved by then – one of your lot, he was – and he persuaded her and her mother it would be her word against the three boys. That was the last I heard of it, as far as I can remember. It was just dropped and forgotten about.'

'Did you ever find out what actually took place?'

'They helped some bloke get in, over the fence, and he gave them ecstasy, I think it was. All four of them had been taking drugs – Darren, Russell, Liam and the girl.' Sanders frowned. 'I never did know her name.'

'What about the name of the person they helped over the fence?'

'Never knew that either.' A shrug. 'She said it was rape, they said it was consensual.'

'Did anyone try to find any witnesses, other people camping around and about? They might have heard something.'

'You'd need to ask the girl and her mother that, I'm afraid,' replied Sanders. 'I wasn't even there.'

'They're both dead,' offered Louise.

'What about the others on the minibus, the other football club members on the trip?' asked Dixon. 'They'd have been camping together, I'd imagine. Can you remember who else went to Glastonbury?'

Sanders looked surprised Dixon had bothered to ask. 'Not really. It was a long time ago and I'm knocking on a bit now, you know.'

'Then we'll need to speak to everybody – first team and under-eighteens. The club keeps records?'

'Yes, it does, and there'll be the team photos on the wall in the clubhouse. We've got every year going back to 1898.'

'Can't be a coincidence, can it? All three of them dead.'

'I should've seen it coming, really.' Dixon's knuckles whitened, his grip tightening on the steering wheel. 'Liam Smith played in the first team at Loughborough University.' He turned the key, the diesel engine of his Land Rover stuttering into life. 'Let's take four people off tracing printer polymer and get them interviewing those football team members. We need to track down everyone who went on the Glastonbury trip and speak to them.'

'I'll ring Mark,' said Louise, reaching for her phone.

'You said the mother and her daughter were both dead?'

'Still to be confirmed,' replied Louise. 'But as far as Mark could find out last night, the daughter took her own life and the mother went to Jamaica to look for her husband, Carl. Died in a fire on a boat. Mark was going to follow it up today.'

'Let's ring Liam Smith's mother as well, find out which solicitor the family instructed.'

'Yes, Sir.'

'I'm not sure I can face sitting through another meeting with a parent telling me their precious son wouldn't do that.'

Dixon drove around the corner and parked on the pavement, listening to Louise's end of the telephone conversations. Away from prying eyes too, Sanders's net curtains twitching.

Motive.

There it was. For the murders of Darren Canter, Russell Lock and Liam Smith. More than enough motive. But what it didn't explain was the murders of Justin Hampton and Andrew Paul first, assuming it was Darren Canter and Russell Lock who'd killed them, of course. There was still no real evidence to support that theory one way or the other.

Dixon had merged the teams at last night's briefing. It was one case, the murders clearly connected, so one major investigation team. Now he wasn't so sure. Or at least it was looking increasingly unlikely.

Hampton and Paul were far too young to have been at Glastonbury.

That said, Darren Canter, Russell Lock and Liam Smith were friends. Longstanding football teammates. Partners in crime, possibly.

Probably.

Louise rang off and was about to dial Mark's number.

'What d'you think of this?' asked Dixon, not pausing to allow her to answer. 'The PCC has his laptop stolen by Hampton, God knows what's on it, but hopefully we'll find out at some point. He's being blackmailed, so he asks Darren Canter and Russell Lock to get it back for him, tells him he'll help them get off their misconduct charge. They go to their friend and techie Liam Smith, who manages to track down the laptop, and you know the rest.'

'Track down the laptop?'

'You can track the IP address, if it was used to send emails. Who knows, but it's certainly plausible.'

'If that's right, it means the Glastonbury thing has got nothing to do with it.'

'It might very well have nothing to do with it.'

Louise cut off the call before Mark had a chance to answer. 'You know, I've never known you do this before, Sir. It's like you're clutching at straws; trying to fit what little we know to some theory. Making assumptions.' She gave an apologetic smile. 'What happened to finding the evidence and going where that leads us? That's what you usually do.'

Dixon sighed. Louise was right, and he knew it, but she clearly hadn't finished hammering her point home.

'What happens if you're wrong about the laptop? If it's completely unconnected to the murders, that means you're wrong about the PCC too, and we're going to look like a right pair of idiots.'

'I'm the one going to look like an idiot.'

'I was being polite.'

She was right. And Dixon knew it. Knew where he was going wrong.

And why.

'What happened to *let's stick to what we know?*' continued Louise. 'That's usually your first question, isn't it? What do we know?'

'Make that call to Liam Smith's mother,' he said, if only to bring the conversation to an end.

Louise flicked on speakerphone, so Dixon could listen in. 'I've got you on speakerphone, Mrs Smith. It's Detective Constable Louise Willmott. We met yesterday.'

'I remember.'

'I need to ask you about an incident involving Liam at the Glastonbury Festival a few years ago.'

'Oh God, that.'

'I'm sorry to bring it up, but as you can imagine—'

'It was terrifying,' said Mrs Smith. 'He was accused of rape, of all things. My Liam.'

Here it comes.

'He would never have done that. Not that.'

Louise glanced at Dixon, her eyes cold. 'We're told that your late husband instructed a solicitor,' she said, working hard to keep an edge from her voice.

'That's right. It was a firm in Bristol. Someone he knew through Rotary, I think. The solicitor came to see us, took a statement from Liam, but then it all fizzled out. The girl withdrew the complaint. Russell's father persuaded the family it was going to be months of torment for all concerned and then the case probably wouldn't succeed at trial anyway. It was her word against theirs, and Liam wouldn't lie, not about something like that.'

'Can you remember the name of the solicitor, please?' asked Louise.

'It was a firm down by the new court building, from memory. His name was Walter, although that might have been his Christian name, I suppose. I really can't remember. It wasn't our usual solicitor. He did crime, and we'd never needed a criminal lawyer before.'

Dixon was already on Google. Walter, Beer and Warburton Solicitors. Must be.

'Did Liam ever talk to you about what happened?' asked Louise.

'He said Darren and Russell got a bit carried away. That was years later he told me that. They were high as kites, apparently, not that that's any excuse. But he swore to me he never touched her and I believed him.'

'Anything else?'

'He said she was too far gone to remember what happened anyway.'

Dixon snatched the phone from Louise's hand. 'If she was too far gone to remember what happened then she was too far gone to have consented. And that makes it rape.'

'I hope you're not suggesting . . . like I said, he swore blind he never touched her.'

Louise snatched her phone back from Dixon. 'Mrs Smith, I'm going to end this call now, thank you. We'll be in touch.'

Chapter Twenty-Six

One firm of solicitors was much the same as any other. Different offices, of course, some posher than others, but the procedures were much the same. Dixon knew them inside out. File storage, retrieval. Destruction dates too.

Walter, Beer and Warburton. Established 2009.

Dixon couldn't understand the fuss. If they'd been established in 1809 then perhaps announce it to the world with suitable fanfare, but 2009 was nothing to shout about, surely?

The office was on the ground floor of a new building opposite the court. An Entryphone, one of the ones with a little camera lens above it. To keep the riff-raff out.

Criminal lawyers, so they'd be suspicious of the police, the office manager waiting in reception in the time it took him to open the front door.

'How can I help you?'

Dixon kept it short and to the point, emphasised it was a multiple murder investigation. That he'd be back within the hour with a warrant if they chose not to assist the enquiry.

'Our files are kept in storage at our old premises in Whiteladies Road. We send our office junior over there once a day and he's been today. Would tomorrow be any good?'

'What d'you do if you need a file urgently?'

'He makes a special trip.'

'Sounds ideal. I'll wait.'

He was standing in the window, looking out through a gap in the blinds at Louise, sitting in the driver's seat of his Land Rover, blue light on top, hazard lights flashing. She was checking the mirrors regularly, keeping an eye out for traffic wardens.

He sent her a text:

Better switch off engine. It's going to be a while.

Although, the office junior had a moped, so maybe not.

Dixon was listening to the phone ringing on the reception desk, the receptionist resolutely refusing to answer it. Perhaps she recognised the number. The firm Dixon had trained at had its regulars too. It sounded glamorous, practising criminal law, but he knew the harsh reality, wasn't taken in by it.

Cases where the client was genuinely innocent? Once in a lifetime.

Murders? A couple in a whole career, if you were lucky.

The rest of the time spent representing the guilty, doing their grovelling for them in court, although the technical term was 'entering a plea in mitigation'.

Soul-destroying by any stretch of the imagination, even allowing for his unhealthy dose of cynicism.

'Would you like a coffee while you wait?'

'No, thank you.'

It reminded him of that job interview; corporate finance lawyer at some posh firm in Taunton. Kept waiting twenty-seven minutes. Walked out in the end.

It had been the biggest lie of all. 'Do a law degree and you'll be able to do anything you want,' they'd said. 'The world will be your oyster.' Far from it, as it turned out. All he could do with a law degree was become a solicitor or a barrister.

The next thing he knew, he'd been standing in front of a photocopier, the lot of a trainee.

But he'd found a way out in the end.

Now, here he was a detective superintendent, looking for a way out of that too.

'He's found the file,' said the receptionist. 'He's on the way.'

Time flies when you're pondering the meaning of life. Actually, it wasn't all bad; if he hadn't joined the police, moved back to Somerset, he'd never have met Jane. Never have walked Monty on the beach. Those were the important things; the things he'd remember on his deathbed.

There you go. Death again.

The door adjacent to the reception desk opened, the office manager appearing with a file in his hand. 'We've got the electronic version, so you're welcome to take it.'

'Thank you.'

It had only been half an hour, but it was still too long. Too much time to think.

'We've found the dark SUV used in the Liam Smith killing,' said Louise, when Dixon climbed in the passenger seat of his Land Rover. 'Turns out it's Russell Lock's.'

'Where was it?'

'In a field over near Stanton Wick. Burnt out, sadly, so there'll be nothing, although it's on the way over to Scientific now, so we'll see, I suppose.' Louise turned the key. 'There's front end damage consistent with a pedestrian collision. Always makes me

222

wonder, when people dump cars in the middle of nowhere, how they get home?'

'An accomplice,' replied Dixon. 'Or a folding electric bike.'

'You're taking the piss now, aren't you.'

He was reading Liam Smith's witness statement in the solicitor's file. A privately paying client, a couple of hours' work, reflected in the bill, paid without question by a family just grateful it was all over. It may have been for them, but it hadn't been for the victim and her family. Their nightmare had just begun.

Five pages. Dixon flicked through the statement. Most of it lies, probably, Smith downplaying his role, reducing it to that of spectator, although there was a word for that in this context.

And there it was. The single word that unlocked the whole thing. Possibly.

Not a word.

A name.

Dixon read aloud. '"We pitched our tents along the fence in South Park 2. The campsites were all full and it was the only space left, but it meant we were a long way from the Pyramid Stage. There was a man outside the fence, trying to get in. He was hiding in the bushes, trying to attract our attention. He was about thirty years of age. Asian. He was wearing blue jeans and a Coldplay T-shirt. He said he would let us have some ecstasy if we helped him get in, so Darren backed the minibus up to the fence. There were very few people around, just a few pitching tents where there were spaces. The festival had started and you could hear the music in the distance. The man climbed the outside of the metal fence and got on top of the minibus. There was a ladder on the back that you could use to load luggage on the roof rack and he climbed down that. Then he gave Darren eight ecstasy tablets and ran off before security could catch up with him. He said his name was Sohail."'

Chapter Twenty-Seven

Dixon was sitting in his Land Rover outside Sohail York's campaign office, waiting for a call from Mark to confirm that the search team was ready and waiting outside York's home address. The search warrants had been granted on the nod, although Dixon wasn't entirely sure what he expected to find.

A 3D printer was unlikely. So was any physical evidence, for that matter. Guns would have been disposed of, melted down. The PCC's laptop would be long gone too, assuming York had ever had it. No, it was about York's own computers and phones. That's where the evidence would be, if there was any.

A drug dealer who'd managed to stay off the police radar; no previous convictions, otherwise he'd be barred from standing in the PCC election.

Clever then.

York had had a busy evening outside Bridewell police station the night before. A speech over the loudhailer – something to do with a police state – several references to policing by consent. Then the press interviews; Dixon had counted three, two for the television cameras. No doubt his assistant had made sure the press knew of the demonstration in plenty of time.

Louise's phone was ringing. 'Yes, Mark,' she said. 'You're in position?'

'Tell him to go in,' said Dixon.

Sohail York saw them coming. He was sitting on the corner of Faith's desk, a mug of coffee in his hand. Dixon could imagine what he was saying, Faith snatching her iPhone off the desk, ready to film the encounter. Fair enough. The two uniformed officers accompanying Dixon were wearing bodycams.

Not that she'd have her phone for long. 'Computers and phones on the premises'; it would be first into an evidence bag.

'This is bloody harassment!' shouted York, for the benefit of the camera, and the few people who'd gathered on the pavement outside his office. 'It's about the demonstration last night.'

'Actually, it's about the supply of class A drugs at the Glastonbury Festival,' replied Dixon. 'And other matters arising from that.'

Took the wind out of his sails, that did, York appearing almost relieved when Faith switched off the camera on her phone and dropped it into an evidence bag being held up in front of her.

Two Scientific Services officers had crawled under the desks and were busy disconnecting the computers.

'Am I under arrest?' asked York, nervously.

'No, Sir. But I am asking you to accompany us to Bridewell police station voluntarily, where you will be interviewed under caution. Having said that, if you refuse to do so, then you will leave me no alternative but to arrest you.'

The crowd outside the office had grown significantly by the time Dixon escorted York outside to a waiting patrol car. Those on the pavement parted to allow them to get in the car, others were standing in the road, banging on the roof, uniformed officers attempting to move them back.

'This could get out of hand quite easily,' muttered Louise.

'And quickly,' replied Dixon. 'Go with him to Bridewell, stick him in an interview room. No doubt he'll want to phone his solicitor as well.'

Louise climbed in the back of the patrol car next to York.

'And keep out of Charlesworth's way,' said Dixon, slamming the car door.

People were banging on the front windows of the office behind him now, more sirens and blue lights coming from both directions.

Faith opened a filing cabinet drawer, took out a loudhailer and stepped out on to the pavement. 'Listen to me. Please go home. Sohail is not under arrest. He is cooperating with the police. There is nothing to see here.' She waited, then tried again. 'Sohail is not under arrest. He will be back in the office this afternoon. Please go home. All of you.'

The crowd started to thin out, people at the back drifting away.

'Thank you,' said Dixon.

'I didn't do it for you.'

Small world, as it turned out. Neil Warburton, from the same firm of solicitors. Balding, sharp suit. Standard stuff.

Sohail York was sitting opposite Dixon, glaring at him while Louise made the introductions for the tape, cautioned him.

'How well did you know Darren Canter?' asked Dixon.

York glanced at his solicitor, who nodded. 'I know the name. He's one of the officers who arrested Faith's sister on New Year's Eve. I've helped the family make a formal complaint and I've been monitoring the disciplinary proceedings. I don't know him, though. I've never met him.'

'Not at Glastonbury, ten years ago?'

The same reaction as before, in his office. Hesitation. 'I've never been to Glastonbury.'

'A man fitting your description supplied Darren Canter with eight ecstasy tablets, which is possession with intent to supply a class A drug. A serious offence.'

'What is the description given of this person?' asked Warburton.

'An Asian male, aged early thirties, short dark hair.'

'And how many people fitting that—?'

'He told them his name was Sohail,' interrupted Dixon. He turned back to York. 'What about Russell Lock?'

'Again, he's one of the officers who arrested Bryony Beech. I've never met him,' replied York, spelling it out.

'Russell Lock was also at Glastonbury.'

'My client has already made it clear he's never been to Glastonbury,' said Warburton.

'Liam Smith.'

'I don't know anyone by that name,' replied York.

'All three of them have been murdered.'

'Hang on a minute,' said Warburton. 'My client was told he was coming here to answer questions about the supply of class A drugs at the Glastonbury Festival. He has attended voluntarily and told you that he has never been to Glastonbury.'

'Actually, he was told it was about that and matters arising from that. The murders are a matter arising from that.'

'Where's your evidence they're connected in any way to what may or may not have happened at Glastonbury ten years ago?'

A good question. Dixon wished he knew.

Warburton hadn't finished. 'And how many Asian men in their early thirties were in the vicinity of Glastonbury during the festival ten years ago?'

'Answering to the name of Sohail?'

'I think we can assume that was a false name,' said Warburton, his voice dripping with sarcasm. 'Drug dealers don't tend to use their real names. Not in my experience anyway.'

Time to try something else.

'Where did the suggestion come from that Justin Hampton and Andrew Paul were drug dealers?' Dixon asked.

'It was common knowledge locally,' replied York. 'Everybody knew. The corner flat in . . . wherever it was.'

'And what made you suspect a vigilante was responsible for their murders?'

'The word on the street.'

'None of our informants mentioned it.'

'Perhaps you need new informants?' York smirked.

The interview was going much as Dixon had expected. Denials were easy at this stage of the game. And it was a game. York thought he was winning. Dixon could tell that from the look on his face.

The game was only just beginning, though. Warburton knew that, even if his client didn't; knew that his client's statement was on the record now. Find him out in one lie, just one, and the second half would be very different.

'I think we're done here,' said Warburton.

Watching too much American television.

'We're finished here,' replied Dixon. 'For now.'

'We're not doing very well, are we.'

It was definitely not a question, Dixon knew that from Charlesworth's tone. He was standing in the window at the front of the station, three floors up and safely out of the way, mercifully, watching York emerge on to the pavement into a small crowd that had gathered outside.

Lots of fists in the air, shouting, laughter.

'We narrowly avoided a riot when you picked him up, and that was thanks to his assistant.'

'He's lying,' replied Dixon.

'Then prove it.' Charlesworth folded his arms. 'In the meantime, leave the bloke alone. How d'you think it makes us look, harassing him like this? If you're not careful, he'll end up getting elected, then we'll all be in deep trouble with him as our Police and Crime Commissioner.'

'Five people are dead, and all I'm concerned about is finding who killed them.'

'Even if he knew them, so what?'

'Why lie about it?'

'He'll say he was worried about police harassment. And who could blame him?'

Charlesworth had disappeared by the time Dixon slid his phone out of his pocket. It had buzzed several times, text messages arriving from Jane, as it turned out.

Popped in to see Sarah. She's spent hours trawling through SY's social media. Found this. He'd deleted it from his Facebook feed, but it was still in a photo album. Twat. Hope it's useful. Jx

Arrived twenty minutes late, possibly, although Dixon wouldn't have mentioned it anyway. Some powder was best kept dry.

A younger Sohail York, grinning at the camera on a sunny day. A selfie, probably. Wearing a Coldplay T-shirt, the Glastonbury Pyramid Stage in the background.

Chapter Twenty-Eight

'There was a laptop and an iPad,' said Mark, appearing at Dixon's elbow. 'They've gone off to High Tech. I know what you're thinking, but the laptop was an old Mac and it was an Acer the PCC had pinched.'

'Anything else?'

'No 3D printers, if that's what you were hoping for. Nothing much else, either. No drugs, ammunition. A couple of old phones with no SIM cards in them in a drawer, probably dumped them there when he got an upgrade. I sent them off to High Tech to be on the safe side. It gets better though.'

'Does it?'

'Not really. Scientific have been working on the traces left behind of the gun that splintered when Liam Smith was killed. They've identified Taulman Bridge nylon filament, which we know came from the barrel because it's on the bullets as well, and e Tech PLA Plus, which is another polymer, possibly from the handle. Do you want it passed over to DS Redgrave and his team?'

'No. I'd rather they focus on the Taulman Bridge for the time being. Talk to me about the girl and her family.'

'Her name was Jessica Burroughs. Known as Jess.' Mark opened a drawer, slid out a file, handed Dixon a picture printed off the internet, the paper curled at the edges. 'Took her own life aged nineteen; threw herself in front of a train. That's supposed to be the last photo of her.'

She looked younger than nineteen. Short dark hair, a nose stud, earrings. Cuddling what looked like a spaniel, although it was difficult to tell. Dixon handed the picture over the partition to Louise.

'I've printed off some old stuff from social media,' continued Mark. 'And there was a website set up in her memory to raise funds for charity. It's gone now, but I found some pages from it in the Wayback Machine, printed them off as well. That one came off the website.' Mark slid a chair out from under the desk and sat down at the adjacent workstation. 'The mother's name was Flora. Looks like they both attempted suicide at one point. There's a police report from a response to their home in Shepton Mallet. Overdoses, and both survived that time.'

'Lou said the mother was dead.'

'After her daughter's death she went to Jamaica, died there. I'm waiting for the records to be emailed over, but the bloke I spoke to confirmed there'd been a fire on a boat.'

'Was there a police report at the time of the rape?'

'A complaint was made. There's a copy on the system and I've printed it off as well. It's marked "withdrawn".'

'What does it say?'

'The gist of it is that boys she knew to be Darren Canter and Russell Lock, Darren and Russ, took turns, while a third boy, Liam, held her down, although she thought he may have raped her as well. The complaint uses the word "boy" but they were all over eighteen by then.'

'What about medical records?'

'The complaint was withdrawn before those were obtained.'

'Poor kid,' mumbled Louise. She was sitting opposite Dixon, listening over the partition.

'Any other family?' asked Dixon.

'There's an aunt,' replied Mark. 'Flora's sister. She's still living in Shepton Mallet. I've got an address for her and a phone number. I've not contacted her yet.'

◆ ◆ ◆

'It's called a coach house, but it's just a way of cramming another dwelling on to the development,' said Louise. 'She's living above the entrance to the car park, basically.'

'Thanks for that,' said Dixon, idly.

'About one-fifty, if you're interested.'

He wasn't, as it happened.

'That's her front door.' Louise was pointing now. 'It's a one-bedroom flat, really. A clever bit of marketing by the developer.'

'Is she expecting us?'

'You told me not to ring. She's in, though. I can see a light on.'

Dixon left his Land Rover parked against the railings of the children's play area. Not that there was anyone in there, the rain seeing to that.

'Rose Coleman.' Louise had her finger on the buzzer. 'She's Flora's younger sister.'

Dixon was peering through the frosted glass, a flight of stairs behind the front door. 'At least they've given her an Entryphone.'

'Who is it?' asked a woman's voice.

'Police, Mrs Coleman,' replied Louise. 'We'd like to have a word with you about Flora and Jess.'

Silence.

'Mrs Coleman?'

'They're dead.'

'We know.'

'You'd better come in.'

The lock buzzed, Louise snatching the door open.

Rose was waiting for them at the top of the stairs. Fifty or so. Gave herself a hard time, by the looks of things; wine and cigarettes. Corduroys were an odd choice. Warm though. A handknitted pullover, sagging around the waist and sleeves.

The flat was small, Louise had been right about that. A bedroom, a bathroom, the rest open plan. Kitchen against the far wall, although the estate agent had probably called it a kitchen*ette*. Dixon was getting the hang of it now, the relentless property speculation. Not that he'd start watching *Homes Under the Hammer*. He wouldn't go that far.

There was a cat flap in the front door, but no sign of a cat, apart from a small bowl of water on the floor.

The television was paused on some true crime documentary or other, a large red 'N' in the top corner of the screen. Dixon recognised the man hunched in the corner of the interview room. Hardly entertainment, but he could understand the fascination; human nature, really. Nothing more. Unless you were up to your neck in it every day. For real.

'That's Ted Bundy,' said Louise, looking at the screen. 'My husband watches the true crime stuff.'

'Went to the electric chair.' Rose was lighting a cigarette, her lips glistening in the glow of the flame, still moist from the large swig of white wine. 'Shame there's not a bit more of that in this country.' She picked up the wine glass, waved it in Louise's direction. 'Would you like a glass?'

'No, thank you.'

'I would offer you a coffee, but I haven't got any milk.'

Plenty of wine, thought Dixon, an open crate on the floor next to the fridge, so that was six bottles, more in the fridge probably. He was standing between the windows, looking at the photographs

233

on the wall. All of them framed, different sizes, different heights; it resembled a patchwork quilt.

'They're all of Flora and Jess,' said Rose, exhaling as she spoke. 'The only real family I had left.'

'You never married?' asked Louise.

'Twice.' Rose shrugged. 'Couldn't have children, so they both left me for younger women who could. Said they wouldn't, but they did. Tossers, the pair of them.' Another swig of wine. 'So, now I'm the crazy cat lady drinking herself to death. That's what they call me round here. I know they do. I've only got one cat. Hardly *crazy*, that.' She stood up, swaying just a little, then tottered over to the kitchen, refilled her glass from a box of wine by the sink, the plastic tap hanging over the edge of the worktop. Red, this time.

'Did you have any other brothers and sisters?' asked Dixon.

'No, there was just me and Flora. Like this we were.' She was trying to cross her fingers, index over middle finger. Left hand too, a full glass of wine in her right.

'Try it the other way round,' said Louise.

Middle finger over index. 'Oh, yeah. That's better.'

'Here, let me.' Louise took the glass of wine, placed it on the table by Rose's armchair.

'We were aristocracy, you know,' said Rose, slumping down into the chair. 'Practically. My father was a distant cousin of an earl and we grew up on a farm the other side of Wells. Lost the lot, though. My mother had expensive tastes; flew everywhere business class, even when we went on holiday. Dad couldn't keep up. Sold the farm to pay off debts, then started running up more. And here I am, living in a car park.'

'Tell me about Flora,' said Dixon. He was standing with his back to the photographs now, Louise sitting on the sofa, in between the piles of magazines and the cat's bed.

'She was the wild one and I was the sensible one, not that it got me anywhere. She married young, divorced young. Then she had a fling with Carl. You can imagine it, can't you? My parents, when she took him home. She'd told me they were coming so I'd made myself scarce, but it wasn't pleasant, by all accounts.'

Dixon waited.

'My parents were living at Hemyock at the time. In a rented cottage. And then Flora brings home Carl. My mother locked herself in her room. Carl had played cricket in the West Indies, even had a trial for Somerset at one point, so at least they could talk about cricket. Sad thing is, though, that was the last time they saw Flora. She never went to see them after that. Even when Jess came along they didn't want to know. Carl buggered off back to Jamaica, left her in the lurch, so it was just Flora and Jess. She did her best to bring up Jess on her own. Working two jobs, renting, they were doing fine until . . .' Rose's eyes glazed over and she began fumbling for another cigarette.

Dixon looked at Louise and nodded.

'I know this is going to be difficult,' she said. 'But we really need to ask you about what happened at Glastonbury.'

Sobbing now. 'I know, I know. Have you got the bastards?' she asked, looking up.

'They're dead,' replied Louise.

'All four of them?'

Dixon could guess, but left it to Louise to ask the question.

'Four?'

'I'm including the one who supplied the drugs.'

'Three of them are dead,' replied Louise.

'Jess was a happy little girl. Always smiling. I used to babysit for her all the time. Then she grew up. Went to college, decided she was going to Glastonbury and off she went. Afterwards it was . . . hell.'

'Did she tell you what happened?'

'Flora did. Jess retreated into herself. Didn't speak for a long time.' Another trip to the wine box, stalling more than anything. 'They gave her drugs, ecstasy tablets they'd been given for helping some shit over the fence. Then they took it in turns. Russell, Darren and Liam, their names were.'

'All three raped her?'

'They did. I know one of them tried to say he didn't touch her, but Jess was quite clear about that. They all raped her.' A sneer. 'Russell and Darren tried to make out it was consensual but how could it be? Jess wasn't capable of consenting after they'd drugged her. Then they just left her in the tent and went off to watch the music. For all they knew, or cared, she could've been dead. Anyway, she woke up later and managed to crawl to the St John's Ambulance first aid station. They'd got a marquee set up. A couple of people did stop and help her get there, thank God. The police were called and she was taken to hospital.'

'A complaint was made to the police?' asked Louise.

'Yes, it was, but it never went anywhere. Flora said she'd been told the CPS wouldn't pursue it, that it was Jess's word against the boys'. They kept referring to them as "boys", as if it was some prank. They weren't *boys*, they were animals, and you know what, I'm delighted to hear they're dead. Fucking delighted.' She raised her glass. 'You've made my bloody day.' She stood up, tottered over to the picture on the wall, reached out and touched the face of her niece with her fingertips. 'They're dead, Jess. What goes around, comes around. Karma, they call it, don't they?' she asked, spinning round, swaying.

'They were murdered,' said Dixon.

'Oh, good. So, there's someone I can thank. Who did it?'

'We don't know yet.'

'Well, be sure to thank them for me, won't you, when you do find them.'

236

'We understand Jess committed suicide,' said Louise.

'Jess took her own life,' snapped Rose. 'We don't say *commit* suicide, these days. You *commit* crimes, and suicide is not a crime. Say ended her own life, killed herself, but she didn't *commit* anything.'

'Sorry.'

'She tried a couple of times after the . . . after the gang rape. I call it that because that's what it was. She withdrew into herself, stopped eating, became anorexic. Poor Flora tried everything. Counselling, saw loads of different psychologists. She never gave up on her daughter, I'll give her that.' Rose perched on the edge of her chair, reached round and picked up her wine glass. 'First time it was an overdose, Flora took one too, but they were found in time, thank God. I hoped at the time it wasn't a serious attempt, just a cry for help, but it wasn't, as it turned out. A few months later Jess tried again, got talked down off a multistorey car park. We got these tattoos done after that.' She put down the glass, rolled back the sleeve of her pullover to reveal her left wrist. 'We all had it done – me, Flora and Jess.'

A black semicolon. About half an inch long.

'There's a charity for suicide survivors and this is the logo, the symbol they use. Me and Flora had it done in solidarity. It's supposed to represent the writer who decides to end a sentence, then changes their mind and keeps going.' Rose's eyes glazed over. 'We hoped Jess had decided to keep going. Turned out she hadn't.'

A rattle from the bottom of the stairs. It sounded like the letterbox, until a tortoiseshell cat appeared on the landing.

'Here she is,' said Rose. She walked over, picked up the cat.

'What's her name?' asked Louise.

'Jess,' replied Rose, indignant almost, as if it should have been obvious. 'She threw herself in front of a train in the end. Flora got there too late. Poor kid was already dead, but out of pain, I suppose. Not that's it's much consolation.'

'Flora went to the West Indies afterwards?'

'A year later, maybe. She wanted to try and find Carl, which she did. They even got back together for a time, until the fire. They were living on a boat and it went up. They thought it was the generator. They recovered the bodies. I had her ashes flown home. I've got some of Jess's here as well, Flora scattered the rest.' She reached inside the collar of her pullover, pulling on two chains, pendants hanging from both. One pink, one turquoise. 'The pink one is made from Jess's ashes, and turquoise was Flora's favourite colour.' She gazed at them momentarily, before dropping them back inside her pullover. 'Keeps them close to me,' she said, her voice tremulous, hollowed out by grief that had come roaring back.

'What about your parents?' asked Dixon.

'Both dead.'

He turned back to the pictures on the wall, leaving Louise to ask the difficult questions.

'We have some dates and need to check your whereabouts—'

'Here,' interrupted Rose. 'I'll have been here. I never go anywhere, do I? I even have my shopping delivered, for heaven's sake. There's me and Jess.' The cat jumped out of her arms, sat next to Louise, claws tearing at the bed.

'One last question before we leave you in peace,' said Dixon. 'Who's this?' he asked, pointing at the one male figure in the pictures on the wall.

Rose swallowed hard. 'That's my nephew. Flora's son by her first marriage. I haven't seen him for years. We don't speak. "Estranged" is the word, I think. I don't talk about him, don't waste my time thinking about him.'

'Why the estrangement?'

'He was jealous of Jess and the time she took from Flora. He'd left home by then anyway, the little shit, but that's what it was about. Jealousy.'

'Where is he now?'

'Bridgwater, last I heard. He's one of your lot now; a police officer.'

Chapter Twenty-Nine

'Do we know him?'

Louise unplugged her phone, left the cable dangling in the passenger footwell of Dixon's Land Rover. 'He was at both carnivals, apparently, and the cider farm the night Nige killed that bloke. I doubt you'll recognise him, though. I can't put a face to the name.'

Dixon had stopped in front of the electric gates to the staff car park at the police centre at Express Park, Bridgwater. His home station. Usually.

'His shift starts at ten, so he should be here by now,' continued Louise. 'Mr Bateman said he'd put him in an interview room until we got here.'

Dixon had spent much of the drive over from Shepton Mallet deep in thought. He was trying to make some sense of what he knew, but that was becoming more difficult by the hour, each new piece of information confusing things further. Confusing him too.

'Still think the PCC has got anything to do with this?' Louise had asked. A simple question that had started the ball rolling in his mind. He'd dodged the question, instead asking her to ring the duty inspector at Express Park, find out where they might find Police Constable Will Smeed.

Different father, different surname. Obviously.

Sohail York had lied about being at Glastonbury. No real surprise, there. People lied all the time.

'What we're missing – what we're *still* missing – is a single motive that covers all five murders.'

'We're not going to find that, are we?' Louise's reply had taken Dixon by surprise; until then unaware he'd been thinking out loud. 'Because it can't exist, can it? Not if Canter and Lock killed Hampton and Paul.'

His response had been curt, at best. 'Chase up those gunshot residue tests, will you?' It was a fair point, all the same. Unless someone had got Canter and Lock to kill Hampton and Paul, and then killed them to cover it up. Someone like Sohail York, for example. Or the PCC. Two separate motives, technically, but connected.

But if that was right, why kill Liam Smith? Although, he could have placed Sohail York at Glastonbury.

'What are you thinking?' asked Louise.

There was time, the electric gates were unusually slow. Time for what, though? Dixon wasn't sure what he was thinking. 'Let's assume we're right about Canter and Lock killing Hampton and Paul—'

'Unless it was this bloke, Will Smeed. He's got motive and he's police. Doris Capel said the police were already there.'

'Two of them.'

'Yeah.'

'And his motive is for the murders of Canter, Lock and Liam Smith. Not Hampton and Paul.'

'Unless there's something we don't know.'

'There's always something we don't know.' Dixon accelerated up the ramp. 'It also means that Sohail York might be at risk, doesn't it? If revenge for the deaths of Flora and Jess is the motive. You heard what Rose said about "all four".'

'He denied being there, didn't he?'

'Bollocks to that. Let's have a presence at his home and office, just in case. Make sure it's discreet. We don't want him complaining of harassment again, do we?'

'No, Sir.'

'I'll tell you what I'm thinking,' said Dixon. 'I'm thinking I may have jumped the gun merging the teams. That there might actually be two separate motives behind all this.'

Louise looked smug, but resisted the temptation to say, 'I told you so'.

Clutching at straws, jumping the gun. Something had changed. And Dixon knew what it was.

'Ah, you're here.' Chief Inspector Bateman had seen them arriving and was waiting for them at the top of the stairs. 'He's in a meeting room on the ground floor. Go easy on him. He's a good lad. One of my best officers.' Following them along the landing now. 'What's he in the frame for?'

'Five murders.'

'Really?'

'We'll see.'

A personnel file had been thrust into Dixon's hand. He turned straight to Smeed's performance reviews while he waited for the lift.

'Is he as good as Mr Bateman says?' asked Louise, jabbing the button with her finger.

'Seems it,' replied Dixon. 'No disciplinaries. Hardly relevant, though, is it?'

'I suppose not.'

Dixon was watching Smeed through the glass partition as he walked along the corridor towards the meeting room. He had seen them coming and stood up. Black trousers and white shirt, open at the neck, the basic uniform, more often than not hidden under a stab vest and hi-vis jacket. He looked nervous, but he was about to be interviewed by a detective superintendent, and he probably knew what about too. Everyone knew about the murders of two uniformed officers, knew who was leading the investigation.

'I do know him,' said Louise. 'Now I see his face. You probably don't remember, but he was there the night Dave . . .' She allowed her voice to run out of steam. Better that than bring back the memory of an officer and friend killed on his own doorstep, dying in Jane's arms.

Dixon didn't remember Smeed, as it happened.

'Why am I here, Sir?' asked Smeed, when Dixon opened the door of the meeting room.

Straight to the point, and who could blame him?

'Sit down.'

Louise made the introductions once she'd closed the door behind her, Smeed impassive. And, no, he didn't want his federation rep present, or a solicitor, not that he was under caution. Happy to cooperate, of course he was.

'Will's fine,' he said, his eyes darting from Louise to Dixon and back again.

'Talk to me about your parents, Will,' said Dixon.

'My mother and my half-sister are dead. My father lives just outside Wedmore. He's remarried and I've got a half-brother and sister. They're both young enough to be my own kids, to be honest, so I feel more like an uncle than a brother. That's what people assume when they see us together, anyway.'

'Families are complicated these days,' said Louise.

'When was the last time you saw your mother?' asked Dixon.

'At Jess's funeral.' Smeed folded his arms. 'I'm guessing you've spoken to Rose and know the background?'

'We need to hear it from you.'

'Look, what's this got to do with the murders of Darren and Russell?'

243

'You knew them?'

'I've been on a couple of operations with them, policing football matches at Ashton Gate, stuff like that. That's all.'

'Darren Canter and Russell Lock are two of three men alleged to have raped your half-sister, Jess,' said Dixon, with an apologetic smile. 'The third was Liam Smith, who was murdered two days ago over at Glastonbury.'

'Those fucking bastards. Good job I never knew, I'd have . . .' Smeed caught himself, let out a long, slow sigh. 'I was over there yesterday, doing the bloody house to house. I'm supposed to be back over there now. All three of them are dead?'

Dixon nodded. 'So, you can imagine what questions we have to ask you, I'm sure?'

'It wasn't me, if that's what you're thinking.'

Louise reeled off the dates and times, the response the same to each. 'I was at work.'

And they'd check, of course they would.

Time to take the conversation back to the original question. 'Your parents . . .' said Dixon.

'They married young, had me, then divorced. My father was in the RAF, an engineer, posted here, there and everywhere. Then Flora met Carl and had Jess.'

Dixon never knew what to make of that. He'd come across it before, rarely as it happened, but children referring to their parents by name was unusual. It was always 'Mum' or 'Dad', 'mother' or 'father'. Rarely by name. Maybe it was just the distance between them, real as well as emotional?

'How long was she with Carl?'

'Not long, which was a relief to be honest. I was only six, so I don't remember much about it, just that he was . . . abusive, we'd call it now, I suppose. I remember being glad when he left.'

'Rose gave us the impression it was only Flora and Jess.'

'I'd gone to live with my father by the time Jess was born. He was out of the RAF and working at Filton. British Aerospace.'

'Did you see much of your mother?'

'Not really. She sort of washed her hands of me. Didn't want to know. That was what it felt like. I went and stayed with them from time to time, but it wasn't easy. All she could afford was a two-bedroom flat, so I had to sleep on the sofa.'

'You resented that?'

'To begin with, maybe. We weren't close, put it that way. Her life revolved around Jess and I didn't fit in, did I?' He was miles away, remembering. 'Jess had issues, looking back on it, so maybe Flora was making allowances. I don't know, but I never seemed to feature.'

'What issues?'

Her medical records were waiting at Bridewell, but Dixon hadn't seen them yet.

'Nothing official, nothing diagnosed. She just seemed to struggle as a kid, at school, you know. Anxiety and depression. She was never happy.'

'What about Glastonbury?'

'Jess was eighteen, so I was twenty-four by then. I went in the RAF to begin with, so I'd have been at Brize. First I heard about it was when Flora and Jess tried to kill themselves. They took overdoses, but were found in time. I took some time off, went to stay with them, but it was no good. It was Jess this, Jess that. Flora didn't seem to want my help so I left them to it.'

'Did they tell you what happened at Glastonbury?'

'Jess did. I knew there were three of them. Knew what they did. She never told me their names, though.'

'Rose said Jess became anorexic.'

'She was bulimic. She'd eat, and you'd think, good, she's had a meal, then she'd go in the loo and stick her fingers down her throat.

245

Weighed under six stone at the end; skin and bone. She tried suicide a couple of times, someone got her down off a multistorey car park once, that's when they got those tattoos. Flora thought it was a good sign, but actually it was just solid police work that got her off the bridge. A temporary reprieve, as it turned out.'

'She threw herself in front of a train.'

'She waited for a fast train at Yeovil station. I'm guessing you've had the lecture from Rose about using the word "commit"?'

'It makes sense,' replied Dixon.

'The train driver might disagree with you.'

There wasn't much Dixon could say to that.

'I went to the funeral,' continued Smeed. 'Let's just say it was *difficult*. Then Flora went to look for Carl not long after that and I never saw her again. We'd fallen out, had words, you know how it is, and I'd washed my hands of her. It sounds harsh, I know, but I had to do it for my own sanity, to be honest.' He rubbed his eyes with the tips of his fingers, the moisture wiped away before it formed tears. 'Sounds bizarre to be talking about my own mother this way, but that's families for you. When I got the call to say she was dead – I was her next of kin, wasn't I? – I told them I wanted nothing to do with any of it. Left it to Rose to make the arrangements. She had her cremated over there and her ashes flown home. Cheaper, I suppose.'

'You don't talk to Rose either?'

'She doesn't talk to me.'

'What did they tell you when they rang?'

'It was a copper from Jamaica; just that there'd been a fire on a boat. It sank and divers had recovered the bodies. Simple as that, really. It was accidental, and what did I want to do with the body? I was still angry, regret it now, but I told them they could keep it.' Smeed was avoiding eye contact now, picking the skin at the base of his thumbnail. 'What does that say about me, I wonder?'

Dixon knew a rhetorical question when he heard one.

'So, there you are. Happy families. And the bastards who raped my sister are dead. Can't say I'm sorry. *Won't* say I'm sorry, but no, I didn't do it. Almost wish I had.' Smeed wiped away a small drop of blood. 'I've got a partner now, two kids, and not a day goes by when I don't remind myself not to make the same mistakes Flora did. Not a single day. Families leave scars. Some do, anyway.'

Dixon dropped Louise home, spent the short drive back to his cottage wondering whether Smeed was telling the truth, or whether he was an accomplished liar. Police officers were good at it. You got that way when you spent your life being lied to.

He wanted to believe Smeed, but could he?

Actually, it was simpler than that. Hope he was telling the truth, assume he was lying; check and double-check everything he'd said.

Doris Capel had said she'd seen two police officers outside Hampton and Paul's flat. When what she'd really seen was two people wearing black trousers and white shirts. Stab vests too, she'd said, but it was dark, the streetlights few and far between.

The gunshot residue tests were becoming more urgent by the second.

Jane was still up, either that or asleep in front of the telly. It sounded like Monty was asleep too. A key in the lock would soon change that.

Soon there'd be a baby to keep them awake.

Turned out the lights were on, but no one was home. Dixon knew some people who were like that.

A text message then:

Where are you? Nx

In the red cow with mum and dad. You coming over?

Getting something to eat.

The pub would've stopped serving food hours ago.

The front door of the cottage opened before the microwave pinged, which meant Dixon would end up sharing his supper with his dog. Not that he minded, of course.

'Getting anywhere?' asked Jane.

'Not really,' replied Dixon. He was leaning on the worktop, watching his curry on the turntable. 'Where are Rod and Sue?'

'Gone home. They thought you'd probably be tired.'

Funny they should say that.

'Was that picture any use?' she asked.

'It arrived twenty minutes late, but it told me what I needed to know.'

'What's that?'

'That Sohail York is lying.'

'I wasn't going to vote for him anyway.' Jane switched on the TV, then lowered herself on to the sofa. 'There was a bit on the local news earlier about the AFR trial. They interviewed a couple of people. One said only villains have anything to fear, and the other said it was an invasion of privacy.'

'A balanced report then.'

'Not really. We came out of it looking like a right bunch of wallies.'

Jane didn't give him a chance to reply, not that he had been going to; best left unsaid. 'I saw Nige earlier. He's got to have an operation on the tendons in his hand. Worried it might put an end to his career if he doesn't regain full use of it. Said there'd be nobody left to keep an eye on you.'

'What about Sarah?'

'On the mend, I think.'

He opened the microwave door, slid the plastic tray out on to a plate.

'Tell me then,' said Jane, flicking channels.

'I'm beginning to think it's two cases after all.' Dixon sat down next to her, Monty resting his muzzle on his knee. 'I've got a rape and the three who did it all murdered. The victim and her parents dead. An aunt and a half-brother, but he's one of ours over at Express Park. Will Smeed.'

'I know him,' replied Jane. 'Nice bloke. Straight down the line. No nonsense.'

'Then I've got two alleged drug dealers murdered, I think by two of the murdered rapists.'

'A tangled web.'

'Yes, but I'm worried it might be me tangling it.'

'You'll get there in the end. You always do.'

'How's life outside the police?' It was a conversation he'd need to work up to. Slowly. 'Missing it already, I suppose?'

'Not really, if I'm honest. To begin with, maybe.'

Jane wasn't daft, Dixon knew that. He was pretending to blow on his curry, watching her out of the corner of his eye.

'You did tell that recruitment consultant to forget it, didn't you?' she asked.

Chapter Thirty

The text message arrived when he was on his way to pick up Louise the following morning.

> *You get 2 weeks maternity support leave. Take it when he's born and we'll talk. Jx*

'He' again, although she'd admitted she had no real idea. And they'd spent most of last night talking.

Life outside the police.

There was one. Jane was just beginning to find that out.

Maybe the answer was a change within the police? Traffic, possibly. Or even just being a proper detective superintendent, sitting behind a desk, spared the blood and death.

That might be preferable to being a newly qualified solicitor. And he was newly qualified, albeit eight years ago now; never practised, either.

He pulled up outside Louise's house, hooted the horn, watching the front door open, a peck on her husband's cheek, and then Lou running down the garden path. A common enough sight of a morning. Dixon had done much the same when he'd left the cottage.

'I've had a message from High Tech, Sir,' she said, climbing into the passenger seat. 'We need to call in there on the way to Bridewell. Something about Sohail York's computer.'

Forty-five minutes, largely in silence.

'I was told to ask for DS Barrett,' Louise said, when they walked into the High Tech Unit. She waited until the receptionist disappeared through the double doors. 'Must be important to drag you all the way here first thing.'

The same thick glasses, pale skin; signs of too much time spent indoors in front of a computer screen. Barrett seemed pleased with herself too.

'I thought I'd catch you on your way into Bristol, Sir,' she said.

'You did.'

'You're going to love this. Follow me.'

Now they were sitting around a computer screen at a workstation in an open plan office. All of the desks were occupied, everybody staring at screens, wearing headphones. The reality of twenty-first-century policing; much of it, anyway.

'Sohail York's computer,' said Barrett. 'Nothing much on it, and he's deleted all his emails. We might be able to recover them, we might not, but that's going to take time, I'm afraid. What he has got is a website. It was built for him by a designer somewhere, not terribly sophisticated, it's just a WordPress blog, really. A front page and then his blog posts, news, events he's been to, going to, that sort of stuff.'

'I've seen it,' said Dixon. Not that it had been terribly enlightening, apart from the link to his various appearances in the press, including the ones where he'd been making the allegations about the vigilante, although those had been deleted after Dixon's visit to his office.

'He's got it set up to auto-forward any messages he receives via the contact page on his website to his email address, and then I'm guessing he replies from there. Unfortunately, he's deleted his email, but what he seems to have forgotten, or never known possibly, is that his website keeps a record of these messages. The designer installed a plug-in called Flamingo that keeps them all in the back end. I found the login details on his phone.' A smug grin. 'I've only got the first message, because as I said, he'd have replied from his email, or phoned the number given, but it's the first message that starts it all, I suspect.'

'Starts all what?'

'The blackmail.'

Barrett had his attention and Dixon was following the clicks on the screen. Trying to, anyway. The trouble with techies was they clicked too fast, the sequence impossible to remember. A login screen, the username and password scribbled in a notebook. Then it asked for a verification code.

Barrett snatched an iPhone off the desk. It was in a plastic bag, but the six-digit code that had arrived by text message was still visible. She tapped that in, sat back and folded her arms in triumph while the page loaded.

'This is his WordPress dashboard. And this is the Flamingo plug-in.' She was pointing to the menu on the left of the screen. 'He doesn't get much via his website.' Click. 'But there's this one, from someone calling themselves Master of the Drift, received four weeks ago:

Hi Sohail

We know, mate.

We know about Glastonbury.

We know about the drugs, and the girl who was raped.

What will that do to your election campaign if it gets out?

Got it all backed up too.

Happy to keep quiet. But it will cost you.

Five grand, that's all.

Ring 07428 900039.

You've got twenty-four hours.

Best,

Master of the Drift

'Whoever it is gave a Gmail address so York would've replied to that and forgotten about this. That's if he replied by email. He may just have rung the number, but I'll check that. The mobile number is offline now; a burner, probably. The IP address is Indonesia, so whoever sent the message was using a VPN.'

'Who looks after his website?'

'There are two admins. A Faith Beech – I'm guessing that's his assistant – and himself, as you might expect.'

'How long will it take to recover his emails?' asked Dixon.

'If we can, then it'll take a few days. He's probably deleted them good and proper, though, so don't hold your breath.'

'Check with Scientific, see if they found anything in Hampton's flat.'

'They would've said if they found anything remotely relevant,' replied Louise.

Dixon had made all the usual noises, gratitude and congratulations, before making his escape from High Tech, and was now on his way to Bridewell.

Sohail York was being blackmailed.

But who by?

It could've been Canter and Lock, possibly, but then it was far more likely to have been Hampton and Paul, Canter and Lock sent to deal with it. It was an easy conversation to imagine.

You owe me. I kept quiet when you drugged and raped that girl. If this gets out it's taking you down as well, etc, etc.

Then what happened?

Perhaps Canter and Lock had killed Hampton and Paul, kept the blackmail money? Sohail York then killed them.

Why Liam Smith though? Unless he helped Canter and Lock find Hampton and Paul. He was a techie, after all.

Speculating. Getting ahead of himself, however much he wanted it over and done with. The first step was to prove it had been Hampton and Paul doing the blackmailing. The rest would follow on from that.

We know about Glastonbury.

How did they know about Glastonbury?

The PCC's laptop, possibly, but that would be long gone, of course. There was a backup somewhere, that much was clear from the blackmail message itself. Where, though?

They hadn't found a phone or laptop in the flat, and he knew Scientific had been through it inch by inch, even if he had asked Louise to check again. An online backup was possible, on the dark web even, but then they'd found no devices of any description to check, no phones either. They were still waiting for records from Hampton's internet service provider, not that they would be much use if it was the dark web.

An external hard drive was possible, or a memory stick depending on how much information there was. Hidden where, though?

The original assessment had been that the scene was staged to make it look like a county lines punishment beating, but there was another possibility. The laptop and backup been retrieved by Canter and Lock, the location beaten out of Hampton and Paul. Tortured out of them would be a more accurate description. Then killed to keep them quiet. It would make sense.

The PCC's laptop. It all started with the PCC's laptop. But, if that was right, what was the information about Glastonbury doing on it in the first place?

Suddenly the pieces of the jigsaw puzzle were fitting into place.

Louise rang off. 'They're going to check,' she said. 'What's the significance of "Master of the Drift", I wonder?'

'There were quite a few motoring convictions in Hampton's previous, from memory. One for dangerous driving,' replied Dixon.

'And?'

'It's where you spin a car deliberately. Skid round corners and roundabouts, burning rubber. Boy racers do it in car parks at night; drives local residents mad.' He remembered the tortuous Neighbourhood Watch Liaison Committee meetings from his short stint as managing DCI at Express Park.

'Hampton must've had a car, in that case,' said Louise. 'We haven't searched that, have we?'

'Where's the Bristol traffic unit based?'

'Roads Policing is at Patchway.'

'See if you can get someone over to Bridewell. Better tell them who and what it's about so they can come prepared.'

Louise was on her phone again, while Dixon was driving into the city centre.

'There's a DS who can come over,' she said, holding her phone to her shoulder. 'Wants to know when you want him.'

'Now, please.'

Chapter Thirty-One

'Charlesworth's in the building, Sir,' said Mark. 'Wasn't looking for you, specifically. Just nosing around.'

'Anything else?'

'I had a call from Donald Watson. The gunshot residue testing has drawn a blank. Darren Canter got his mother to wash his clothes when he got home that night and Russell Lock was in the sea for however long it was, so . . .'

Dixon had expected that; wasn't surprised.

'It was a long shot anyway,' said Mark, ducking down behind his computer.

'You'd better have come up with something else,' said Louise.

'I have, as a matter of fact. Doris Capel said she saw the two officers at the scene of Hampton and Paul's murder getting in an unmarked car out on the main road about an hour before the anonymous tip came in about the murders. And this is a picture of Canter's Beamer taken on an ANPR camera at 2241 that evening, so around about the right time. Not far from the scene either.' He was waving a piece of paper with a flourish.

'Driving to or from?' asked Dixon.

'From.'

'Are we bringing him in?' asked Louise.

'Not yet. I'm not risking him walking out of here and into a jubilant crowd on the pavement again, so we'll get everything in place first. See if we can't find that backup.'

'Who are we talking about?' asked Mark.

'Sohail York,' replied Dixon, his voice hushed, not that there was anyone else in the incident room. It was more in case Charlesworth was creeping up behind him. 'He was being blackmailed by someone calling himself Master of the Drift.'

'Then we've got him.' Mark grinned. 'Git.'

'We need to prove Hampton was Master of the Drift first.'

'The parking area outside his flat. Residents' parking. There was a huge skid mark in a circle. I remember seeing it and thinking someone's been doing doughnuts. Could've been Hampton, couldn't it?'

'He was banned from driving.' Louise had flicked on the kettle, sitting in front of a computer while she waited for it to boil, looking at a list of previous convictions. 'Three years for dangerous driving.'

'We need another statement from the neighbours, Lou,' said Dixon. 'Take Mark with you. I'll hang on here for that DS coming over from Traffic.'

'It's called Roads Policing and Road Safety, Sir,' she replied. 'It hasn't been called *Traffic* for years.'

Dixon could imagine the focus groups, hundreds of thousands spent on rebranding. Another bright idea from a Police and Crime Commissioner, trying to make it look as though he was doing something.

'Can we have a coffee first?' asked Mark.

'No.'

A uniformed sergeant was holding the door for Louise and Mark when they left to interview Hampton's neighbours. A big man, over from *Traffic*, as Dixon was determined to call it. It was a form of gaslighting, really. Rather like changing the name of speed cameras to 'road safety enforcement cameras'; trying to convince people they were something they weren't. There was a lot of it about.

'I'm looking for the super,' said the sergeant.

'That would be me,' said Dixon, ignoring the surprised look. He was sensible enough to know, God willing, there would come a time when he didn't look so young.

'You wanted all the intel we've got on Justin Hampton, Sir,' he said, sliding a file out from under his arm.

'Coffee?' asked Dixon. 'The kettle's just boiled.'

'Thank you,' the sergeant replied, the surprise in his voice this time.

'Talk to me about drifting.'

'It's basically a controlled skid, round corners, round in a circle. Roundabouts and car parks usually. The more smoke and burning rubber, the better. There's quite a drifting *scene* around Bristol.'

'And what's the point of it?'

'I'm not sure there is one. The scrotes who do it will tell you it's fun.' The sergeant gave a dismissive grunt. 'Beyond me, I'm afraid.'

'Was Hampton a drifter?'

'He was until we took his driving licence away from him, although I suspect that didn't stop him.'

'What car did he drive?' asked Dixon, placing a mug of coffee in front of the sergeant.

'A Mazda MX-5. They get them off the scrap heap, really. Trash what's left of them, run them till they fall to bits, then get another one. Basically, you want the engine at the front and rear wheel drive, then you can get the back wheels spinning; after that it's just opposite lock, floor it and round you go. What d'you drive, Sir?'

'A Land Rover Defender.'

'It'll be a mystery to you then, I'm afraid.'

'I did spin the wheels once, on some gravel.'

The sergeant opened the file. 'Hampton first came to our attention for driving without insurance and MOT. That was three years ago. A fine and points on his licence. Then he started popping up on Facebook pages we monitor. Drifting groups, they arrange meets, usually at night. If it's out of the way and posing no risk to the general public we leave them to it, but sometimes it's in a place where the public are at risk, so we have to intervene. Then they shut down the Facebook group, start another one, move on. And off we go again.'

'What was his dangerous driving conviction?'

'Drifting around a roundabout. We had several calls from concerned members of the public. There'd been several near misses, apparently. That was just the tip of the iceberg, really. The little bugger had been doing it all over Bristol, no insurance too, no MOT. The plates on his MX-5 were fake last time he was stopped. We took one car off him, had it crushed, but he just got another. Some of them seem to think racking up driving offences is a badge of honour. We knew he'd been driving whilst banned too, just hadn't caught him yet.'

'Do you know where he keeps his cars?'

'There's a farmer who lets them drift in one of his fields. It was part of an initiative we put together to try and get them off the streets, and it works – some of the time. The adrenaline rush isn't quite the same, apparently.' The sergeant gave an exaggerated shake of the head. 'Anyway, there's a barn and some of the cars are in there. There's a circuit over in South Wales that allows it as well, but the fun goes out of it if it's legal, or so they tell me.'

'Like smoking at school.'

'Something like that. You might find Hampton's car in that barn. We know he still had it because there's a summons outstanding: failing to identify the driver. Picked it up on an ANPR camera and he's supposed to be banned, isn't he? Either he tells us who was driving or he takes the points and pays the fine. Or at least he would if he wasn't dead.'

'Where's this barn then?'

'The other side of Bradley Stoke.'

'You drive.'

'What exactly are you looking for, Sir?' asked the sergeant, weaving down the farm track, trying to avoid the potholes.

'Hampton was murdered because he was blackmailing someone using information he'd found on a stolen laptop. His blackmail note said he'd made a backup of the files and we've torn his flat apart. That leaves his car. We didn't know he had one until now. He's not the registered keeper of a vehicle, according to the DVLA.'

'You're looking for a memory stick then, something small like that.'

'He could have backed it up online, of course, but we haven't got his phone or the laptop, and there was nothing in his iCloud backups.'

'Got to be worth a try.'

The field on the far side of the valley looked more like a race track, a figure of eight carved into the mud by the wheels of drifting cars, several gaps in the hedge where cars had gone through into the adjacent field. Hay bales had been stacked on the apex of the bends, a makeshift crash barrier of sorts.

'There are even competitions, would you believe it,' offered the sergeant. 'Judges give them style marks for control of the drift, speed and fluidity, stuff like that. It's another world, which is fine, until they bring it on to the streets. I should say *back* on to the streets. That's where it started and we're trying to get it off them.'

The barn was little more than a rusting metal gazebo, probably used for keeping hay and straw dry originally. Now there were eight cars, sheltering from the elements.

A small man in oil-covered overalls was working on one of the cars.

'That's Faisal,' said the sergeant. 'He helped us set up the project. He'll know which car is Hampton's. Let me have a word with him.'

Dixon couldn't hear what was being said, but he could tell from the body language, Faisal pointing to the far corner of the barn.

And there it was. A grey Mazda MX-5, the soft top ripped, dents in both wings.

'That's it, at the back,' said the sergeant. 'Shall I get a flatbed out here to bring it in?'

'Thank you,' replied Dixon, climbing out of the patrol car, stepping over the puddles.

'They're all Japanese imports.' The sergeant was following Dixon, dialling a number on his phone, weaving between the cars towards the MX-5. 'They're the best, apparently.' Then someone answered the call and he turned away.

Dixon pulled on a pair of gloves, tried the driver's door.

Open.

Spots of mould on the seats and dashboard. He leaned in, looked in the obvious places: glovebox, storage compartment between the seats.

'Lorry's on the way, Sir,' said the sergeant, appearing behind him. 'I wouldn't try under the seats in case something's living under there.'

It was a good point.

'There are loads of places you could hide something small like a memory stick. Scientific will have to tear it apart bit by bit.'

◆ ◆ ◆

'You want me to drop everything and do this now?'

Dixon had waited at the barn for the flatbed lorry to arrive, gone with the MX-5 to the Scientific Services lab.

'We do cover the whole of Avon and Somerset, not just your cases.'

'Five murders, two of them police officers.'

That did the trick; got the MX-5 into the bay and on the ramp.

'Passenger compartment first,' said the Scientific Services officer.

Dixon didn't know his name, didn't ask. He was too busy scrolling through the messages on his phone. Several from Jane reminding him to eat. More from Charlesworth. He didn't bother listening to the voicemails.

He watched as bits of the car appeared on the concrete floor next to the ramp. Seats, carpets ripped out, door panels, the dashboard.

'There are these plastic panels behind the seats and in the boot. If I get all of them out we'll be able to see under the parcel shelf.'

Dixon wasn't really interested in the details. Just the end result.

Curved plastic panels were being thrown on to a pile, the little plastic clips stuffed into a pocket. The Scientific Services officer was wearing latex gloves, so that was something.

'Hello. What's this?' The Scientific Services officer was sitting in the passenger compartment, facing the rear panels, which would ordinarily have been hidden behind the seats. 'Could you pass me an evidence bag, please, Sir? They're on the side in that crate.'

'What've we got?' asked Dixon. Knowing his luck it would be coins dropped by the driver. Or keys.

'It's an external hard drive. Western Digital by the looks of things. Someone's taped it in this little compartment here, where the seatbelt retainer sits.'

'We need to get it over to High Tech.'

'The van comes round at five.'

'Bollocks to that. I'll walk it over there now.'

'Is it urgent?'

It seemed an odd question, particularly when a detective superintendent had walked in the pissing rain to hand deliver an external hard drive, personally.

Not that Dixon was entirely sure why he had. It might have had something to do with sticking his neck out, merging the teams at the briefing the day before. A decision he had started to regret before the end of the day.

Whatever.

'How long will it take?'

'I've just got to scan it for viruses. Catalogue it and then we can plug it in, see what's on it.'

It didn't take long.

'There's not a lot on it. Just one folder, not even a meg of data.'

'Let's have a look.'

Ten minutes later Dixon tucked a bundle of paper under his arm, slid his phone out of his jacket pocket, sent a text message to Louise.

Can you come over to Portishead and pick me up, please? Quick as you can.

Where will you be?

The PCC's office.

Chapter Thirty-Two

'He's got somebody with him at the moment,' said Julia, when Dixon marched into the PCC's office suite on the first floor. She'd seen him coming, had a chance to draw breath, make a half-hearted attempt to stop him, but that was all he gave her.

He opened the door, walked in.

'What do you want?' asked Napier, looking up.

'Who's this?'

Two young people in civvies were sitting in front of Napier's desk, notebooks open in their laps. They looked startled more than anything.

'They're from the press team,' replied Napier. 'We're working on a damage limitation strategy after you outed the AFR trial.'

'I need to speak to the PCC in private.'

'Now, wait a minute.' Napier hesitated, the press officers closing notebooks and standing up. 'Perhaps you'd better go,' he said. 'We'll continue this tomorrow.'

Dixon waited until the door closed behind him, but Napier beat him to it.

'How dare you come marching in here?'

'Five people are dead and it all starts with your laptop. I said we'd speak again if I found that it did. I'm guessing they call it "opposition research"?'

'I don't know what you're talking about,' said Napier, but he knew. Dixon could tell from the look on his face, the tremble in his voice. 'Have you found the laptop?'

Close, but not quite.

'We've found a backup of the information on it,' replied Dixon. 'Information that was being used to blackmail Sohail York.'

'I told you to leave him alone.'

'There's a team on the way now to arrest him for conspiracy to murder Justin Hampton and Andrew Paul, and attempting to pervert the course of justice.' Dixon was on a roll now. 'You are also under investigation for attempting to pervert the course of justice and you will make yourself available for interview under caution at Bridewell police station tomorrow morning at eleven. You are welcome to bring your solicitor with you. Is that clear?'

'Me?'

'If you fail to attend for interview at the allotted time, a warrant will be issued for your arrest. A search warrant will also be issued for your home and office. And we'll see what the press team make of that.'

'You said there was a backup of the information on it . . . ?'

'A copy of the initial report made by Jessica Burroughs, an eighteen-year-old girl raped by three men at the Glastonbury Festival ten years ago; a witness statement taken from one of the attending St John's Ambulance paramedics, another from the girl's mother. Still images from CCTV on the fence near the campsite. There are also several drug squad documents in a separate folder providing intelligence on a supplier by the name of Sohail, operating in the Crofts End and St Paul's parts of the city. I wondered why there was no police intelligence on Sohail York on the Police National Computer.'

'You looked?'

'I did.'

'You were given a direct order by David Charles—'

'I ignored it.'

'I'll have you—'

'No, you won't. And if you seriously think the ACC is going to come to your rescue then you're very much mistaken.'

'David and I go back a long way.'

'Not that far.'

'But I haven't perverted the course of justice.' Panic was creeping in. 'Yes, I didn't report the theft, but that's not a crime, is it?'

'Deliberate and concerted efforts to suppress evidence in the form of the still image of Justin Hampton captured by the AFR camera. Deliberate efforts to interfere with the police investigation into the murder of Justin Hampton, the man you knew to be guilty of the theft because you'd got a copy of the AFR image.'

'That was to protect the AFR trial.'

'Deleting intelligence files from the system. We'll see what the Crown Prosecution Service makes of all of that, shall we? And then, perhaps, a jury. One thing I can guarantee you, a file will be going to the CPS.'

'Speak to David Charlesworth.'

'I will. I'll be needing a witness statement from him detailing your attempts to interfere with the murder investigation.'

'Look, I wasn't going to do anything with this stuff on my laptop.'

'Not officially, no. I noticed the draft press release leaking the story to the media was anonymous. When were you going to send that, I wonder?' Dixon shook his head. 'Once nominations had closed? Too late for anyone else to stand in his place then.'

'I haven't done anything wrong,' protested Napier.

'If you'd come forward the day of the theft, your laptop could have been recovered in a matter of hours. We'd got a photo of the lad who pinched it, even his name. Instead you did nothing except try to cover your tracks.' Dixon gave a sarcastic smile. 'D'you know, I might stand for election myself.'

'You can't be a serving officer.'

'So much the better.'

A crowd was gathering on the pavement by the time Louise picked up Dixon and they arrived back at Bridewell. Someone had already painted a slogan on a sheet billowing from a street lamp: 'FREE SOHAIL!'

Not this time.

Another was bellowing into a loudhailer.

'Are you responsible for this?' demanded Charlesworth, when they crept in the side door.

'Mr York is under arrest for conspiracy to murder, Sir.'

'They went mob-handed to his office—'

'I sent them to his office, mob-handed, as you call it. And he was arrested peacefully and without incident.'

'You'd better be right about this.' Charlesworth's phone was buzzing in his pocket. 'I've got the PCC on the phone now.'

'You're going to want to take that call, Sir,' said Dixon, turning on his heel and setting off along the corridor.

Twenty minutes later Dixon was sitting in an interview room. Louise was to his left, York opposite with his solicitor.

Louise dealt with the formalities, reminded York he was under caution.

'Right, let's pick up where we left off last time, shall we, Sohail?' said Dixon. 'The Glastonbury Festival. You denied being there, is that correct?'

'Yes. I've never been.'

'So, you've never climbed over the fence, on to the top of a minibus and then down a ladder at South Park Two?'

'I have no idea where that is.'

'Never supplied the young men who helped you over the fence with ecstasy?'

'No.'

There was a nervousness creeping into York's answers, a slight hesitation, perhaps. Louise had spotted it. So had York's solicitor.

Charlesworth probably had as well, watching on the monitor in the adjacent room.

'You see, they gave a description of an Asian man, about your age as you would have been then, wearing jeans and a Coldplay T-shirt, calling himself Sohail, but just to be clear, you're adamant that was not you.'

'I told you, I wasn't there.'

'There's a CCTV image of someone matching that description climbing over the fence. Can't see his face though.' Dixon slid a piece of paper from a folder, placed it on the table in front of York. 'Can in this one though. Is this a picture of you?'

Silence. York looking at the photograph, then his solicitor, then back to the photograph.

'You see, the thing with Facebook, Sohail – and I must confess, I don't understand it at all, but we have people who do, obviously – is that when you upload an image to your timeline it also goes in a photo album. And to get rid of it you need to delete it from both, to make sure it's really gone. Even then it can be recovered.' Dixon looked up, fixed York in a steely glare. 'Is that you?'

'Yes.'

'Can't really deny it, can you? After all, you took it. Haven't changed a bit, have you?'

A selfie with the Pyramid Stage in the background.

'Who was on stage at the time?'

'I don't remember.'

'Yes, you do. It was Coldplay, wasn't it?'

'If you say so.'

'So, here's what I think happened. You took the photo, uploaded it to your timeline or feed or whatever they call it, for all your friends to see. Then, when you heard about what those lads did to the girl after they'd taken the drugs you'd given them, you quickly deleted it from your timeline, but forgot your photo album, which is where we found it. How am I doing?'

Dixon waited.

'Let's be clear, Sohail, I'm not interested in any drugs offences you may have committed. Let's say you had a small amount, for personal use only, and shared it with them because they helped you over the fence. Would that be fair?'

'No comment.'

'Their names were Darren Canter, Russell Lock and Liam Smith. Do those names ring any bells?'

'No.'

'Okay,' said Dixon. 'Nothing happens then for ten years. It's all conveniently forgotten, isn't it? The girl and her mother are both dead, Darren Canter and Russell Lock are police officers, and you're standing in the election to be the new Police and Crime Commissioner.' Dixon slid another piece of paper across the table. 'Then you receive this email.'

Both York and his solicitor leaned forward, reading it slowly; York breathing deeply through his nose.

'I've never seen that email before.'

'Yes, you have,' replied Dixon, offhand almost. Dismissive. 'You had the email at your website set to auto-forward any incoming messages to your Outlook email. So you must've seen it.'

No response.

'Careful to delete those emails, of course, but you forgot the copy kept in the back end of your website, didn't you?'

'Faith deals with the website.'

'Our High Tech Unit will most likely be able to recover the full email exchange, if there is one. Or did you just ring that number?'

'Of course I rang the number. It was just some kid. He said he'd pinched a laptop and it had all this stuff on it. Offered it to me for five grand.' York straightened, indignant. 'It was either that or wave goodbye to my PCC election campaign. A lot of people have put a lot of money into it. How could I let them down?'

'So, you paid?'

York nodded.

'For the tape.'

'Yes.'

'Where did you get the money from?'

'Campaign funds.'

'Did they give you the laptop?'

'I never met anyone, never saw anyone. I left the money by a dog bin on Clifton Downs, found the laptop by another. I threw it in an incinerator. Then a few days later they came back for more. Said they'd kept a backup, wanted more money for that.'

'And what did you do?'

'I called the police, which is what I should have done in the first place.'

'You called the police?'

'I rang Police Constable Darren Canter. Reported the blackmail to him and he said he'd deal with it. Next thing I know I get a call telling me there's nothing else to worry about and I can forget it. PC Canter said he'd dealt with it.'

'How did he deal with it?'

'I have no idea. I didn't ask and he didn't tell me.'

'So, you didn't ask Darren Canter to kill Justin Hampton and Andrew Paul?'

'Who are they?'

'They're the two young men who stole the laptop and were blackmailing you. You were at pains to tell everyone who'd listen that they'd been killed by a vigilante cleaning up the streets of Bristol, when actually they were killed by Darren Canter and Russell Lock. Tortured first, to get them to hand over the backup. Seems they must've made more than one, which is how we found it.'

'News to me. All of it. I don't know anything about any of this. All I did was report the blackmail to a police officer. Isn't that what we're supposed to do? What Darren Canter did after that is down to him, not me.'

'Where did the vigilante story come from?'

'I made it up, for the free publicity. Got quite a bit of news coverage off the back of it too.'

'Did you meet Darren Canter at any point?'

'No. I rang him.'

'You had his phone number?'

'His name was familiar to me from the Bryony Beech case, so I rang and left a message for him to call me, which he did. I wanted to speak to someone I knew for obvious reasons.'

Dixon must've looked blank, fleetingly.

'The election,' continued York. 'I needed to impress on him the sensitive nature of my situation. He asked me to forward the email to him, which I did.'

'You knew Darren Canter because of what happened at Glastonbury.'

'No comment.'

'Promised you could help him with his disciplinary proceedings. Make them go away even; get the family to drop their complaint.'

'No comment.'

'Look, Superintendent, my client has made his position clear, I think. He reported the blackmail to the police and knows nothing of what happened after that.'

Chapter Thirty-Three

A packed incident room; Charlesworth and Deborah Potter sitting at the back, both on their phones.

'Right, what have we got on Canter and Lock?' asked Dixon.

'There's no record of a call coming into Bridewell from any of Sohail York's numbers; not from his home, office or mobile,' replied Mark. 'What we have got is a request for a mobile phone trace on the number in the blackmail note. The form was signed by Darren Canter and gives "suspected car theft" as the reason for the search. Then, when he'd got his trace, the complaint was marked "withdrawn".'

'When was that?'

'Two days before the murders of Hampton and Paul.'

'Did you check with the complainant?'

'Doesn't exist.'

'We've also got Canter's BMW on a traffic camera leaving the vicinity of Hampton's flat. Anything else?'

'What Darren's parents said about him arriving home late is corroborated by their Wi-Fi router, Guv.' Dixon recognised the officer sitting at the front of the incident room, but her name was a mystery to him. 'All our phones are set to connect to our home Wi-Fi automatically when we get within range, and the router keeps a log of connections,' she continued. 'Darren Canter got home at nine minutes to one in the morning, just like they said.'

'No smoking gun, though.'

'Well, actually, Sir, there is,' said Redgrave, looking pleased with himself. 'The Canters have got a wood burning stove and Scientific found traces of melted polymer in the bottom. It had been cleaned out, the ashes gone in the grey bin, probably – they did check the compost heap in the garden, but there was nothing there. Anyway, there were traces. Confirmed to be from the same batch of Taulman Bridge as the 3D printed gun that killed Hampton and Paul.'

'Melts down the murder weapon, but makes the mistake of doing it in his own wood burner,' muttered Mark. 'Idiot.'

'They did remember to leave their mobile phones in Russell Lock's car,' said Redgrave. 'Both their phone signals give the Rudolph Street car park as their location until gone midnight. Then we've got Canter dropping Lock back to his car on CCTV at twelve-ten.'

'Seems you were right then, Sir,' said Louise.

'Let's get pictures of Canter and Lock in front of Hampton's neighbour, Doris Capel. See if she recognises them as the officers she saw outside the flat an hour before the anonymous call came in.'

'Done that, Guv, and she didn't. They were sideways on almost, walking away from her at the time, she said.' Another officer Dixon didn't recognise. 'She did say it was a large green car they got into out on the main road, though, so that's something. I showed her a picture of Canter's BMW and she said it could've been that car.'

'Anything else?'

'High Tech rang to say they've finally got access to the iCloud backups of Canter and Lock's phones, so "watch this space" was the message,' said Redgrave. 'The phones themselves probably went in the River Avon down at Portbury, of course, but the backups should give us plenty. They would've backed up the night before on their home Wi-Fi, so we'll only be missing the last twenty-four hours.'

'Someone's been using burner phones too,' said Mark. 'We've got the call data from their mobile phone companies and there are calls to and from unidentified numbers. Probably Sohail York.'

'And the gunsmith?' replied Dixon. 'How far have we got with the polymer?'

'Nowhere yet, Sir. There's not enough of us, frankly.' Redgrave shrugged. 'We've traced and interviewed twenty-seven individuals, but so far, nothing to report.'

'Right, let's be clear. Given what we now know about what took place at the Glastonbury Festival, if we had Darren Canter and Russell Lock in custody downstairs, then we'd have enough to go to the CPS for a charging decision for the murders of Justin Hampton and Andrew Paul.' Dixon looked around the room. 'Anyone disagree with that assessment?'

'No, Guv,' seemed to the gist of the murmuring.

'Good. So, we'll proceed on that basis and I'll update the Policy Log accordingly. Darren Canter and Russell Lock murdered Justin Hampton and Andrew Paul. What that leaves us with is the murders of Canter, Lock and Liam Smith.'

'Sohail York has to be in the frame for that,' said Redgrave.

'He is,' replied Dixon. 'He's still in custody downstairs and will remain there until we're satisfied one way or the other.'

He glanced at Charlesworth, who was looking out of the window, craning his neck to see the crowd in the street below. The chanting was clearly of greater concern to him than it was to Dixon.

'Phone records, messaging apps, location data are all going to be critical. He admitted in interview that he contacted Canter and Lock when Hampton and Paul demanded more money.'

'He said he used campaign funds to pay them the first time.' A voice coming from behind a workstation. 'And there's a withdrawal of five thousand pounds from his election account dated two days after he received the email.'

'He'll have to resign, then. At the very least,' said Redgrave.

'I want him for conspiracy to murder. He doesn't just resign and walk away from this.'

'No, Sir.'

'We've probably got enough for a fraud charge, but that's not enough.' Time to stick his neck out. Again. 'It goes back to Glastonbury. It must do.'

'Are you saying York didn't kill them?' Redgrave again.

'He's in the frame for conspiracy to murder Hampton and Paul but I don't believe he killed Canter, Lock and Smith, no. Not just to tidy up a mess that he's lived with for ten years already. Canter and Lock certainly weren't going to say anything, so why kill them? And if he was tidying up, why kill Liam Smith? Smith wasn't involved in the murders of Hampton and Paul. I thought he might have been at the start, that they might have needed his tech skills to track down Hampton and Paul, but we know they did that with a simple mobile phone trace now, don't we?' Dixon was pacing up and down in front of the double doors. 'Smith knew something was going on, so Canter or Lock must've warned him York was being blackmailed about Glastonbury. That might explain why he didn't set foot outside his house, but apart from that, he was just sitting at home, minding his own business. Either that or he put two and two together when he heard Canter and Lock had been murdered and assumed he was next, which he was.'

'It's two separate cases after all, then?'

'Two separate motives, but they both start with Glastonbury and the theft of the PCC's laptop.'

'The dickhead.' An anonymous whisper from behind a computer monitor; saying what everyone was thinking. Dixon heard it, but couldn't tell which workstation it came from. Charlesworth heard it too.

'Hampton and Paul were killed because they were blackmailing York about what happened at Glastonbury,' said Dixon, spelling it out. 'Canter, Lock and Smith were killed *because* of what happened at Glastonbury.'

◆ ◆ ◆

Dixon had expected it.

'Montpelier Room. Now, please.'

Charlesworth looked angry, or exasperated perhaps; Deborah Potter more apologetic, if anything. At least Charlesworth waited until Dixon had closed the door of the meeting room behind him.

'I've spent the last two hours trying to persuade the PCC not to resign,' he said, dropping his phone on the table.

'He needs to resign, Sir. And he needs to do it now,' replied Dixon. 'As I've already said, you would be well advised to distance yourself from him as quickly as you can. Leaving aside the question of how confidential police intelligence material concerning a private individual found its way on to his laptop, leaving aside the question of how it came to be deleted from the Police National Computer, there is the question of his course of conduct following the theft of his laptop.'

'Yes, but—'

'He also had a copy of the Glastonbury rape file. There are no *buts*, Sir.' Dixon glanced at Potter, who was nodding her agreement, mercifully. 'If it was anyone else, you'd expect me to submit a file to the CPS, and that is what I intend to do. If you or I accessed that material for personal use it would be gross misconduct. Then we've got deliberate attempts to suppress the AFR image – evidence in a murder investigation – which looks an awful lot like attempting to pervert the course of justice to me.'

Charlesworth pulled a chair out from under the table, slumped down.

'The CPS might even decide to add a misconduct in public office charge,' continued Dixon.

'Just tell me he didn't kill anyone.'

'Not as far I'm aware, Sir.'

'York gave a good account of himself in interview,' said Potter, more to give Charlesworth time to process the situation.

'He's had plenty of time to get his story straight,' replied Dixon. 'And he's not frightened of the police, hardly fazed by being in an interview room; cautioned.'

'Thinks he's going to be the PCC, doesn't he?' Charlesworth gave an acid smile.

'All that crap about reporting the blackmail to the police,' said Potter. 'He rang his mates, Darren and Russell, which is hardly making a formal report of a crime. He'd have known that.'

'It's going to be hard to prove a conspiracy,' said Dixon. 'You can bet there'll be no emails or messages. It'll have been phone calls only, burners, no traces. He'll stand up in front of a jury and expect them to believe that a candidate to be the PCC was naive enough to think he'd made a formal report to the police and that the killings were down to Canter and Lock. He'll say they had their own motive for the murders, had even more to lose than he did if the rape allegation came out; killed Hampton and Paul to cover up the beating they gave them.'

'It needs to go in front of a jury.'

'It does, Ma'am,' replied Dixon. 'But we need more to get that far. As it stands now, the CPS are unlikely to authorise charging him with anything more than perverting the course of justice and fraud.'

'We need to release York, on bail if needs be,' said Charlesworth. 'Listen to that crowd out there. It's a public order matter and we can't put the general public at risk of rioting.'

'Since when do we release people facing a possible conspiracy to murder charge?' demanded Dixon.

'Since the crowd outside doubled in size.' Charlesworth was holding one arm of his glasses between his teeth, and was massaging the bridge of nose. 'Have we got enough to put it to the CPS for a charging decision? Yes or no?'

'Not yet, Sir.'

'How long has he been in custody?'

'Four hours.'

'How long d'you intend to keep him for?'

'As long as it takes.' Dixon was bridling now. Time to try another tack. 'Look, Sir, if I'm right about the motive for the murders of Canter, Lock and Smith, then he's next in line. He supplied the drugs they used to rape Jessica Burroughs. We need to keep him here for his own safety.'

'Talk to me about the brother. He's another one of ours.' Charlesworth puffed out his cheeks. 'Can't say I can put a face to the name.'

'He's Jessica's half-brother, by the mother's first husband,' replied Dixon. 'Estranged from that side of the family, or so he says.'

Potter looked up sharply. 'You don't believe him?'

'I don't believe anything anyone tells me.'

'We're going to have to let York go,' said Charlesworth, sliding his glasses back into position.

'Let's be clear, Sir,' said Dixon, firmly. 'He conspired with Canter and Lock to kill Hampton and Paul, then he tried to deflect attention with that crap about a vigilante on the loose.'

'He says he didn't, though, doesn't he? And at the moment you can't prove anything one way or the other. I'm sorry, Nick, but public order trumps all. You've got until ten tonight to come up with something – interview him again, by all means, put it to him about his personal safety – but if you can't charge him at that point, you'll have to let him go.'

Chapter Thirty-Four

'There she is at the front, Sir,' said Louise. 'With the loudhailer.'

Dixon and Louise had crept out of the side door of Bridewell police station, through the car park and down the ramp into the road. Now they were standing on the pavement at the back of the crowd, listening to Faith Beech leading the chants.

'What do we want?'

'Free Sohail!'

'When do we want it?'

'Now!'

A few stones had been thrown at the front windows, Charlesworth and Potter watching from the fourth floor.

Two hundred and fifty people, possibly. A few journalists, a TV camera van on the far side.

'There's another crowd outside his office, apparently,' said Louise. 'Smaller, though.'

It wouldn't take much for a riot to start, and they'd be along in a minute – the trouble makers, shit stirrers. The first shout had gone out on social media twenty minutes earlier, according to the monitoring team at Portishead.

'I need to have a word with her,' Dixon said. 'You wait here. Keep an eye on me and call it in if I get into any trouble.'

Two vans from the Tactical Support Group were parked within shouting distance but he didn't want police in riot gear wading in unless it was absolutely necessary.

He took off his tie, stuffed it in his jacket pocket, turned up the collar, then walked around the side of the crowd to the front. It turned out a small flatbed Transit van had been parked on the double yellow lines outside the police station, Faith standing on that.

'I need to have a word with her,' he said, to one of the men blocking his approach to the van.

'Who are you?'

'She knows who I am.'

Glaring at him now. A tap on the leg had got her attention, a finger jabbed in Dixon's direction. Faith went to the far side of the van's deck, squatted down.

'What?' she asked, when Dixon appeared in front of her, between the van and the locked revolving doors at the front of the police station.

'Sohail is helping us with our enquiries,' said Dixon.

'You arrested him,' she snarled back.

'We did. He supplied class A drugs to three young men at the Glastonbury Festival ten years ago. Ecstasy. They used them to drug and rape an eighteen-year-old girl. Like I say, he's helping us with our enquiries.'

'He supplied drugs?'

'I take it you didn't know?' Dixon was standing on tiptoe, shouting into Faith's ear.

'No.'

'All three men involved in the rape are dead, shot at point blank range in the head. So, you'll understand, I hope, we are not *harassing* Sohail. He has questions he has to answer.'

'Where's the victim?'

'She killed herself.'

Faith rocked back on to her heels, blinking furiously, trying to take it all in.

'Did Sohail tell you he was being blackmailed?' asked Dixon.

'No.' Eyes wide now.

'He received a message via his website four weeks ago. Used campaign funds to make a payment of five thousand pounds. Who has control of the bank account?'

'He does.'

'Are you a signatory?'

'Yes.' Faith was kneeling down now, her knees getting wet from the rain. 'Does that make me liable?' she asked, over the flashes and bangs of fireworks being let off on the far side of the road.

'Only if you knew.'

'I didn't know. He never told me anything about it.'

'So, he never told you he arranged to have the blackmailers killed?'

Silence. From Faith anyway.

'Justin Hampton and Andrew Paul,' continued Dixon. 'The two young men he said had been killed by a vigilante.'

'What d'you want me to do?'

'Tell these people to go home. Then we'll have a chat back at your office.'

It took a while, a few stragglers reluctant to move on. Uniformed officers had been about to arrest them, until Dixon stepped in. There might have been a dispersal order in place covering the area outside Bridewell police station, but now was not the time to enforce it.

'I've had to borrow a computer,' said Faith, pushing open the office door, speaking over the jangle of the bell. 'You lot have taken all ours. What is it you want me to look at?'

'How often d'you log in to the campaign website?'

It was a trick question. Dixon knew the answer. It was all in the server logs.

'I think I've only done it the once. Sohail was having trouble uploading an image. The file was too big, so I optimised it for him then tried again.'

Telling the truth then; about that anyway.

'The blackmail message came in via the website.'

'Then it would have been forwarded to his email.'

'Does he have any other phones?'

'You've got his iPhone.'

'Apart from that. Have you ever seen any other phones around the office, seen him using one, perhaps? Personal assistants know everything there is to know, apparently, and you're more than just his assistant, aren't you?'

Faith thought about it, but decided to let the remark go.

'Two of the young men he supplied the drugs to were Darren Canter and Russell Lock,' continued Dixon. 'The officers who arrested your sister on New Year's Eve.'

'He knew them?'

'It was them he turned to about the blackmail.'

'All the fucking time, he knew them. Months we've been pursuing that complaint and he never said a thing. Not even when we saw them at the misconduct hearing.'

'You went?'

'With Sohail.' Jaw clenched now. 'The bastard. I could bloody well—' Faith thought better of it. 'He did have another phone, a cheap thing, twenty quid probably; disposable. He hid it in his office.'

Dixon followed her into the room at the back of the shop. She stepped up on to the chair, then on to the desk, before removing a light fitting.

'Better wear these,' he said, handing her a pair of latex gloves.

Faith was up on tiptoe now, feeling above the plasterboard, her hand through the hole in the ceiling.

The phone was small, no bigger than a box of matches. Thin too. A tiny screen and buttons. She dropped it in the evidence bag being held up by Dixon.

'Thank you,' he said.

'I saw him using it a couple of times. He'd always go quiet when I came in. I just thought he was seeing someone else, which was fine. I was just using him anyway.'

An hour was all Faith had asked for; time to get her stuff out of Sohail York's flat. An easy enough request to grant.

Dixon would be interviewing York again before he let him go. Briefly, probably, his answers almost certainly 'no comment' this time. The burner phone might get a rise, but Dixon wasn't holding his breath. It would take a while to get the call data off it. Longer than Charlesworth had given him anyway.

The ACC was still hovering, presumably to make sure Dixon really did let York go.

Louise dealt with the formalities, once York's solicitor had put in an appearance.

'Right, then, Sohail,' said Dixon. 'We have mobile phone data from Darren Canter and there are multiple calls to and from this phone.' He placed the evidence bag on the table in between them. 'What were those calls about?'

'My client has already told you he contacted Darren Canter to make the initial police report of the blackmail.'

'Why the burner phone?'

York cleared his throat. 'I wanted to keep it separate from my office phone in case it leaked to the press.'

'I can understand that,' replied Dixon. 'And that might explain the calls *before* the murders of Hampton and Paul. What about the seven calls that came *after*? What were those about?'

'No comment.'

'You knew they were dead at that point, because you made five of the calls *after* you'd spoken to the press and told everyone they'd been killed by a vigilante.'

'No comment.'

'Did you conspire with Darren Canter and Russell Lock to murder Justin Hampton and Andrew Paul?'

'No.'

'My client has already answered that question, Superintendent,' said the solicitor.

'Were your statements to the press an attempt to pervert the course of justice?'

'No.'

Dixon sighed. 'You're going to be released on bail, Sohail. That's if you'd like. You can also remain here in custody, if you'd prefer. It seems to me that Darren Canter, Russell Lock and Liam Smith being dead, you're next in line.'

York gave a humourless laugh. 'You are joking?'

'I'm not, as it happens.'

It took half an hour to complete the paperwork, Dixon watching from the ground floor window as York stepped out on to the pavement from the side entrance. His solicitor must have made a call or two, because there was a small crowd waiting to greet him. A couple of journalists too, but no sign of Faith.

'I have an announcement to make,' said York. 'Due to ongoing and intense police harassment and intimidation, I have no alternative but to resign as a candidate in the upcoming election for the new Police and Crime Commissioner. I feel very strongly that the people of Bristol need a voice, that Avon and Somerset Police do not police by consent – you only have to look at facial recognition technology being used on the streets without any of the proper safeguards in place to see that – and it had been my intention to act as a bridge between the community and the police, if I had been fortunate enough to have been elected. That will not now be possible. I apologise to anyone and everyone I have let down and very much hope that a suitable candidate from the Bristol community will step forward to take my place. Someone needs to hold the police to account.'

No doubt the press would've got that word for word, judging by the iPhones recording the speech, but it would be the 'intense police harassment and intimidation' that Charlesworth would be concerned about most of all. That said, the Police and Crime Commissioner's resignation might distract him a bit.

Napier had blamed it on the handling of the facial recognition trial, according to the piece on the *Bristol Post* website, and he took sole responsibility. Made no mention of the perverting the course of justice charge hanging over him.

Funny that.

'You've been a busy bunny, haven't you?' said Jane. She was standing in the open back door of the cottage when Dixon arrived home just before midnight, watching Monty sniffing around the wheels of his Land Rover. 'The PCC and that fellow Sohail York. I take it their resignations were down to you?'

'I didn't make the PCC access confidential information on the police national computer, didn't make him pervert the course of justice.'

'Not about the facial recognition trial, then?'

'No.'

'The other candidates must be shitting themselves. Unless anyone else comes forward, there'll only be two to choose from on the ballot paper. They've got a fifty-fifty chance of actually getting elected.'

'How was your day, dear?' asked Dixon, dutifully.

'Don't take the piss.' Jane took a step back to allow Dixon into the kitchen. 'Someone came to fit a smart meter and I took Monty for a walk.'

'You're going to have to stop doing that,' said Dixon. 'He pulls on the lead like a train; won't be doing you any good at all.'

'. . . *in your condition.*'

'Exactly.'

'That's why we went to Berrow beach. I just opened the boot and off he went.'

Dixon had lost track of the tides, not that Jane should be taking her car on to the sand anyway.

'You eaten?' she asked.

'Lou and I got something when we were out and about.'

'Getting anywhere with the case?'

'We've closed half of it.'

'Half the case, or one of the cases?'

'It's all connected. Separate motives; blackmail and the original events giving rise to the blackmail.'

'I've never been to the Glastonbury Festival.'

'We're too old now.'

'Speak for yourself. I'm only thirty-three.'

Chapter Thirty-Five

Detective Chief Superintendent Potter loitering in the reception area at Bridewell police station. At this time in the morning.

Not a good sign.

Dixon had been getting used to the commute into the middle of Bristol. Leave early, dodge the traffic; it took a fraction of the time. Meant that Monty only got a turn round the field behind the cottage, if he was lucky – no more riding along in the Land Rover either – but then he'd got Jane at home now. None of that leaving him alone with just the TV for company, that crestfallen look when Dixon closed the door behind him. The dog had been getting the hang of it all the same, beginning to understand that he'd always come back, simply because he always had.

'Can I have a word, Nick?' asked Potter, when Dixon negotiated the revolving doors.

Two workers had been outside on the pavement, pressure-washing more slogans from the pavement and front windows of the building. Nothing broken this time, though. No shattered glass.

'I think you should know DS Redgrave made a complaint to the ACC yesterday.' Potter's voice was hushed, just carrying over the whirr of the coffee machine. 'He said the team was lacking leadership and direction, that you were never in the incident room, always out and about.'

'That's the way I work,' replied Dixon. He was watching her trying to snap the lid on to a paper cup without spilling the coffee. 'And the team has a very clear direction. Everyone knows what they should be doing. Everything that should be being done, is being done.'

'That's what Charlesworth told him.'

It seemed to be a metaphor for life, really. This investigation too. One bit clicked into place only for it to pop up on the other side.

'These bloody things,' muttered Potter, giving up and dropping the lid in the bin. 'Look, Nick, it's just sour grapes, I suspect. We thought he might be trouble at the outset, loyal to DCI Hunt, but watch him. You're getting results now, and while you're doing that you're fine. Charlesworth will back you to the hilt.' Potter had balanced her coffee on the banister and was emptying a sachet of sugar into it. 'Just be careful, that's all I'm saying.'

'Thank you.'

A one hundred per cent record, according to the former PCC's personal assistant. They kept a league table. Who knew? More importantly, who cared?

'Who's the new PCC?' Dixon asked.

'The Assistant PCC will stand in until the election. It's only a matter of weeks away now anyway. He's put his name forward as a candidate as well.' She was stirring her coffee with a pen now. 'What's the plan for today?'

'The Glastonbury rape allegation is the focus now, so we're re-interviewing everyone connected with that. The football team; what's left of the victim's family. We should have the iCloud backups of Canter and Lock's phones by now as well. I'm hoping they've become available overnight.'

'Not forgetting the gunsmith,' said Potter.

'We're still tracking down the batch of polymer.'

'Good.'

They were in the lift now, Potter jabbing buttons two and four.

'Just watch your back. Get a quick result and I can put DCI Kendall in charge of tidying up; you can go and get on with your honeymoon.'

'What's left of it.'

'You're in early.'

'Staying in Bristol, Sir,' replied Mark, with a mischievous grin directed at the detective sitting opposite.

Her face reddened.

Dixon found himself staring at her. Shoulder-length dark hair, a few curls, blue eyes. Late twenties, possibly. Yes, just about the age Jessica Burroughs would be now, had she lived. Eighteen, ten years ago, would have made her twenty-eight now.

Had she lived.

'Have we had the inquest file on the rape victim's death?' he asked.

'Not yet, Sir,' replied Mark.

'Chase it up. Go and fetch it if you have to.'

'Yes, Sir.'

'What about the papers from Jamaica?'

'They promised them on the email today.'

'Why is it taking so long?'

Mark shrugged.

'Ring them again,' said Dixon.

'They'll be asleep over there now.'

'Wake them up.'

He turned for the kettle, the whispered 'Is he always like that?' just carrying over the dull thud of his footsteps on the carpet tiled floor.

No, he isn't.

Mark hadn't replied, unless he just shook his head. Or nodded. He might have nodded, possibly.

'We have got the iCloud backups, Sir,' he said. 'Came in overnight. Some very interesting stuff on Russell Lock's. Looks like he had an Apple Watch, but there was no mention of it being found on him.'

'It records all sorts of stuff in the Health app, Guv,' offered the officer sitting opposite Mark. She quickly corrected the 'Guv' to 'Sir'.

Dixon could imagine the look Mark must've given her.

'This is DC Helen McMahon, Sir,' said Mark.

'What sort of stuff?'

'Heart rate,' she replied. 'Distance walked, number of steps, flights of stairs.'

Dixon could see where it was leading. 'Anything tally with the night of the Hampton and Paul murders?'

'Increased heart rate from about eight onwards, rising to a pitch at about ten-thirty. Starts to fall after that and it looks like he went to sleep just before two in the morning. It recorded five hundred and thirty steps just after ten, which might tally with where Doris Capel said the car was parked and the walk from there to Hampton's flat. I was going to check that today.'

'Good work.' And it was.

'There's nothing for the night of his own murder because he hadn't been home. It only backs up when it connects to Wi-Fi.'

'Anything else?'

'There are a couple of interesting messages in Darren Canter's backup, Sir,' replied Mark. 'The number he's talking to is unidentified, so a burner, probably. But, the first one says, *Drop off £1000 in orange bag in bin at boardroom.weddings.duet.* I checked and it's a What3Words location. There's a bin in the corner of the car park at RSPB Greylake, out on the Levels.'

'The gunsmith.'

'Sounds like it. The next message is half an hour later and says, *Pick up orange bag under stone finishing.bring.lifestyle,* which is down a lane off the A372 at Middlezoy. Looks like a farm gateway between two drains. I'm guessing that's where he left the guns. Gave Canter the location when he'd picked up the money.'

'Which means the gunsmith was in the Greylake car park between those two times.'

'Ahead of you there, Sir,' said Mark. 'I'm checking the nearest traffic cameras now.'

'What's the significance of the orange bag, I wonder?'

'Visibility, probably.'

'A Sainsbury's carrier bag, possibly,' said Helen. 'The nearest one is Bridgwater.'

'Any location data on the mobile number he was messaging?' asked Dixon.

'The request has gone in, but I wouldn't hold your breath. If he's this careful, then he's unlikely to have switched it on at home. That would be too easy.'

'Have you thought any more about Faith Beech and her family, Sir?' asked Helen. 'She's got motive for killing Darren Canter and Russell Lock, surely? So have her parents.'

'Why would they kill Liam Smith, though?' asked Mark, saving Dixon the trouble. 'He had nothing to do with the arrest on New Year's Eve. He wasn't even a copper.'

The incident room was starting to fill up, officers drifting in, most carrying large paper cups of coffee with lids securely in place.

The phones were oddly silent, although everyone seemed to be checking something on their mobiles. Facebook, probably.

Mark snatched the phone off his desk when it rang. 'Mark Pearce. He's here. Really? Fuck. Yeah, I'll tell him.'

'What is it, Mark?' asked Dixon, when he rang off.

'Sohail York is dead, Sir. Single gunshot wound to the head.'

Chapter Thirty-Six

Dixon hadn't been to Sohail York's flat before. He'd got a warrant, sent in Scientific Services, but he hadn't seen it for himself.

Faith Beech had been there the night before, collecting her stuff, she'd said. It would be interesting to know if that was all she did, and she'd be waiting at Bridewell for him when he got back, whenever that might be. She'd just have to be patient.

She had motive for killing Darren Canter and Russell Lock. Sohail York too. She'd certainly been angry enough the night before. But what about Liam Smith?

Dixon was missing something. That much was painfully obvious. To him, and everyone else for that matter.

He'd waited for Louise to arrive before setting off. Missed the rush hour too; the worst of it anyway.

It would be an interesting conversation with Charlesworth when the time came, although he suspected the ACC would be keeping out of his way for a few days. Every cloud, and all that.

'Bet Charlesworth's kicking himself,' Louise had said.

'Saves me the bother.'

'If we'd kept York in custody, he'd still be alive.'

There hadn't been much Dixon could say to that. And the worst part about it – well, not the worst part, a man was dead, after all – was the nature of the chain of command; people would think it had been his decision to release York. That he was somehow responsible for the man's death.

Louise knew the truth, though. And so did Charlesworth.

Not that it mattered.

Several sets of traffic lights had given him plenty of time to think on the way.

Who was next?

It was one question that leapt out at him, a patrol car despatched to sit outside the house of Russell Lock's father. A long shot, possibly, but the ex-police officer responsible for persuading Jessica Burroughs to drop the case seemed next in line, if someone was intent on revenge. And they certainly seemed to be.

The three young men who'd taken part in the rape.

Now, the man who'd supplied the drugs.

Simple revenge. There was no more powerful motive. Not even greed. Not in Dixon's experience anyway, and he had plenty. Too much.

'It's the first floor flat,' Louise said, breaking the silence.

Dixon had been allowed through the police cordon with a wave of his warrant card, not even winding down the window.

Roadblocks at both ends of the street. Scientific Services vans, a tent already blocking the communal entrance, officers in overalls carrying in equipment. Arc lamps had been set up inside the flat, the telltale bright white light streaming out through a gap in the curtains in the bay window at the front.

It was a gloomy morning. In more ways than one.

The pathologist was there, leaning on the back of his car, snapping on a pair of latex overshoes.

Hari Patel looked up from his clipboard, gave a visible sigh.

Dixon was old enough to remember the good old days, when it had been *his* crime scene. The SIO's crime scene. Not any more. Some bright spark had put a stop to that. Now there was a gatekeeper, with an irritating habit of getting there first.

'Overalls are in the box,' said Hari, when Dixon walked across the road. 'You'll have to wait until Scientific are ready for you.'

'You been in?'

'Whoever killed him got past the Entryphone. So, either he knew them and let them in, or someone else did. You'll need to check with the other flats. They've all been told to stay indoors for the time being.'

'The front door might have been open,' said Louise.

'It's unlikely at night,' replied Hari. 'But you'll need to ask the residents.'

'Where is he?' asked Dixon.

'In the hall of his flat. The front door is standing open, so it looks like he opened it and *bang*. Neighbour from the top floor flat found him this morning when she came down for her milk.'

'Can Lou go in to speak to the neighbours?'

Another sigh. 'Yes, go on,' replied Hari. 'Overshoes and don't go near flat three. Remind the residents they still can't come out.'

Five buttons on the Entryphone. Dixon could see that from the back of the tent, which was as far as he'd been allowed in. And he'd only got in that far because of the rain that had started falling. Two flats on each floor, flat five in the rafters.

York had first floor front, with the bay windows.

'Parking's round the back,' said Hari. 'There's nothing in flat three's space.'

'He hasn't got a car,' replied Dixon.

Louise hadn't reappeared by the time Dixon was allowed in. The pathologist, Leo Petersen, was already in there, kneeling on a stepping plate adjacent to Sohail York's head. 'Single gunshot wound to the head.' He spoke without looking up. 'No exit wound.'

Dixon could see that for himself, a hole in the middle of York's forehead; no blood spatter to speak of, no blood and brains soaking into the carpet underneath the body.

York was lying on his back, his hands by his sides. Dead before he hit the ground, almost certainly.

'Been dead between ten and twelve hours, I'd say.' Petersen still hadn't looked up. 'So, that's late last night, between ten and midnight.'

Dixon had done the calculation; thought it best not to say so, all the same.

Louise was standing out on the landing now. 'You only let people you know in at that time of night,' she said. 'Sometimes wish we had an Entryphone at home. Our first flat had one. First morning after we'd moved in, we got Jehoved. It was useful during elections too.'

Petersen looked up. 'There are no powder burns, so the gun barrel wasn't pressed to his forehead. What else do you want to know?' he asked, turning to Dixon.

'Who did it?'

'Yeah, right.'

Barefoot, jeans and a 'Vote Sohail York' T-shirt. Not gone to bed, by the looks of things. The television was still on in the living room, but the screen had gone dark.

'The set top box switches itself off after a while,' said the Scientific Services officer prowling around the room, camera in hand.

There was a tumbler on a glass coffee table, in front of a brown leather sofa. Dregs in the bottom of the glass, next to a bottle of Irish whiskey. Half empty – everything was half empty at the moment.

No phone anywhere, apart from the landline, but then it was still at High Tech. Dixon had been promised call and messaging data off it today. Too late, as it turned out.

'There was a camera lens on the Entryphone,' he said.

'Doesn't record.'

'Typical.'

'Next door's got a doorbell camera. That might've picked something up. There are several cars outside with dashcams too, motion activated, probably.'

'Got any eggs?' asked Dixon. 'You can teach me to suck them while we're about it.'

'Sorry.' The Scientific Services officer shrugged. 'Just trying to help.'

Seemed vain, did York. All of the photographs on the wall were of him doing something: water-skiing; there was a framed centrefold from the *Bristol Post*; a feature about him announcing his candidacy in the Police and Crime Commissioner election. Some of the quotes had even been highlighted.

'A dedicated servant of the community.'

'Role model for youngsters growing up on the streets of Bristol.'

Some of the people, all of the time.

But then they hadn't had access to the Police National Computer. Unlike the PCC.

Biding his time until nominations closed; an anonymous press release and suddenly Napier would have had one less candidate to worry about on the ballot paper. Dixon wondered whether the Assistant PCC knew about the 'opposition research'? Whether the plan had been cooked up between them?

The Assistant had been appointed by the PCC. Terence Lake, although Dixon learned a long time ago that people weren't who they said they were. Ever.

They're who we know them to be.

And that made a world of difference.

An Assistant PCC, out of work after the election, now the PCC who had appointed him had resigned; suddenly finding himself standing in, the incumbent, taking Napier's place on the ballot paper too.

'You finished in there, Sir?' Hari was standing out on the landing now, looking along the corridor into the living room. 'Only, it's three max and I've got a mortuary technician who wants to come in and photograph the body.'

'What do we know about Terence Lake, the Assistant PCC?' asked Dixon, a few minutes later. Louise was sheltering in the tent outside, watching him wriggle out of his hazmat suit.

'Nothing, really.'

'Let's find out everything we can about him. Then we'll go to Portishead, see what he's got to say for himself.'

Louise frowned. 'Yes, Sir.'

'Let's have the *former* PCC in too.'

'The ACC will love that.'

'What have we got for house to house?'

'There are six from uniform and DS Redgrave is here with four of his team. He's organising them now – looking for cameras, before you ask.'

Not that it would do any good. Everyone knew to hide their face, these days. Perhaps not in the heat of the moment, but this was their fourth murder, and the killer was getting good at it. Knock on the door, raise the gun, pull the trigger. There couldn't have been any hesitation; York hadn't even had a chance to turn away.

No hesitation.

A professional hit, possibly. That was something he hadn't seriously considered; it had crossed his mind, but he'd dismissed it. After all, what professional would take the risk of a plastic gun exploding in his hand?

'Have we ruled out a professional?' he asked.

'I thought so.' Louise looked surprised. 'Why would they be using 3D printed guns? They'd use a real one, surely?'

301

It was a good point, and explained why it hadn't been addressed before. 'They make a different sound, it's low velocity, there might be all sorts of reasons. Easy to dispose of.'

'I'll check with Mark. I don't think our informants came up with anything, but that's never conclusive, is it?'

'Don't bother,' said Dixon. He rolled his overalls into a ball, dropped them in an open plastic crate. 'There's rage here. You can feel it. This killer hasn't employed someone to do it for them. The case is about revenge and they're doing it themselves; relishing every minute of it.'

Chapter Thirty-Seven

Charlesworth's text arrived when Dixon was driving back to Bridewell police station:

Montpelier Room at 1.30, press conference at 2. Thank you.

Louise read it out, placing his phone back on the dashboard, the charging cable still plugged in.

'You've got ten minutes,' she said.

Just enough time to park and get a sandwich from the canteen.

'Any news?' asked Charlesworth, when Dixon sat down. He ripped open his sandwich carton, scattering grated cheese across the conference table.

'We haven't made an arrest, if that's what you mean, Sir?' he replied.

'It's not going to be an easy press conference. There'll be lots of questions about the PCC, his resignation, the election, Sohail York, that sort of thing. I'll make it clear at the outset that we won't be answering any *political* questions, and the reasons for the PCC's resignation are entirely a matter for him. You can take any questions on the investigation. Apart from that, if I have to shut it down early, I will.'

'Four murders outstanding and we're still no nearer to making an arrest,' said Vicky Thomas. The press officer was never usually far from Charlesworth's side, following him around like his shadow. Or a bad smell, possibly.

'Six,' said Dixon. 'If you include Hampton and Paul, but we know who killed them.'

'Two of our own,' said Potter, not that anyone needed reminding.

'I'm not entirely convinced this press conference is such a good idea,' said Charlesworth, looking around the room for some encouragement. 'At most I think we should make a statement, but not take any questions at all.'

'You can try that, but there's someone on the loose with a 3D printed gun and the press are bound to have questions,' replied Vicky Thomas.

The next twenty minutes were spent cobbling together the statement.

'What can we tell them about progress in the investigation?' Potter asked.

'Nothing.'

'The usual flannel it is then.' Charlesworth was avoiding eye contact, staring at the notes in front of him as he slid his pen into his inside jacket pocket. 'Look, Nick, I feel I owe you an apology. You wanted to keep Sohail York in cust—'

Dixon raised his hand, silencing him mid-sentence.

'Well, if it comes up at the press conference I will deal with it. All right?'

It turned out that Bridewell had a purpose-built press suite, Dixon's phone buzzing as he sat down in front of the cameras.

A text from Jane:

You're live on the Beeb! Jx

Best poker face on.

Charlesworth made the introductions, read out the prepared statement, finished with a reminder they wouldn't be answering political questions.

'How close are you to making an arrest?'

Dixon didn't know any of the journalists in Bristol. He knew a few from Bridgwater and Taunton – knew to avoid them would have been more accurate, possibly.

'We have several lines of enquiry, and expect to be making an arrest in the near future. In the meantime, I would ask anyone with any information to come forward. In particular, we would very much like to speak to the person in this photograph.' Dixon turned, gestured to a screen behind him. 'This image was captured on a doorbell camera in the vicinity of the murder last night of Sohail York. We are keen to identify this person and eliminate them from our enquiries.'

Always nice to have something to give them.

'Whose decision was it to release Mr York from custody last night?'

'Mine,' replied Charlesworth. 'Made in collaboration with the investigation team.'

Twat.

'Can you comment on his allegation of intense police harassment and intimidation?'

'Mr York was under investigation in connection with a number of offences arising from events that took place at the Glastonbury Festival ten years ago,' replied Charlesworth. 'He had been interviewed several times and search warrants executed at his home and office. Those were legitimate enquiries, but he was perfectly at liberty to characterise them in the way that he did.'

Dixon couldn't have put it better himself.

'What about whoever is printing these guns?'

'Our forensic team has established that the polymer used to print the weapon or weapons used in the murders came from the same batch, and we are tracing everyone who bought from that batch,' said Dixon. 'If any member of the public has purchased either Taulman Bridge nylon filament or e Tech PLA Plus within the last two years, they are asked to make themselves known to the investigation so that they can be eliminated from our enquiries.'

'Is there a serial killer on the loose?'

That old gem. The press do love giving killers a label, thought Dixon. 'Not in the conventional sense, no,' he said. 'There is nothing random about these murders.'

'Why did Hugo Napier resign?'

'That is a political question,' replied Charlesworth, stepping in. 'And I'd refer you to Mr Napier for his reasons.'

'Was he involved in the murder of Sohail York?'

Charlesworth looked at Dixon, his eyebrows raised.

'I can't comment on individuals,' replied Dixon. 'And it would be irresponsible of me to do so. Whether and, if so, when an arrest is made, an announcement will be forthcoming.'

Charlesworth stood up, turned for the door at the side of the small platform. Dixon followed.

'I was expecting you to say no, when they asked you about Napier's involvement in York's murder.'

'I can't.'

'You're not seriously expecting me to believe that Hugo . . .' Charlesworth clearly thought better of it. 'I've had the Chief Con on the phone. Asking me to consider whether the time has come for a more experienced officer to take over the investigation. He's concerned by the public order issues that have arisen.'

'Aren't we all?'

'I told him we weren't there yet.'

'Thank you, Sir.'

'You haven't got long before his patience runs out.' Charlesworth shook his head. 'You're even going after the Assistant PCC now, I gather?'

'He's going to be on the ballot paper in place of Napier, which itself raises questions. Convenient too, don't you think? Selected by committee last minute; no time for a ballot of local party members. I'm also making legitimate enquiries into the murder of one of his opponents in the election.'

'And you're no nearer finding the gunsmith. We have to get those guns off the streets, Nick.'

'Until the next moron buys himself a printer and sets himself up in business.'

'You haven't forgotten Faith Beech is downstairs.'

Dixon hadn't, as it happened, but it was a timely reminder all the same.

'Why am I here?' she demanded, standing up sharply when Dixon and Louise walked into the interview room.

'You've heard what happened to Sohail?'

'Yes.'

'That's why you're here. You're helping us with our enquiries.'

'I wasn't given a lot of choice.'

Dixon tried a disarming smile, not that it did any good. He gestured to the chair, sat down opposite. 'Would you like a solicitor?'

'I haven't done anything wrong,' replied Faith, sitting back down nervously. 'Why would I need a solicitor?'

An answer given by two categories of interviewee, in Dixon's experience at least. Those who were genuinely innocent and, at the same time, naive enough to believe the police would get it right.

Then, the more interesting category perhaps, those who were in it up to their necks and arrogant enough to believe they could beat the system.

'Where were you last night between ten and midnight?' he asked.

Faith folded her arms tightly across her chest. 'Aren't you going to caution me?'

She had worked in York's office long enough to know the score. Long enough to have developed a deep mistrust of the police, if she hadn't already had one. All the more strange then that she didn't want a solicitor.

'I can if you want me to,' replied Dixon. 'Will if I need to.'

'I collected my stuff from Sohail's flat, like I told you I was going to do. There wasn't a lot. One bag. Then I went home. My parents will confirm.'

'What time did you get there?'

'I don't know. Seven, maybe. Eight at the latest.'

York had been in custody until gone eight. 'How did you feel when you found out about Sohail's involvement with Darren Canter and Russell Lock?'

'Betrayed. Bloody angry. You know that.' Faith shrugged. 'It's why I moved out of his flat. Not that I was living there. I hadn't moved in or anything, just stayed there most of the time. And I'm still angry, if you must know.'

'Did you kill him?'

'No, I didn't.'

'What about Canter and Lock?'

'I was with Sohail that night. You checked with him, and my parents.'

'You were in a relationship with Sohail. And alibis given by family members can be taken with a pinch of salt.'

'When will I get my phone back?'

'When we've finished with it, Faith,' replied Dixon. 'Did you give them the passcode?'

'Yes.'

'That'll make it quicker.'

'What are they looking for?'

'Evidence.'

Faith shifted in her seat. 'They won't find any, because there isn't any. I get it. I do. There's a motive for me killing Canter and Lock. Sohail too, after he betrayed me, betrayed Bryony. But what about the other bloke? Why would I kill him? I don't even know his name.'

'Tell me about your parents.'

'What about them?'

'Their health.'

'My father is in the early stages of motor neurone disease. He can just about walk, but uses the wheelchair to get around. He's had a few falls, so . . .' Her voice tailed off into a shake of the head. 'My mother has glaucoma, so sits in the dark. Has to wear special glasses if she goes out. They're more like goggles, actually.'

'Does the name Jessica Burroughs mean anything to you?'

'No.'

'Have you ever been to the Glastonbury Festival?'

'I go every year. Why?'

'Where d'you stay?'

'South Park Two, usually. It's miles from the stage, but it means you can find a space easily enough. If you get there early, anyway.'

'Your first year?'

'Coldplay were headlining.'

'Who did you go with?'

'A couple of friends. We took Bryony that year, I think. She came with us a couple of times; struggled with the large crowds, but enjoyed it. She said she did, anyway.'

'Do you remember an assault that took place in a tent on South Park Two?'

'Yeah, there were rumours going around that someone had been raped, but I never knew who or anything like that. Never saw any police either. That's all, really. Then the festival just ended and everyone went home. That was the last I heard about it.'

'The names of the friends you went with that year?'

'Emma Simpson and Laila Napier. Laila Stevens she is now; got married. She's a solicitor at the Community Law Project. Helping us sue you over Bryony's death.'

'You've been a busy bunny again,' said Jane, when Dixon opened the back door of the cottage just before six. Monty had his face buried in a bowl of food, pushing it around the kitchen floor. The dog looked up, wagged his tail, then carried on eating.

'Thank you for your text message. It came at just the right time.'

Jane stifled a chuckle. 'Your tie was crooked.'

'No it wasn't.'

'Dad came over and put up the cot, so you don't have to worry about that.'

'Has he been out?' Monty had finished his food and was now jumping up at Dixon.

Priorities.

'We went to the beach earlier, but didn't stay long. It pissed down with rain and I wasn't getting wet.'

'Pub?'

'If you must.'

A pint of beer, a tonic water, fish and chips twice. Nice and easy. Their usual table in the corner, by the fire, had been free too.

'Any nearer finding whoever it is printing these damn guns?' asked Jane.

'Not really. We know he's charging a thousand pounds each for them. And that he's using What3Words – drop off the money here, pick up the gun there. That's about it, really. Remote locations, obviously, so the camera coverage is non-existent.'

'Nothing on the batch of polymer?'

'We've interviewed twenty-seven people so far. More this afternoon, probably. I'll have a look in the morning.'

'How would you go about buying a gun?' asked Jane.

'You've got to know the right people.' Dixon took a swig of beer. 'Two uniformed officers on the streets of Bristol would've had no trouble.'

'What about the ammunition?'

'Standard nine millimetre, according to Ballistics. Open up the cartridges, take out some of the powder to reduce the velocity. That's if they're new. It's not difficult, if you know what you're doing.'

'Have you tried gun clubs?'

'That was the first thing they did. Weeks ago.'

'At least Hunt managed to think of that.' Jane took a sip of tonic water, turned up her nose. 'What about the rest of the case? There'll soon be no one left to be the PCC.'

'Turns out Napier's daughter is the solicitor helping sue the police over that death in custody on New Year's Eve.'

'He kept that quiet.'

'Charlesworth knew she was a local solicitor, but didn't know what she did.' Another swig of beer. 'She was at Glastonbury too. Same campsite.'

'Perhaps you're getting somewhere after all?'

'Doesn't feel like it. I was just beginning to narrow it down a bit and then suddenly the list of suspects gets longer than it was before.'

'And you still don't know whether it's two cases or one.'

'You know just what to say.'

Jane raised her glass. 'Thank you,' she said. 'It's part of being a devoted wife.'

'Now you're taking the piss.'

'There'll be something.' Jane kicked off her shoes, resting her feet on Monty who was stretched out in front of the fire. 'Something that connects the whole thing up. You've just got to find it.'

'Yeah.'

'You've probably already seen it, just haven't realised the significance of it yet. That's the way it usually works, isn't it?'

Their food arrived with the inevitable reminder the plates were hot. They ate in silence, Dixon mulling over what Jane had said. *Probably already seen it.* Perfectly possible, of course. He'd read everything, seen everything. Taken it all in, discarded the bits that didn't seem relevant, hung on to the rest. Jumbled, maybe, but it was all there. Somewhere. Going round and round in his head.

Something that connects the whole thing up.

'The new smart meter's fun,' Jane said, as they strolled the fifty yards home, half an hour later. 'You can see what you're using in real time, how much it's costing.'

'You need to get out more,' replied Dixon, idly.

'Bit difficult at the moment.'

'Course it is, sorry.'

'Actually, I'm loving it, but don't tell anyone I said so. We need to get some more DVDs though. I must've watched *Went the Day Well?* about eight times. I can tell you what they're going to say next.'

'I thought you'd subscribed to Netflix? And there's always daytime telly.'

'Piss off.' Jane waited while Dixon opened the back door of the cottage, then she stepped inside and switched on the light. 'See,

312

look. You get this screen thingy and it tells you how much you've spent. One pound ninety-seven today so far.'

'All day?' he asked. He was outside in the yard, waiting while Monty cocked his leg on the wheel of his Land Rover.

'That's the fridge, telly, a few lights but they're LEDs, and I did a load of washing. Charged my phone too, come to think of it.'

'One pound ninety-seven?'

'It's one pound ninety-eight now.' Jane was filling the kettle, the noise carrying through the open back door. 'That's just the electricity. There's gas too, don't forget. I had the heating on all day. We'll have to keep the cottage warm for the baby.'

Dixon appeared in the kitchen. 'Got to go. Sorry,' he said, kissing her on the cheek. 'I've got Monty in the Land Rover.'

'Where are you going?'

'To arrest the gunsmith.'

Chapter Thirty-Eight

Burtle.

One junction south on the M5, then east on the A39. Twenty minutes, at most, one hand on the steering wheel, foot flat on the floor, his phone pressed to his ear.

No good ringing Mark Pearce, he'd be getting his leg over in Bristol.

'Louise Willmott.' She sounded sleepy, but then Dixon had told her to go home and get an early night.

'Lou, I know who the gunsmith is. I'm on my way there now. I'll need backup. Armed Response. No blue lights on the approach, no sirens. He's going to be armed, so I'll wait for them before I go in. Ask everyone to rendezvous in the pub car park, The Duck at Burtle, used to be the Tom Mogg.'

'Who is it?'

'You remember we went to see that custody officer, Ed Grady?'

'The one who looked after you when you spent a night in the cells?'

'That's him. He's suspended pending the IOPC investigation into the death of Faith Beech's sister, making a bit of money on the side.'

'How d'you know?'

'He's got a smart meter. We went to see him at ten in the morning and the electricity reading was eleven pounds twenty-seven. He's running a 3D printer in there. He's not going to be using that much electricity sitting up all night on his games console, is he?'

'Yeah, but—'

'Think about it. He knows Canter and Lock, doesn't he?'

'I'll make the call.'

'We'll need uniform to close the roads too.'

'Leave it with me.'

Dixon had time for a beer, and the pub was open. Instead he was standing in the rain, watching the blue lights out on the A39, listening to the sirens, all going dark when they turned off the main road. At least that message had got through.

Three marked cars in convoy. Dixon recognised the one at the back: Armed Response. They were going to earn their money tonight.

Chief Inspector Bateman climbed out of the lead car. 'I thought I'd better come in case there's a siege,' he said.

'He lives alone, so I'm not expecting him to have anyone in there.'

'Do you know him?' asked Bateman.

'We've met.'

He nodded his understanding. 'I've always thought he was bit odd, to be honest. Seemed to enjoy his job a bit too much, if you know what I mean?'

Dixon had been on the receiving end of it, but resisted the temptation.

'It's down there on the right,' said Bateman. 'I've got a car coming in from the other side of the village to block the lane at that end. We'll block it from this end, then send the AR team in.' He popped open the boot of the patrol car. 'I brought you this,' he

315

said, handing a set of body armour to Dixon. 'I'm guessing you'll want to be right behind them when they go in.'

They crept along the front of the terrace of cottages. Two Armed Response officers in front, then came Dixon, with two uniformed officers behind him. The lead AR officer was carrying the battering ram, his assault rifle slung over his shoulder.

It had been an easy decision. There'd be no warning given.

Either side of the front door now, the lead AR officer counting down silently, mouthing the numbers. Then he stood up; one swing of the battering ram and the door frame splintered, the door swinging open.

'Armed police! Come out with your hands up!'

They moved into the hall, kicked open the door of the front room.

'Clear!'

'There's a doorbell camera,' muttered Dixon. 'He'd have known we were coming, probably got an alert on his phone. Fuck it.'

'Clear!' shouted an AR officer from the kitchen at the back.

Dixon was following the other up the stairs.

The bathroom was standing open, the lights off. The loft hatch on the landing was open too, the ladder pulled up, if there was one, although it looked possible to stand on the banister and climb up.

'Armed police! Come out with your hands up!'

Front room first, the officer kicking the door open. He checked under the bed, the wardrobe. 'Clear!'

Back room it is, then, thought Dixon. That's where the 3D printer had to be. There was nowhere else. Not even a shed in the courtyard at the back.

Another shout of 'armed police', another door kicked in.

The AR officer appeared in the doorway, his machine gun slung down by his side. 'Clear, Sir, I'm afraid. But you're in the right place. Have a look. I'll check the loft.'

And there it was. A square pine table with a large glass case sitting on it, cables running to a computer on a camping table. The curtains were closed, held together with pegs.

The nozzle was moving from side to side on a steel rod, what looked like the handle of a Songbird gradually appearing beneath it, layer by layer.

Two more plastic handguns were lying on the table next to the computer keyboard, Dixon picking one up in his latex gloved hand as he listened to the AR officer pull the ladder down from the loft, then climb the aluminium rungs. 'Loft's clear too. There's no one here. It's open to next door, though. Bollocks.'

Dixon pushed the barrel out of the side of one of the guns. Loaded. He pulled back the hammer; a firing pin too. Looked like a nail.

Nice.

Gun parts were strewn all over the table and mantelpiece. Triggers, several barrels, some white, one pink. An open box of cartridge cases. There were several spools of PLA in different colours, a packet of nails, a bag of elastic bands. A drill, files, sandpaper, squashed tubes of epoxy glue. Cable ties.

A pair of chainmail gloves.

'You need to come and see this, Sir!' There was an urgency in the AR officer's voice, coming from the front room now. 'There are some pictures you need to see.'

Several, as it turned out, Sellotaped to the mirror on a chest of drawers next to the bed.

Several pictures of Jane; most taken from a distance, covertly, some in the canteen at Express Park, some outside; some even more recent, enough for the bump to be visible.

Dixon ran to the back room, stood in front of a cork noticeboard that was hanging over the mantelpiece on a picture hook, a yellow Post-it note pinned to it. A What3Words location.

He slid his phone out of his jacket pocket, took a screenshot of it, then opened the app.

jetted.handyman.quote

'Sir, the helicopter is reporting a motorcycle leaving the village at speed.' The shout came from the bottom of the stairs. 'It's going north-west towards Mark Causeway.'

He clicked on the microphone, said the words out loud.

Three options. The first – the exact match – near Brent Knoll. He clicked on it, a sick feeling rising in the pit of his stomach, watching as the map zoomed in, the line pointing to a cottage on Brent Street.

Opposite the Red Cow.

His cottage.

Chapter Thirty-Nine

Accelerating hard on the A39 now, orders given as he'd sprinted back to his Land Rover, parked outside the police roadblock, mercifully.

The Armed Response vehicle had overtaken him on the run down to Bawdrip, and was already out of sight before he reached the traffic lights. The helicopter was no longer in view. God willing it still had the motorcycle in sight.

Dixon had his phone pressed to his ear, but there was no reply from Jane. Come to think of it, the washing machine had been on when he left. Cheaper at night, she'd said.

And she was probably watching *Went the Day Well?* for the umpteenth time.

Out on the M5 now, two patrol cars flying past him, sirens wailing, blue lights flashing. More coming in from the north as he approached the off-slip.

Braked late at the top of the slip road, short at the best of times. He followed a patrol car through the roadworks, went across the grass to avoid the roadblock at the junction with Brent Street. Hammer down again, engine screaming in protest.

Bateman had beaten him to it, set up a cordon. And there was no getting past that. Dixon screeched to a halt in front of the patrol cars blocking the road, slid his hand in to his coat pocket, pulled back the hammer on the Songbird, cocking it. Then he pushed Monty into the back of the Land Rover.

'You're not coming, matey. You'll only get yourself killed.'

Walking towards the roadblock, Armed Response officers squatting down behind the bonnets of the cars, assault rifles pointing along Brent Street, his cottage maybe a hundred yards away. More cars were parked a hundred yards or so beyond it, their headlights illuminating a motorcycle, lying on its side on the pavement.

Right outside.

'You can't go any further,' said Bateman, his hand squarely in the middle of Dixon's chest.

'I've got body armour on. Watch me.'

He pushed past Bateman, only token resistance given. He knew Dixon was going in, he'd seen him do it before.

He walked along Brent Street, watching out of the corner of his eye as an officer took up position in the car park of the Red Cow behind a van, a loudhailer in his hand. A negotiator, presumably.

Negotiate?

Fuck off.

No room for hesitation. Not this time. Dixon walked straight up to the front door, turned the handle.

He saw Jane first. Kneeling down at the bottom of the stairs. A figure in black was standing behind her.

'Here he is,' said Grady, making sure Dixon could see the Songbird in his hand. Bright pink, cocked.

The television was still on, a young Thora Hird scribbling messages on eggs.

'Help!'

It was a familiar feeling.

Jane's knees were apart, both hands between her legs. Sobbing, a cut on her cheek, her hair straggled, tangled, ripped from its usual ponytail and matted with blood. She looked up at Dixon, pleading, trembling, raised her right hand, her fingers covered in blood.

Her own blood.

'Don't do anything stupid, Ed,' said Dixon. 'All you're facing at the moment is the manufacture and sale of illegal firearms.'

'Twelve years. I looked it up.' Grady's curly dark hair was wet, matted with blood, and he kept touching the side of his head, looking at the palm of his hand.

Jane had hit him with something.

Red in the face, nostrils flaring. 'And you'll try and pin conspiracy to murder on me, so that's a life sentence, isn't it?'

There was a vase on the floor, the flowers Jane's mother had brought that afternoon strewn on the sofa, water soaking into the rug. Solid cut glass; as good a weapon as any.

'Whose idea was it, printing the guns?'

'Darren's. I met him at the misconduct hearing, said I'd got a 3D printer. He offered me a grand for two, so I thought, why the fuck not? Downloaded the instructions off the internet. Easy, really.'

'Two?'

'Made a few more since then, mind. Supply and demand, isn't it?'

'What's this all about then?' Dixon looked at Grady quizzically. 'Have I offended you somehow? In a past life, perhaps?'

The curtains were drawn and Dixon had closed the door behind him, so no one outside could see what was going on. Shame. One of the AR officers might have taken the shot, put Grady out of his misery.

'You've got it all, haven't you? Everything I ever wanted.'

'What?'

'Her,' replied Grady, jabbing the back of Jane's head with the barrel of the gun. Her head jolted forward and she let out a soft groan. 'She never gave me a second look. And now she's married *you*.' He leaned over Jane's shoulder, shouted in her ear. 'What the fuck did you have to go and do that for?'

'That's just an excuse. You've fucked up and now you're trying to make out it's someone else's fault.'

'And you, you prick.' Grady was pointing the gun at Dixon's head now.

Fine by me.

'You never batted an eyelid when you were in custody. Most people shit themselves.'

'I'm a solicitor. And I was innocent.'

'All night I watched you on the screen.'

'That's more than you did for Bryony Beech.'

Angry people made mistakes. Dixon knew that. And if Nigel Cole could pull the trigger when he had to, so could he. Someone was going to have to take the shot. *He* was going to have to take the shot. All it was about now was timing.

'It was New Year's Eve, for fuck's sake.'

'You were the custody officer on duty. Her welfare was your responsibility.'

Next time he puts his hand up to the side of his head, thought Dixon.

'You need to get that looked at,' he said. 'Looks nasty.'

Grady put his left hand up to the side of his hand, stared at the blood in the palm of his hand.

Dixon took his chance, slid his hand into his coat pocket, drew the Songbird and pointed it at Grady's head.

'If I'm going anywhere, I'm taking her with me,' said Grady, grinning. He was pointing the gun at the back of Jane's head now. 'You're destroying my life, I'm going to fuck up yours. I'm looking at life anyway.'

Actually, you're looking at death.

Then Dixon heard the shot.

Chapter Forty

Heard the shot before he pulled the trigger. Felt like it anyway.

Grady fell backwards, blood spurting from his neck. He dropped his gun, clutching at his throat with both hands, the blood pumping, spraying up the wall. He was lying on the bottom few stairs now, coughing, gurgling.

Bleeding out.

Jane reached forward, trying to pull herself up on the arm of the sofa. She was reaching out for Dixon's hand, leaning over, doubled up in pain. Groaning.

'Listen to me,' she said, taking his hand, squeezing, blood oozing from between her fingers. 'If they find out you brought the gun with you, you're in deep shit.'

'It was by his computer.'

'Did anyone see you take it?'

'No.'

'Then he turned up here with two guns, one in each hand. We fought and he dropped one on the rug.' Jane winced. 'In front of the television. You saw it, picked it up and shot him. All right?'

Silence.

'I'm not having my husband, and the father of my child, in prison.'

'All right.'

The gurgling had stopped now, Grady dead. The loudhailer outside crackled into life.

'Is everyone all right in there?'

Jane looked up at Dixon, pain etched on her face. 'The gun was on the rug. You saw it when you came in, picked it up,' she said, spelling it out. 'The rest of the story stays the same. Say it.'

'The gun was on the rug. I picked it up.'

'Good. Now get me to the hospital.'

'3275 Superintendent Dixon,' he shouted, through the open front door of the cottage. He was holding Jane up, his arm clamped around her shoulders. 'Grady is dead. The scene is secure. I'm coming out with Detective Sergeant Winter.' Then he scooped up her legs, carried her over the threshold, out rather than in, into the glare of the lights and rain. 'I need to get her to a hospital.'

Bateman had run forward, Armed Response officers still aiming their weapons at the cottage. 'There's an ambulance on the way.'

Jane was resting her head on Dixon's shoulder. 'I'm haemorrhaging. I need a maternity unit. Weston's nearest.'

'A patrol car in that case,' offered Bateman. 'Williams is pursuit trained and you can blue-light it.'

Eleven minutes. Just enough time for Dixon to ring ahead.

Jane was lying on the back seat, her head in his lap, her eyes closing.

'Stay awake,' he whispered, gently tapping her cheek with his fingertips.

Siren wailing for the last mile or two, the car screeched to a halt, the rear door opened from the outside and an unconscious Jane was pulled from his arms, carried on to a waiting trolley.

'Are you the husband?' asked one of the nurses.

'Yes.'

'We've got an operating theatre on standby and she'll be going straight in. We've got to get the baby out. Have you got someone who can come and wait with you?'

That had been one text message, Poland's response immediate.

On way.

Chapter Forty-One

The waiting room was much the same as any other. Armchairs around the walls, a coffee table covered in shredded magazines. Noticeboards covered in posters only the truly bored bother to read.

Dixon heard the footsteps in the corridor, then the familiar ping of a text message arriving. Poland walked in, holding his phone.

'It says there's a body, gives your home address.'

It took about ten minutes to give him the whole story, from the top. The race home from Burtle, finding the gun on the rug in front of the television, pulling the trigger.

Killing a man.

Jane unconscious in the back of the car.

Surgery.

Poland tapped out a reply to the text message. 'I've told them to send my assistant, Davidson,' he said, dropping his phone into his coat pocket. 'Let me go and see what I can find out. There must be a coffee machine as well.'

Voices, murmuring down at the nurses' station.

'I got you a can of fizzy pop,' said Poland. 'The coffee's terrible, apparently. Jane's going to be a while. They'll let us know when there's any news. Have you told her parents?' He took a plastic cup from the water tower, handed it to Dixon.

'Thought I'd wait.' He shrugged. 'Don't want to give Rod another heart attack.'

'Good thinking. There's nothing they can do anyway.'

Dixon snapped open the can of fizzy orange. 'I killed a man, Roger,' he said.

'Would you rather he'd killed Jane?'

'No.'

'There you are then.'

There'd be a lot of that. Dixon knew there would. Lots of pats on the back, being told he'd done the right thing, but it still felt . . . wrong, somehow. Maybe that was the lie about the gun? Something else he'd have to live with. And he would; he could. If, God willing, everyone came home in one piece. Then it would have been worth it.

'The best laid plans.' Poland tried a reassuring smile. 'Try not to dwell on these things would be my advice. When was the last time you checked your blood?'

'I had some pastilles before I went into the house at Burtle.'

'There's only crisps and chocolate in the machine. And some revolting flapjack thing.' Poland was looking at the clock on the wall. 'How long's it been?'

'An hour, maybe?'

'A caesar takes an hour at most. They'll have to stop the bleeding first, though.'

'You're not really helping, Roger.'

'I'll just sit here and shut up.'

'Thanks.'

He lasted about five minutes.

'Where's Monty?'

'Louise has got him,' replied Dixon. 'She'll drop him to Rod and Sue's tomorrow, if I'm not back by then.'

'What's the procedure in this situation . . . when a police officer . . . ?'

'Suspended on full pay pending an IOPC investigation.'

Poland nodded. 'You'll be exonerated, of course you will. In the meantime, treat it as paternity leave.'

'Yeah.'

'Nick Dixon?' asked a nurse wearing dark blue scrubs. She'd appeared in the doorway silently.

'That's me.'

'Congratulations,' she said, smiling. 'It's a boy. Would you like to come and see him?'

He tried to reply but the words caught in the back of his throat.

'He does,' said Poland, standing up. 'Can I come too?'

'What about Jane?' asked Dixon, hesitating in the middle of the corridor.

'The doctor will be along to see you in a minute.'

'Softening me up with the good news first?'

'No, it's nothing like that.'

They followed her into a private room behind the nurses' station, a single incubator occupied.

'He's what we call "moderately preterm". Almost, anyway. Five pounds two ounces, though, so a good strong lad.'

'What's that tube?'

'Oxygen. Just a precaution, don't worry.'

Poland put his arm around Dixon's shoulders. 'This is a day you'll remember for the rest of your life, old chap,' he said.

Actually, it was a day he'd spend the rest of his life trying to forget, but that was something else best left unsaid.

'You're the husband?' Tall; light blue scrubs this time. Poland probably knew the significance of them, but they were lost on Dixon.

'Yes.'

'Angela Smith. I operated on your wife. We were able to stop the bleeding fairly quickly. She's lost a lot of blood, but we've given her a transfusion, and her vital signs are good. We'll be keeping her in intensive care overnight, and all being well, she'll be on the ward in the morning. She's had a caesarean section, so that'll knock her out for a bit, but she's as strong as an ox. Fit and healthy, which helps.'

'Can I see her?'

'Of course you can. She's out for the count, though, so you won't get much conversation out of her.'

'Can I bring our son?'

An anxious look between nurse and doctor. 'That should be fine. Not long though.'

Both of them were asleep. Like mother, like son. Jane's mouth was hidden behind an oxygen mask, cables running to machines on the wall.

Poland had switched into doctor mode. 'All looks good to me,' he said, watching the line bouncing across the screen.

Dixon perched on the edge of the bed, holding his son in his arms. He looked down at Jane, her eyelids fluttering.

'Look what you've gone and done,' he said.

Chapter Forty-Two

Dixon had ended one life and now, here he was, responsible for starting another.

Life suddenly seemed so fragile. He'd spent much of the night leaning over the incubator, checking his son was still breathing. Getting in the nurse's way. That, and sitting in the armchair next to Jane's bed in the ICU, watching her eyes open, then close again, her eyelids fluttering from time to time.

He'd slept for a couple of hours too, but it had felt more like five minutes.

There'd been one lucid moment in the early hours. 'Where is he?' Jane had asked.

'In an incubator. Five pounds two ounces.'

Then she'd smiled herself to sleep again.

It had only occurred to Dixon later that Jane had known she'd had a boy. Maybe she'd overheard something in the operating theatre, or the recovery room, perhaps?

Poland had left just before two in the morning, with a promise to be back first thing. And he would be. He had to be.

There was somewhere Dixon had to go, and he wasn't leaving Jane alone.

There was always her parents, but that call would have to wait until she was on the ward, out of danger. Even the mention of 'intensive care' and Rod might find himself back there.

Dixon already had enough on his conscience.

Poland had brushed it off, almost. 'Would you rather he'd killed Jane?'

An easy question to answer.

'There you are then.'

Right, of course. And Dixon knew it.

He'd never been much of a soul-searcher. Things were either right or they were wrong; legal or illegal. And what he'd done was both right *and* legal. Apart from bringing the gun with him, possibly. That was possession of a firearm; manslaughter even, if the Crown could prove he'd gone there intending to kill Grady.

He hadn't. He'd gone there intending to save Jane, never really gave much thought to whether or not he'd have to kill Grady. Jane had been haemorrhaging, so he hadn't had time to muck about. He couldn't even recall having pulled the trigger, but he had. There had been no conscious decision to do it, put it that way.

How do I explain that to a jury?

Fucking 3D printed guns. Dixon had been aiming at Grady's head, hit him in the neck. Inaccurate, even at eight feet. Random thoughts, popping in and out of his head all night as he dozed in the chair. He'd even found himself wondering whether it would be covered by the house insurance. New carpets, decorating, a deep clean.

And what the hell would he put on the claim form?

Dixon woke to find the doctor standing at the end of Jane's bed, checking the clipboard and screens.

'She's doing well,' she said. 'We'll be moving her in a minute. We've got her a private room, off the ward, and she can have the baby's incubator next to her. Hopefully, she'll feel like some breakfast too. Got to get her strength up.'

'Peter's incubator,' said Dixon. 'After a friend of ours who . . .' He didn't feel the need to finish his sentence.

'Nice.' She hooked the clipboard over the end of the bed, disappeared.

'Have you told my parents?' Jane asked, her voice weak. She'd turned her head on the pillow, was trying to focus on Dixon.

'Not yet,' he replied, taking her hand, careful not to dislodge the cannula. 'I need to ring Lucy as well.'

'It was that custody officer from Express Park, wasn't it?'

'Edward Grady.'

'Is he dead?'

'He is.'

'They're going to be wanting statements from us, and you remember what we said.' Jane had recovered enough to fix him with a steely stare. 'He asked me out once. A long time ago, before you came down from London. Pushy sod. I thought he was a bit creepy, to be honest, so I said no, although it took him a while to get the message.'

'A bit creepy,' said Dixon, shaking his head.

Nurses arrived, started disconnecting machines.

'I'll go and make those phone calls outside, catch up with you in a minute.'

'She'll be in the Ashcombe Birth Centre,' said one of the nurses. 'First room on the right.'

Dixon stepped out into the darkness, his phone pressed to his ear. The first glow of dawn was just visible behind the streetlights in the car park. Lucy would be on the train home from Manchester, probably, and he needed to tell her not to go to the cottage. Needed to tell her she was an aunt too.

She took the news of the dead body at the bottom of the stairs in her stride, started screaming when Dixon told her Peter had arrived. Then he'd used the words that had been touch and go for a while, not that Lucy needed to know that.

'Mother and baby doing well.'

'I'm just getting on the train now, I'll change at Bristol, get a train to Weston and take a taxi,' said Lucy.

Always nice to have a plan. Dixon had one too. It was something Jane had said in the pub. He'd been going over it in his head – over and over it. For a time there it had looked like it might have been their last evening together. And she'd just come out with it.

'There'll be something that connects the whole thing up.'

It had only hit him at four in the morning. When he was standing over Peter's incubator. Now the challenge would be keeping out of Charlesworth's way long enough.

One more call to make, Rod answering, mercifully; less chance of screaming.

Dixon had hoped to get away without telling him the full story, instead opting for an abridged version: 'I got home and found her losing blood, so I put her in the car and drove her straight to the hospital.'

One thing led to another, though.

'We'll call by the cottage and pick up some of her stuff in that case.'

'Er, no. Don't do that.'

'Why not?'

The whole story then.

'I'll leave it to you how much of that you tell Sue,' said Dixon.

'You killed him?' asked Rod.

'I did.'

'Good for you. Tell Lucy she can stay with us if she needs to. You too. I expect they'll be keeping Jane in hospital for a few days and it sounds like you won't be going home for a while anyway.'

A kind offer. Poland had said much the same, and his offer included whisky.

Dixon stepped back behind the bushes as he rang off, a patrol car sweeping into the car park, stopping in front of the main entrance.

Charlesworth and Potter.

Best avoided.

For a few hours anyway.

There were always taxis hanging around the hospital, dropping off and picking up, even at that time in the morning.

Dixon opened the rear door of one that had just dropped someone off at A&E, slid into the back.

'Oi, I've got another job.'

'Where?' he asked.

'A pickup in Burnham.'

'Then earn some money on the way, drop me off in Brent Knoll.'

'You're supposed to ring the office and book.'

'Cash.'

It turned out to be the magic word.

The road through Brent Knoll was still closed, but he'd left his Land Rover outside the cordon, walked the rest of the way the night before. The taxi driver dropped him a discreet distance away, leaving him to walk along the pavement, avoiding the streetlights and anyone who might wish to report his presence, want a witness statement. Or to suspend him on full pay pending an IOPC investigation into the death of Edward Grady. It was all coming.

Just, not yet.

He'd sent a few text messages from the back seat of the taxi. Two, actually. To Louise and Mark.

Severn Beach.

A convenient spot and close to where he needed to be anyway. He'd added a line to the one to Louise:

Please bring Monty.

He was sitting on the low wall forty minutes later when Monty appeared, his lead trailing. Louise was not far behind, examining the fingers of her right hand.

'The little bugger nearly had my arm out of its socket when he saw you,' she said. 'And he slept on the end of my bed last night.' Then she caught herself, remembered. 'How's Jane?'

'Fine. Peter is doing well too.'

'How big?'

'Five pounds, two ounces.'

'Not bad, for eight weeks early.' Louise perched on the wall next to Dixon. 'Charlesworth turned up after you'd gone. Went in. He didn't say much.'

'More worried that Grady was one of ours, I expect.'

'I left about three in the end. Scientific were crawling all over the place. You're going to need a new carpet.'

'Ahead of you there.'

'Yeah.'

'When were they bringing Grady out?'

'This morning, they said. Davidson was there when I left, not that cause of death will be very difficult.'

'You lucky sod,' said Mark, appearing behind them. 'Suspended on full pay. It could be months.'

'Thanks.'

'Oh, and congratulations. I'd have got you a big fat cigar but there wasn't time.'

'It's fine. Really.'

'My phone's ringing again,' said Louise, looking at the screen, ignoring the alert. 'That's the fifth time already this morning. All they want to know is where you are.'

'Mine's on silent,' said Dixon. 'I know it won't be Jane anyway, we left her phone in the cottage.'

'So, what are we doing here?'

'We're going to finish this thing.'

'Well, we can't go back to Bridewell,' said Mark. 'That super from Professional Standards was looking for you.'

'Carlisle.'

'That's him. He had that weasel of a DI in tow.'

'They'll want a statement from Jane,' said Louise. 'As soon as she's feeling up to it.'

'I saw Charlesworth and Potter going into the hospital.' Dixon slid off the wall, picked up Monty's trailing lead. 'I was in the car park, on the phone, as luck would have it.'

'Took some bottle to shoot him like that,' said Mark, curling his lip.

'He was holding a gun to the back of my wife's head,' replied Dixon. 'What else was I supposed to do?'

'Why the neck? Word has it you shot him in the neck.'

'I was aiming for his head. These bloody plastic guns are useless, even at short range, which might explain why every killing so far has been point blank. That's what I thought, anyway. But there's another reason.'

'What?' asked Louise.

'Rage. Our killer wants it point blank; wants to look into their eyes when they die.'

'You know who it is?'

'Jane said it last night. We were in the pub and she said there's something that connects everything.'

'And is there?' asked Mark. 'Something?'

'Not some*thing*,' replied Dixon. 'Some*one*. I'm standing there in the maternity unit, looking down at my son in that incubator, and suddenly it all made sense.'

'Where are we going then?' asked Louise.

'The Police and Crime Commissioner's office.'

Chapter Forty-Three

'Everyone's going to know where you are now. That's for sure,' said Mark.

They were sitting in Dixon's Land Rover – all three of them crammed on to the front seats, Monty in the back – watching the gatekeeper at Avon and Somerset Police headquarters, in his guardhouse, on his phone.

'Bet they asked him to ring if you turned up here,' continued Mark.

'You make it sound like I'm on the run,' said Dixon.

'You are. Sort of.'

'Do the honours, will you?'

Mark opened the door, slid out. Then he walked over and raised the barrier. Dixon accelerated forward, stopped. Waited.

'Oi!' The shout was half-hearted, the gatekeeper lowering the barrier, watching as Mark climbed back into the Land Rover. Then he picked up his clipboard and walked over to the car behind.

'He was never going to stop us,' said Louise.

'I haven't got time to hang about,' said Dixon. 'I want to get in there, make the arrest before I'm suspended. Then I need to get back to the hospital.'

'Yeah.'

His phone was buzzing in his pocket as he accelerated along the drive, ignoring the '15 MPH' signs, bouncing over the speed humps. He parked outside the main entrance, put the blue light on the roof and his hazard lights on – token gestures – then walked in.

'Can I—?'

Straight past the receptionist. It was all about time now, and the element of surprise.

Up the stairs, across the landing, heading for the double doors, 'Office of the Police and Crime Commissioner' etched on to the glass.

Louise and Mark were wearing body armour beneath their coats. Dixon hadn't bothered; left it in the Land Rover. There was only one bullet in a Songbird, and only one place it would be going. It would be his job to stop that if he could. To manage the situation, if he couldn't.

The PCC's office door was open, the Assistant PCC sitting behind the desk. Standing in until the election, name on the ballot paper now. Dixon gestured to the door, Louise walking over and closing it.

Napier's personal assistant, Julia, was there, standing beside her desk. Coat and gloves on, handbag slung over her shoulder.

'I was just nipping over to the canteen. Can I get anyone anything?' she asked.

'You've always got your gloves on, Julia,' said Dixon. He leaned over her computer, double-clicked the mouse, the screen lighting up to reveal the feed from one of the CCTV cameras, the one covering the front entrance. 'Knew I was coming, I see.'

'I said I was just going over to the canteen.'

'Of course you were, Flora,' said Dixon, flatly.

She took a step back.

'Always got your gloves on when I come in,' he continued. 'I thought it was just coincidence to begin with. Then I thought you were covering up a hand injury; we know the gun exploded when you killed Liam Smith, but it's not about that at all, is it?' Dixon turned back the cuff of his left wrist with his right index finger. 'There'll be a tattoo, right about there. A semicolon.'

Silence. Face reddening.

'Rose has got one. Jess had one. You've got one too.'

Flora gave a sad smile. 'How did you know?'

'It came to me last night, when I was standing by my son's incubator watching him breathe. I knew then what a parent would do for a child; felt your rage.' Dixon hesitated, an air of resignation descending on Flora. She seemed to crumple, the blood draining from her cheeks.

'Rage,' she said, her voice barely a whisper. 'A good word.'

'I killed a man yesterday. He was holding a gun to the back of my pregnant wife's head, and I shot him. So, I came to tell you I understand. I really do.'

'Thank you.'

'I have to stop you, all the same.'

'I know.'

Dixon took a small step forward, matched by a step back from Flora.

'Who did you kill?' she asked.

'Edward Grady.'

'So, you found the 3D printer as well. The little shit.'

'I'm guessing you met him at the misconduct hearing? Napier said he'd sent you to take notes.'

'You don't miss a thing, do you.'

'Who was it on the boat with Carl, the woman everyone thought was you?'

'Just some tart he was seeing behind my back. He thought I didn't know about her, but I did. The fire was accidental, though. I had nothing to do with that.'

'I believe you,' said Dixon. 'So, then you came home to get revenge on those you blamed for Jess's death?'

'Not originally. I just came home, moved to Bristol, got a job, tried to get on with my life. But then I started working for Hugo, found two of the men who raped my daughter were police officers and that drug dealer was suddenly *respectable*; standing for elected office. It was as if Jess had never existed, that what they'd done to her didn't matter. I felt . . . no grief, no sadness. Only rage.'

Flora reached into her handbag, drew a Songbird and pointed it at Dixon.

'I'll be leaving now,' she said.

'You've got one bullet and there are three of us. How far d'you think you're going to get?'

'I'm going to be with Jess.'

Suddenly, Flora was pointing the gun at her own temple.

'I'm guessing you knew what was on the stolen laptop, the intelligence about Sohail York,' said Dixon, determined to keep her talking. 'There's nothing a PA doesn't know about their boss, is there?'

'Yes, I knew. Then I saw the facial recognition image in Hugo's email – someone at Facetech sent it to him. It had Hampton's name on the top of the picture, so I knew who'd stolen it; didn't take long to track him down. I made sure he knew the importance of the information. The *value* of it.'

'So, the blackmail was your idea?'

'I watched Sohail York suffer, just as Jess had done before she took her own life. Enjoyed every minute of it, watching him squirm.' Flora shrugged. 'Next thing I know, they're there, at the misconduct hearing, sitting right in front of me. Darren Canter and Russell Lock, two of three who attacked Jess. You just couldn't believe how seriously fucking stupid these people were, sitting

342

in police headquarters, outside a misconduct hearing, talking to Grady about printing guns.'

'Then Hampton and Paul are found dead,' said Dixon.

'That's when I knew I had to do something. They had to die. I got in touch with Grady and he wanted a thousand pounds each for the guns, but that hardly mattered. I had to sleep with him, though, which made my skin crawl. Then I followed Canter and Lock when their shift ended; found myself at Portbury Docks of all places. They must've had some scam going on the side. There was a container full of boxes.'

'You had two guns, I take it?'

'One for each of them. They thought I was robbing them at first, until I said, "This is for Jess." Then they knew. Canter I shot first. He fell back on to the boxes and I got Lock to close up the container. Then I marched him out to the river, made him look me in the eye, pulled the trigger and he fell into the water.' A wry smile crept across Flora's face. 'God, it felt good. Worth everything.'

'Worth what comes next?' asked Dixon.

'Oh, yes. It was always going to end this way anyway.'

'Dumping Canter's BMW in Wales was a clever bit of misdirection.'

'You saw through it straight away, didn't you? But it was a nice trip down memory lane. Jess loved those tearooms.'

The landing outside the glass doors was filling up with people. Armed Response officers, paramedics at the top of the stairs, peering over the balustrade.

'Tell them to stay back,' said Dixon.

Louise opened the door, said something, closed it again.

'Lock the door, Lou.'

Click.

'Why Liam Smith? My understanding is he didn't rape Jess, but that came from his own witness statement.'

'He did rape her. Said he just held her down, but he was as guilty as the others. Made a hell of a bang when I hit him with the car. I thought that might have killed him, which would've been a shame, because I wanted to look into his eyes as I pulled the trigger. He was still alive, as it turned out, and I made sure he knew who I was, why he had to die, before I shot him. You can't put a price on it, you really can't.'

'A price on what?'

'The feeling you get.'

'What about Sohail York?'

'He supplied the drugs, didn't he? The drugs they used on Jess. Didn't know who I was, would you believe it? Did by the time I'd finished with him.'

'It has to stop, Flora,' said Dixon.

'I suppose it does. I knew you'd come, but I had hoped to get one more before you did.'

'Who?'

'Russell Lock's father. The bastard doesn't deserve to breathe the same air as the rest of us.' Flora shook her head, still holding the gun against her temple. 'I can still remember the look on his face when he told me Jess had been asking for it, that a jury would see through her in seconds. I'd dearly loved to have looked into that man's eyes when I shot him.'

'You need to put the gun down now.'

'I don't think so.' She gestured to the computer on her desk. 'I haven't updated the spreadsheet yet. You're still on a hundred per cent.'

'The gun might misfire.'

'At this range, it'll still do the job.' She took a deep breath, exhaled slowly through her nose. 'I wanted to thank you.'

'What for?'

'Understanding.'

Then she pulled the trigger.

Chapter Forty-Four

All hell broke loose after that.

Banging on the door, Louise opening it; Armed Response officers and paramedics rushing in.

Dixon was looking down at the body of Flora Burroughs, eyes wide, mouth open; almost a smile, but not quite. A single trickle of blood coming from her right temple.

No exit wound.

The gun still in her hand.

Paramedics rolled her on to her back, started CPR. Protocol, but pointless, all the same.

'You all right, Sir?' asked Louise.

Dixon nodded. 'Like she said, it was always going to end that way.'

'Yeah.'

'You did your best, Sir,' offered Mark. 'Kept her talking, which was the right thing to do. And there was no way she was going to be taken alive. You could tell.'

He spotted Charlesworth and Potter in the foyer when he reached the top of the stairs. 'Time to face the music.'

'It just gets better and better.' Charlesworth was watching the throng on the landing above; civilian staff who'd come out of their offices being directed down the stairs by armed officers.

'Two uniformed constables, a custody officer, and now the PCC's personal assistant. Not to mention the PCC himself having to resign.'

Potter took Dixon by the elbow, led him to a quiet corner.

'Nick, there's going to need to be an IOPC investigation into the death of Edward Grady. I'm sure you know that. You're to be suspended on full pay, effective immediately, pending the outcome of that investigation. I'm sure none of this is coming as a surprise.'

'No, Ma'am.'

'Liz Kendall can take over the team, tie up the loose ends.' Potter looked hopeful. 'I'm assuming that's the end of it?'

'It is.'

'Good. In that case all I need from you is a detailed witness statement, and then you can go and be with your wife and child.'

'Thank you, Ma'am.'

'We went to the hospital this morning, looking for you as it happens, but he's a lovely little lad, isn't he? And Jane seems to be doing well, in spite of everything she's been through.' Potter put her hand on Dixon's shoulder. 'We're all on your side, you do know that? You did what you had to do.'

'Thank you, Ma'am.'

'You'll be back,' said Potter, smiling. 'You're the best of us.'

Four hours at Bridewell police station, sitting in front of a computer, typing out his witness statement.

There was a gun that I now know to have been a 3D printed handgun, known as a Songbird, lying on the rug in front of the television. I picked it up and pointed it at Grady. He was still pointing his gun at the back of my

*pregnant wife's head. He said, 'You're destroying my life,
and I'm going to fuck up yours,' so I pulled the trigger. I
do not recall making a conscious decision to do so, and I
had not gone there intending to kill him, but I believed
my wife and unborn child to be in imminent danger of
death and I acted to preserve their lives.*

He printed it off, read the declaration four times before he
signed it.

*This statement (consisting of 11 pages each signed by me)
is true to the best of my knowledge and belief and I make
it knowing that, if it is tendered in evidence, I shall be
liable to prosecution if I have wilfully stated anything in
it which I know to be false, or do not believe to be true.*

He'd never looked at the wording that closely before.
Never had to.

Never lied before.

Life was going to be about grey areas from now on.

He'd acted to protect his wife and child, and everyone was busy
patting him on the back.

Flora had acted in revenge for the death of her child and that
was murder.

Michael Lock had acted to protect his child by convincing Jess
and Flora to drop the rape case. Nobody would be patting him on
the back for that.

Grey areas.

Files going to the Crown Prosecution Service for charging
decisions would be someone else's problem too. If Dixon had his
way, there'd be one for the PCC on a perverting the course of
justice charge, and another for Michael Lock. Same charge, with

a misconduct in public office thrown in for good measure. That said, the CPS might decide he'd suffered enough, losing his son in the way he had.

Dixon uploaded his witness statement to the system, emailed a copy to Potter, then shut down his computer.

Grateful that he wasn't the one having to make these decisions. His job stopped when the evidence was collated and the file sent in.

Although now it had just stopped.

'You off, Sir?' asked Louise.

'Going to the hospital.'

'Good for you. Tell Jane I'll pop in and see her on my way home.'

It was a full house when Dixon arrived in the Ashcombe Birth Centre. Lucy was leaning over the incubator, drumming her fingers on the top, smiling down at Peter. Sue was sitting in the armchair, Rod standing at the end of the bed.

'Here he is,' said Jane, raising herself up on her elbows.

Rod started welling up, standing in front of Dixon with his hand outstretched. 'Jane's told us what happened,' he mumbled. 'Fancy having the presence of mind to pick up the gun and shoot him.'

'I didn't really have time to think about it.'

'Bloody good job.'

'Let's go and get a coffee,' said Sue, giving Dixon a hug on the way out. 'Give them a minute. You too, Lucy.'

'Oh, yeah. Right.'

Jane waited until the door closed behind them. 'I'm guessing you saw Charlesworth and Potter?'

'I was on the phone, ducked behind the bushes; ended up taking a taxi home, picking up my car.'

'They didn't say anything, but they were looking for you. Made all the right noises, though. Congratulations, isn't he lovely, blah, blah. You can imagine it, can't you?'

Dixon sat down on the edge of the bed. 'They caught up with me at Portishead and I'm suspended on full pay. I went back to Bridewell, did my statement.'

'I've got someone coming to see me tomorrow afternoon,' replied Jane. 'You stuck to what we agreed, I hope?'

'I did.'

'They'll never be able to prove you had the gun. You'll be fine.'

Dixon stood up, leaned over the incubator. 'How is he?'

'I had him out earlier to try a bit of a feed, but I'm going to express and he's got a feeding tube. It's just for the first couple of weeks while he's in hospital.' Jane took Dixon's hand, squeezed. 'Roger's been and gone again. Said he'd come back this evening.'

'I'm staying at his place tonight. I called in at the cottage on the way here. Grady's long gone and Scientific have finished, but it's a bloody mess. I'm not sure I could stay there anyway, after what I . . . after what happened.'

'It was Grady's decision to do what he did. He knew the risk he was taking, how it might end. Fuck him. He got what he deserved.' Jane sat up. 'Anyway, we'll sort the cottage out. You'd better ring our insurers in the morning. And have you rung your parents?'

'Not yet.'

'You'd better do it this evening,' said Jane. 'Your mother will only moan. What about the case, is it over?'

'It is.'

'How did it end?'

'Exactly as I thought it would. With another body.'

'You have had a bellyful of it, haven't you?' She pulled him towards her, kissed him.

'Enough to last a lifetime.'

'You can get him out of there if you like. Just be careful with the feeding tube.'

Dixon lifted the lid of the incubator, picked up Peter and sat back down on the edge of the bed, cradling his son in his arms.

'They offer counselling to firearms officers who've taken a life,' Jane said, softly.

'I've got my dog. I'll be fine.'

'Maybe being suspended for a few months isn't such a bad thing?'

'Let's hope it's not too long, otherwise I can't see myself going back to it.'

'Try not to worry about that now. Let's just be parents for a while, get used to that, one step at a time.'

Chapter Forty-Five

'Come in. Sit down.' Carlisle waited, watching the pair of them shuffle in, sitting down nervously. 'Thank you for coming. My name is Carlisle and I am a detective superintendent in the Professional Standards Department. This is Detective Inspector Larkin. We are investigating an incident that took place seven days ago and resulted in the death of custody officer Edward Grady. This interview is taking place at Express Park Police Centre. It is being recorded, but you are not under arrest, nor have you been cautioned. Is that clear?'

'Yes, Sir.'

'State your name for the tape.'

'My name is Rhys Webber and I am a sergeant in the Armed Response team.'

'And who is this with you?'

'Police Sergeant Malcolm Fleetwood. I'm Sergeant Webber's federation rep.'

'Fine.'

'Rhys, tell us about the incident,' said Carlisle. 'Starting with when you got the shout.'

'I've given a detailed witness statement,' replied Webber, nervously.

'You have, but there are certain matters we need to clarify.'

'We got to Burtle in a convoy of marked cars. The timings are all in my statement.'

'Don't worry about the times.'

Webber nodded. 'Acting Detective Superintendent Dixon was waiting for us in the car park of The Duck, although he might've been parked on the grass verge outside. We waited until we got the signal that the road had been closed at the far end and then moved in. It was a fairly routine scenario for us; occupant of the house possibly armed, so we went in cold, no warning.'

'Who's "we"?'

'Me and Jack.'

'Constable Jack Wells?'

'He opened the door with the battering ram and I went in first. Jack was behind me, then came the superintendent. I went into the room on the left, turned out to be the living room, shouted a warning, but it was clear. Jack had gone through to the back, shouted "clear" from the kitchen, so up the stairs we went. I was in the lead, Mr Dixon behind me.'

'Which room did you go into then?'

'The front room first, but it was clear. Actually, the whole house was clear. Grady had done a bunk before we went in.'

'What did you see in the front room?'

'At that stage, just a wardrobe, chest of drawers and a bed. It was clear, so I moved on to the back room.'

'And what did you see in the back room?'

'There was a desk with a computer on it. A 3D printer on a small table. That's about it, really. I was only looking for the occupant of the house, to be honest. After that I checked the loft.'

'Where was Acting Superintendent Dixon while you did that?'

'In the back room. A 3D printer was what he'd been looking for, so . . .'

'And the loft was open to next door?'

'We think that's how Grady got out. I came back down the ladder, had a look in the front room, and that's when I saw the photographs.'

'Of DS Winter?'

'That's right. I called to Mr Dixon and he came to have a look at them.'

'What else did you see in the back room?'

'There was loads of crap, really. It looked more like a workshop. There were gun parts, triggers, moulds for making bullets, and what have you. Elastic bands, tools, spools of polymer.'

'Guns?'

'Yes.'

'In your original witness statement, Rhys, you said there were two handguns on the desk, near the computer keyboard.'

'That's right.'

'And yet the inventory in the Scientific Services report only makes reference to there being one.'

'No, there were two. Definitely two.'

Author's Note

Thank you for reading *Blue Blood* and I do hope you enjoyed it.

I must confess that I found the research a touch disturbing this time; the ease with which a 3D printer can produce a workable firearm is quite horrifying. And there was me thinking the availability of crossbows online was scary enough.

On the plus side, I had a lot of fun playing with What3Words, although I should clarify that whilst the locations at Newport and out on the Somerset Levels are real, the geographic coordinates given for Nick and Jane's cottage are not. Go there and you will find yourself visiting the Burnham-on-Sea Low Lighthouse out on the beach. A lovely spot and well worth a visit, if you've never been, but do check the tides before you go and take your dog.

It really was a joy to find myself writing Nick and Jane's wedding (at long last) and I hope they'll both be very happy!

There are lots of people I would like to take this opportunity to thank.

I am always on the lookout for unusual ways to find the first body (rather than relying on another poor dog walker) and am most grateful to the Burnham-on-Sea Gig Rowing Club for their open evening. I am yet to take them up on their kind offer of a taster session on the water, but hope to do so one day.

To my wife, Shelley, for her unwavering support. It never ceases to amaze me that Shelley remains delighted to drop whatever it is she is doing (without complaint) and read the manuscript on a daily basis.

To my dear friend Rod, who, as well as being my harshest critic, also doubles up as Jane's father!

Once again, David Hall and Clare Paul have been incredibly generous with their knowledge of Somerset, Land Rovers and guns. Thank you both!

Lastly, to my editorial team at Thomas & Mercer for their patience and professionalism: Sammia Hamer, Eoin Purcell, Victoria Haslam and Ian Pindar.

Damien Boyd
Devon, UK
February 2025

About the Author

Damien Boyd is a solicitor by training and draws on his extensive experience of criminal law, along with a spell in the Crown Prosecution Service, to write fast-paced crime thrillers featuring Detective Inspector Nick Dixon.

Follow the Author on Amazon

If you enjoyed this book, follow Damien Boyd on Amazon to be notified when the author releases a new book!
To do this, please follow these instructions:

Desktop:

1) Search for the author's name on Amazon or in the Amazon App.
2) Click on the author's name to arrive on their Amazon page.
3) Click the 'Follow' button.

Mobile and Tablet:

1) Search for the author's name on Amazon or in the Amazon App.
2) Click on one of the author's books.
3) Click on the author's name to arrive on their Amazon page.
4) Click the 'Follow' button.

Kindle eReader and Kindle App:

If you enjoyed this book on a Kindle eReader or in the Kindle App, you will find the author 'Follow' button after the last page.

Printed in Dunstable, United Kingdom

63663622R00211